"WONDERFUL . . .
Patchett writes with a simplicity of style and clarity
of voice that make one eager for her next book."
Entertainment Weekly

"This book pokes a little finger into the soft part of your
heart and probes the secrets you keep."
Detroit Free Press

"In an assured, warm, and graceful style, a moving novel
that touches on the healing powers of chance sanctuaries
of love and fancy in the acrid realities of living."
The Kirkus Reviews

"A compelling story, rich with emotion and
characterization."
The Cincinnati Enquirer

"Exceptionally good."
Nashville Banner

THE
PATRON
SAINT
OF LIARS

Ann Patchett

IVY BOOKS • NEW YORK

Ivy Books
Published by Ballantine Books
Copyright © 1992 by Ann Patchett

Library of Congress Catalog Card Number: 91-41584

ISBN 0-8041-1151-0

First published by Houghton Mifflin Company.
This edition reprinted by arrangement with Houghton Mifflin Company.

Manufactured in the United States of America

First Ballantine Books Edition: June 1993

The author gratefully acknowledges the following people and foundations for their support in the writing of this novel: the Fine Arts Work Center in Provincetown, Michael Glasscock, the Millay Colony, the Corporation of Yaddo, James Michener and the Copernicus Society, and the Henfield Foundation. Also, Ann and Jerry Wilson, Jill Birdsall, and Adrian LeBlanc for their help with this project, and Elizabeth McCracken for her endless patience and hard work, thank you.

$=$ HABIT $=$

Two o'clock in the morning, a Thursday morning, the first bit of water broke through the ground of George Clatterbuck's back pasture in Habit, Kentucky, and not a living soul saw it. Spring didn't care. Water never needed anyone's help to come up through the ground once it was ready. There are rivers, hundreds of them, running underground all the time, and because of this a man can say he is walking on water. This was a hot spring that had broken loose of its river to make mud in the grass, and it kept on till it was a clear pool and then a little creek, cutting out a snake's path toward the Panther River. Water will always seek out its own.

George Clatterbuck found it when it was already a pretty steady stream. It was only fitting that he should be the one, seeing as how it was his land. It was 1906. He was hunting for his family's dinner. He smelled the spring before he saw it, foul and sulfurous as spoiled eggs. He thought it was a bad sign, that it meant his land was infected and spitting up bile for relief. The water was warm when he dipped in his hand, and he wiped it off against the leg of his trousers. He was thinking about it, thinking what he ought to do, when he saw a rabbit on the other side of the field. It was as big a buck as he'd seen, and he knelt down slowly to get off his shot. He had to shoot on his knees. His father taught him that way because he was afraid the rifle's kick would knock the boy off his feet, thought George would be safer close to the ground. But since that was the way George learned, that was the only way he could ever do it, and now here he was, grown with a family, going down on his knees like a man in prayer to shoot a rabbit.

He blew the head clean off and didn't disturb the pelt. He thought he would tan the hide and give it to his daughter, June,

3

for her birthday. June, like many little girls, was partial to soft things. By the time he'd tied the legs onto his belt he'd forgotten about the water altogether.

It wasn't long after that times turned hard for the Clatterbucks. Both plow horses came down with colic, and Betsy, the horse George rode to town, got a ringworm thick as your thumb that no amount of gentian violet could clear. Not a week after, every last one of his cows came down with mastitis that left them all drier than bones. George had to get up every three hours in the night and bottle-feed the calves, whose crying put his wife beside herself. "Sounds like a dying child," she said, and she shivered. George didn't say this to her, but he was thinking he might have to slaughter the calves and take his losses. Bought milk was more than he could afford.

Then, if he didn't have enough to worry about, the horses broke free of the corral. George took some rope and set out to bring them back, cursing the rain and the mud and the stupid animals with every step. He found them at that spring he had forgotten, drinking so deeply he thought they'd founder. He was frightened then because he thought such water would kill them, and where would the money come from to buy three new horses? But the horses were fine. Betsy's hide was smooth where the ringworm had been and the other two were past their own disorder. George knew it was the spring that had done this, but he didn't know if it was the work of the Devil or the Lord. He didn't tell a soul when he drove his sick cows down to the water, but by the time they came home their udders were so full they looked like they might burst on the ground.

Then little June took sick and laid in her bed like a dull penny. Doctor came from Owensboro and said it wasn't the pox or scarlet fever, but something else that was burning her alive. She was slipping away so fast you could all but see her dying right before your eyes, and there sat her parents, not a thing in the world to do.

So George goes out in the middle of the night with a mason jar. He walks in the dark to the spring, fills up the jar, and heads home. He goes to his daughter's room and looks at her pale face. He prays. He takes the first drink of water for himself, thinking that if it was to kill her he'd best die, too. It is foultasting, worse even than the smell of it. He lifts up June's head from her sweaty pillow and pours the water down her throat, the whole jarful. He only lets a little run down the sides of her face. He wonders for a moment what it would be like to feed a child from his own body as his wife had done, but the thought embarrasses him and he lets it go. The next morning June is fine, perfect, better than new.

When the spring had saved his livestock, George kept it to himself, not wanting to look foolish, but when it saved his daughter he felt the call to witness. He went into the streets of Habit and told what he had seen. At first the people were slow in believing, but as hardships came to them and they went to the spring for help, all was proved true.

Tales of what had happened spread by word of mouth and before long people were coming up from as far away as Mississippi. The truth was stretched out of shape through all the telling, and soon the lame showed up wanting to walk and the blind wanting to see. The spring can't do everything, the townspeople said. It's wrong to expect so much.

And then one boy died right there at the water's edge. He was that sick by the time his folks brought him. He's buried in Habit now, two hundred miles away from his own kind.

One of the people who got word of the spring was a horse breeder named Lewis Nelson, who lived in Lexington. Lewis' wife, Louisa, had rheumatoid arthritis and her hands froze up on her even though she was only twenty-two. They set off to Habit to see if the water couldn't do her some good. The Nelsons were rich, and when they came to town they were looking for a hotel, but there wasn't one. George had made a vow to never make a cent off the spring, and Habit said that was only fitting. So when visitors came they were taken in with charity, many times by the Clatterbucks themselves. This put the Nelsons ill at ease, since they were used to giving charity and not receiving it.

June was seventeen that summer. She had grown up as well as she had started out. She was a kind of a saint in the town, the first one saved by the spring, but all that really meant to June was that there were few boys bold enough to ask her out, and the ones who did thought it would be a sin to try and kiss her. She gave up her room for Mr. and Mrs. Nelson and slept on the sofa downstairs.

After her second trip to the spring the use of Louisa's hands came back to her and she taught June how to cross-stitch. Her husband was full of joy. Lewis was a devout Catholic with a head for figures. He saw the hand of God in the spring and thought the thing to do would be to build a grand hotel in the back pasture. No one was ever sure how he changed George Clatterbuck's mind, but probably it was by telling him that a lot more people could be saved if there was a bigger place to stay and that George was being unchristian by denying them. It's easy to imagine that Lewis had seen how well the hot-springs hotels had done in Arkansas and Tennessee and knew there was some real money to be made. Not long after that the architects came with their silver mechanical pencils, and after them the builders and the gardeners. In 1920 the Hotel Louisa opened its doors. They'd wanted to call it the Hotel June, but June, afraid of scaring off the few dates she had left, said thank you, no.

When the roses on the wallpaper were still in their first bloom and the carpet was soft and springy beneath your feet, there wasn't a hotel in the South that could match the Hotel Louisa. People came from Atlanta and Chicago and New Orleans, some to be healed but most to play tennis on the grass courts and dance in the fancy ballroom. Lewis sent for his collection of horse prints in Lexington, and Louisa picked out velvet to cover the settees for the lobby. There were two formal dining rooms where people ate with real silver and drank champagne smuggled down from Canada. At five o'clock everyone went out and stood on the front porch to drink bourbon and soda. No one from Habit ever went inside after the opening day. It made them feel like they weren't quite good enough. Even the Clatterbucks, who were supposed to be partners in everything, kept to the other side of the woods. You couldn't see their house, not even from the third-floor rooms. The guests never knew they had ever been there at all.

The crash of the stock market in 1929 and the great drought that came over the land were so close together that it was hard to separate one from the other. Everything was coming to an end, and the spring would not except itself. Maybe there was a reason for it, that things got so hot that even the water underneath the ground felt the pull of the dry air. In no time it went from a trickle to a strip of mud and then not even that. But whatever it was, the town of Habit took its leaving as a sign, just as they had taken its arrival.

For the spring this was no hardship. It was just going back, folding into one of those underground rivers. It would break through later, years from then, someplace else. Next time people might not be around for miles. It was very possible that no one would ever drink from it at all.

Not long after all this, people stopped going to the hotel, though it would be hard to say if it was because of the spring or because they were the kind of people who had kept their money in banks. June used to walk across the field in the evenings and look at the place in the ground where her salvation had come from. She saw men in suits and women in silk dresses carrying out their own bags and taking hired cars north to catch trains.

The Nelsons tried for a long time to get the water to come back. They hired people who said they knew how to coax it out of the ground. But the spring was long gone by then. They stayed on in the hotel alone until the middle thirties, hardly coming out for anything. You could trail them as they moved from room to room, one light going off and another one coming on. People said they could set their watch by what window was bright at the time. Then one day the Nelsons packed up and left without saying good-bye.

Word came soon after that the Nelsons had made a gift of the Hotel Louisa to the Catholic Church, and this put the fear of God in everyone. It was one thing to have rich people in your pasture, but when the Clatterbucks thought of Catholics, they saw statues of the Virgin Mary going up in the yard, ten feet high. The Clatterbucks could have kept the Catholics off, since they owned the land, but nobody told them that. When the lawyers came and knocked on their door, there was nothing for them to do but look at the ground and shake their heads. A few weeks later two buses pulled up, and a group of little old women in white dresses were led or carried up the front stairs. The church had changed the name of the Hotel Louisa to Saint Elizabeth's and turned it into a rest home for old nuns.

But the nuns were miserable. They'd been dirt poor all their lives, following the word of their church. The idea of spending their final days in an abandoned grand hotel made them restless. Soon the tiny women started wandering over to the Clatterbucks' in their bathrobes, searching out a simpler way of life. The Clatterbucks, good Baptists every day of their lives, took pity on the old Catholics and overcame their fears. They served them platters of fried mush with sorghum, which were received with heartfelt prayers and thanks. It made the family feel needed again; the old women's dependence called to mind the early days of the spring when the sick were healed. They thought that God had seen again what was best.

But the church did not agree, and two years later the buses returned and took the nuns to Ohio. Mrs. Clatterbuck cried when they left, and June touched the medal around her neck of

Saint Catherine of Siena that Sister Estelle had given her. She wore it all her life.

The Hotel Louisa was getting worn, fretwork slipped from the porch, shutters hung down. In any other town it would have been ransacked, people breaking out windows and carrying off furniture in the night. But the people of Habit were true to their name and just kept on avoiding the old hotel like they did in the days when they wouldn't have had the right clothes to go inside for a cup of coffee.

The Clatterbucks waited and watched. Then one day a station wagon pulled up the front drive and two nuns, dressed in what looked to be white bed sheets, and five big-bellied girls got out. June and her mother were just coming through the woods at the time, out for their daily walk.

The nuns cut across the dried creek bed, not knowing a thing. They didn't know how the hotel had come to be or that they were standing on top of what might have been the closest thing to a real miracle that any of them was ever going to see. They were occupied, unloading the car.

"Pregnant girls," Mrs. Clatterbuck said. "They've gone and made it into a home for pregnant girls."

═ ROSE ═

===== 1 =====

I WAS SOMEWHERE outside of Ludlow, California, headed due east toward Kentucky, when I realized that I would be a liar for the rest of my life. There was plenty of time to think about things like that, headed into the desert alone, windows down, radio up. I imagined that it was possible for people to have talents, great talents, that they never stumbled across in the course of their lives. Somewhere out there, maybe in one of those African countries where all people have time to do is starve to death, was a painter who had never seen a canvas. Maybe he scratched simple pictures into the dirt with a stick, and it felt right to him even if he didn't know what it meant. So maybe I was born to lie, and it just took me twenty-three years to find the reason to do it. I started out with a lie of omission, which some people might see as easier, but I think is actually more complex. I left my husband with only a note.

> Dear Thomas,
>   I am unhappy and it cannot be resolved. Do not try and find me. I will not come home. I'm sorry about taking the car.
> Rose

I reworked it two dozen times, but it was still not a good note. Writing is not my talent. It was stiff and formal, given the fact that we had been married for almost three years and that he was, at every turn, a good man. But I thought the smallest bit of kindness would send him out looking for me, and since he wouldn't be able to find me, what kind of life would that be for him? Wandering in the desert, showing my picture in gas stations, pinning fliers that gave my height and weight, the place I

11

was last seen, onto telephone poles. The hardest part was knowing how to sign the note, because *Love* wasn't right and anything less *(Sincerely, All best,)* was worse than nothing. So I went with nothing.

But like I said, I started with omission, which means the contents of the note were true, but there was a larger, unmentioned truth which I took with me from Marina del Rey. I was pregnant. The beginnings of a child, his, mine, slept between my hips, a quarter-size life beneath the steering wheel of the blue Dodge Dart. Maybe you could trace the lying back further than that, to the darker issue of lying to myself. I lied to myself for three months, thinking that my period had gone someplace from which it would quickly return, that my body had simply forgotten and would remember. I lied to myself about wanting to be married, too. But I forgave myself that.

Forgiveness was at the heart of everything. Because I could not ask, I could not be forgiven. What would be the point in confessing a sin for which you had guilt but no remorse? Bless me, father, for I have sinned, I have lied to my husband, left him never knowing he will have a child, and would do it all again in a heartbeat. Bless me, for I will continue to lie until I go the way of all the earth. Bless me in my absence of remorse.

At nineteen I had been to Tijuana three times, drank mescal with high school boys, bet them money on dart games and let them kiss me, never anything else. I was saving myself for that one person who would be mine alone in all the world. That's what I thought at nineteen. There was one out there who was looking for me like I was lost. I had been to Los Angeles a dozen times, and farther, up the coast to Malibu and Zuma and Ventura, names so beautiful you'd think they were someplace else, and all the time I watched the waves and let the boy who drove me put his arm around my waist and slip the ends of my hair into his mouth as if they'd just blown there by accident, I never cared. Never cared for any of them. I would go into the water all the way through late November, even when the waves were high and cold enough to cut you in half. I would swim out with long strokes while the boy quickly drifted back toward the shore, shivering in the daylight, looking for his shirt. He would try again, go up to his ankles, his knees, but the water would push him back as fast as it pushed me out. As long as it's a regular day, not too rough to begin with, the ocean is pretty smooth once you make it out past that first set of waves. That's why people are afraid to swim in the ocean. They try to jump over those waves and get slammed down to the bottom and pulled across the sand like a piece of shell. You've got to go through them, dive under just when they're rising up for you, set your direction, close your eyes, and just swim like hell. Once you get through that, you'll find there isn't a better place for swimming because it's the ocean and it goes on forever. You don't have to see anyone you don't want to. If you look out, away from the beach, it's easy to imagine that there's no one else but you in the whole world, you and maybe a couple of sea gulls.

I never turned and waved to the boy. I felt how cold the water was, but never like I felt him watching me. I knew how my arms would look, how a lump would rise in his throat as I dove down again and then stayed under too long. I swam until I got tired, and I didn't get tired fast. By the time I walked out of the Pacific Ocean I could be sure he would remember this, and that I would remember it too: the swimming, not the boy.

In church I prayed to God. Every morning on my way to school, every morning before going to work when it wasn't on my way anymore, I stopped and knelt before a rack of candles. The flames would tremble inside their red glass cups when my elbows pressed against the railing. I would pray for the soul of my father, who I said I could remember but could not, that his young and handsome face from my parents' wedding picture was watching over me. I would pray for the exams I had not studied for and the small ruby ring in the window of Cantrell's Jewelry. I would pray for high-heeled shoes, my girlfriends, and permission to do as I pleased. I would pray to be noticed, beautiful, and loved, but mostly for that sign to which I was rightfully entitled. Every candle I lit, every long wooden match I gave a dime for and struck against the bottom of the coin box, making a small disruption of sulfur and light in the church, was by way of reminding God that I was still here, waiting. I knew that it could come at any time, and that any time could be a long way off, but I thought that by constantly placing myself in God's presence, He might be more inclined to think of me sooner rather than later. I did not ask for more than my share, one sign. That which was by rights mine because I believed and was so ready to listen.

Sometimes I prayed for Holy Orders, so that I would walk away from them in a way that would make me amazing; the strength of my will sanctified by God. Father O'Donnell had said that God called us to our vocations, in some kind of dog whistle voice that only we would hear, and if we kept our heart open, our ear to the ground, we would know what to do. Nun or Wife, my choices loomed above me like giant doors, and I waited, listening, for God to give me the word. But God was quiet in San Diego in the middle sixties. If He had an opinion as to which way I should go He kept it to Himself, or maybe He said it while I was in the shower, humming something, and the moment of my lifetime passed me by. But I was like a woman lost in the desert, her eyes trained for water for so long that she begins to think she could drink the reflections of light on the sand. What I finally accepted as my sign came in the form of Thomas Clinton, as Father O'Donnell told us God can come to us in many ways and we should never be quick to discount anyone. I was nineteen and working as a secretary at Simms candy factory on Pacific Avenue. I ate the lunch I brought from home on the beach. Thomas was in college, went to our church, and asked if he could take me to dinner some Saturday night.

"Which Saturday night?"

My mother was happy because he didn't wrap chocolates or drive a truck. I said yes because it seemed so hard for him to ask me. I wondered how many Sundays I had walked by him while he watched me, how many times the words had come up in his throat, or he had started to reach out to touch the sleeve of my dress but I was past him already and he would have to wait another week. You think that sounds conceited, you think that maybe it was the first time he had seen me, thought to ask at all. But any girl who tells herself the truth knows differently. So I said yes to Thomas Clinton and later thought that I had said yes to God and later still realized I had said yes only to Thomas Clinton.

My mother and I had our own lives, our own schedules. Sometimes it seemed like the only time we managed to spend together was in the bathroom while one of us was getting ready to go to work or out for the evening. "This is going to be a good date," my mother said. She said it every time, regardless of who I was going out with. "I have a feeling." She was sitting on the edge of the tub, still wearing her dress from work. She sold cosmetics at I. Magnin's. She used to work in hosiery. Cosmetics was a big promotion because she made a commission, and my mother knew that no woman thought she was beautiful, or beautiful enough, or beautiful in the right way. "They look into the mirror and all they can see is a collection of flaws,'' she used to say. "I can fix that." She sold to them gently, she soothed them. When they said their eyes were small, she did not deny it, but instead brought up a thin blue pencil from someplace deep beneath the counter and showed them how to draw themselves on. "There's no sense worrying about what you're given," my mother would say. "The important thing is what you do with it."

I was working on my face from the vast collection of samples my mother brought home, overused testers with just enough left for us. She rubbed a Kleenex over the top of a lipstick and handed it to me.

"It's too light," I said.

"It's not too light."

My mother liked to watch me get ready, like I had watched her get ready when I was a girl. After my father died when I was three, after enough time had passed, she would get ready to go on dates herself. I would pick out her earrings, sniff the bottle of Rive Gauche which was her. The women at church were always telling my mother she should marry again, that she should give me another father. "Rose has a father," she told them. "She doesn't need another one." My mother took marriage very seriously. It was a sacrament, the same as communion. It was a long time before she decided that maybe being married to someone who was dead wasn't as binding as being married to someone who was alive. By the time I had graduated from high school, she had pretty much settled with Joe, who handled claims forms for an insurance company. But then it wasn't a date anymore, only a series of nights she went to his house and nights he came to ours and they made dinner and watched TV and went home late but always went home.

"Your blush is too high."

I looked in the mirror again and started to wipe it off. I had stopped fighting with my mother, at least over make-up, a long time ago. It was the thing she knew, I could give her that much.

There was a way she watched me when I was looking in the mirror. She thought I didn't see her. She would stare at me so intently and I knew she was trying to see me like a stranger would, to judge me as harshly as the world would judge me. If she had that information, she thought she could prepare me somehow for what was to come. "Pretty girls have it harder," she said while I brushed out my hair.

"What?"

"People think it's the other way, that the ugly girls, the plain girls even, they're the ones to feel sorry for. But they don't have so many"—she stopped and pushed her eyebrows together, trying to think of the word—"distractions, I guess. There will always be people there to tell a pretty girl what she should be doing or thinking. At the counter, it's the pretty girls you can always sell the most to. They never know their minds."

"You don't know what you're talking about." My mother loved to talk about things like that, but I wasn't in the mood. I was going to be late. I pressed my mouth against my hand and then washed it off.

"You're a pretty girl," my mother said. "I was a pretty girl. I know what I'm talking about."

My mother was a pretty girl. I had seen the pictures, her dark hair sweeping off her forehead in a wave, her head tilted imperceptibly to one side, her mouth open to show the rows of small, perfect teeth. There was a picture of her in her confirmation dress, standing on the steps of the church, another waving from the bow of the *Queen Mary*, a snapshot taken on a guided tour, her sunglasses on, her gloved hand raised to the camera. But as she grew older my mother became beautiful. I could never find the exact moment it happened. In the pictures she changed, her face had lost its sweetness but taken on another thing. You can see it best in the photograph taken at my father's funeral. Who would have had the nerve to make a picture then, or how it came to be in her possession, I never knew, but there she was in a black dress, walking toward the camera but looking away from it. The cemetery is only a backdrop, the trees making an arch behind her, the headstones arranged like lilac bushes. She is more beautiful than a bride. Once, when I was ten and intent on finding every photograph of my father ever taken, I ran across this one. When I showed it to her, she closed her eyes and turned away. "Keep that if you want it," she said, "but I don't ever want to see it around. Do you understand me?" For the rest of the day she was quiet, and while I later understood it was because she didn't want to remember the day she watched them bury my father, at the time I thought she was ashamed, ashamed of the beauty that seemed somehow to break apart the grief around her. I put the picture in my Bible between the Gospels of Luke and John. I took the Bible with me when I left. It is the only picture of my mother I have.

I left her in the bathroom and went into the closet, turned on the light, and shut the door. There was a full-length mirror inside and I wanted a minute to look at myself without my mother watching me. What would she say if she saw me coming to her counter? Would she run her fingers along the sides of my face as I had seen her do to other women and tell me what could be done about the shape of my mouth or the length of my nose? And would I think what all those other women must think, that no matter how beautiful she made me, I would never be as beautiful as her?

"I'm going to wear your blue dress," I called out through the door.

"Sure," my mother said, "that'll look good."

I pulled the dress on over my head, and for a minute I thought about staying. Locking the door from the inside for no good reason other than I couldn't remember for a second what Thomas Clinton looked like. But then I did.

It was a night that at nineteen, in southern California in May, was like every other night you had seen so far, but a night that when you remember it years later in a place without an ocean, is like a powerful dream. Everywhere you went you heard the water, the same way you had always heard your breathing, and would later hear the highway, or trains, or women's voices. But the sound was so much a part of everything that you couldn't hear it at all then. This is what I took for granted: The sound of the water. The light on the water, day or night. The way you could look out for so long you couldn't tell the difference between the water and the sky. The sand that blew onto the highway in sheets and formed small dunes against the curbs. The smell of the water. The tough grass that grew from nothing. The soft, hot tar and the birds which never occurred to me would not be everywhere I went. I am saying this from memory and there are things I am forgetting. But I remember this: I wore that blue dress of my mother's which was spotted with holly leaves because I knew that when the wind caught it and blew it back, the skirt would press against my legs and be as big as a sail. I knew we would walk along the beach that night and he would have to remember the sight of me in that dress. I wore it because he went to college, and I liked the way he had to keep looking away from my face when he spoke to me. I knew that dress would break his heart.

Thomas Clinton was about my height, but there was a lightness to him, the size of his bones, the width of his shoulders, that made him seem smaller. Everything about him made me think he had been born late, that he would have been better off being his father, or my father. I could imagine him in a wide-brimmed felt hat, a newspaper folded beneath his arm. I could see him gladly giving up his seat on the bus to anyone who seemed to want it.

He picked me up in a blue Dodge Dart with wide bench seats. My mother and I didn't have a car, and to ride in one was always an occasion. I rolled down the window and leaned my face into the night air while he drove me to dinner in silence. The streets were wide and lined with small houses, every one of them exactly alike except for some small thing: a hedge around the front, a bay window, a garage. They were painted in sherbet colors, pale orange or pink, a creamy yellow. The lawns and the sidewalks made neat lines. You could count on everything being just so. I looked at a house and then closed my eyes for a minute. When I opened them again, I would see the same house, a full block away. It was a game I liked to play whenever I was in a car, especially when I was in a car with a date who had nothing to say.

Words came hard to Thomas Clinton. He managed to tell me before our dinner arrived that he was studying to be a math teacher. He would have been better, I think, drawing equations on napkins to show me how he felt. What percentage of his heart he had given to me already, as opposed to percentages given to his family, his work. He was fluid in numbers, he could explain them, but in an Italian restaurant, pushing a veal cutlet from side to side on his plate, he was lost. It was not a romantic place, where long silences are full of meaning. It was bright and clean and the waitresses wore uniforms that made them look like nurses. Our waitress came by too often because it was late and all her other tables had paid up and gone.

"Don't you like that?" she said to Thomas, pointing at his dinner. "If something's wrong, you'd tell me, right?" She was a woman in her early fifties, whose bright blond hair looked like candy spun onto her head.

"It's fine," he said, and cut again at the meat. "It's good."

"Well, I hope so. Your girlfriend liked hers. Look, she's almost finished." She leaned over toward me, like she wanted to tell secrets. "The cheesecake is good," she said. "You're skinny, you can eat cheesecake. If you have the room, you should think about it."

There was something about the way she talked, her easy manner, that made our silence singularly unbearable. "I'll just have coffee," I said.

"That's why you can eat cheesecake," she said, and sighed. "Because you don't. That's the way it works."

As soon as she had gone I wanted her to come back. I was no stranger to first dates, to their special kinds of horrors, but the ones I'd had tended to talk more often than not, to try and make an impression any way possible.

"I know you work at Simms," Thomas said finally, his eyes fixed down. Our plates had been taken away, but the waitress had insisted on bringing him his dinner packaged up, even though he'd said he didn't want it.

"You might not want it now," she said, leaving the folded white sack on the table between us, "but tomorrow for lunch, you'll want it."

"I work at Simms," I said. "I schedule deliveries."

"I know because I saw you once, going into the building in the morning. I drove past you." He stopped and I waited, thinking there had to be something more.

"And you knew me from church?"

He nodded. "I've seen you at church. You go with someone."

"My mother."

"Your mother," he said. "I thought it was probably your mother."

I looked out the window because I was afraid I would embarrass him if I looked at him too long. I felt genuinely bad for him, not angry or bored the way I did with so many of the others. I wished I had an idea what to say myself, but somehow the tone had been set; the passage of words would be difficult between us. "I think I'd like to take a walk," I told the window.

So he paid the check while I waited by the door and the waitress said good night and then came after us in the street to give Thomas the sack of cutlets he had left on the table. "You two look real cute," she said. "You have a good night."

I was right about the wind, but by then I was sorry about the way it made my dress into a flag that waved behind us. It was a dark night, and darker as we walked across the highway and down toward Imperial Beach, and I was hoping he wouldn't notice it. There was only a little light on the waves, no stars. As hot as the day had been, it had cooled off, and I could smell the smell that wasn't exactly sand or salt or water, but all three together. When we stopped I put my hand on Thomas Clinton's shoulder to balance myself and take my sandals off, and I felt

him tense, almost as if I startled him, as if he had forgotten I
was there, but when I pulled away he put his hand over mine
and held it there near the collar of his shirt. We stayed there,
just like that. There was something about the gesture, which
was so strange and unexpected, that I think I would have just
stood there all night.

"I knew it was your mother you went to church with," he
said finally. He was facing the water. His voice was low so I
had to lean in to hear him over the sound of the waves. I didn't
ask him to speak up. I knew if he stopped talking he'd never be
able to start again.

"I knew it was your mother and I knew where you worked
and I knew where you lived. I drove behind you one morning,
all the way from your house to Simms."

I looked at him, thinking it had to be a joke but then knowing
for sure it wasn't. The wind was high and it pushed the sand
around. It threw my dress out straight behind me. "More than
one morning," he added quietly. "Don't think I'm crazy, I'm
not. My God, there is nothing crazy about me. It's something
about you, Rose. When I saw you in church. I saw the way you
put your forehead on your hands when you're kneeling there."
He ran his fingers along my fingers. His hand was shaking. "I
would sit right behind you. The back of your neck. The back of
your dress." He pressed my hand into his shoulder, but he
wouldn't look at me. "Every week I thought I would talk to you
and then I finally did. And tonight. All night I just sat there and
in my mind I was telling you everything. Things I had thought.
It's been seven months. You'll think I'm crazy, but I couldn't
not tell you this."

My heart was beating so fast and all I could think of was, fast
as his. My heart is beating as fast as his.

"I had to wait until the thought of not telling you was worse
than the thought of telling you. Does that make sense? Once I
saw you eating lunch by yourself. It wasn't too far from here. I
hadn't even been looking for you but you were there. I used to
think if I just had your picture that would be enough. Then I
could look at your face. Your beautiful face."

He stopped and drew in his breath. He was still watching the
ocean. The waves were high from the wind. They were as black
as the night was black, the same way they had been blue like
the sky that afternoon. My eyes had adjusted to the darkness
and I could see him. He wore small wire glasses and had pale
hair. He was handsome. I hadn't really thought about it before.

I remember I started to cry, though I'm not sure why anymore. Maybe it was just that I had waited such a long time to hear someone say those things to me. It was romantic. What a thought, to be nineteen and be willing to give up everything in your life because someone says something to you on a dark beach that sounds romantic.

He didn't make a move toward me, and somehow that made it all the more spectacular. All those boys I'd turned away, all those boys who when they kissed me slipped my blouse out of the back of my skirt and tried to run their hands along my stomach. All the boys who said what they wanted, told me my breasts, my neck, the sides of my legs. I was stronger than all of them. I could twist myself away and walk into the water, demand that they take me home, or take myself home. But I didn't know until that night how they must have felt, wanting to press the side of their face against my breast bone and hold me. The comfort that would come from that, and I gave them so little. It was dark and Thomas Clinton could have been anyone, but I thought he knew me like God knew me. The longer we stood there in silence, my hand caught between his hand and shoulder, the more my memory set about improving his words, until they churned through my stomach and over my chest, spreading down through my arms and legs like my own blood. It was my own blood. The plainest form of nineteen-year-old sexual desire on a dark beach of the Pacific Ocean in southern California in May. And I knew so little that I took it to be a sign from God.

I faced him, pressed in chest to chest, bent his neck down with my hand, covered my mouth with his mouth, moved his hand down my back, pressed in like I was trying to pass through him, my whole body through his. I stood on one foot and wrapped my other leg behind his. I knew from every time I'd stopped before what the other body wanted from me. My hand raking up hard from the nape of his neck to the crown of his head, then down, inside the collar of his shirt, then back between us, working down the front of my dress until my arms came out of the sleeves and went back to his waist. Where was he? God help me, I don't remember him, not until the point he held my arms and pushed me back. Held me there and looked at me, and when he was afraid and couldn't look again he folded me back into my clothes and buttoned my dress and looked for the two buttons that were gone but couldn't find them in the dark, in the sand. He picked up the white sack with his dinner which had fallen from his hand and brushed the hair out of my face

and took my hand and led me back to the car. He drove me
home without saying a word and walked me to my door and
didn't kiss me good night. He called me the next night for a date
and the night after that and the night after that. He married me
at the end of the summer in Our Lady of Lourdes and Father
O'Donnell said the mass and his parents and his two sisters
came down from Victorville and we moved into the married
students' apartments and my mother cried but did so quietly in
the kitchen while I took out the last of the boxes, and the next
year he got a job teaching math in a high school in Marina del
Rey. That is everything. That is all there was to know.

═══ 2 ═══

My mother knew how to drive but didn't. She said she'd forgotten. She'd forgotten how to ride in a car as well. She would walk everyplace she possibly could. If it was raining, she would wear jeans and a sweatshirt, wrap her work dress in a dry cleaner's bag, and put it in with her shoes and purse in one of the large, plastic I. Magnin's bags we kept stacked beneath the kitchen sink. If she had to go someplace far from home she took the bus, but she didn't like to. She said it was dirty and crowded and she didn't like to sit next to strangers. If there was an emergency, a terrible emergency, she would call a cab or Mr. Lipton, the superintendent of the building, to come and drive her. She did the night I was five years old and my eardrum burst. She did when I was fourteen and ran a fever so high I couldn't tell her who she was, even though she asked me over and over again. They took my appendix out, and when I was well Mr. Lipton drove me home, but Mother walked, because going home was not an emergency.

It's no great mystery. It was because my father had died in a car. But he didn't die in a car. He died later, in the hospital, which is the thing that makes the story tragic instead of just very sad. The car got away from him somehow, forgot gravity despite its weight, and flipped three times before digging itself into a sidewalk where no one was walking. His spine was nothing but dust. "Bone dust," my cousin told me secretly in the back yard of my uncle's house when I was seven. He was the one who gave me the details. I never got them from my mother, I never asked. It took him five weeks in intensive care to finish what had been started. It was there my father died of pneumonia, which, from what I understand, is like drowning.

But I loved to drive, the way people love forbidden things.

23

Thomas taught me soon after we were married. He was a patient teacher and loved the fact that he could do something for me, though I wondered if later he regretted ever showing me how. We would sit on the cement steps in front of our apartment building, next to the red hibiscus that the gardener was always having to clip back so it wouldn't completely block the front door. I rolled my shorts up as far as I could, trying to get a little color on my legs while Thomas quizzed me from the safety manual. "At what point in a rainstorm are the streets most dangerous?" he asked. "Who would go through the intersection first, if two cars arrived at the same time?"

While I was taking the test, he went and bought me flowers and I wondered if the high school girls were in love with him. If they wrote their names next to his in a notebook during math class.

For a long time I couldn't bring myself to drive in San Diego, for fear of passing my mother on the street. It was a ridiculous fear because I knew every route she walked and when she walked it. But once we moved to Marina del Rey, I drove everyplace I could think of to go. I would drive to the electric company to pay the bill in person, drive to one grocery store that had good prices on staples and then another one across town because the produce was nicer. I would take Thomas to school in the morning and wait in the long line of carpooling mothers to drop him off at the door, then rejoin the line at three, or five, depending on whether or not he was coaching basketball. But then one day I missed. I was too far away, driving up the Pacific Coast Highway, listening to the radio. I was looking at the hills, thinking about the fire that had swept through last year and left them a charred pile of prickly black sticks. Now here they were, one year and a couple of floods later, as thick and green as they had ever been. The hills were the reason I was so late, and when I was sure it was impossible for me to make it back in time, I simply didn't try. Thomas was worried, he waited at school for a long time, then walked home and looked there. Then he started to think that he had possibly missed me, and that I was waiting for him, so he went back to school.

I can't remember Thomas ever getting angry with me. Sometimes, in bed at night, he would retell the story of those seven months before we met, when he would watch me.

"I remember one day you wore a red dress to church," he would begin.

"I never had a red dress," I said, my head on his chest, his arm around my shoulder.

"It was a red dress with half sleeves and a round collar. You had on flat black shoes and a black belt."

"It must have been my mother's," I said. "I don't remember it."

"You sat right in front of me. I would always get there late, so I could sit near you, but that day you came in after I did. You were alone. And you sat down right in front of me. I could smell your perfume, and your hair wasn't completely dry. I never heard a word Father O'Donnell said."

His sadness was a powerful thing then, and he never forgot it, the way my mother never forgot the Depression and so was forever saving little bits of things that might be useful later. Thomas said he made a promise to God and even though he never said exactly what the promise entailed, I knew it went beyond to love and honor and obey. This was a promise with desperation in its origin, the kind of deal Jonah cut in the belly of the whale. The difference being that I'm sure Thomas kept his promise, in the years I knew him.

So if my driving bothered him, he didn't say. If my lateness bothered him, sometimes all the way through dinner, he didn't tell me. I did try to be on time, and nearly every day I was. It's just that I had found a tightness in my chest. Some nights it woke me up, and I would lie there, taking shallow breaths. I would listen to Thomas, who slept so quietly beside me, and feel the warmth of his body in bed with me, and I would think, what makes something a sign from God? What makes something right? I didn't even know what I was thinking of, but I could feel it pressing down on me when I slept, when I ran the vacuum, when I picked out the wallpaper, bought cereal, wrote home.

The only time it seemed to go away was when I was driving. The world moved because of the directions of my hands. I rushed it past my windows as fast as I wanted. At first I knew where I was going. I would make up excuses, little reasons that took me farther and farther away, and then I gave up. I was never going anywhere and there was no sense lying to myself. People think you have to be going someplace, when, in fact, the ride is plenty. I loved to drive early in the morning, before the traffic started up. I loved to drive in the hard rains and see the world blur and clear beneath my windshield wipers. When it was dark I could see the lights of the other cars speeding by me and when it was sunny I would roll down the car window and look for the islands, Anacapa or Catalina, through a tangle of my own hair. I bought maps in every town, stuffed the glove compartment with directions. When I studied them late at night, after Thomas was asleep and the pain in my chest had gotten me up again, I was never interested in where I might go, only the contours of the roads, the kind of lines they made, their shape and width, the views I imagined they would afford me. This is what I was looking for.

I continued to light my candles up and down the Pacific Coast Highway, though I was less sure now of what to ask for. The first sign had simply changed the shape of my life, left me sharing an apartment with one person instead of another. There was a loneliness in being answered, as if God and I had less to say to each other now. I put in my coins and took my match from the box, pressed my forehead to my hands in prayer, but all I could think about were the candles that were already lit. Who had come here before me and what did they want? Did girls still want to be married and loved? Did they want to never be alone? Or had the priest lit these himself, a primer to bring the faithful from the street like moths? I could have prayed, Dear God, please keep me from Carmel, where every day my car was headed. It was a full day's drive. I would have to sleep over and come home the next morning, and how would I explain that? And what if I went and Thomas never asked me where I'd been for fear I might go away again and come back in two days or three or not at all? Would I head on to Oregon, or south through Mexico? I had the maps. But I could not pray for what I didn't want. I was careful with my prayers, now that they had been answered.

This is how the days passed, weeks and months. Places I could get to in time to come home. I worked as a temporary secretary and would call in to the placement office when the money I had didn't seem like enough. I would stay in a job for two days, a week, typing or filing, answering the phones, until whoever was missing came back and I had time to drive again. I didn't always stay on the freeways. Some things can be seen only by going off onto the secondary roads: the migrant workers moving through the strawberry fields, the palm trees. I liked to go down side streets, looking at the houses and the bicycles in the yard. Sometimes I would drive all the way to San Diego just going through neighborhoods. When I got into town I took my mother out to lunch.

"Why aren't you home?" she said. "Doesn't Thomas worry about you? My God, I hate to think of you just driving around out there."

"I only drive to see you," I said.

"I'd feel better to think of you home," she said. Even though I knew which home she meant, I liked to think it was with her.

My mother had married Joe the spring after I left, and it made me sad in a way, not her marriage, but the fact that she felt she had to wait for me to go. "Who'd have thought we'd be a couple of old married women having lunch?" she liked to say to me. My mother was happy being married. It was a gift she had given herself, the permission finally to live again the way she thought was natural. Her life was good. She was doing well at work. She had regular customers who refused to talk to anyone but her. I tried to talk to her, to tell her about the pain in my chest that could be eased only by a drive, to tell her that May reminded me so much of October and this year of last year, but I couldn't say things I didn't have words for yet. All I was sure of was that I loved her, her red lipstick, her delicate hands. Sometimes I drove all the way to San Diego but would only stand in the accessories department, watching her over a counter of scarves while she told another woman how to be beautiful.

After I left the doctor's office, after he had shaken my hand and said congratulations, I drove the car out onto the freeway and couldn't remember how to drive. I pulled over into the breakdown lane and pressed my forehead against the steering wheel. I closed my eyes and listened to the sound of the traffic whipping past me. I kept thinking, someone is going to open the passenger side door and tell me what to do. Not Thomas, not anyone I know. Someone is just going to get in the car beside me and say, Martha Rose, this is what we're going to do here. And I'd have done it, I swear to God, but no one came. Not even a cop to see if I was okay. For three years I hadn't been able to say what was wrong with my life, but at that moment it all became very clear. I had married a man I did not love. I was mistaken in my sign. I would have to have something else because this could not possibly be my life.

In a way I thought it would get easier from then on, because knowing is easier. But how I would have rather known three months before, when I could have left with nothing inside me but guilt and sorrow. I kneaded my flat stomach with my hand. I dug the heel of my hand into the skin until I could feel a small pain, and then I pressed harder.

I slept at home that night and never said a word. In the morning Thomas sat at the breakfast table, grading a stack of papers. He was teaching summer school. "Show your work," he wrote on the top of a paper, and then worked the problem at the bottom the way it should be done, line after line of numbers and letters I couldn't understand. I had never done well in geometry.

"She got the answer right," he said. "See that."

I looked at the paper. The girl had nice handwriting. I wondered if she was in love with him.

"Are you going to work today?" he asked.

"At a lawyer's office," I said. "It should last all week."

"Rose, Rose," he said and leaned over the table, over the cereal bowls and cups of coffee, and kissed my cheek, my mouth.

A lump came up in my throat. He was never a bad man. No one will ever say that Thomas Clinton was a bad man. "Come on," I said. "We need to get going."

When we got to school he told me not to worry about picking him up. "It's a nice day," he said. But in Marina del Rey they were all nice days.

"Make them all smarter," I said, because it's what I said every morning when he left.

"I'll do my best."

And then he was gone, mingling in with a sea of children. He was twenty-six years old.

When I went to Father O'Donnell, it was not to confess but to make him my accomplice. I needed the name of a place to go, someplace far away, where women had babies and left them behind, like pieces of furniture too heavy to move. A place that gave the babies to remarkable people, so fit to be parents that their sterility was unconscionable. I also wanted him to tell Thomas, when he came looking for me, that my desire to leave was sincere and he should let me go without ever telling him where I had gone. I'm making this sound very easy, when in fact it was not. It was sad enough to change my life for good, to make the blood reverse the course of its flow in my veins.

I was going to Saint Elizabeth's. Father O'Donnell had a file, which he brought out with great difficulty. It contained fliers, nearly advertisements, that addressed the problems of unfortunate Catholic girls. Words like *comfort* and *prayer* were scattered through the texts, along with *moral guidance*. But I was interested in the location more than the description. Saint Elizabeth's was in Kentucky, a state whose capital I did not know. I had never wondered about Kentucky, never imagined it as a girl the way I had New York or Houston or Paris. No one I knew had ever been to Kentucky, or was planning on going, and so I thought it would be the last place anyone would look for me.

"Tell me you'll wait until tomorrow," Father O'Donnell said. "Go home to Thomas, just for tonight, or go to your mother's. This isn't a decision to be made quickly."

Father O'Donnell had baptized me and given me my first communion. He had buried my father and married me. I had been in love with him when I was a girl. I had wished he was my father. Maybe once he wished I was his daughter, because it was plain that my news was hard for him to hear. His face was flushed and damp, and there was a trembling around his mouth not unlike my own. I may have made a mistake in going to him, though it seemed right at the time. California was full of priests who would try to dissuade me but not feel disappointed in me. It was his house, not God's, that I had come to in my moment of confusion. His windows full of saints, his pews, his rack of candles. Whenever I kissed a boy in school, cut a day of classes, argued with my mother, over what I can't remember, it was not God's forgiveness I sought, but his. He was the one I told. We sat in a small room behind the altar which he used to dress in before mass. His vestments hung on wire coat hangers from the doorjamb, great satin robes that looked ridiculously beautiful with no one in them. The window in that room had plain glass in it, meant for looking out over the parking lot and not for inspiration. There was a crucifix over the washbasin where anyplace else there would have been a mirror.

"I have to go today," I said. "I've made a mistake and if I don't leave now I might not be able to straighten things out."

"Divorce is a sin, Rose, I can't tell you otherwise. People today think that whatever they want, right at that moment, will be fine. But there are larger things to consider. Can you not see that?"

It was a strange thing, but I never even considered divorcing Thomas. I was only leaving him. For some reason that seemed different, even if I couldn't say what the difference was exactly. "I'm doing the only thing I can do," I said.

When I wrote down the address of Saint Elizabeth's, my hand was shaking. I asked if he would write a letter, telling them I was coming. "Don't tell them about Thomas," I said. I thought

the fact that I was married might disqualify me from a home for
unwed mothers.

I stood for a long time at the door, looking around the altar
to the church where I had spent so much of my life. Mrs. Mar-
nez was there lighting candles, as I had done year after year,
asking God to show her His will. Old Henry at the front railing
on his knees. A few people I didn't know.

"What about your mother?" he said.

"Don't tell her either."

"Are you going to let her think you're dead?" he said. His
voice was a whisper but it carried, as the voice of a good priest
carries.

"Don't ask me this."

"You've asked enough of me today, now I'm asking you,
Rose. What will you do about your mother?"

I turned around to face him, but I shouldn't have. I understood
then why confessionals were dark places where you told your
secrets through screens. "I'll give her up," I said, and went out
to the car. The second I said it I knew that would be my penance,
the worst thing I could bear. I was doing a terrible thing, but I
would pay the price. If I gave up the thing I loved most in the
world, then maybe God would respect my desperation.

Elizabeth was not the saint I would have chosen to name a home
for unwed mothers after. She had wanted a child, prayed for
one for so many years, and when John came to her late in life
she was filled with joy. But then again she was a woman who
found herself pregnant when she did not think that such a thing
was possible. Maybe that was the part they wanted us to remember. I have always taken names very seriously, people or places.
It's because my mother took them seriously. It was my father
who wanted to name me Rose. My mother told a story of being
pregnant with me. "Big as a ship," she liked to say. She would
lie on a chaise longue in the little garden outside their apartment,
her swollen feet sunk into a sea of pillows, and argue with my
father over names. "He was sure I was giving birth to a flower,"
she would say. "Lily, Iris, Daisy, those were the kinds of names
he was interested in." My mother believed that a name should
come from the Bible or at least a saint. She settled on Martha,
despite what Jesus had said. She understood how Martha
felt, wishing her sister would give her a little help in the kitchen.
Anyone would rather sit and listen, but there are some things,
like dinner, that needed to be attended to. So I was Martha

Rose, Martha until my father died and Rose after that. My mother had a sudden change of heart then. She saw my father's need for a name that bore no more significance than the bush that grew alongside the house. A name that was as important as beauty itself. Elizabeth lost her child, too, in the end. That was another thing.

But I didn't think about any of this for a long time, until I was nearly across the California state line. Until then I was crying for my own mother with such a fierceness that I twice had to pull the car over to the side of the road because I couldn't see.

August was a lethal time to attempt such a drive, but there was no waiting. A seasoned liar, like the one I became, is in no hurry. But the one I started out as that day in the doctor's office, my knees pressed together tightly, had hands that shook. I looked over my shoulder, cried easily. All of that is gone now.

The backseat was lined with water bottles and they made a gentle sloshing sound that was almost like an ocean. It was all I could think of to bring. My life, the car's life, were completely intertwined, and water, I thought, would save us both. The sun made waving lines of heat across the black highway. The land was so desolate, so untraveled, that I couldn't imagine why they had built a highway there at all. It was not so much a place as much as a place to get through, a stretch you had to cross if you were ever going to get to where you were going.

It turned out I had a little money saved. I had started putting some aside when I was taking so many trips. I thought, what if something ever happened when I was on the road, something could break down. I kept a bank envelope under the tarp that covered the spare tire and whenever I had a job I'd put in ten or twenty. I didn't take a dime from Thomas when I left, but I took his car. That car had become my best friend. I could leave my husband but not his car. By the time I pulled into a gas station in Barstow I had spent the little bit I had in my purse, and so I took out the envelope. There was more than six hundred dollars in there, and I kept thinking, I must have known, all the time I was slipping in money, never looking to see how much I had, part of me was planning to leave.

But worrying about the car made me careful, and most nights I just pulled over to a rest stop and put the water bottles on the floor and slept in the backseat. If something happened to the car I'd be wiped out, stuck in some desert town with no way to go on. In Barstow I asked a station attendant with the name Dwight stitched on his shirt in red cursive letters to look under the hood for me.

"I'm going a long way by myself," I told him. I leaned under with him, trying to get a little of the shade. It was sickeningly hot, 105, maybe more. "I just wish you'd check to see if everything's all right. I don't want to get out in the middle of nowhere by myself and have something happen," I said.

Dwight slipped his finger down into one of the belts, gave it a little tug. "Woman shouldn't be traveling alone," he said.

I knew it could go either way. He could help me out or drop an aspirin into the battery which would send me limping back to him as soon as I was five miles out of town. "I could use your help," I said. "I'm going to have a baby." It was the first time I'd just said it out like that. It was the first time it occurred to me that it could be something to use. "I'm headed just past Las Cruces. My husband, he's stationed out at Fort Bliss. He didn't want me to come alone, but he couldn't get leave to get me."

He looked at me under the hood. My dress was loose and blew around, there would be no telling for sure. "You're in good shape," he said, touching the spark plugs. "I'll fill up the radiator, but you keep an eye on that. Pull over every hundred miles or so and check it. The water, it's got to be up to here. But don't touch anything. If it overheats, you just stand back and wait." I thanked him. I meant it. When I got back into the car he came back and leaned in my window. "People will tell you your transmission's going to go. But don't listen to them. Your transmission is good."

There were so many things I needed to know, how to fix a car, how to lie. My mother taught me how to put on eyeliner without smudging it, but life was going to take more than that.

This driving was not a game. My back ached down into my hips and I tried moving to one side and then another. Only the week before I had thought I wanted nothing more in the world than to drive in one endless direction. Highway 40 was exactly that. East was an endless direction. The radio came in and out in waves. I ran out of songs I knew the words to and then sang them all over again. I played games with myself. At the next town I'll stop. I'll take off a whole day, get a motel room, sleep. But the next town would come and I'd say, You've made it this far, you might as well keep going, one more hour won't make a difference and that will be an hour you won't have to drive tomorrow. When I did stop, it was to get gas, check the oil, fill the radiator. I would walk around the car a couple of times, lift my hands up over my head, stare at the landscape that looked the way it had on the stop before and the stop before that. I did not know how to keep going and I did not know how to stop, so I kept going.

I had started to doubt my body. When I got so tired that the cars in front of me began to sway on the road, I remembered my mother saying how tired she had been when she was pregnant, and I would think, so you're not really tired. When I felt sick at my stomach, I wondered if I was actually sick, or if that was just part of it, too. Anything I could attribute to this baby I could dismiss, because I'd decided somewhere along the road that I was going to have nothing to do with it. I was following through on my part of it. I would see this pregnancy out, but that was it, no sickness, no side effects. It was enough that I was going so far to have it, and that I would see it delivered into the hands of those decent parents whose complete and wholesome lives I liked to contemplate. There was a difference, I knew, between being pregnant and being a mother. I was pregnant.

The steering wheel was so hot I couldn't move my hands around. That was one of the worst parts about stopping, making a cool place for your hands again. I tried writing letters to my mother in my head, but they weren't any better than the note I'd left for Thomas. I wanted to do better for her. I knew she'd been a good wife to my father, that she was a good wife to Joe, even if she could never love him in the same way. She took marriage seriously, as she had taken motherhood seriously. She would find a way to love me even if I told her the truth, but I could feel her disappointment like a hot wind on my neck. The truth was something that would have to be mine alone. It was something that receded as I drove east.

There was a time in my life when I'd wanted to know everything. I wanted to read the brutal details of every local murder. I wanted to know exactly how my father had died, the extent of damage to the car, the very place it happened. Facts had a certain irresistible quality. No matter how deeply they disturbed me, I thought I was better off knowing. But learning is easier than forgetting. The fact that my mother, that Thomas, didn't know where I had gone or the reason, made my life easier, but I liked to think it made things easier for them as well. The world is full of things we're better off not knowing.

But that didn't mean I couldn't lie to her. Late one night, after eating eggs and toast in a truck stop in New Mexico, I got all the quarters the cashier would give me and called her up. The phone was in the parking lot, and when I shut the door to the booth it gave off a blue fluorescent light. I put the change in a napkin and fed it steadily into the phone. When Joe answered I was so surprised that for a minute I couldn't think of what to say.

"It's Rose," I told him.

"Rose? Rose?" He didn't speak to me but dropped the phone on the bed and called out for my mother. Both of us were crying when she picked up, and it made it harder to understand what was being said.

"Come home," my mother said.

"I can't."

"You will," she said. "I love you. I'm not going to have you lost out in the world. You're my daughter."

I put a hand over my other ear, trying to block out the sounds of the traffic. "Things just weren't right," I said. "My life, it wasn't right. I can't tell you about it now, you're just going to have to trust me. I'm doing what's best." It was almost exactly what I had written on the postcards I hadn't mailed. It sounded every bit as wrong when I said it.

"Whatever this is, we'll fix it. Thomas is going crazy. He's terrible, Rose. You can leave if you have to but not like this."

I looked out at the traffic going along the highway. "I'm already gone," I said.

I stayed in the booth for a while after I hung up. Then I opened the door, which automatically snapped off the light. I had promised myself I would stay in that town for the night. But I didn't.

There was nothing behind me and nothing ahead of me. The world consisted of as much road as I could see in either direction. I found myself looking forward to towns, counting down the miles to Albuquerque, Tucumcari, Amarillo. When I got close to a city I felt almost euphoric, as if I had finally arrived, but five minutes later I would be on the other side, looking at the mileage for whatever was ahead. I was disappointed in myself because it used to be I'd never care at all. But now I was tired in my bones. It was important for me to have something to concentrate on, because when my mind wandered it went to my mother, or worse yet, Thomas. I would picture him sitting in our house, the lights off, trying to watch television. I could see him going through my dresses in the closet, running his hands along the sleeves. The worst was to think of him eating. The thought of him at the table alone, trying to finish dinner, was nearly enough to make me turn the car around. Once I did, just before Oklahoma. I drove back twenty-five miles, and then turned around again just as quickly, because nothing looked any different. To be truly brave, I believe a person has to be more than a little stupid. If you knew how hard or how danger-ous something was going to be at the onset, chances are you'd never do it, so if I went back I would never be able to leave again. Now that I knew what leaving meant.

Just over the Oklahoma border, thirty-five miles outside Elk City, I picked up a hitchhiker. I told myself I wouldn't do it. It went against everything I believed about driving as something best done alone. But the sight of Oklahoma scared me to death. I pulled into a rest stop to refill my water bottles from a public spigot and spread the map across the hood. Arkansas was as far away as China.

"Where you headed?" a man said to me. He looked young, maybe nineteen or twenty. He was wearing jeans and a white tee shirt. His hair couldn't have been more than a quarter of an inch long in any one place. He didn't look like the kind of person who'd kill you. He looked like he knew how to drive.

"East," I said, my hand trying to block out enough of the sun so I could see him.

"East isn't a place," he said.

"Well, I'm going east."

"You taking Forty into Arkansas?"

I looked around. There were no other cars in the parking lot save one station wagon loaded up with kids. Someone must have left him there. I nodded.

"I could use a ride," he said, "if that's the way you're going. I'd kick in for gas."

Any other time in my life I would have said no, but I didn't see that there was anything left to lose that I hadn't already lost. "Sure," I said. "Come on."

He looked so pleased, and when he smiled, seemed even younger, sixteen maybe. "You know how to drive?" I asked him.

"You bet."

"Good," I said, "you're driving." I threw the keys over the hood and he caught them. It was a stupid thing to do, but I figured if something bad was going to happen, it would happen if I was driving or not. It would happen if I was awake or not. He got in the front and I got in the back. I asked him his name.

"Billy," he said.

"Listen, Billy, keep an eye on the thermostat. Don't let it overheat. Stay on Forty the whole time, promise. I'm going to get some sleep."

We got into the car and shut the doors. He asked if he could play the radio and I told him that would be fine. He looked carefully before pulling onto the interstate and then got quickly up to speed. If he played the radio at all, he waited until I was asleep. Asleep and driving at the same time. It was like a wonderful dream.

When I woke up it was dark and we weren't going anywhere. I thought that I had just pulled over to go to sleep, but then I remembered I hadn't been driving. I remembered Billy and felt a wave of panic moving up from the soles of my feet to my throat. When I looked out the window I saw him standing in a bright light, talking to another man. We were at a gas station. Billy gave the man some money and got back into the car.

"You're awake," he said. "I hope I didn't wake you up."

"Where are we?" I pushed the hair out of my face. I wanted a bath.

"Maybe a hundred miles west of Fort Smith. You've been asleep a long time."

I got out of the car and told him to slide over and let me drive for a while. He made sandwiches and cut up apples and we drank water out of one of the jugs.

"You didn't tell me your name," he said.

"Mary."

"It was nice of you to pick me up. I'd been waiting at that rest stop a couple of hours. I had a real good ride before that, almost six hours. Some trucker hauling oranges from California. But it wasn't as good as this ride, though." He stretched one arm out of the open window and let the wind blow it back. "I love to drive," he said. "Not everybody'd let you drive their car, but I've been driving since I was ten years old." He spoke quickly and his voice was anxious and high. "That's when my dad taught me. Soon as I was big enough to reach the pedals and see over the dashboard he had me driving a car. By the time I got my license it seemed almost funny, you know, 'cause I'd been driving for so long without one. That's what makes me so careful, all those years I drove without one. I had to make sure I never got pulled over 'cause then there'd really be hell to pay.''

He looked happy, all fresh-faced and young, like he could stay up all night. I kept thinking I wasn't that much older than he was, but I felt like I could have been his mother. "Where did you say you were coming from?'' I asked him.

He looked out at the road for a little while, trying to decide how much to tell me. "West,'' he said. "Just like your east.''

"I've been west,'' I said.

"I'm going to see my folks,'' he said, still watching the road. "They're right before the Tennessee border, not too much off Forty, if you're going that far.''

"I'm going that far.''

"My father needs me at home. I got older sisters, but they're all married and gone. It's not like he's so old, my dad, but the place is too much for him and my mom to handle by themselves. I shouldn't have gone away in the first place. I'm all the help my dad's got now, nearly three hundred acres to work. It would be too much for anybody. Don't you think that's too much?''

I nodded, then took my eyes away from the road for a minute to look at him. "That's a lot,'' I said. You could tell what he would have looked like when he was young, the same way you could tell what Thomas was going to look like once he was old. His hair would have been redder, where it was nearly brown now. He would have been skinny with milky skin. "You're right to go back if that's what you think you should do.''

Then he leaned back against the door. He seemed relieved somehow, like all he needed was for one other person to tell him, to forgive him for running away. It didn't take a lot to figure out he'd left the army someplace. "What about you,'' he said. "Why are you going east?''

"I'm going to get my sister Lucy down in Pensacola.''

"She in trouble?''

"It's her husband,'' I told him. "He's been drinking a lot. It's gotten to be pretty bad for her. She's got kids and everything. But she's scared to go, you know how that is. She doesn't know what she's supposed to do. So I told her I'd come and get them.''

"Where're you going to take them?''

"Home to live with me and my husband in New Mexico. We've got plenty of room. Maybe they'll want to stay on, I'm not sure. We'll have to see how it goes.''

"One of my sisters' husbands ever crossed her, I'd kill him,''

Billy said in a tired voice. "That is, if my dad didn't kill him first."

I thought about this for a while. I had always wanted a sister. "I may kill him," I said. "I'll have to wait and see." But he didn't hear me, he'd already fallen asleep.

I ended up driving Billy right to his parents' place in Crawfordsville, Arkansas. It wasn't too much out of the way, and he said if I wanted to come in for something to eat and rest up for a while, that he was sure it would be all right with his family. "I've never had a ride like this before," he said. "To-your-door service."

The house wasn't much, but there was a whole lot of land. I stayed in the car while he went up to see his parents. He would be telling them a lie, some lie about getting out that he would have to keep up with for the rest of his life, if he was never caught. You could see on their faces how glad they were to have him back, how much they'd missed him.

"You shouldn't have been picking up hitchhikers, young lady," his father said to me. "But you couldn't have picked up a better one than this fellow here."

I couldn't seem to get enough to eat at dinner, even though his mother brought out food like she'd been expecting us. I ate like I was desperate. I wanted to touch everything in the house, the backs of the chairs, the family photographs, the bowls that lined the cupboards. It seemed like the first time I'd been someplace in years, even though I'd had a home of my own just four days before. When they asked me to spend the night I was grateful. I was only a day's drive away from Saint Elizabeth's and suddenly I felt I had all the time in the world. What would the difference be, a day or two? My stomach was still flat, though harder now. I looked at it for a long time in the bathtub that night, deep in the hot water, beneath a film of soap, and thought, remember this, it won't be like this again. I went to sleep in Billy's sister's room, in a single bed with a yellow flowered bedspread. I went to sleep in a girl's room in her parents' house, where people talked in quiet voices downstairs and the windows were open and the night blew in from the fields. I slept like his sister would have, without trouble or dreams.

Billy woke me up, shaking my shoulder, saying, Mary, Mary, in a whisper. He was kneeling beside my bed in his pajamas. Maybe he was only ten or twelve. Maybe he woke up in the night and was afraid and went to his sister.

"I have to tell you something," he said.

It was such a deep sleep, I had a hard time coming up. I wasn't afraid, or even surprised to see him there. "What is it?" I said softly.

"I didn't tell you the truth," he said. "I went AWOL. I just left and bought these clothes. I buried my uniform back in Arizona."

I reached out and touched his head, ran my hand along the side of his face. It was still warm from sleep. I wanted to take him to bed with me, just to keep him under my arm until he could rest again. "Don't worry," I said.

"I've got to worry. What if they find me?"

"They've got lots of guys," I said. I didn't want to wake up, not completely.

"You think I should tell my folks?" he whispered.

"You should do whatever you want to, whatever you can live with best."

He sat back on his heels and looked at me. He reached out very tentatively and touched my hair. "I know you're lying, too," he said quietly. "And if you need to stay here, I think it would be just fine." He stayed for a while longer, just looking at me. Then he got up and left the room, shutting the door behind him.

In the morning I didn't know for sure if he'd been there or not. I never knew for sure. I left before anyone was up.

I GAVE Interstate 40 up in Nashville. When you don't have a home, it's easy to get attached to things, people, highways. Wherever you are the longest starts to feel like the place you're supposed to be, and I had been on 40 since California. Now I was on 65 going north. Then the Green River Parkway up toward Owensboro. I had good directions. You'd think I would have known by then that all roads are more or less the same, but as I pulled off the exit for Habit I started to think there was a lot out there I hadn't seen, and I wondered if maybe I should.

I found a gas station off the highway and went in to ask about Saint Elizabeth's. I knew how to get to the town but not more than that. There was a woman sitting in front of the station, sunning herself while three children who I guessed were hers sat dully in a small inflatable swimming pool half full of water. They were dark-haired and tan and they all three looked to be about the same size. It was hard to tell because they were sitting down. One of them tried to splash me as I walked by, but the water fell short, making a little muddy spot in the dust.

"Excuse me," I said to the woman. I was waking her up. I didn't want to, but I didn't know what else to do.

"Ma!" one of the children screamed. "Somebody wants gas."

The woman blinked her eyes open and pulled up the top of her blouse, which she had down below her shoulders to get some color on her chest. She looked exactly like the children in the pool. They were only smaller, tanner versions of their mother. She shook the sleep off of her. "Sorry," she said. "I drifted off."

"No," I said. "It's so hot. I know."

She stood up and stretched her arms over her head. I imagined

40

she didn't do a lot of business. She looked over to the pool. One of the girls was trying to hold another girl's face under the water, but there really wasn't enough water to do it right. The boy sat on the edge, watching. "Stop that," the woman said to them without much enthusiasm.

"What I need are directions, really," I said. "I'm looking for Saint Elizabeth's."

The woman's expression changed. She looked back at her children again and then back at me. "Up there," she said, her voice flat. "Three miles past town. On the left." Then she turned around and headed inside the station.

"Can I get some gas?" I said. I had half a tank, but I didn't want to have woken her up just for directions.

"You got enough to get you there," she said, and went inside.

"Boo," one of the girls in the swimming pool said.

It wasn't until I was back in the car and driving again that I realized what had happened. That just by saying where I was going she would know all of my business. She didn't like it, either.

If I drove through a town, I didn't see it. Habit was nothing but two stores and a dozen or so houses that were closer together than the others. Saint Elizabeth's, on the other hand, would have been nearly impossible to miss. I came over the top of a hill and there it was, sitting back from the road. It was giant and white and looked more like a natural phenomenon, like the Grand Canyon, than a home for unwed mothers. I guess there was nothing peculiar about it as a building. It was beautiful because it was impressive; spires and latticework, jutting balconies, arched windows. It was just so completely out of place. Kentucky had been all mountains and fields of tobacco so far. I couldn't imagine who would have built a place like this here. Who would have looked all over and come to the top of this hill in Kentucky, driven down the first stake and said, here's the place we're putting it.

But I got my answer soon enough. I pulled the car up near the front steps and got out to read a brass historical marker. That's where I first heard the history of Saint Elizabeth's, the Hotel Louisa and the spring. It told the story of how the Clatterbucks and the Nelsons came together, about a child named June falling ill and the wealthy horse breeder who built a hotel for a spring that eventually dried up. The letters were tiny and they managed to pack a lot of information on the sign. When I finished, I looked up to the massive front double doors and felt a sinking feeling all the way down to my feet. There was no more time, no more traveling. I had arrived. I read the sign again and then again. I thought about getting back into my car.

I must have made a sorry picture standing there, taking such an incredible interest in the hotel's history. The suitcase beside me was so small it looked like something a child would take to spend the night with a friend. I rubbed my ankle up against it.

"It's an interesting history," a woman said. I turned and found a nun beside me, one who was obviously skilled in moving quietly from place to place. She wasn't much more than five feet tall and was completely covered in white cloth, head to foot. She was clearly of a different breed than the nuns I was used to seeing in California. "You've come to stay with us?" she said, keeping her eyes on the sign, possibly so as not to frighten me off.

I told her I was.

"We always know the girls who are coming to stay," she said. "Of course, sometimes you can just tell, but even when you can't, they're the ones who read the sign. We used to wait for them to come inside themselves, but they could read this sign for hours. Once a girl stood here halfway through the night, then she just went away and we never saw her again." She reached down and picked up my bag. "Didn't bring much, did you? Well, that doesn't matter. Clothes are the one thing we have plenty of." She asked me my name.

"Rose," I said, "Martha Rose Clinton."

"I'm Sister Bernadette," she said, and then she stopped and looked at me. She tilted back her head, so that the light fell under her visor. She was possibly thirty herself, with small, bright eyes. She reached up and pushed some hair that had fallen into my face back in place behind my ear. "Mother Corinne hates to see girls with hair in their eyes. And you have such a pretty face, Rose." She touched my cheek for a moment and smiled at me. "You'll be glad," she said.

I wondered what I would be glad about, having the baby, giving the baby away, coming here at all. None of them seemed like particularly joyful things. I followed her up the stairs and into the main lobby, keeping my eyes on the long black rosary that swung in and out from the folds of her skirt. Then I looked up and saw a sea of pregnant girls.

If you see a pregnant girl on the street, maybe you notice. There could be some brief registration in your mind about her or her child, and then it goes. But this room was full of girls, sitting on sofas, reading magazines, talking quietly among themselves, and each was more pregnant than the last. One girl's size served only to exaggerate another's. Their bellies were so uniformly large they overwhelmed the room, so that it wasn't the girls you saw at all, only a gathering of distended abdomens, overinflated balloons from which small wisps of girls were attached. I felt that surely I had come to the wrong place, that whatever these girls had was not what was wrong with me. I was thin, flat, tall, and when they looked up at me, you could tell that was the very thing they were thinking. Or possibly they were thinking, wait and see.

Sister Bernadette pulled me through without introductions. I must have looked pale, and I felt pale. I knew now what was coming, my body was going to rebel, take on a life of its own, make decisions without me. All of this leaving, this sadness, this driving, had been about having a baby. I was going to have a baby. Until that exact moment I hadn't understood this fact at all.

We went behind the elaborately carved registration desk, where a hundred wooden boxes stood without keys. Sister Bernadette knocked lightly on a door that read O F F I C E. "Mother?" she said.

The nun who answered the door was as tall as I was but three times my size. She was a big woman in every sense, heavy-boned with weight besides. Her face was soft and red and a tuft of iron gray hair jutted coarsely from beneath her wimple. Her breasts were as noticeable and as awkward as the stomachs of the girls who filled the lobby. They created a shelf that ensured that anyone meeting her would have to keep their distance. I couldn't help but think a nun must be embarrassed by such breasts.

"What have we here?" she said, as if I was another delivery, a carton of milk, a sack of flour.

"This is Martha Rose Clinton," Sister Bernadette said.

"Yes, of course, from California."

"California!" Sister Bernadette said. "What a long way to come."

Mother Corinne made a strange movement, almost as if she was bowing her head for a moment, and Sister Bernadette was silent. She left as quietly and completely as she had arrived. "Come in, Miss Clinton," she said, and I followed her into the office.

It must have been Lewis Nelson's office. There was still a picture of a horse on the wall, along with paintings of Saint Elizabeth and the Sacred Heart. It was an office built by a man who was playing at running a hotel. The desk was big enough to sleep on, the chairs were leather, the big picture window looked out to the place where water once came from the ground.

"So you know Father O'Donnell?" she said.

"Yes, in San Diego. Did his letter come?"

"No, there's been no letter, but he called. He had several interesting things to say about you." She toyed absently with a silver cross that hung around her neck.

"What did he have to say?"

"That would be between Father O'Donnell and myself," she said, opening up a file I couldn't see. The distance created by the desk was formidable. She kept her eyes on the paper in front of her.

"Do you know Father O'Donnell?" I said. It never occurred to me that he might know people here. But she didn't answer my question. I got the feeling Mother Corinne was in the habit of asking questions, not answering them.

"Do you know for sure that you're pregnant?"

"Yes," I said.

"So you brought a medical report."

"No, but why would I lie about a thing like that?"

Mother Corinne looked up at me and shrugged. "It's happened. You're not showing and people will lie about strange things. Most girls wait until they truly need our services before they arrive, so it's quite easy to tell. Other girls are vagrants, looking for a place to stay for a while."

It had been a long drive and I was tired enough to want to kill her, but at the time I remember thinking she looked like someone who would never die. "You spoke to Father O'Donnell?" I said.

"Yes."

"Then you know at least I'm not a vagrant." I paused, wondering how to address the rest of it. "I'll try to show as soon as possible," I said.

"Don't be fresh, Miss Clinton," she said, marking something in the file and then closing it. "I'm here to look out for the welfare of all the girls, you included."

I stared at the face of Saint Elizabeth, an older woman, so happy to be pregnant.

"About the father," she said.

"Yes?"

"What became of him?"

"He's dead," I said. "It happened in a car."

She sighed and shook her head, reopening the file and making yet another mark. "Dead," she said. "Yes, of course."

Then suddenly Sister Bernadette was back and leading me up the stairs to my room. What if he had been dead? That would make me a fairly sympathetic case, a pregnant girl with a dead lover, that deserved at least a few words. Sister Bernadette opened a door to what must have once been a lovely room. Now the worn bedspreads and thinning carpet seemed depressing. At least there was a bed, which meant I could sleep.

"You'll be sharing a room with Angela," she said. "She's a sweet girl, you'll do fine with her. You get some rest now, Rose. After a while I'll bring you up a tray."

I sat down on the edge of the bed. I was suddenly too tired to say anything, even to thank her.

"You'll be fine," she said, and patted my shoulder.

I dreamed of my mother at the cosmetics counter that afternoon, an endless line of women waiting as she tiredly told each of them how to apply their make-up. When I woke up I was crying, as I would do for many years whenever I dreamed about my mother, and there was a dark-haired girl sitting on the edge of the twin bed opposite mine, watching me cry.

"Hey," she said quietly. "You okay?"

I wiped my eyes on the corner of the sheet.

"You don't need to do that. Here, look here." She handed me a box of Kleenex and I took one. "I'm Angie," she said. "I'm your roommate. Did you have a bad dream, or are you just crying?"

"It was a dream," I said, and blew my nose, but I couldn't seem to stop crying. It wasn't anything much, but it wouldn't stop.

"I wake up that way sometimes," she said, "lately, you know. I didn't used to." She leaned across the gap of our two beds. "It makes me feel a little crazy, like there's all this stuff going on in my head that I don't know about. It seems like a person ought to at least know what was going on in their own head."

"It seems that way," I said, and sat up. This was two times

in a row now I'd woken up with someone watching me. I was starting to think that I was more interesting in my sleep.

"You're not showing at all," she said, looking at my stomach. "I'm not much, but you can see it." She pulled her thin dress tight across her stomach to show me the little roundness that was there. "We must be pretty close together. That's how they decide on who rooms with who. If they put a real pregnant girl in with a new girl, the new girl freaks out when the other one leaves, or she gets real scared about having the baby and all. Someone said that once a girl tried to do herself when her roommate had her baby."

"Kill herself?"

"No, no, kill the baby, you know. She drank a whole bottle of castor oil. Can you believe that?"

I said I couldn't.

"Well, who knows what's true around here. The stories you hear. They told me your name was Martha."

"It's Rose."

"That's just the kind of thing I'm talking about. Rose. That's a lot prettier. Where did you come from before?"

"California." My head hurt, and I had that feeling that I'd been having lately, like the room was rocking.

"California? Well, why did you come all the way out here? Don't they have places like this in California?"

"I wanted to get away," I said. I wasn't quite up to being questioned. I wasn't quite up to anything, so I lay back down on the bed.

"Did something bad happen to you?"

"My husband died," I said.

Angie began to giggle a little, and she covered her mouth with her hand. "I sure hope you didn't tell Mother Corinne that."

"Why not?"

"Because that's what everybody says, stupid. Everybody says they had a really great husband but he died, in a car crash or something. Except now girls say he got shipped out to Vietnam and stepped on a land mine. Usually one of the older girls tries to tip you off before your interview. They say it's best if you just look down at your hands and act all sad and penitent."

"Great."

"Don't feel bad, you figure things out here in no time. I've only been here eight days and it already seems like my whole life."

I tried to think of that, being here my whole lifetime. It made my head hurt worse. "So what do I need to know?" I said tiredly.

"Sister Bernadette and Sister Serena are the ones you want to go to if you've got something on your mind. Sister Evangeline is sweet but she's older than time and pretty much blind. Sister Loyola is a snitch. She seems nice enough when you meet her, but she takes everything from your lips right to Mother Corinne's ears."

"And Mother Corinne?"

"Well, you already met her. And you can bet that anything you thought about her was right on the money." Angie looked at me. "I wish you'd stop crying," she said.

What I couldn't understand was why, in a place with nearly a hundred rooms and only twenty-five girls, we had to have roommates at all. I asked it carefully, making sure Angie understood it wasn't her I minded, I was just wondering. She told me that years ago they used to have the whole place set up like a hospital ward, with all the girls in rows of beds in the grand ballroom, but then one girl got the pox and they couldn't control the spread at all. "All those little babies born blind or missing arms," she said. "Can you imagine just waiting on that? All the girls in front of you having crippled babies and you know you will too but all you can do is sit around and wait for it to happen. After that they put people in rooms. They say we can't have our own rooms 'cause of the heating costs, that they don't like to open the whole place up, but really it's because they don't like for us to be alone, or they 'don't think it's natural,' as Mother Corinne likes to say."

I had never shared a room with anyone but Thomas.

I put on a clean dress. Billy's mother had washed and ironed the few things I had before I left Arkansas. The only vestige of the days of the grand Hotel Louisa was that people still met on the front porch at five o'clock in the warm months. The bourbon and sodas were strictly forbidden, but we went there as if pulled by tradition, just to sit in the chairs and look out over the Clatterbucks' back pasture.

"You've got to be respectful to the girls ahead of you," Angie told me as we were walking downstairs. "The farther along a girl is, the nicer everyone will be, like fixing her plate at supper and giving up chairs. It's only right, you know, we're all going to graduate sooner or later. There are three girls now, Charlotte

and Nora and Lolly, who are already two weeks late. That's a
lot to have late at the same time. Everybody's real nervous about
it.''

The stairwell was lined with grand paintings, mostly of a
beautiful, dark-eyed woman I later learned was Louisa herself.
Louisa with her hair up, standing in front of the fireplace. Louisa
with her hair down, walking through the gardens. Louisa with
Lewis, his hand resting gently against her shoulder. I don't
imagine she had time to do much else but sit for paintings. At
the bottom of the stairs was a small dish of holy water nailed up
to the wall. Angie dipped in her fingers without looking down
and crossed herself, and after thinking about it for a moment, I
did the same.

We walked onto the porch in the late August afternoon of
Habit, Kentucky. It was hot, but not like Flagstaff and Amarillo
and Oklahoma City. There had been good rains all summer and
the grass in the pasture was heavy and dark. I had never seen
such thick banks of trees, such softness growing from every
surface of a field. Kentucky was another country, and in that
country, Saint Elizabeth's was a country unto itself, where on
the porch of a grand hotel, twenty-five pregnant girls drank
sweaty glasses of iced tea and watched the sun set west while
their loose dresses blew around their hips and pressed against
their huge stomachs. I couldn't imagine which ones were two
weeks overdue. They all seemed two weeks overdue to me. I
watched their faces carefully; they looked like they had forgotten
themselves and maybe for a moment thought their husbands
were upstairs changing in the room, and would soon come onto
the porch and kiss them and look proudly over the beginnings
of their family. Every now and then a girl broke away from the
group and walked down the front steps and into the field, where
she could imagine herself to be the only woman in the world
about to have a child.

At six o'clock the one that Angie said was Sister Loyola
stepped onto the porch and rang a small bell. The girls hoisted
one another up from their chairs with exaggerated effort and
laughed. ''That damn bell of hers,'' Angie whispered to me.
''You think she could just say that supper was ready.''

As I turned to go in I saw a man walking up toward the hotel.
He was the only man I had seen since my arrival, and I wondered for an instant if he was coming to get someone. ''Who's
that?'' I asked.

''Oh, that's Son,'' Angie said, and waved to him. He waved

back to her and smiled. He was a giant man, maybe six foot six. He wasn't fat, but as big and broad as an oak. His arm swept through the air like the branch of a tree. "He fixes things. Everybody's in love with Son."

I didn't know how she meant that, really in love, or as a kind of joke, but she had gone into dinner before I could ask her.

We said our prayers standing beneath chandeliers, Bless us, O Lord, and these Thy gifts.

At dinner we sat with girls who were closest to our class. Your class was the month you were due in, so I was the class of February. Charlotte, Lolly, and Nora, the class of August, sat at the head table with a couple of girls who were due any day. It made an odd kind of sense, their not wanting to get too close to the ones who were just coming in. By the ninth month, they were saturated with the things they were going to have to give up: their friends, their home, their child. They had no cause to take on new alliances. We sat with a girl named Regina, who was due in January, and Beatrice, who was due in December. Beatrice was a big-boned, strong-looking girl who claimed to work in the mines alongside the men in eastern Kentucky.

"I bet you worked 'long side the men," Angie said, laughing at her own joke. I was surprised at how bold she was, having been here only eight days herself. Beatrice was clearly a girl who could give you trouble if she was so inclined. But she laughed a little herself and poured another glass of milk. She was showing nearly as much as the girls in the class of October.

"Twins run in my family," she said, and smiled to show her big white teeth, which were miraculously straight and even. "My grandmother was a twin."

"What a nightmare," Angie said.

"If I have two," Beatrice said, "I might just take a mind to keep one for myself." But no one laughed at that, and Regina, who was quiet anyway, turned her head. Even at the end of my first day I knew enough to know that keeping a baby wasn't something to be joked about. None of us would. That's why we were here.

We ate the rest of our meal quietly. The food was not good, vegetables were overcooked, the meat sat in thin pools of grease, but there was a limitless amount of everything. "Sister Evangeline does the cooking," Beatrice said to me in a low voice, as if that would explain everything.

I pushed back my plate, suddenly unable to go on. "Eat, eat, eat," Angie said cheerfully. "That's the war cry around here. I've gained four pounds in a week. 'The success of a girl can be measured in the pounds gained,' that's what Sister Loyola says."

She looked so thin to me, all knees and elbows. I couldn't imagine where she put those four pounds.

"Can't you just see what this place must have been like?" Beatrice said. "I mean, with white tablecloths and white napkins and fancy china that all matched. There must have been a guy in a white coat coming around with little bowls of water, asking you if you wanted to rinse off your hands. My sister ate dinner in a real fancy restaurant once, down in Lexington. She said that's what you do."

"That's crazy," Angie said. "Everybody washes their hands before they go to dinner."

"Hey, she ate there, not you," Beatrice said, helping herself to another slice of bread.

"Well, I like to think about what I'd wear, you know, if this was still a fancy hotel. Something low-cut with little pink beads on it. Something that kinda caught the light when I walked through the room."

"I'd wear black," Beatrice said. Her hair was thick and black and her eyes were nearly black. It would look nice on her. "I wanted to make myself a black dress once, and my mother nearly threw a fit. 'Why do you want your one nice dress to be something you can only wear to a funeral?' she said."

"Black is very stylish," Angie said. Then all at once all three of the women looked at me. "How about you, Rose. What would you wear?"

But somehow I just couldn't get into the spirit of things. The idea of a pretty dress in a beautiful restaurant made me want to cry. We were all through with pretty things. We were all through turning heads, being young. "I don't know," I said. "I wouldn't care. I'd just wish it was a little darker in here."

"Candlelight," Angie said softly. "We forgot about the candles."

Then there was a commotion in the front of the room, and Lolly stood up and then sat back down again. Then other girls stood up and came to her table, and then the sisters came out, taking quick steps, their habits sailing out behind them, telling everyone to sit down and be quiet. A girl from the table in front of ours leaned over and whispered to us. "Water broke."

"I can't believe this is happening on your first night here," Angie said. "I've been here eight days and nothing like this has happened to me before."

In fact, it was happening to everyone. My throat closed up in such a panic I thought it was me they were coming to take away. As we watched Sister Bernadette and Sister Serena guide Lolly out of the dining room, we knew what was ahead of us. Lolly passed right by me, so close I could have touched her. She was younger than I was. She had a wide pink satin ribbon in her hair. Her hands were shaking. The back of her dress was soaked through.

"They'll take her to Owensboro," Regina said in a dreamy voice. It was the first time she'd said a word all evening. "I used to live in Owensboro."

"What will happen?" I asked Angie that night when we were both in our beds. The room was dark, as dark as anything I had ever seen before in my life. The town was too far away for the lights to come to us, no streetlights, very little moon.

"They'll take her to the hospital, that's almost an hour away, and she'll have the baby. The sisters stay with you the whole time. They'll even go in the room with you and hold your hand if you want them to. Then after, they give you something to make you sleep, and in the morning you wake up and the baby is gone."

"Doesn't anybody ever keep it?"

"Hardly ever. Lots of girls say they're going to, right before their time, they say they're going to get married and all sorts of crazy stuff. Everybody always says they're going to have their baby without making any sound, get through their whole labor right here at Saint Elizabeth's without any of the sisters finding out. That way they'd have to call for an ambulance and you could ride all the way up to Owensboro holding your baby. But no one's ever pulled it off. They get scared about something going wrong or they can't keep from calling out, and so they wind up going and having the baby in the hospital."

"Then what?"

"What do you mean, then what? Then you go home."

"I don't understand, if you had to come to a place like this, I'd think you wouldn't have a home to go back to."

Angie sighed, like she was tired of girls from California being so stupid. "When you leave you tell everyone a lie. You tell them you're going to take care of your sick aunt, or you won a trip to Europe or something, then you come back six months later and get back your job and have dinner at your parents' house and see your old boyfriend and everything's just the way it was. Just exactly the way it was.''

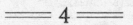

4

"GIRLS AT SAINT ELIZABETH'S are the recipients of charity," Mother Corinne informed me. "But that does not mean they are not expected to work so long as they are able."

Clearly I was able. I kept my discomforts to myself. When I was sick, I was sick quietly and privately, so that even Angie commented that I wasn't like the other girls. I was sent to work in the kitchen with Sister Evangeline. It was a job that few people were able to keep for long, as the smell of food sent them reeling sooner or later, but I found it comforting somehow. The kitchen was huge, with long steel tables for preparation, twenty-six gas burners and half a dozen ovens. Giant copper pans hung from the ceiling, and the bone handles of good knives jutted up from wooden blocks. The kitchen was the one part of the hotel which had maintained its glamour.

It was a room Sister Evangeline rarely left. She tied the middle of her habit with a piece of string to keep it from falling into the food and rolled up her white sleeves past her doughy elbows. Even when the meal was prepared, she wandered back and forth, touching things, moving the cinnamon back into line, checking the produce in the giant walk-in refrigerator. She was somewhere around seventy-five, and gravity had pulled at her through the years, making her heavier and closer to the ground with every step she took. Often her glasses would steam so badly while she was working that it was impossible to see her eyes. But Sister Evangeline, whose prescription had been out of date for years, didn't seem to notice. When she was tired, she would sit in a chair next to the stove or next to the freezer, depending on the season, and say her rosary until she fell asleep.

I was not much of a cook in those days, but the kitchen inspired me. At night I would bring the heavy cookbooks back to my room and read them in bed while Angie talked dreamily about her favorite foods from home. I knew that even if I made mistakes, I could still do better than Sister Evangeline. She was nearly blind and very good-natured, so she never minded, or saw, when I slipped pans off the fire and went to work on them myself.

"You're going to have a baby," she said to me one day after I had been there several weeks.

I told her I was.

"Well, let me see it," she said, and motioned with a big wooden spoon for me to come toward her.

I dried my hands on my skirt and walked over to her. There wasn't much to see, but there was something. Proof had pushed against my skin and made me nearly as round as Angie. She covered my stomach with her hands and began to knead me gently like a delicate dough.

"It's a girl," she said, and smiled hugely, so pleased about the news. She leaned over and pressed her ear to my belly. "Oh, you sweet girl," she said. "I love little girls. All God's children, but little girls are so nice."

She straightened up and pulled down my head so she could kiss me. Her face felt cool against my cheek. "God's blessed you, Rose, just like Elizabeth." Then she said in a whisper, "Mother Corinne doesn't like me to tell the girls about their babies. That's why she put me back here in the kitchen. But I used to be mother superior." She smiled and put her hand back on my stomach, as if she couldn't get enough of it. "So I say, if a girl comes into my kitchen I can tell her what I want."

I felt uneasy. "You can't really tell, can you?"

"Oh, don't you doubt it for a minute. I've never been wrong, not even one time. It's God's gift to me, that I can hear the babies. I was born in Kentucky, you know, the only sister here who was. When I was growing up, folks liked to say we were the only Catholics in the whole state. People were afraid of Catholics back then, thought we were witches. Then here I come along, telling everybody about their babies and then they're sure, like it's all no good. But my mama never bade me stop. She knew I was with God and she was proud of me. She was a listener herself, heard voices in the garden sometimes. Folks grow up around here, they know things, like your baby's going to know things."

I didn't like to think about the baby that way. I didn't like to think about it all. The more that it was just something taking up space in my body, the easier it would be. If I thought of it as being something, a girl, a boy, mine, Thomas', it all became too confusing.

"Never you mind, dear." She rubbed my stomach like a lucky charm. "You've got a good girl. You'll do right by her."

"I'm giving her up," I said quietly. "I'm not keeping her." I didn't like it. Her. It made me shiver.

Sister Evangeline laughed and headed off toward a pot of something boiling. "Not you, Rosie. Everybody else, but not you."

That night in bed I tried not to think about it. I had never thought about it, what it might be like to keep this baby. I whispered to Angie in the darkness what Sister Evangeline had said.

"Lord," she said back quietly. We had to keep our voices down, as the halls were checked for sounds, stray words seeping out underneath the doors.

"Do you think she knows anything?"

"They say she does. They say she knows about babies. I didn't know about her being mother superior though. That's something."

I was always happy to be able to give Angie a piece of news she didn't have before. "I wish I didn't know about the baby."

"I'd love to know. A boy or a girl. You could picture what it was going to look like once it grew up. You could know for sure what you'd name it. What would you name it?"

"I don't think about it."

"You can't keep yourself from thinking of things. It used to be if I had a girl I was going to name her Sharon, just because it's a beautiful name." She stopped for a minute. "But now I'd name her Rose of Sharon. Maybe I'd just call her Sharon, but her name would be Rose of Sharon."

It was all talk. Angie and I would never name our children, but her saying that put such a tightness in my throat I couldn't reply.

"And if it was a boy I'd name it for my boyfriend at home."

"Who's that?" I whispered.

She was quiet for a long time and I could hear her steady breathing. She wasn't crying, because no matter how softly she did that, I could always tell. "Duane," she said.

"That's the father?" There were girls who told stories about the fathers. They were the ones who said he was away and would come back and marry them the day the baby was born, but no

one ever really told the truth. The truth, I imagined, was almost
uniformly the same, someone who said he loved you but didn't,
someone who loved you but got scared. Within that truth were
an endless number of stories, each so personal that no one could
believe theirs was like anyone else's, as I believed mine was like
no one else's. Maybe I should have asked, we were so careful
not to ask things, but in that dark room I felt like a girl telling
secrets.

"No," she said, "that was Mr. Price. He owned the drugstore where I worked. I mostly worked the fountain, making
sundaes and milkshakes and stuff like that. Sometimes I worked
up front." She rolled over onto her side to face me and pulled
the blanket way up over her shoulders. Angie got cold when it
wasn't cold at all. I put my face right to the edge of the bed and
listened.

"Duane's my boyfriend. We've been dating pretty steady since
I was fifteen and everybody thought me and Duane would get
married. I guess we probably will. He's a really good guy, you'd
like Duane. But we never, you know, did anything, 'cause we
were going to wait." After that she just trailed off, and for a
while I thought she might have gone to sleep.

"What about Mr. Price?" I whispered.

She reached her hand out and touched the edge of my mattress, ran her fingers back and forth along my sheets. "You
won't ever tell?"

"Promise." And I wouldn't, we were friends. It all happened
so fast it hardly made sense to me. I had never had a girlfriend
like this before. But that's the way it was at Saint Elizabeth's. It
was like the army. It was like the war. You stuck with people
because your life depended on it.

She tucked her hand back inside her covers. "Mr. Price was
older. He was a little older than my dad, and he was married. I
went to school with his daughters. We all went to the same
church. That's why he gave me the job, but later he said he gave
me the job because he liked my ass. He'd say things like that to
me, you know, after. He told me I was beautiful. He said I
wasn't like any other woman in the world. God, nobody ever
said something like that to me before. I felt so daring, so . . .
so, grown up. The first time, it was a slow day. I'd been working
there for months already and he was always real professional,
like he didn't notice me at all even though he was always polite.
There was no one in the store and he came up behind me and
put his hand on my chest. Didn't say a word, just touched me.

I was so scared I couldn't move, I didn't pull away from him. I just stood there, so then he ran his hand under my sweater and went inside my bra and then he sort of pressed me back against him. Anybody could have walked in, his wife, his daughters, but he didn't seem to care. I guess I'd always had a sort of crush on him. He was smart and good-looking, but I never really thought about it. Duane was so good to me, and there I was, letting Mr. Price put his hands in my clothes. It didn't even happen that time. He never said anything to me about it. It made me so nervous, I kept thinking I should just quit the job, but that feeling, it didn't leave me. Every time he'd tell me to do something he'd stand real close and I could feel him breathe on my neck, I'd think I was going to pass out.

"The next time I was behind the back counter. I was waiting on somebody, and he came up behind me, crawling, and he starts running his tongue along the backs of my knees. He was licking my knees. I thought I was going to buckle, fall over on the floor. There's a customer right there and everything. Then he pulled down my underwear and started touching me, real lightly. Duane had never tried to touch me there, I wouldn't have let him, but Mr. Price was. When that woman left he kept going, running his hand all over me. I never told anyone this. I never said it in confession: he had his head up under my skirt.

"The crazy part is neither of us said a word about it, it just kept happening, until one day he says he has to leave early and he wants me to close the store for him. He left, and at five o'clock I changed the sign and turned out all the lights and locked the front door. It was winter then, so it was nearly dark outside. We always went in and out the back way, but when I get back there he's waiting for me. He was leaning up against one of the storage shelves, all those bottles of pills, and he tells me to take my sweater off, just like he would tell me to ring up an order or take out the trash, he says, 'Angie, take off your sweater now.' And I did it. Then he told me to take off my shoes and stockings. He didn't make a move, he just watched me. He told me piece by piece, until I wasn't wearing anything, and then he came over and put his arms around me and kissed me and said my name and that was it. He had never kissed me before. We did it right there, in front of a half a dozen different brands of birth control."

"And that's when it happened?"

"Not the first time. We went on like that for a while. I wonder sometimes what I could have been thinking about. I sure wasn't thinking about Duane or Mrs. Price or my family. I'm not even so sure I was thinking about him. It was more just me, the way I felt. I'd been such a goody-goody, you know, but all of a sudden I was walking around town and I'd think, none of you know what I'm doing. I thought I was such a big damn deal. I thought I was so in love."

"What did he say when you told him?"

"He said he'd pay for everything." She drew in her breath. "Part of me thought, what does it matter? If I'm the kind of girl who'd sleep with a married man, then I can be the kind of girl who doesn't have a baby, too. But I couldn't, you know, when it came right down to it I just couldn't do it. None of us could," she said. "That's why we're all here. So I told my mother I was pregnant. I didn't say who, but I knew she'd think it was Duane. She said, 'Does Duane know?' and I said no, so she made up some big lie about me going off to my cousins' and she sent me here, so that when I came back everything would be just the same."

I lay there for a while, thinking about Angie, her brown eyes and heart-shaped face, her dark hair that fell halfway down her back. It was like my mother used to say, about the pretty girls having it harder. I finally understood what she was talking about.

"Promise me something," she said.

"You bet."

"Promise you'll take me to see Sister Evangeline, so she can tell me if it's a boy or a girl."

"Sure," I said.

"I'd feel better. If I knew that much I'd feel better."

"We'll go tomorrow."

"Rose," she said.

"Yes."

"What about you? What was the name of the boy you slept with?"

"Thomas," I said.

"Did you love him?"

I waited for a minute, because I saw a light pass by our door, Sister Loyola out looking for wakeful girls. "No," I said. "I didn't."

When I went to the kitchen the next morning long before breakfast to start baking rolls, I found Sister Evangeline and Son peering in between the stove and the cabinet.

"I dropped my rosary," she told me. She kept folding and

unfolding her hands, which seemed helpless and small. "They were around my wrist while I was stirring something and they just slipped off."

Son was shining a flashlight into the slim divide, trying to see, but there was no telling. "Are you sure they went in here?" he said.

"Right there. Right down in there." She leaned over his shoulder, as if she was trying to see. "They were my mother's," she said. "She gave them to me when I entered the convent. I've had them forever."

Son asked me to get him a yardstick and I brought one out of the pantry. He stuck it down into the crevice and tried to slide it back and forth. He paid close attention to his work. His hands were so huge that they made the yardstick into a twig. I didn't know Son much at all then, other than to say hello when passing him on my walks. He seemed to bear all of our pains. When he saw any of the girls his face looked just for a second as if he understood that it was a man who had led us here, and he took the burden of that upon himself. He was only forty-five then, but I thought he was ten years older. The sun and wind and work had shaped him like the bed of the dried spring. He was a man who could never commit a crime because everything about him was so recognizable, his enormous height, the way one of his feet turned in and gave him a little limp, his hair that had grayed only on one side. I had never seen him wear anything but overalls and white shirts, and his boots looked like they would hold an entire watermelon.

Soon there was a jingle, and the rosary shot out across the floor. I reached down to pick it up. The little wires that connected the beads and the metal crucifix on the end were hot from the stove. I held them for a second to cool them and then gave them back to Sister Evangeline.

She hugged Son, barely coming up to his waist. "I thought I could do without any one thing," she said. "But not these. It would have broken my heart to have these gone." Then she went off to show them to the other sisters. What was lost is now found.

Son wiped the dust off the edge of the yardstick and put it back in its place. "I worry about her down here," he said to me. "Too many hot things, too many knives. But I expect it would kill her quicker to be taken out of the kitchen. This is the only place she feels to home. But you seem like a smart girl, and Sister Evangeline, she sings your praises, so you'll watch out for her."

"I watch out for her," I said. It was early, not even light outside, and I asked Son if he wanted some breakfast.

"That would be nice," he said, "if you've got the time."

He had left his house, which was the old groundskeeper's cottage behind the hotel, when Sister Evangeline had called him, breathless and frightened for her beads. He didn't take the time to get himself some coffee, so I poured a cup for him and put it down on the small table we sat at to shell peas.

"You're not from around here," he said.

"No, I'm from out west, California." How many times had I said that already? Kentucky wasn't a place you could just be in, you had to be from there, or everything about you was strange.

"I could tell from the way you talk." He took a long drink of his coffee. "Well, it's not just the way you talk, it's the way you move around too, look people right in the eyes, hold your head up. You don't see too much of that around here."

"We're all pretty much alike," I said.

Son shook his head. "These girls get all round-shouldered, like they've been broken down. It's a sad thing to see. Used to be, when I first came here, I'd holler out to them sometime, say hello or something, and it liked to scare them to death. I felt so bad. It was like I had murdered somebody."

"How long have you been here?"

"Oh, Lord," he said, smiling a little, "a long time, since I was eighteen. Who'd a thought, you know? I was just bumming around, wandering, taking in odd jobs where I could get them. I thought I'd go all over the world, but I just kept going around Tennessee and Kentucky." He laughed. "Like I didn't have a sense of direction, I kept going in circles."

"Maybe you didn't want to leave," I said.

"Well, I guess you may be right."

"How did you come to Saint Elizabeth's?"

"I came to Habit first, and I met somebody who sent me down here. Sister Evangeline was running things then, and I asked her did she need some work done. Anybody could see she needed work done, this place. A mess. You think it's not so great now, but before I came here, the pipes were half rusted through and the lights only worked if you jiggled the sockets, and the roof. Lord. So she says I could stay on a few days, until

I could straighten things up, and here I am, still straightening things up."

"So you never saw the world," I said, putting down a plate of eggs in front of him.

He went to the cupboard and took out a little bottle of Tabasco, which he poured over his food like it was catsup. "I suppose I saw as much as I was meant to see. Not as much as you, though. California."

I rinsed out my pans and started work on the rolls. Saint Elizabeth's would be waking up soon, and the girls who didn't get sick in the morning were always fiercely hungry. "I used to drive a lot," I said. "But I was never very good at getting anyplace, so I guess I was like you. Lots of moving without covering a lot of ground."

"You got this far," he said.

It was nice to have a man to talk to while I worked. I could understand what Angie meant, about all the girls being in love with him. It wasn't love, but the relief that came in a moment of something different. Our days were very much the same. Charlotte and Nora had had their babies, though they left without any of Lolly's production. Once they had gone, they sent us notes from the hospital saying they were fine, and then we didn't hear from them anymore. They didn't come back. Now there were new girls at the head table and we talked about when they were due. We talked about our sore backs and our hair, which seemed to grow an inch a day. We invented secret histories for the nuns and played Scrabble in the afternoons, but we didn't talk to men. In fact, we talked very little about men. Having Son in my kitchen made me feel extremely normal somehow, normal in the way my old life had been, fixing breakfast for Thomas. It comforted me.

He took his dishes to the sink and washed them, thanking me for the breakfast, saying my eggs were better than Sister Evangeline's but I was not to tell her. Then he reached out his hand to shake mine. It was an awkward gesture. When I took his hand mine was lost, swallowed whole. "You let me know if you need anything," he said, and then he lumbered out of the kitchen. That was just the word I thought as I watched him go, lumbered.

By the second rising of the dough, Sister Evangeline was back, happy and clucking, her beads attached to her belt tightly. All morning she touched her hip to check them, make sure everything was still in place. I had made breakfast alone, and quiet Regina and a new girl named Helen I had never seen before came in to serve it. Helen was already showing as much as I was. I imagined she stayed home as long as she could, wore loose dresses and stood behind counters. I hoped someone had told her not to say anything about a dead husband. I had forgotten to, when she was right there.

After the dishes were washed and put away, Angie came into the kitchen. Her hair was up in a high ponytail and she had on a couple of those cheap, dime-store bracelets that Mother Corinne was always yelling at her about wearing. She looked so impossibly young, like a girl who had stuck a sofa pillow under her dress as some kind of joke. "This is what I'd look like pregnant," she would say to her friends, and they would all laugh until their sides ached.

"Did you ask her?" she said to me in a low voice.

"Ask who?"

"Sister Evangeline, about my baby." She was clearly irritated that I had forgotten.

"It's been a big morning," I said. "Lots of kitchen drama."

I went over and asked Sister Evangeline, who was trying to find some cream of tartar, if she wouldn't have a talk with my friend's baby.

"Now I'm not supposed to do that, Rose. I told you that's how I got in trouble, that's how I wound up here in the kitchen." She laughed and put her hand on my wrist. "I get in trouble again, they'll have me out back mowing the lawns."

"Angie's sweet," I whispered, "a lot sweeter than I am. And she can keep a secret." I doubted the last part was true, but I knew the first was.

"Well," she said, still so happy from her morning's misfortune and good turn of events, "I always like to see the babies."

I introduced them. They would have met before, but as Sister liked to say, so many girls coming and going. They all start to look the same. Which in our case was true.

But when she put her hand on Angie's stomach, I knew it was all a mistake. Sister Evangeline's face dropped and her eyes half closed behind her glasses.

"What is it?" Angie said, meaning the sex of the child.

"It's hard to tell," she said quietly.

"I want to know." Her voice was impatient and high. "You told Rose."

Sister Evangeline leaned over to touch her cheek to Angie's stomach, but it was more like she was trying to touch her cheek to the burner of the stove. All she could do was bump against her lightly, and even that seemed to cause her pain. I held onto her arm and helped her straighten up. "It's a girl," she said.

Angie clapped her hands and kissed me and kissed Sister. "I knew it would be. I knew it would be all along. Rose of Sharon." She kissed me again. "Rose of Sharon."

"Take me to sit," Sister Evangeline said. "This tires me out. I shouldn't do this at all." But before she left she touched Angie's face. "You're a sweet girl," she said. "God will stay with you."

I told Angie to go on, that I was going to take Sister Evangeline to her room, but once she had left, Sister said to just take her to a chair. She sat down heavily.

"Are you going to tell me?" I said.

"The baby dies," she said. "Not until the very end." Her voice was half choked and her cheeks were flushed. Yesterday I doubted what she had said about me, but today I believed.

"Maybe she won't know," I said. "She'll be asleep and they'll take the baby from her and she'll never know."

"You always know," Sister Evangeline said.

Sister Evangeline did go to bed. She tried to find comfort in cooking, but she was tired and I took her to her room. It was a maid's room, down the back hall from the pantry. It was small and spare with white walls and a little bed near a window. I knelt on the floor and undid her heavy black shoes. I helped her under the blankets and covered her up like a child.

"Stay with me awhile," she said. I sat on the edge of the bed and held onto her hand. "Tell me something," she said.

"What do you want to know?"

"Anything," she said. "Tell me about your mother."

It caught me off guard. My mother. It would be the thing she would think of now, the thing we all had in common. "My mother is beautiful," I said.

"How is she beautiful?"

"The way her hair smells, the way she crosses her hands over her knees, like this." I thought about it. I saw her sitting on the edge of the tub, laughing. "The way she always came home from work telling stories about something that happened that day."

"And you miss her." Her voice sounded small. I reached over and took off her glasses and put them close beside her on the night table, near a glass of water.

"Yes."

"I know," she said, and squeezed my hand.

I stayed there until I thought she was asleep. I looked out her window and saw fall coming up in the back pasture. I thought about my mother. I wondered if she would still be waiting for me to come home or if she would have given up hope by now. As much as I wanted her to be able to go on with things, the thought of her forgetting took my breath away. I stood up from the bed and started to go back to the kitchen.

"Rose?" Sister Evangeline said.

"Yes."

"Sing me something."

"I can't sing."

"That's all right," she said.

So I sang her a song, but I don't remember what it was now, and by the time I was finished she had fallen asleep.

I was only responsible for working one meal that day, but I did all three. I chased the others girls away when they came in to take their turns. I was becoming more and more like Sister Evangeline. The only place I felt safe now was in the kitchen. I labored fiercely. I cooked with anger. I thought, damn you all, I'll feed you and make you strong, I'll feed you until you can't eat another bite, until you drop your forks and push your chairs away. I'll feed you until you want for nothing in your lives. I'll feed you until you're able to save yourselves. I pounded out the chicken with a spiked mallet until the breasts were as thin as writing paper. I brought out frozen chunks of stock and melted them into soups. I filled the pots with potatoes and carrots and celery. I was careful to remove all the bay leaves, any tough ends. No one will choke on this food. No one will be hurt by what has come from my hands. I made rice pudding. I put in as many raisins as they might dream of having, made it sweet and warm, food to send you to sleep. Food to keep you safe.

I'd hardly looked at my car since my arrival. I'd had enough of driving, but tonight I thought of getting in, driving every-place, never coming back. I could drive back to California, see Interstate 40 with the sun setting ahead of me rather than behind. I could go into I. Magnin's, where my mother would be selling lipsticks, and stand on the other side of the counter in my big winter coat, which would be far too warm, and she wouldn't notice this baby. All she would see was her baby. The joy on her face. I closed my eyes and savored it. I wanted to never comfort. I wanted to be comforted. I wanted to be wrapped and held and kissed and rocked.

I stayed in the kitchen. At five o'clock the residents of Saint Elizabeth's went onto the porch without me and drank their tea, even though the evening was turning cold, and pretended that someone was coming for them. They looked at the red leaves, on certain trees so bright already they made you look away, and thought of last fall. Where had these girls been then, with their flat stomachs, never thinking how much could go wrong? I stayed in the kitchen and made their dinner, sent it out to the table, and waited to wash their dishes. And when the last dish was put away, Mother Corinne came in and told me it was not up to me to decide who should have a day off from work and that we were to keep to the schedule and all I had to do was look at her, simply raise my eyes from the sink I was scrubbing out and meet her eyes, and she left without a word.

When it was dark I went out to my car and got inside. I took a map out of the glove compartment and spread it over the seat, leaving the car door ajar for a little light. California was so far away. I wondered if Billy had told his parents. I thought maybe I would go to see him, sit at his bright kitchen table while his mother made coffee and cut us thick slices of cake. For a minute I thought about Thomas, and I wondered if things were easier for him by now, but then I stopped because I just couldn't. There was no place to go but away. I looked at the maps for a long time, tracing my finger along roads, trying to imagine that there would be someplace I could go and not know about Angie. Someplace I could go and not be pregnant, as the thing I wanted most to get away from was inside me.

I got into the backseat of the car. I pulled the old wool blanket over my shoulders and fell asleep.

I woke up to a tapping on the window. I could hear a man saying my name and in the darkness I thought it was Thomas. "Rose. Rose."

I sat up and peered out the window. It was Son. He had a flashlight but was careful not to shine it in my face. I unlocked the door and slid over. An old habit, sleeping with the doors locked. He leaned inside.

"They sent me to find you," he said.

I nodded.

"You're gonna freeze to death out here."

"Is it late?"

"Naw, only ten or so, but they don't like you just wandering off. Why're you sleeping in the car, Rose?"

"I just wanted—" I stopped and rubbed my face. I was crying again. "I don't know," I said.

"Wait here," he said, and headed back toward the hotel. I pinched the bridge of my nose and took deep breaths, trying to quiet myself down. After a while Son came back and handed me a heavy jacket. "I told them I found you. It's Sister Bernadette doing bed check. I told her you wanted to take a little walk."

"I want to take a walk?" I said.

"Come on. Come on out of the car."

I got out and put on the jacket. It was one of Son's and it came down to my knees. It was so heavy I put my hands in the pockets, thinking they must be loaded down with sand, but they were empty. The weight of it felt good, it seemed to push me into the ground. We walked straight across the back pasture, not out toward the road where I went for my walks in the mornings but out toward the bank of trees we watched from the front porch. Son was pulling in his steps, going slow so I wouldn't have to fight to keep up with him. He kept the flashlight in front of us. The dew was already starting to come up, and it soaked through my shoes and chilled my feet. When we got to the other side of the pasture, he showed me a break in the trees and we followed a path into the woods, the same path George Clatterbuck had taken the morning he found the spring. Son put his hand under my elbow, lightly, as if he were afraid he might frighten me, and led me over the fallen logs and around the blackberry branches. I was still half asleep, and it never occurred to me to ask where we were going, or to think there might be something unusual about the groundskeeper leading me off into the woods in the middle of the night. I just wanted to follow.

When we got to the other side of the woods, I saw a small white farmhouse, all lit up. "I wanted you to meet a friend of mine," Son said.

"Isn't it a little late to be visiting people?"

"Miss June's always up," he said. "I've never been by here when she hasn't been up."

He knocked on the door and sure enough, the woman who answered looked like she'd been expecting us. She was a thin woman of maybe sixty-five or seventy, with her hair done up in an elaborate twist on the back of her head.

"Miss June," Son said, "this is my friend Rose. Rose, this is Miss June Clatterbuck."

She took my hands and pulled me inside, saying how glad she was to meet me. "I can always count on Son to make my day. It used to be girls came down from the hotel all the time, but I'm starting to think that back pasture must be getting wider. No one comes to visit now, it's not like the old days at all." She put me down in an old flowered armchair and went off to get us some drinks.

"So do you like living at the hotel?" June called out to me from the kitchen. I wasn't exactly awake yet. I wasn't sure what I was doing there at all.

"It's fine," I said.

"Not something a person could get very excited about, I suppose," she said happily. "Living in a home for unwed mothers and all."

"No," I called back. "I suppose not." I shot Son a look. He nodded at me. I took it to mean that everything was all right.

"Miss June owns Saint Elizabeth's," Son said.

"I do not," she said.

"Well, you sure own everything under it. It was criminal the way they took that place from you. If you ask me, they ought to at least be paying rent."

"What am I going to do with rent from the church? It's not the kind of money a person can enjoy." She came back in, carrying a tray that she put down on the table. "When I'm dead," she said, "they'll find a way to get it once and for all." She seemed a little too bright about the proposition, like she'd cheerfully resigned herself to both facts: her death and the Catholic Church winning out. "You've just got to promise me, Son, you won't let them take down my sign."

"Not while I'm around," he said, putting a couple of cookies on a napkin and handing them to me.

"Oh, they hated that sign," she said, and laughed. "Did you see it?"

"First thing when I came in," I told her. That's when I put it all together. This was June Clatterbuck, the little girl. She was the three-year-old whose father made her drink the water and saved her life. She was the reason Saint Elizabeth's was there at all.

"I had that sign made after my mother died. Cost me a fortune, solid brass. I had it made up to look just like one of those historical markers the state puts up.'' She stopped and poured herself a Coke. ''She wouldn't have liked it, my mother, she would've said I shouldn't do anything that might upset the sisters, but that was only because she was afraid of the big one. But I did it as soon as she was gone. They're fine over there, they do good by you girls, but no one likes to admit that Saint Elizabeth's used to be the Hotel Louisa, and that before that it used to be my father's field and my father's spring.''

''They were supposed to call the place the Hotel June,'' Son said. He was sitting on the couch, which was too small for him. His knees came up nearly to his shoulders.

''There never would have been a Hotel June, I wouldn't have stood for that, even at seventeen. There aren't too many people who remember the spring anymore. I'm not saying it was any sort of miracle, mind you. It was a long time ago, maybe it wasn't anything at all. But it did put Habit on the map for a while, and I think folks ought to be respectful of that.''

''That's right,'' Son said.

''Catholics think they've got the market cornered on miracles. Fátima, Lourdes, that's where they want to see their miracles. If something happens in their own back yard, which just happens to be a Baptist back yard, well then, that's really not worth a thing. When Lewis and Louisa Nelson first came here and they saw all the spring had to offer, the first thought in their heads was, let's make it Catholic. Sort of like America trying to get to the moon so we can say it's ours. I keep thinking, I just bet the Pope is doing a slow burn over this one. He'd like to send some priests up there and say the moon was Catholic.'' She looked at me and smiled. ''Are you a Catholic, dear?''

''I am, actually,'' I said.

She put down her Coke on the table next to her. ''I don't mean any offense,'' she said. ''Why, some of my best friends are Catholic. Sister Evangeline, up at the hotel. Do you know her?''

''Rose works in the kitchen,'' Son said for me. ''She and Sister are thick as thieves.''

''You bring her by for me,'' she said. ''It's getting hard for us to make the walk alone. I don't see her as much as I'd like to anymore. They keep her too busy over there.''

''Things are better for her,'' Son said. ''She's got Rose now.''

''I like nuns,'' she said. ''Of course, not all of them. That would be like saying you liked all people flat across the board, and that would be foolishness. We used to have a lot of nuns around here, back when Saint Elizabeth's was a retirement home. They were the best thing that spring ever brought here, not that you girls aren't fine, but I loved those old nuns." She paused and thought about it all. "Sometimes I think that maybe I'll become a Catholic and become a nun, just so I could retire with women like them. Course, with my luck, Mother Corinne would retire in the bed right next to mine."

We stayed for a while, but I was tired. June had enough energy to burn a hole in the carpet. It wore me out to think a woman three times my age was wide awake past midnight.

"Best stay with us," she said at the door.

"I've got to get her home," Son said. "I shouldn't have kept her out this long."

"Listen to me," she said, and took my hand, " 'cause this is important. You come back here. You visit me."

"Yes, ma'am," I said.

"I'll watch for you, from this window right here." She kissed us both good night, and Son led me back through the woods, toward the Hotel Louisa.

"She's a live one," I said. "I'm glad you took me there."

He stopped before we got to the front steps. He looked up at the hotel, like he was trying to get what he wanted to say exactly right in his mind. "They'll have you thinking that what's going on right now is the only thing happening in the world, but there were all those other people living here before you, and there'll be a lot of them here after you. Go on now," he said. "Go on up to bed." And then he headed off toward his house, the beam of his flashlight cutting a path into the darkness.

I went up to my room. Suddenly I was so tired I could barely make it up the stairs. I got into bed without taking off my dress.

"Where have you been?" Angie said.

"I fell asleep in the car."

"What were you doing in the car?"

"I don't remember."

"Well, Lord, I've been wanting to talk to you all day. I got so excited about what Sister Evangeline told me, about the baby being Rose of Sharon. A girl, we're both going to have girls."

"Yes," I said softly.

"She seemed awful depressed about the whole thing, though. Sister Evangeline, that is. I thought maybe she goes into some

kind of trance or something when she's talking to the baby. Was
she that way with you, too?''

"Yes," I said.

"Well, good. I was a little worried at first."

"Don't be," I said.

"Good night, Rose," she said.

"Good night, Angie."

"Sleep well," she said.

But I didn't sleep at all.

5

I DID NOT KNOW my own body. I thought of all those years I hadn't known my mind, didn't come close to understanding what I wanted, but my body was completely my own. I knew how to glance up at a man for just a second and then look away. I knew the weight of my hair and how it would fall against my neck when I turned my head. I knew the way my hand looked holding a glass and how my shoulders looked when I stretched. Through movement I could bring people toward me or make them turn away. I understood the way I worked, but in six months all of that was gone.

My breasts were the first to defect, swelling over the neck of my dress, as if trying to warn me of what was ahead. They were followed out by my stomach. Every day it was harder to ignore, harder to think this child did not concern me. It kicked and pressed against my back, my sides. It went back and forth like a Channel swimmer. I was a tenement building, a place to live. It made me hungry and tired and sick. It made my hair thick and my skin pink. At night I would lie on my back and run my hands tentatively across the great expanse of my skin. It wasn't my own life anymore, it was a life splintered off from mine. It would grow beyond me. It would need so badly to grow it would leave my body and go into the arms of that good mother who would raise it, watch over it, turn on night-lights, wait for its cry. It would reach for her breasts instead of mine.

"Why won't you talk about it?" Angie said to me. She was sitting on her bed cross-legged, her stomach resting in her lap. She was crocheting a baby cap, but she never looked down at her hands. She knew the movements in her sleep. The needle dipped mechanically in and out of the thin pink yarn.

"There's nothing to talk about."

"Look at yourself, Rose! Don't you ever look in the mirror? Don't you ever look down? God, sometimes I think you must take your baths with your clothes on, if you don't mind me saying so. This is supposed to be a happy time. The baby picks up on that, all your thoughts, everything. It goes right to her. Right along with the blood and the food and that stuff. You've got to act like you're excited about this. I mean, if you're not, then fake it or something."

"If the baby knows what I'm thinking, then don't you think it would know if I was faking it?" I was brushing my hair, which had become somewhat of an obsession with me. The consolation prize for the end of beauty was that my hair had become as thick as a horse's tail and nearly as long.

"It's not that specific and you know it. You've just got to act pregnant every now and then. Knit something, do something." Her crochet hook kept up its rapid pace. She never slowed down for a minute. She'd already made a dozen sweaters, tiny socks, embroidered the collars of sleepers with rosebuds ("For my Rose of Sharon," she would say). "Right now, I'm her mama. I'm all she knows in the whole world. I've got to do right by her. What do you think?" She held up the pink cap, which dangled from a strand of yarn. "It's so much more fun now that I know she's a girl. I can get the colors right. Do you like this one?"

"It's nice," I said.

"I'll make one for you."

I shook my head.

"Jesus, you don't think you could send your baby girl out into the world with a few things?" Angie was putting together a box which she planned to leave with the head nurse at the hospital. I did my best to never think of Angie's baby not surviving, never getting to wear those clothes. If I thought about it, I found I couldn't talk to her at all, about anything, for fear of it coming out somehow. I could not stand to think about it.

"I'm sure that anyone who went to the trouble of adopting a baby would go to the trouble of buying clothes for it," I said. "I'm not keeping it. I'm not going to fool myself." Angie's face darkened and she wrapped her hands tightly around her work, pressing it into a ball. "Oh, God. Don't look like that. Honey, all I'm saying is you do what's right for you and I'll do what's right for me."

But it was too late, she was already crying. It wasn't a bad thing. We all cried at the drop of a hat in those days. Our emotions were tripped by the simplest things. A sentimental commercial on TV could leave us sobbing for hours. I put down my brush and went and sat beside her on her bed. She put her arms around my neck and buried her face in my hair, crying like a rainstorm. I held her. She was still so thin. Her back all but disappeared beneath my arms. I kissed her hair. It was like holding a bird, a little life.

"This is all I've got," she said, her voice breaking on every word.

"I know," I said. "I'm sorry."

"I can't not," she said. "I can't not."

"I know." I rocked her and laid my cheek against her head until she started to settle down. Maybe that was all we wanted. Maybe that was why we cried, so someone would scoop us up and hold us in the soft cup of her arms. "The cap is so pretty," I whispered. "She'll have the nicest things of any baby in the world."

Angie took a couple of deep breaths and I handed her a Kleenex. She rubbed her eyes and blew her nose. "I'm such a waste," she said, and laughed a little. The storm had blown over as quickly as it had come in. "Can you imagine me being a mother?"

"You'd cry every time the baby cried."

"The two of us sitting on the floor, howling at the top of our lungs."

"Not a pretty thought," I said.

"But this baby's going to have one hell of a mother," she said, sniffing a little. "I dream about her. She has blond hair. She's a real big woman, you know, big-boned like Beatrice and tall as you. All she's ever wanted in her life is my baby."

"And the father is a doctor."

"Exactly," she said, so happy that I was going along for once. She stayed close to me on the bed, held my hand. "But he's home a lot. Crazy about kids."

"They have a swimming pool."

She thought about this for a minute. "Not just yet. They'll build one later, you know, when she's old enough."

I was pleased by her foresight. I wouldn't have thought of that. "That's good," I told her.

"And what about you? Do you think about your baby's mother?"

"Yes."

"And?"

I thought about her all the time, her good sense, her unfailing patience, her little quirks. The way she would sing when she washed the baby's hair. "She's my mother," I said.

Angie nodded, understanding completely. "And the father?"

But there hadn't been a father. In all of my daydreams, he was gone. "I don't know," I said, "I'll have to think on that."

On one hand, our days were so relentlessly the same they were barely worth mentioning. We ate, we slept, we went for walks. Now that the weather was cold we drank our tea in the main lobby and clustered near the windows to look outside. On the other hand, the world changed every minute. I had seen three months of classes leave, almost every one of them in the night without good-byes. Girls simply were not at breakfast the next morning and were replaced by other girls, their rabbit eyes round with fear as they walked past us the first time. They pressed their suitcases against their stomachs. They looked away. Then slowly they blended in, grew to fit us, took their seat at the back table and began to move up. I didn't know them well. I kept to my own class, the girls a month ahead of me or a month behind. After three and a half months I'd nearly forgotten what had brought me there in the first place, and when, from time to time, I felt my wedding ring, which I had slipped into the lining of my purse, I had to stop to remember what it was, what it meant.

More and more I spent my time in the kitchen, and the girls who had been there awhile commented often on the fact that the food had gotten better. Whenever I saw Sister Bernadette in the hall she would stop and take my hand happily inside both of hers. "You're going to make me fat, Rose," she said. "I worry, I don't want Sister Evangeline to think that we haven't appreciated her cooking all these years, but I have to tell you, that chicken. What was that chicken?"

"Piccata."

"A wonder," she said. "God has given you a talent."

"Thank you, Sister."

"Rose," she said quietly, looking around a little over her shoulder, "you seem to be awfully good at the desserts. Do you know how to make napoleons?"

"I think I could figure it out."

"My mother," she said softly, "made napoleons. I haven't had one in years."

"Then you leave it to me," I said. I always had a special fondness for Sister Bernadette because she had been so good to me the first day I arrived. Nothing would have pleased me more than to make a napoleon for her. It was almost as if I could see her roll my promise around in her mouth.

"Thank you," she whispered.

As for anyone worrying that Sister Evangeline's feelings were being hurt by the sudden popularity of the food, nothing could have been further from the truth. She just didn't get it, and no one would have been so unkind as to explain it to her. She reveled in her newfound attention. Suddenly the kitchen was full again. After every meal a stream of pregnant girls poured through, all generous in their praise. Girls came by to help, or sometimes just to sit on one of the long steel tables and talk while we worked. After all of Sister Evangeline's years of exile in the kitchen, Saint Elizabeth's had finally rediscovered her.

Even Son started having his dinners in the kitchen. At first he came by just as we were finishing up, leaning back against the counter and talking about the shingles or the paint until we asked him if he'd like something to eat. Then after a while it became so regular I fixed a plate for him and set it aside. "Why don't you eat in the dining room like everyone else?" I asked him. He didn't eat until we were finished, until I was back washing dishes and putting things away. It wasn't right.

"I didn't know I was hungry before," he said, running a piece of bread across his plate.

"This is every night for two weeks now," I said.

He brought his plate to the sink and washed it carefully. "If you've got plenty, then I'm much obliged to eat here. If you don't, I'll head home."

"It doesn't have anything to do with the amount of food. You know that."

"Good," he said. "I'll see you tomorrow, then."

I asked Sister Evangeline about it. "He's not a dog," I said. "He shouldn't be waiting until everyone else finishes to pick up the scraps."

"And there would be no other cause for him to want to wait and eat in the kitchen?" she said.

But there was no cause I could think of.

Now that her kitchen was full, Sister Evangeline had more time to do what she loved best, which was talk to the babies. "Oh," she said, taking a spoon of white clam sauce from the pot. "Oh, taste this," and she took it to Clara, eight months, and slipped it in her mouth. "This baby likes fish, anything from the water. He'll go to sea someday." She tapped Clara's huge stomach with her finger. "You wait and see."

Sister had a good sense of who wanted information on her pregnancy and who didn't. To some girls she told long stories, whole lives, to some she would merely say boy or girl, and to others, nothing at all. What was said in the kitchen remained in the kitchen, that was the policy. "Think of me out there mowing lawns," she would say. The only thing Sister never seemed to grasp, or at least would never speak of, was that we were all giving our children away.

"Rosie," she told me one night when we were washing dishes, "we're a team. You and me, we work the best together."

"I think so," I said. We weren't alone as often anymore, and when we were I found myself staying close by her side. She was the only other person who knew about Angie's baby, and while we had never discussed it again, after that first day, it gave me comfort to have one secret I did not bear alone. But it was more than that: we cared for each other. I liked the way she held my arm when we went on walks. I took her to see June Clatterbuck in the afternoons as I had promised. They went to each other like long lost girlfriends, not two women separated by a short field.

"Why haven't we been together every day?" June said.

"Time gets away from us," Sister said.

Sometimes I would stay with them for a while. I liked to sit and listen while they talked about the way Kentucky had been when they were girls.

"Things were better back then," June said. "Folks came to the house all the time. People looked out for you. Now, some days, it feels like a person could just get lost in the world."

I couldn't imagine how June's life had changed at all. There she was, still living in the same house she'd been in since she was born. The view out her window the same, same trees, same pasture. She hadn't had to watch highways or shopping malls go up beside her.

"Her family's gone," Sister Evangeline explained to me later. "That's more change than anyone should have to bear."

They liked to watch their soap opera together and cluck their tongues over moral indiscretions. "That Blaire," June would say, "wearing a dress like that in the middle of the afternoon. You know she's up to no good. Four husbands just since I've been watching." They never considered the drama that lay just across the pasture in a hotel full of unwed mothers.

We had quietly switched our places, Sister Evangeline and I. Now she was shelling peas and stirring soups while I put things together. Some days she would be my mother, and on other days I was hers.

"You know how to cook," she said. "You don't just read the books, you understand food. Me, I never really got it, not entirely. Of course, nobody knew, but your talent is in food, the same way mine's with the babies. That means you go with God."

I took eight chickens out of the freezer and put them into the refrigerator to thaw slowly overnight. "I've been thinking," I said to her. "Maybe I could get a job as a cook once I get out of here." As far away as my departure seemed to me, I knew it would come. I had left Thomas so I could begin my life, and I knew it was high time I figured out what it was I should do with myself. Unlike the other girls, I couldn't just go back, flat-stomached and full of innocence, as if nothing more had happened than I had temporarily lost my mind and run away. I would have to drive again, find a place, live my life.

"Oh, you'll work as a cook all right." She laughed to herself and started throwing the silverware randomly into different drawers. I always had to come down in the morning and sort out what she had put away.

"Don't get all psychic on me," I said. "If you've got something to tell me, just tell me."

"You don't want to know," she said, "you don't like knowing. Besides, you're a young girl, you should have some surprises in your life. The excitement of just finding out." She closed her eyes and nodded her head. "I remember that, when I was young, not having any idea what was going to happen." She smiled and reached up to pat my cheek, a gesture that had become less of a pat and more a series of short slaps the longer I knew her. "Boy, that was something, not knowing. I used to go around waiting for God to tell me what to do. Do I join the sisters or marry Timmy? I used to ask that every morning when I woke up."

"Timmy who?" I said. I'm sure it was possible, but it was hard to believe.

"Timmy somebody or other. I don't remember exactly."

"So what happened?"

She spread out her arms, as if to say, have you not noticed

these black beads, this white dress, which was, at the time, smeared with a red sauce.

"But how did you know?" I asked her.

She cocked her head, sure that a question so easy must be some kind of a trick. "My sign from God," she said.

God came to us in the form of Father Bernard, who made the drive down from Owensboro three Sundays a month to say mass in the grand ballroom. He came around two o'clock, after his Sunday duties were completed at home. First he listened to confessions in the coat checkroom, which had a small wall that separated it from the front desk. It meant that everyone had to stay out of the lobby while waiting her turn. I never went myself, but Angie told me she could hardly keep from laughing, thinking of him sitting on a small folding chair that once must have held a young girl in charge of putting mink coats on hangers. "It's not the best setup," she said. "He keeps saying, 'What? What?' "

It was a difficult day all around, as many of the girls refused to eat before communion, leaving them irritable and nauseated. The minute that mass was over they flocked to the kitchen and picked at dinner until there was nothing left, then wanted something else to eat before bedtime. Sister Evangeline and I worked overtime on Sundays.

Except for the first Sunday of every month, that is, when the ladies' auxiliary sent down the church bus to collect us early and bring us to the Church of the Incarnation in Owensboro. Although Saint Elizabeth's was funded by the archdiocese, the government, and several substantial private donors, the women of Incarnation's Saint Vincent de Paul Society saw us as their special project. They saved their maternity clothes for us, had bake sales to fund special medical needs, and sent us all their old magazines. We were their good deed, and in return for their charitable work they expected to see us clean-scrubbed and heavy with child at the front of their church once a month, with two nuns in front and back of the line.

The average age of a Saint Elizabeth's resident in 1968 was twenty-three years old, but on those Sundays we all felt fourteen, schoolgirls told to be quiet and walk straight. We were the lost lambs brought back into the fold. Our immorality was past tense, and in this bath of forgiveness we were washed clean of our sins. Twenty-five pregnant virgins on parade. The pews were hard on our backs, and kneeling was just impossible, though we felt obliged to try. The girls in the early classes went right to their knees, but the further along you were the more difficult it was. You didn't want to admit that last month you'd made it down fine, and this month you were sliding the pew into the small of your back, pushing the knees you couldn't see out in front of you, and praying you would make it. Even if you could get down, forget about getting back up again. I saw girls suffer the entire mass wedged in at a slant, neither in their seat nor on the ground. The mass seemed endless, and I kept my eyes on the rack of candles where so much of my youth had been spent. What could I have been thinking of?

Saint Elizabeth's was full of girls who were not Catholic. They said they were, because it was a lying time in our lives, and no one pressed the point. They had no place else to go, as there were no homes for unwed Protestant girls in those days. At mass they took communion to avoid questions. You could see it flash across their faces for a moment as the priest reenacted the Last Supper, said, "This *is* the body of Christ. Happy are those who are called to His table." They would be joining up with us, the flesh eaters, the people who believed not in the symbol but actually claimed to digest the thing itself. Body and blood. But maybe, they thought, if I keep it clear in my mind, my portion will remain bread and wine and no one will be the worse for it. Better to just eat the damn thing and have a roof over your pregnant head. They dropped their Baptist chins to their Baptist chests and said, "Lord, I am not worthy to receive You, but only say the word and I shall be healed," then scooted sideways, uncomfortably, through the pew and up the aisle to balance the savior of the world on their own pink tongues.

Except me.

I had not received the sacrament since I left Thomas. I could not confess my sin because I was not remorseful, and I could not take communion without confession. For a person whose life was comprised of lies, this was the one thing I felt dead certain I had to be honest about. It would be fatally wrong to lie on the altar of God, to say I was clean and at peace when I was neither. I'm sure that to second-guess God is the greatest sin of all. I decided He had no right forgiving me and I held my ground. It put Mother Corinne beside herself.

"What you do at Saint Elizabeth's does not please me," she said, her voice completely without inflection, which was her way when she was angriest. "But that is among us, in our family.

When, however, we are at the Church of the Incarnation, you are to take your place in line with the other girls. Is that understood?''

"Understood," I said, and waited for my dismissal. It was the same exchange we had at the first Sunday of every month. There was no point in arguing with her, or trying to explain. I would simply agree and know the next month we would go through it all again. I was pregnant, and there were only so many first Sundays left on my calendar.

"You're a liar, Rose," Mother Corinne said to me. She kept her voice steady, but I could feel it straining, I could see the tender veins rising on the sides of her temples.

"Yes, Mother."

"You admit it, then?"

"Yes."

"But this time I'm telling you to promise. You must promise to take communion on Sunday."

"Yes," I said. "I promise."

And on Sunday I would twist my swollen stomach to the left and make the other girls climb over me. I didn't enjoy it. I didn't care about the embarrassment, it was a quality you had to lose to survive such an outing in the first place. I simply missed communion, that feeling of walking back to your seat with the host in your mouth, certain that God was with you now. Once Mother Corinne sat beside me and dug her nails into my wrist deep enough to draw blood while one by one the others whispered amen to each body of Christ. She couldn't possibly have thought that would be all it would take to make me join them.

After mass we were given doughnuts and milk in the church basement and made small talk with the women there as part of our responsibility to charity. The room was long with gray cinder block walls. There were metal tables and folding chairs set up for us. The ground-level windows were above my head and were nearly covered up with banks of leaves that had blown in front of them. On the wall were the old felt banners from masses and Sunday school projects, crayon drawings of Daniel and the lion. The social was harder on us than the mass, as many of the women had babies and small children and in the basement we were close enough to smell them. Once I saw a woman give her baby to Angie, laid a newborn gently in her arms, putting Angie's hand beneath his head, and said how sweet he looked there. I thought at first she must have been insane, when in fact she was only thoughtless. Angie stood pale and rigid, the weight of this child resting on top of her own. "You make such a pretty mother," the woman said to her, and fixed the blankets around the baby's neck. It was like seeing Angie attached to an electric fence, able neither to let go nor to hold on, to simply be there while a thousand volts of current cleaned her veins.

"Let me," I said, and took the child from her cold arms. Angie slipped away, stumbled toward the front of the hall, and was gone without a word. It was, perhaps, the only truly good thing I had ever done in my life, because now the pain was mine and I wanted it not to be. The baby wasn't more than a month old, and somewhere far away I heard the woman talking about her long labor. That sweet face. The domes of her cheeks. The milky smell. I ached to put its hand inside my mouth, my face on its chest. It was as if I had never held a child before. "Please," I said finally, wanting her to take it, wanting her to never take it.

"They get heavy awfully fast," she said. "Come back here to me," she said.

I said something, made sounds, and went toward the doors where the air was. I felt broken.

"I want to get completely fucked up," Angie said once I found her outside. "Goddamn ladies. Goddamn Incarnation charity cases. Fuck them." Her hands were shaking as she reached in her huge purse and took out her bracelets and long earrings, which Mother Corinne would not let her wear inside. She turned and faced the church. "Fuck you," she said.

There were no bars in Owensboro, Kentucky. The town was dry. If there had been one, it wouldn't have been open on Sunday anyway. It had been a long time since I'd had a drink, but if we'd found a bar that Sunday we would have taken down the town.

After the social we were given an hour and a half to walk around town and spend whatever money we had. We were given a small allowance from the sisters, and some of the girls got money from home every now and then. I still had part of my travel money, which I kept safe in the trunk of my car in case I ever had to leave again in the night. Not much was open on Sunday, a Woolworth's, the drugstore, a small grocery. Two or three other stores would open up for us for that time and we would wander up and down the aisles, just happy to look at

things, pick them up and smell the store-bought smell. I tried
to remember the I. Magnin's where my mother worked, one
whole department for purses and scarves and gloves. A hundred
different pairs of gloves, every color, kid or cotton or satin that
went up to your shoulder. There was a woman there who asked
you what size your hands were. Some days I would pick my
mother up from work and we would go and try on the hats.
I remember a jade green cocktail hat with two feathers that
came down along one side of my face, a little wisp of veil.
My mother pinned it into place and said it looked so perfect
that she would buy it for me with her discount. "Even if you
never have a place to wear it, everyone should own a hat like
that once in their lives." But I didn't let her. It seemed too
far beyond me.

Now I was looking at a rack of mittens and stocking caps,
warm and practical, thinking about those two green feathers. I
would have liked to have that hat, maybe wear it alone in the
bathroom while I brushed my teeth, just to have a beautiful
thing.

How each girl spent her money changed over time. Beatrice,
who bought detective magazines at first (the kind she loved the
most, the kind the ladies from Incarnation never sent in their
monthly boxes), now spent her money on cocoa butter and hand
creams. Angie, who used to buy lipstick and perfume, now
spent every cent on yarn and embroidery floss. I didn't change,
though. All I ever bought were postcards to send to my mother,
which I wrote on and then tore up later. We all bought candy. We
all said we would make it last through the month, but inevitably
it was nearly gone by the time the bus pulled back into Saint
Elizabeth's.

Angie and I were both in bad moods that Sunday coming
back. We'd gone through the stores quickly, picking up a few
things we didn't want: a spool of black thread, a package of
emery boards, paste. Then we spent the rest of our time sitting
on a park bench in silence. In a few days we would be full of
regret, think of a half dozen things we needed, but for the time
we felt too hurt to enjoy such luxuries as shopping. Holding that
baby had hurt us, made us angry and full of longing. I looked
out the bus window and watched the Kentucky landscape speed
by. It was the first Sunday of December, and the trees were
black and bare and wet along the road. In southern California,
such a day would have been unimaginable, but in Kentucky, it
was the beginning of winter like the beginning of every winter.

The air hung over the fields like a heavy gray marsh; you'd have to cut it to get through. If I was going to buy anyone anything for Christmas, I would have needed to do it that day, and I had forgotten. I had wanted something for Sister Evangeline, for June, for Angie.

"You have a car," Angie said. "Why don't you go later? You could go all the way to Louisville if you wanted."

But that was the point. I could go all the way to Louisville, or Lexington, or Cincinnati. I was afraid if I went anywhere, I wouldn't be able to stop going. I was nearly seven months by then and the baby was kicking me hard. I shifted my weight around in the seat.

Beatrice leaned over the aisle and offered us some of her Junior Mints. She was so huge that her stomach nearly touched the seat in front of her. The doctor said it was one baby, one giant baby, but Beatrice swore it was twins, and Sister Evangeline backed her up. "That's four feet in there," Beatrice said, "not two."

I let the candy dissolve slowly in my mouth, and in truth it cheered me up a little. It was a time in my life when a Junior Mint could mean the difference between happiness and unhappiness.

"I want you two to help me," Beatrice whispered.

"Help you what?"

"I've made up my mind. I'm going to have the babies at Saint Elizabeth's."

"You're crazy," I told her.

"No I'm not. I can take pain. I broke my arm once, clean through, and I didn't cry out at all. I want to see these babies, you know, for a little while. It takes a good hour to get to Owensboro. That's all the time I need."

"Beatrice," Angie whispered, "if you're so sure you're having two, then don't you think you ought to go to the hospital?"

"It's only the first one that's hard. That's what my grandmother said. You pay the full price for the first one and the second one just comes out free. I got me a book on midwifing at the library," she whispered. "I read it through. If you read it, you'll know how to tie off the cord and all."

"Don't say this," Angie said.

"I am saying it. I'm going to do it. Regina can't help me, she'd be too afraid. I need you two."

Regina was Beatrice's quiet roommate, who walked the halls

at night in her sleep. Beatrice had taken to putting a chair in front of the door before they went to bed so that she could catch Regina before she got out and the nuns found her. Being found like that, asleep and lost, embarrassed Regina so badly that she wouldn't eat in the dining room for days. Beatrice was right in thinking she'd be no good in a crisis.

"All right," Angie said, rifling through her purse. "We'll do it."

"What?" I said.

Angie kicked my shin, and Beatrice settled back in her seat. "Good," she said. "Thanks."

Angie scribbled something on the back of a paper sack and handed it to me.

"She won't do it," the note said. *"No one does."*

Back at Saint Elizabeth's, Regina and another girl named Luanne waited for us on the porch. They were both from Owensboro and so they never came along on Sundays for fear of being seen. Everyone in Owensboro thought they were off visiting relatives somewhere. No one suspected they were in Habit, not even Luanne's aunt, who was a member of the Incarnation's Saint Vincent de Paul Society. They had their coats and hats on, as if they had meant to come along and had somehow missed the bus. Their faces looked chapped and cold. I wondered if they had been waiting outside the whole time.

They stood at the door of the bus and waited for us to get off. Regina waited for Beatrice. You never saw Regina without Beatrice. If Beatrice was out alone, that meant that Regina was waiting for her in their room. I thought how hard those Sundays must have been for Regina, and how hard January would be, after Beatrice delivered and left her with a month to wait alone. Beatrice had brought her back the box of hairpins and the pad of drawing paper Regina had given her the money to buy, as well as six rolls of butterscotch Life Savers and two Clark bars as a present.

I was tired and restless. On the Sundays we were away we had a cold supper, which Sister Evangeline took care of by herself so I didn't even take off my coat and go inside. I set off through the back pasture, at first toward June's and then away from her, not really going anywhere but through the woods. The ground was frozen hard already. The first light snow had been that morning, just a little bit blowing around. I was up early, working in the kitchen, and by the time the rest of the girls got up it had already melted and gone. It was the first snow I had seen in my life, and I opened the window and put my arm outside, letting it fall on the sleeve of my sweater. Walking in the woods that evening I thought about what it might be like to be home, having Thomas make me dinner and put pillows under my feet, telling me I could do no work whatsoever, having my mother take the bus up from San Diego to stay with me in the final weeks. There would have been baby showers with party favors and long talks about names and somewhere my mother would have found the christening gown that had been my father's, and somehow that all seemed worse. Walking through the woods alone in northern Kentucky, wearing a man's overcoat that someone had donated to Saint Elizabeth's, I felt strangely better off.

When it started to get dark I headed back to the hotel, taking a different path through the woods. I came upon the grounds-keeper's cottage unexpectedly, turned into a clearing and found it there. It was small and square and smoke came through the chimney and made the air smell like fall. The light from the windows fell in long yellow lines across the ground and I could see Son sitting at a table. He looked as lonely as me. He wasn't reading or eating, just sitting there quietly, staring at his hands. He turned them over from time to time, and I watched him watch his long fingers, his broad palms. To be in a well-lit room at night is like being in a movie, and I could see him as clearly as if I were standing next to him, but he never saw me. Even if he had looked up, he wouldn't have been able to make me out in the night. I wondered about him. It was as if he had no life at all, that he fixed things during the day, took orders and did the work well, but at night went home and simply waited. Waited for the night to be over and morning to come, when he would be needed again. His face looked so empty and lost in the bright kitchen light that I wanted to touch it, not to be there with him, exactly, but just to be behind him for a moment and put my hand on his cheek. Sundays must have seemed endless to him, with no one to say his name.

That night I wrote a card to Father O'Donnell back in San Diego and told him I was doing well. Then I wrote my mother and told her I missed her. I told her I was sorry not to be coming home for Christmas, but that I had a good job and couldn't get away just yet. "Don't think that I am gone forever," I told her, "I just need more time." Then I added, "I never drive at all anymore." One truth. I decided for once to mail them off and wrapped the postcards in a sheet of paper that said, "Please mail these." Then I put it all in an envelope and sent it care of the main post office, Chicago, Illinois. I hoped that no one was looking for me, but if they were, it would be better to have them look in Chicago than Habit.

There was a weight to missing. It was as heavy as a child.

===== 6 =====

CHRISTMAS came and went. The sisters tried, even Mother Corinne was cheerful. They wound green tinsel boughs up the heavy banister in the main lobby, strung large colored lights across the windows. The Hotel Louisa had taken the holidays seriously, and the attic was laden with boxes marked "X-Mas." We had three full nativity scenes, each as complicated as a chess set. Kneeling lambs and wise men and camels spread across the tabletops. I was forever stepping on some little animal on the floor and putting it back in its place. June had Son cut down a big spruce from the edge of the property and sent it over to us with a red bow on top. But we all had our own way of decorating trees. There were the ones who thought it should be done right away, others whose families had always waited until Christmas Eve. We made popcorn and cranberry chains until our fingers bled from sticking the needles in them so often.

The ladies of the Saint Vincent de Paul Society sent a gift for every girl and the sisters decided what most suited each individual and wrapped them and put them under the tree. Sister Bernadette wrote our names on the gift tags with a flowing hand. Many of the girls got boxes from home, but they kept the presents upstairs in their rooms, hidden under the bed so they could drift away in a private moment and open them alone. In spite of the carols and the red candles, the tufts of holly at each place setting and the great exchange of cards, we were uniformly heartsick. We wanted to be home.

My mother had a real tree for a long time after my father died, but every year it got smaller. Then one year, when I was twelve, it was only a little potted shrub, not even an evergreen, I don't think, and my mother and I laughed so hard trying to decorate it we couldn't see straight. We ate all the popcorn we meant to string and went out and bought an aluminum tree at the after-Christmas sales. We kept it in the hall closet of our apartment. With its branches folded down it looked like a large, prickly umbrella. My mother and I just didn't take it all very seriously. Christmas meant that I. Magnin's was closed for the day and my mother had a moment of peace between the last-minute shoppers and the people coming in to get cash refunds for sweaters that didn't fit. Christmas meant that I was out of school. After we went to mass we exchanged our gifts and went to the movies. One Christmas we saw four movies in a row and didn't get home until past midnight. It was a day we gave over to enjoying ourselves completely. We felt daring and wild, making so little out of the holiday, doing exactly what we wanted to do for the whole day. And the thing we wanted to do the most was be together.

I didn't think much about the later years, when Thomas and I were married and my mother was with Joe. We all spent the morning together and then drove to Victorville to see his family. Of course, it wasn't the same. My mother relented and started buying a tree again and the day became normal and structured, a real dinner with a ham and pineapple sauce. But even then it was all right because my mother would look at me a thousand times and smile, as if to say, Remember when it was just the two of us? Remember when we ate the whole box of chocolates every employee of I. Magnin's received along with their bonus, and how we threw the ones we didn't like out the window, the jellies and the marshmallow creams, one corner bitten off?

We were a family at Saint Elizabeth's, but on that day we seemed makeshift and uncomfortable to one another. We wanted our own families. One by one we would wander into another room and take deep breaths to try to keep from crying, or cry.

I had a little pastry gun that pumped out perfect butter cookies. Sister Evangeline came behind me, doing whatever she wanted, pushing in red halves of maraschino cherries or dusting their tops with red and green jimmies.

"Dammit," I said. The gun had clogged. It was the third time.

"Don't swear," Sister Evangeline said, not looking up.

"I can't work like this. I can't do my job if nothing works."

"The cookies are fine," she said, so happy, so glad to be making Christmas cookies.

"Don't be so nice," I said, suddenly choking up. "I can't

stand it. Don't be so nice anymore." I put down the gun and held onto the counter.

But she didn't come to me. I thought she would, touch my stomach and try to make me laugh. "Come on, Rose," she said. "Get back to work now." She handed me the gun. "Lots of girls out there wanting their cookies. Lots of girls who feel as bad as you. You're not the only one in the world who misses her mother at Christmas."

I stared at her. I was nearly a full foot taller than she was and from where I stood all I could see was a white draped head bobbing up and down over the sugary lumps of dough. "Do you miss your mother?" I asked her.

"Every day of my life," she said. "Every minute."

The other thing that made Christmastime so tense was that we were all waiting on Beatrice. She had moved up to the head table, the first seat. She was so pregnant that her stomach seemed to tremble when she was sitting still. Two girls who were due after her went on ahead and delivered out of turn, one going out on Christmas Eve.

"I'd hate for my baby to be born on Christmas," Angie said. "You've got to know you'll never get any good presents if you're born on Christmas."

The doctor swore that Beatrice was fine, not dilated, not even close to dilating. He drove down twice a month to check us all. One of the bedrooms had been set up with an examining table, and he brought his own nurse.

"It's going to be a big baby," he told Beatrice.

"It's two," she said.

"Not this time." The doctor folded up his stethoscope and slipped it in his pocket. "Anyone else, I'd say we'd take it C-section, but you're a healthy girl." (" 'Heavy girl' is what he meant to say," Beatrice told us when recounting the story later.) "You'll do just fine."

The doctor said I was still looking like early February to him. He said this while I was lying on the table, staring at a single bulb on the ceiling with my knees spread open. That I looked like early February.

Sister Evangeline gave me a holy card for Christmas. It looked to be as old as she was, but carefully preserved, not a single bent corner. On it was a picture of a beautiful woman, her chin tilted up toward heaven, a ring of stars in her hand, a swirl of clouds beneath her feet. "It's Saint Ann," she said, her face anxious, afraid I wouldn't like it. "The good mother. Don't show it to anyone for a while. I feel badly that I don't have something for all the girls."

Angie gave me a sweater she had knitted herself. It was the color of the ocean at night, and there was a single pearly button at the neck. "It's going to be too small for you now," she said. "But I thought, hey, you're not going to be pregnant forever."

"When did you do this?" I held the sweater up over my stomach. It was beautiful, as fine and stylish as a green cocktail hat.

"I worked on it while you were asleep, or in the kitchen. A couple of times I was knitting on it right in front of you and you never even noticed."

From the ladies of Saint Vincent de Paul I got a hardbound copy of *The French Chef Cookbook*, which I was happy to have.

June came over for Christmas Eve dinner. She came into the kitchen, stamping the slush off her boots. I had invited her. I knew there were plenty of people who liked June, but I wasn't sure that any of them asked her to Christmas Eve dinner. The little family she had left was far away now. I had told her I would come over and get her, but she said no, the walk would do her good.

"Merry Christmas, girls," she said to Sister Evangeline and me.

We wished her a Merry Christmas. I had never seen June at Saint Elizabeth's. "When was the last time you were here?" I asked her. I was thinking a couple of months. Maybe it had just been last week and I had missed her.

"Not since they took the old nuns away," she said, hanging her coat up on a hook by the door.

"That's more than thirty years," I said.

"That isn't so, June," Sister Evangeline said. "You came over when Sister Mary Joseph and I first came. You brought us a pie. Don't you remember that?"

June nodded. "Maybe I did," she said. She looked around the kitchen, let her eyes wander over every pot and pan hanging against the walls.

"It's still pretty much the same," she said. "The refrigerator, that's new."

"Stoves, too," Sister said. "Bunch of the burners died out on us in 1955."

It didn't make any sense to me. We were so close. We were literally in her own back yard. "Why don't you come over?" I said.

June picked up a cookie, looked at it, and set it back on its plate. She shrugged. "I never came here. I did when they were building it, and then maybe a couple of times after that. Opening parties, you know. We weren't so welcome here, the Clatterbucks."

"But you're welcome here now," I said.

"Old habits are hard to break." She laughed a little. "That's what we used to call the old folks in town when I was growing up. Old Habits. Guess I'm an Old Habit now. I'll tell you, though, I used to go to the edge of the woods at five o'clock and watch the folks come out and have their drinks on the porch. This is way back, when it was the Hotel Louisa. I used to think that they would all be sick people come to drink from the spring and there they'd be, all decked out like a fashion magazine. High-heeled shoes, suit jackets. Healthiest-looking group of sick people I'd ever seen. I guess it kind of burned me. I just stayed away."

"Well, you're back now," Sister Evangeline said, tossing the whole thing off. "Rose and Son. They brought you back."

It was Son who gave me the biggest surprise of all that Christmas. After dinner he came into the kitchen and slipped an envelope on the counter. It was tied with a green ribbon. "What's this?" I asked him.

"Open it up."

It was a drawing of a chair, a little pencil drawing of a straight-backed chair. It was good, really. The chair just floated on the paper without benefit of room or floor. The drawing was careful and clean. On the back it said, *"Merry Christmas to Rose, from your friend, Son. 1968."*

"This is nice," I said, feeling surprised and a little bad because I hadn't gotten anything for him.

"It's your chair," he said, looking away from me. "It's back at my house. I figured you could get it before you go, if you have room in the car and all. I didn't want to bring it over now. You know, that would look pretty stupid, me walking in here with a chair."

"You made me a chair?"

He nodded.

"This chair?"

"It's not a big deal or anything. I make a lot of chairs, tables, stuff like that."

I turned the card over and read the back again, then I looked at the drawing. "I'd like to see it."

"Sure," he said, "any time you want. I have it for you."

"I'd like to see it now," I said.

"Ah," he said. "It's Christmas Eve, maybe you best stay here. Y'all be doing stuff tonight."

I went back into the pantry and put on the heavy sweater I kept on a hook near the flour. "I want to see it now," I said.

We headed out into the darkness, into the light snow. Silently we went across the field to his little house, where I had seen him sitting alone. I could tell that he was limping more than he usually did. I wondered if the cold weather bothered his leg, and I wanted to ask what had happened to him, but I imagined that it was none of my business. I felt nervous somehow, almost like I was going to the house of a man I didn't know alone at night, and not to Son's house to see a chair. I folded my hands across my stomach. I was six weeks away from delivery, and there could be no doubt that he was not bringing me out to his house to kiss me, to tell me I was beautiful. I was not beautiful.

We wiped our feet carefully before going inside. It was like a doll's house. The little living room I had seen with a table right in the middle of everything, then three rooms in front of us, a kitchen, a bath, a bedroom. All the doors were open. Everything was neat and put away, almost as if he had been expecting someone to come. There was a painting of a horse over the couch, one of the leftovers from the days of the Hotel Louisa, I assumed, and the curtains seemed washed and pressed. It was careful like the drawing, everything just in its place, so if he was to leave quickly it would seem like no one had been there at all. It was too small for him. He made the furniture into miniatures just by standing beside it. He'd had to bow his head to come through the door of his own home.

"There," he said, and pointed to the chair next to the sofa. "That one's yours."

I would have known it. It was the chair in the picture. It was sturdy and graceful, made of a dark wood. There was a needlepoint cushion on the seat that tied onto the back of the chair.

"Miss June made that for you. She told me not to tell you she did it, but I didn't want you to think I did it."

I went over and sat in the chair. It was comfortable. It was the right height.

"Get up for a second," he said. I stood up and he grasped the chair by the leg and turned it over like a book of matches.

Under the seat, in the exact same writing, were the words *"Merry Christmas to Rose, from your friend, Son. 1968."* He had carved it there. "That way you'll always know it's your chair."

I thanked him and touched the letters with the tip of my finger.

That night I thought more about the chair than anything else. It was like coming back into the world, owning a real thing. There was a time I had chairs. Chairs and lamps and a mattress and box spring, plates and books and records. All of that was gone now. Until that night I had owned nothing that would make me think I could one day have a home again. And now I owned a chair. And it had my name on the bottom, proof that, no matter what, it would still be mine.

It was three days after Christmas and everything seemed stale. The tree would stay up until New Year's Day, as would the decorations, but Christmas was over and we wanted it behind us. We ate turkey sandwiches and turkey soup and a turkey potpie. We were trapped inside the house with Christmas leftovers. There had been a heavy snow on December 26, and even short walks were difficult. The sisters discouraged us from going out at all, telling us how we could fall, how other girls had fallen, what had happened. As ambivalent as I had been throughout my pregnancy, I now had a sense of coming into the closing stretch. I had made it this far and the idea of something happening to me now kept me inside, watching my step. From the kitchen window I could see my car, wrapped in a white blanket of snow. It was as if it had gone to sleep for the winter.

Angie came into the kitchen just after lunch. She was due the week before I was. It was impossible to believe that her baby was going to die, the way it kicked and grew. She was so fine-boned and small that the pregnancy seemed bigger on her than on me, as if what she had was not so much a part of her, but merely stuck on.

"Come on, Rose," she said, "I need to talk to you."

"Then talk," I said. I was tearing up lettuce into a plastic waste can, the only thing I could find big enough to mix so much salad.

"I want to talk to you *upstairs*," she said.

Sister Evangeline and I both looked at her. Her fists were clenched, her face full of rage. "You go on now, Rose," Sister Evangeline said. "I'll finish here."

I dried my hands and went to Angie, but before we were out the door, Sister Evangeline called to us. "I know about these things," she said. "My mother knew. I'd like it better if it could happen another way, but you call me if you need me."

Angie stopped dead and looked at her.

"Go on," Sister Evangeline said. "I was just telling you."

Angie pulled me up the stairs by my wrist. "It's Beatrice," she whispered harshly.

"What do you mean, it's Beatrice?" But I knew.

"She's having the baby here. She says she's going to do it."

It was all I could do to keep myself from lunging for her. "You said she wouldn't. You said nobody did."

"Well, I was wrong, okay? I can't talk her out of it. There's not a damn thing I can do but do what she wants."

"We could go tell Mother Corinne," I said. "That would stop it."

"You just do that."

"Look, I don't want to, but this isn't a game. We have to do what's best for her."

"She's all grown up," Angie said. "She's made her own choice about what's best for her."

We got to her door and stood for another second in the hall. I held her hand. "Did you read that book?" I asked.

She nodded and we went inside without knocking.

Beatrice was sitting on her bed, her feet stretched out in front of her, reading a detective magazine. Regina was sitting beside her quietly, watching.

"Hiya," Beatrice said.

We came inside and closed the door.

"Tell her not to do this," Regina said.

"Don't do this, Bea," I said.

"Well, you tried. I've got to give you that much." Beatrice flicked through the pages of her magazine. " 'Dead Girl Found Strangled in Pool of Blood That Is Not Her Own.' That's the one I've been saving as a distraction, for when things get bad."

"When will that be?" Angie asked, sitting down on the opposite bed. Beatrice and Regina had one of the nicest rooms in the hotel. The honeymoon suite. It had a window seat with a beautiful view of the pasture and a separate sitting room. I wondered if the honeymoon suite had always had twin beds or if they'd moved those in later.

"Hard to say," Beatrice said, "I haven't done this before. I had the first one this morning around six o'clock, forty-five minutes apart. Now they're twenty minutes."

"Twenty-two," Regina said, holding up her wristwatch.

"Twenty-two, whatever. My water just broke a little while ago, though, that's why I called y'all. It could be sooner or later, either way."

Beatrice had her black hair up in a ponytail right on the top of her head, so that it made a black fountain down the sides of her sweaty face. She didn't have her socks on, and her feet were so swollen that her toes seemed to run together.

"This is so much better, being here," she said. "My own bed, all of you. I'd say you all ought to do it this way, too, but they'll crack down after I make it. It'll be a lot harder to do. They don't expect it now, they're not—" Then all of a sudden she stopped and closed her eyes. Angie, Regina and I held our breath. Beatrice took Regina's hand and squeezed it so hard you could tell it hurt. Her face contorted with a pain so pure it made me want to cry out. It lasted too long, it seemed to go on forever.

"Seventeen minutes. That was only seventeen minutes from the last time." Regina was paler than Beatrice, her own light brown hair slicked back with sweat.

Beatrice exhaled and smiled. She was a little bit shaken, you could see it, but mostly she was proud. "See there, I can do this. I told you I could do this." She laughed. "Hurts like a son of a bitch, ladies. I'm sorry to have to be the one to tell you, this is pain. They say you forget all about it, though, once you've got the baby."

That made me think that the four of us would never forget then, that we would have to carry that pain around with us forever because there would be no reward for our labor.

"Stop staring at me," Beatrice said. "Y'all are acting like I'm some kind of sideshow. This is gonna be you here in not so very long."

"It is not going to be me here," Angie said. "I'm going to be in the hospital, like any civilized person."

"Suit yourself," Beatrice said. "But you drop me a note when your time comes and tell me that you didn't want to ride all the way to Owensboro in an ambulance holding your baby."

I turned away from them, toward the window, looking for comfort and finding snow.

Beatrice went back to her magazine and the three of us sat there, waiting. Finally she shut it. "Look," she said, "it's not that I don't appreciate this and all, but you're making me nervous as a cat here. Go do something. I'll call you when I need you.''

"We can't just leave you here," Angie said.

"Get," she said.

So we left. I went back to the kitchen and Angie went to polish silver. Only Regina stayed on, because it was her room, too. It would have been beyond her to leave Beatrice, anyway.

"How's she doing?" Sister Evangeline said.

"Who?" I knew she knew, but I just didn't want to get into it with her. She was a sister, after all, and I didn't want to incriminate her in any way.

"All right," she said, peeling an apple, "be that way."

I couldn't settle down. I would try to read from the cookbook, but then I'd put it down and head back up the stairs. I caught Beatrice in the middle of one, panting like a dog. Regina had a wild look about her, her eyes were big and round, her shirt was soaked through.

"Wow," Beatrice said, settling back.

"That was eighteen minutes, but the one before that was thirteen. It doesn't stay exactly the same."

"Why do you keep looking at that damn watch, anyway?" Beatrice said. She was getting tired, you could tell.

"I have to have something to do," Regina said.

All afternoon I tried to think about Beatrice, but I kept thinking about myself. That was where I was headed, the panting and pain of it. Like Christ in the olive garden, I prayed for deliverance. I wanted the birth to pass over me.

At six o'clock everyone came down to dinner, including Regina and Beatrice. I couldn't believe it, but there she was, her face not nearly as pale, her hair brushed neatly. "I fixed her up," Angie whispered to me as we walked in. "I think she looks pretty good. It took nearly all the blush I had, but she's got some color in her."

"Why are you here?" I said to Beatrice.

She smiled weakly. "If I skip dinner they'll know something's wrong. They're watching me pretty close, you know."

So we sat at the table and took turns eating off of Beatrice's plate, though none of us was hungry. Sister Bernadette came by and put her hand on Beatrice's shoulder. "How are we doing tonight?" she said.

"Fine," Beatrice said. "I'm a little tired. I stayed up all night reading."

"No signs yet?"

"Not yet," she said. "I don't know how much longer this kid thinks he can hold out."

Sister Bernadette laughed and patted her arm. Then she wandered off to the other tables, checking, asking.

I was impressed by the fluency with which Beatrice lied. She was no beginner. I suddenly wanted to hear her story, know just what had happened to her in that mine where she worked with the men, but it hardly seemed the right time to ask. I wanted all of this to be over, and yet I knew that once it was she would be gone and I would never see her again.

It seemed clear that everyone knew exactly what was going on except the nuns. The other girls looked at our table, nodded when they caught our eye. They were telling us they understood and would be ready to help when the time came. A light currency connected us. We were all in the same boat. We knew.

When her first contraction came at dinner we laughed and she put her hands over her face as if she were embarrassed. I could see the veins rising in her arms, her shoulders trembling, and then it passed. Her blush was streaked with sweat, and Angie leaned over to wipe her cheek with her napkin.

Beatrice stayed all the way through dessert. She had another contraction just as the plates were being set down. But she was not even the first to leave the dining room. When she did go, she went slowly, stopping to talk to people while Regina stayed close at her side.

"You'd think we were staging some kind of prison break," I whispered to Angie. "This is ridiculous."

I went back into the kitchen and Son ate his dinner while I cleaned up. When the serving platter slipped from my hands, he was there before it hit the floor. He caught it in one giant hand and laid it on the sink. "Sit down," he said, taking my shoulders and guiding me over to the chair. "You don't look very good."

"I don't feel so well, I guess." Sister Evangeline wasn't around. She had taken to drifting off somewhere after dinner.

"I'll tell you what," he said. "I'll clean up and you can sit and talk to me for a change."

"You've worked all day," I said, but made no move to get up. Son reached down and picked up my feet in his hands and set them lightly on the chair in front of me. There was something so familiar about the gesture that it made me shudder.

"You want to tell me what's wrong," he said, starting in on the dishes.

"This," I said, and pointed to my stomach. "It wears me out."

His face flushed and he turned away from me. "Then you shouldn't be working yourself so hard. You chase the other girls off, take it all on yourself. You've got to think about what's going to happen when you're gone. Sister's gonna need a new girl and now I don't know but what she won't be able to stand it. You've been with her all the time."

I had never thought about it, that what I was doing might not be what was best for Sister Evangeline. I looked down at my hands.

"Look," he said, "I'm not bawling you out or anything. I'm just saying give it some thought. You're not like the other girls, Rose." He stopped, the sponge in his hand was suspended on the plate. "You're half running this place now. Everybody's come to count on you, they're getting attached to you. Do you understand that? You're going to be leaving soon. They've got to be able to stand on their own once you go." He looked at me and for a minute I was sure he was going to say something else. He was such a big man. He was nearly as old as my father would have been if he were alive. The bib of his overalls was wet with dishwater by the time he put the last dish in the rack. "I need to go home now," he said, as if there was a reason to go, that someone might have been waiting for him that one night. "You just give it some thought. Don't let it bother you, just think about it."

"I will," I said.

After he had dried his hands and buttoned his coat he came and stood beside me. He reached out for a second, I thought to touch my hair, and then pulled back his hand. "You all right?" he asked.

"It's just been a long day," I said.

But the night was years longer. We went back to our rooms and waited under the covers for bed check. "Good night, God bless," Sister Bernadette said into the darkness, and we said the same to her. Once her footsteps were far away we got up quietly and went to Beatrice's room. The contractions came closer and closer, but there was still no baby. It seemed that Beatrice would scarcely catch her breath before another one broke over her like a wave. "Read to me," she said, and tapped the magazine on her bedside table. "I think this would be a good time."

All of her hardness had washed away. The pain had pushed a

sweetness into her, made her nearly docile. I picked up the magazine. "You want the pool-of-blood one?"

"Definitely."

" 'On the night of November 16, 1967, the body of Carrie Holcome, aged sixteen years, was found in an alley outside of Big Jimmy's Restaurant in Waco, Texas, by José Díaz, an employee of the establishment.' "

"This is going to give me nightmares," Angie said. "I can't stand stuff like this. Look, the hairs on my arms are up already."

"So when you have a baby you can hear what you want," Beatrice said, fading off into another contraction, which seemed ridiculously close to the last one.

"Read it," Regina said.

" 'The coroner's report showed clearly that Miss Holcome had been strangled, possibly with a telephone cord, at approximately nine P.M.' "

"It's always a phone cord," Beatrice said dreamily, the pain having left for a minute. "Have you ever noticed that?"

"Jesus," Angie said, and covered her eyes.

" 'But the detectives that arrived on the scene were quick to notice that Miss Holcome lay in a pool of blood, even though she had no cuts on her body. After careful analysis, it was discovered that the blood under Miss Holcome's body was not her own.' "

"You mean to tell me that somebody killed this girl, poured a bucket of somebody else's blood on the ground, and laid her in it? That's too sick," Angie said. "That's even worse than just killing her."

"Dead is dead," Beatrice said. "How can it get worse?" But then she went off again. The only noise she made was something like a squeak, high and thin. She was holding Regina's arm with both her hands now and I prayed to be away, to not see it.

We went on like this through the night, close but not there. The pool of blood was something from meat, steaks, I think, that had been thrown into the alley from the kitchen door. It was the girl's boyfriend who'd killed her, dropped her there because she would not say she loved him, or so he said in his confession. He knew nothing about the blood.

"What a hoax," Beatrice said. "I thought it was going to be better than that."

We stayed awake all night. Even if we drifted off for a second, we were awakened by Beatrice every seven minutes, then five, then three. She did not call out, but the fact of every contraction pulled us to her bed. By the time the sun came up I was half out of my mind. I had crossed the line from exhaustion to being so completely awake I was aware of every time I blinked my eyes. I was suddenly afraid of everything. I didn't know how we could get through breakfast, I didn't know how we would ever get back any peace in our lives. It was as if everything was ruined now. It could not be reversed. The night we lost would never be regained.

At five-thirty that morning Beatrice started to move in her bed, pulling up her legs and twisting her head from side to side. "This is it," she said.

But we were wrecked. Angie started to cry, her hands were shaking. I got up quickly, quicker than I had in two months, and went down the dark stairs and through the dark corridor past the kitchen. I knocked on the door at the end of the hall. "Sister," I whispered, "help me."

A voice asleep but not tired like my own called me inside. There was a small old woman in the bed, short and round beneath her blanket. She sat up and started looking for her glasses. Her hair was completely white and it fell halfway down her back. She had on a flannel nightgown with a row of forget-me-nots around the collar. "Rose?" she said.

I could not get over the sight of Sister Evangeline, who was not a nun but any woman in her bed. "I need help," I said.

She clicked on the little lamp beside her bed and we stared at each other in disbelief. "Oh, Lord," she said, "look at you."

I looked down and saw my hands were shaking like Angie's. I felt like I couldn't stand up. "Help me," I said.

She got up and covered her head and immediately looked like herself again. I was so relieved to see her face framed inside the coife. It made sense to me now. She pulled on her bathrobe and went into the bathroom and got a bottle of rubbing alcohol. Then she went through the kitchen, picking up a stack of clean dishtowels, a ball of string, and her favorite knife, the one with the black handle she used for cutting tomatoes.

"I wish you girls hadn't done this," she said, not with anger, but as a matter of fact. "It's been a long time. I don't imagine it's something you forget, but I'd rather, well, that doesn't matter now. This is what we have to do and we'll do it."

We climbed back up the stairs and went into the room. In the few minutes I was gone everything had changed. Beatrice had crossed the line. The contractions counted for something now. Regina had taken on a new clarity. She seemed alert and calm, wiping off Beatrice's forehead with a damp washcloth. "You're fine," she said sweetly. "Everything is fine."

"I've never done two," Sister Evangeline said. "I don't even think my mother did two." She washed her hands in the sink again and again until I thought her skin would bleed.

"I don't think I'm going to be able to keep quiet about this much longer," Beatrice said.

"It doesn't matter, sweetheart," Sister Evangeline said. "You sing out if it makes you feel better. You're too far along to move now. You're going to have your way." She peered down between Beatrice's legs and slipped two fingers inside her. "Right there," she said, "all ready to go. Two fine boys. The next time you push. Next time you're ready, you get one out."

"I don't want to do this," Beatrice said, and took short breaths. Angie came and stood beside me, and we held to each other like drowning men. Only Regina seemed completely calm, whispering and sponging, staying right on the bed beside her.

What can I say about this? I had never seen a birth. I'm not sure I had ever really imagined it. It was like a movie that made you close your eyes and then open them again, until you were unable to either watch or look away. I remember that birth had a smell as heavy and salted as blood itself, and I remember that Beatrice never cried out, even after Sister said she could. It was a point of honor. She said she would be quiet start to finish and she was.

"There's so little to do," Sister Evangeline said, easing out the first shoulders. "They do it all themselves."

When I saw that first wet fish, its slickness, its blue cord, I pressed my hands against my stomach. The gates were open now to every longing Angie talked about late at night. This baby. My baby. To think I would be in a hospital asleep and when I woke up she would be gone. Never gone. I thought, never, never.

Sister Evangeline tied string in two places on the cord and drew her knife through what connected Beatrice to her son. Her hands were fast and sure the way they'd never been in the kitchen. She turned him over and loosened the fluids from his throat and he cried as his mother had not. Regina took him from Sister's hands and carried him to the sink with complete certainty and Beatrice laughed, as loud and coarse as she ever had in her life.

The second one was not free, as Beatrice's grandmother had told her, but it came more easily. Beatrice turned her head to the side. The light sounds she made seemed almost like desire, as if things had come full circle, and her face again contorted the way it had that night nine months ago. Regina gave me the first baby so she could take the second. She had wrapped him tightly in a pillowcase. His was a face one minute old. A face more exhausted than my own.

Mother Corinne came in just as the second cord was being cut. She looked at the knife and the blood across Sister Evangeline's blue terry cloth robe. You could tell by her face that at first she simply didn't understand, thought that what had happened revolved somehow around that knife.

"Evangeline," she said.

"It came on her so fast," Regina said. "She just had them. She was fine and then she just had them. I woke up Angie and Rose and they got Sister Evangeline. There was no time at all."

"Why didn't you come to me?" Mother Corinne said to me. She was furious. The blood had soaked through the mattress, onto the carpet.

"I was asleep," I said. "I just went to Sister Evangeline. I couldn't think. By the time she got up here to see what was wrong it was all happening."

Regina was washing out the baby's eyes, rinsing the blood from his open mouth. Girls started coming down the hall. Suddenly the world was up and pressing into the room. Every pregnant girl come to see her fate, and Beatrice laughing, laughing, a son in each arm. Sister Bernadette came and Mother Corinne told her to call for an ambulance. It would take an hour to arrive at least. Sister Evangeline pressed down into Beatrice and kneaded her abdomen until the afterbirth pushed out, and then she scooped it up in her hands and carried it to the wastepaper basket to throw it away.

I followed Beatrice to the door of the ambulance and then followed the ambulance down the road. It was snowing hard and the tires slipped a little as they turned. Maybe someone called to me and I didn't hear them or maybe they didn't call. It was as if everyone was wandering blind and I happened to be the one who went outside. Or maybe other girls were outside. If they were, well, what could I do for them? I had lost my capacity for worry, had used up every ounce of worry I had in me over the last twenty-four hours. Beatrice, Angie, Sister Evangeline, poor Regina. I should have been worried for them, but instead I watched the ambulance fade into whiteness, until all I could see were the red lights, spinning, and after a while, not even them. I pulled my bathrobe closer to my throat. I had put on my shoes at some point, because I saw them there. I knew it must be cold, but all I felt was wet.

Without worry to protect me, every thought that came into my mind received real attention. For the first time I saw myself clearly, waking up in the hospital the next morning alone. I would not be brave like Beatrice. I would not win those few hours. Even if I could, they would not dent my need. I could go back to Thomas. He would take me still, I was sure. I could make the drive, brush the snow off my car. How amazed he would be to see me like this, how he would fall to his knees to have me back, both of us back. Or I could go to my mother's, who would hide me from Thomas, or back to Billy's in Arkansas. I could go someplace where I could keep this baby. I saw those good parents crying. "Our girl," they'd say. But there were other girls for them. Saint Elizabeth's raised them, rich, fertile fields of babies. I was through with giving things up. I wanted something of my own.

I kept going through the snow, as if the place I was going was someplace I had to walk to. My feet got heavier as the snow started caking to my shoes. But I couldn't see where I was going. It was white in every direction and the dark lines around the edges could have been trees or hotels or towns. I should have been worried about that, too, but like I said, I just couldn't. I was thinking about the candles, about all the years I waited for my sign from God. I thought about it long and hard, and then I made a decision.

"I'm not counting that one," I said. "I took it the wrong way. There hasn't been a sign. I was really good, You know. For a long time. You shouldn't forget that."

I shoved my hands in my pockets and started walking in small circles. "I'm saying that I'll do what You want me to do if You just give me some kind of hint about what that is. Do You hear me?" I was shouting, the snow was filling up my mouth. "Your will be done. Okay? Tell me what in the hell that's supposed to be."

"Rose!" a voice called.

I looked up but didn't see anything at first. I was hoping for a quick answer.

"Jesus, girl, I've been looking for you everywhere."

The figure that came toward me in the whiteness was huge, big enough to be the Son of Man. He who so loved man He sent His only Son.

Son took off his coat and wrapped it around me, bundled me

like newspapers, firewood, and lifted me up. "Who were you talking to? What were you saying?" But I didn't answer him. I was watching the snow go past me, the dark bank getting closer. I was riding. Being carried. I am five feet ten inches tall. I had not been carried since the night my appendix burst, when the superintendent struggled under my weight to take me down the stairs to his car. It was summer and hot and I was burning up with fever and I felt him try to shift my weight in his arms, but now the snow beat down on us so hard it stung my face, and I was huge, two people in one, me and my daughter in those arms and the arms never faltered. They were bigger even than us. He took such giant steps. I looked down and saw the footprints rushing behind us, filling up with snow as they receded, being swallowed back into the smooth white landscape like we had never walked in this pasture at all.

We went to Son's house because it was closer than the hotel. Son laid me down on his bed and took off my shoes. He rubbed my feet in his hands, my hands in his hands. He pulled off his sweater and unbuttoned his shirt and put my feet against his warm chest. He rubbed my legs and covered me in blankets. He was full of motion, never stopped moving.

"Don't freeze up on me," he said to my calf. His voice was shaking.

And at that moment a little bit of me came back because I was worried about him. "I'll be all right," I said.

He looked up, embarrassed at being overheard. "You need to change clothes, get out of those wet things," he said. "Can you do that?"

I nodded.

He brought me a shirt and a sweater and some long underwear and socks. Even in my present condition they would be too big. "Put these on," he said. "I'll get you in front of the fire."

I peeled off my wet clothes and tried to dress, but everything about me was slow. I couldn't think enough to make my hands work, to see the difference between shirt and socks. I worked my way slowly into the fabric, wrapping myself again and again in blankets. I had started to shiver. I could finally feel the cold and it was brutal.

Son came back in and carried me to the sofa, which he'd moved right in front of the fire. "You don't have any frostbite that I can see," he said, going back to work on my hands. "What could have possessed you to go out like that in your nightdress?"

"Beatrice," I said, but I didn't say anything else. I didn't feel like talking. I just sat and watched the fire for a long time and then went to sleep.

When I woke up, it was dark and the snow had stopped. Son was sitting in my chair, watching. He had stayed awake and kept the fire going.

"Angie's going to think I'm dead," I said.

"I went over there and told them. They said to just let you sleep for a while. They wanted to take you into the hospital, but I said you were fine. I don't think you were out there very long."

"Is it late?"

"No, no. Not even suppertime. But you've been asleep all day, since eight o'clock this morning."

My sense of time had been destroyed in the snow. This was still the same day. This morning was still connected to today. I sat up and shifted my blankets around me. You have never seen so many blankets in your life. "I don't know what I'm going to do," I said.

"About what?"

"The baby." I yawned and shook my head, trying to force the sleep out of me.

"What do you want to do about it?"

"Keep it," I said, out loud and clear for the first time in my life. "I'm going to keep it and I don't know how."

"Stay here."

"I can't stay here, they wouldn't let me."

"Stay here," he said. "Marry me and they'll let you stay."

I turned around and looked at him. He looked at the fire for a minute and then turned to me. "Marry me, Rose," he said. "I'm not going to try and talk you into something you don't want to do, but it makes good sense. We'll stay here. We'll bring the baby up together."

I thought about it for a minute. Maybe this was the way it was supposed to be for me. God was telling me He was right after all. I was supposed to be married, live a small life with a man I didn't love. My old life seemed so far away at that moment that I figured the last marriage had been erased somehow, that I had come far enough to negate it. "All right," I said.

Son looked at me, puzzled, then smiled. "Really?"

"Really."

He stood up, his head nearly touching the ceiling. The look on his face was so completely happy that I realized for the first time that he was in love with me. The dinners in the kitchen, the chair, that he was the one who went to find me in the snow. He loved me, and I was sorry about that. It would only make things harder between us.

"I guess I'll take you home then," he said. "We'll work out the details of all of this later."

"No," I said. "I want to do this now. Tonight. If you want to marry me, then marry me tonight."

"But there's no time to plan anything. You'll want to call someone, your family. You'll want to get a dress to wear."

"I don't need a wedding," I said. "I need to get married. I don't care about anything else."

Son sat down beside me. He thought it over. "I know there's a justice in Owensboro. If we called him now he might stay open for us."

"Then call," I said.

Son spent a couple of minutes on the phone and then came back. "He said he'd wait for us."

"Good." I got up and Son brought me his coat. "Do you have one?" I asked.

"Sure," he said, "I've got something in the back."

We walked out to his truck and climbed inside. My shoes were soaking wet and cold. "I'll drive you over to the hotel so you can change," he said.

"I don't want to change." I didn't want the time to stop or think. I just wanted to go.

"You're going to get married in my clothes?"

"It looks that way."

So we headed toward Owensboro. The road was covered with snow, but it didn't seem to bother Son. He was a little worried, happy about the way things were turning out, but took my clothes and lack of desire to plan as troubling signs.

"We can get a bigger place in town," he said.

"Later, maybe. Your place is fine with me for now. The baby won't need her own room for a while."

"Her?"

"Sister Evangeline told me. It's going to be a girl."

Son smiled. "A girl," he said. "That's something, all right." He looked at me for a second, me or my stomach, it was hard to tell. "I'd like to give her my last name, if that suits you."

"That would be nice," I said, and then thought about it for a minute. "What is your name, Son?"

"Abbott," he said. "Wilson Abbott."

"Wilson," I said, and nodded.

"You don't have to tell me about the father. That's your own business. As far as I'm concerned, we start from right now, right this minute. Whatever's in the past belongs to you. Private."

"I'd like that."

"So if you want, this baby can be yours and mine, you know, as far as she's concerned. I think that would be easier on a kid than knowing the truth."

"I think so."

"I've always wanted a baby, Rose. I'll be a good father."

"I know," I said. "That's why we're doing this." I should have been kinder to him. He was changing his life for me, some woman he really didn't know at all, but I couldn't seem to bring a kind word out of my mouth. I wanted him to know what this was all about for me, so that if he wanted to change his mind he could. I didn't want to think I was tricking him in any way.

The driving was slow because the roads were still bad, even where the plows had come through. I hardly ever got out at night. I thought about going to the movies as a teenager, out to dinner. I was getting married. I tried to remember something about my first wedding, but I couldn't, not even the dress I wore.

We weren't in Owensboro until seven. The judge told us he was just about to give up. "I've got a family," he said. "I can't be waiting around on folks all night."

When I took off Son's coat he stared at my stomach and then at Son. "So that's all the rush," he said. "Looks like you coulda got here a mite quicker."

"We just want to get married," Son said.

"Have to is more like it from where I'm standing." He was a man in his fifties who wore a dark suit and red tie. He was so happy to see scandal, so pleased for a little diversion. "Most times we see a girl like that she's got her papa holding a shotgun on some poor boy. But you're no boy, mister. You could be this girl's daddy yourself."

Son put his hand on the man's shoulder. The hand said, Remember how small you are, how easy this would be. Get about your business.

"I'll have to call my wife and my son over to witness," he said, dialing the phone. "They just live around the block. I told them you'd be coming. They're waiting on you, too." The man rang up his wife and by the time we were comfortable in our chairs they had arrived, a short, round woman with tight curls and a boy who was tall and thin and not bad looking. I wondered if they had picked him up at Saint Elizabeth's eighteen years before, as he bore no resemblance to his parents.

"Take your places here," the man said, and arranged us in front of his desk, Son and I standing together, his wife beside me, his son beside Son. They looked bored. They were tired of marriage, had seen it all before. The woman pulled at a thread on her dress which came out and out without end. She snapped it off and dropped it to the floor. She was trying hard not to look at my clothes, Son's clothes. I had a hand up underneath my sweater, holding up his long underwear, which was dingy from too much washing and a little frayed around the seams. The man opened his book and started reading quickly. I remembered those words. Dearly beloved. Honor and obey. Sickness and in health. Until death do us part. I had said them before and for that second I wondered if Son had as well. When the man asked me my name so that he could say, do you, Wilson Abbott, take, I said, Martha Rose Clinton, and Son looked at me surprised. He didn't know my name either and had been too polite to ask. I thought about giving my maiden name, Sloan, but I was used to Clinton. There were people who knew me by that name, and consistency is the most important part of a lie.

When the service was over the man started in on the paper-work, and his wife and son said good night and shook our hands and wished us luck. "It was a real nice wedding," the woman said to me. "Prettiest I've seen in a while." Her voice sounded like a record. Her kind words were part of what you bought. They were meant to leave a good taste in your mouth, so that for the next marriage you would remember to come back and try them again. The boy smiled politely but was quiet. Then they were gone.

"I'll need to see birth certificates," he said.

Son took his out of his wallet and unfolded it. I said I didn't have mine.

"Don't have it?" the man said. "Then what did we just go through all of this for? No birth certificate, no marriage. It's as simple as that."

"She's from California," Son said, by way of explanation.

"I don't care if she's from France. A person needs a birth certificate to get married in this state."

Son sighed and reached into his wallet. He laid five ten-dollar bills on the desk. The man touched them with his finger. "Plus the cost of the service. That's twelve dollars."

Son counted out twelve dollars. A five and seven ones, and

put his wallet back into his pocket. The justice showed us where to put our names and then signed the paper with a flourish. "Done," he said. "Married."

Son and I stood out in the snow and looked at each other for a minute. "So," he said.

"Well," I said.

There wasn't much to say in the car going back. "Martha is a pretty name," Son told me.

"I never use it," I said.

"That was my sister's name, Martha."

I thought about asking him about his brothers and sisters, his family, where he was from, but there would be all the time in the world for that. I rested my head against the glass and watched the dark white world.

"Well," he said when we pulled up in front of Saint Elizabeth's, "I guess I'll see you tomorrow, dinner for sure."

"What do you mean?" I asked him.

"Well, you're going to go to bed, right? It's getting late."

"I'm coming home with you."

"Tonight?"

"You married me, Son. I guess that's the way it should be, unless you'd rather I didn't."

He rubbed his neck uneasily. "No, no. You should do whatever you want. I mean, of course you're welcome with me. It's your house, too. I just thought you might not want people to know."

"We haven't done anything wrong. They'll all know sooner or later."

"Sure," he said. "You're right."

"I want to tell Angie is all."

"I'll wait for you."

"Go home," I said. "I may be awhile. I'll walk over later."

"I'll wait for you in the kitchen," he said, and we went into the Hotel Louisa through separate doors.

Angie was asleep when I came in, and I wondered if she had gone to bed early or if she had been asleep all day. I sat down on the edge of her bed and looked at her pretty face. Asleep she was a child. You could almost read her dreams across her forehead. I touched her hair. "Hey," I said.

She opened her eyes, blinked, and smiled. "I was so worried when you left," she said.

"I'm okay."

"Son told us he found you out in the snow. You must have gone a little crazy, huh?"

"A little."

"Me too," she whispered. "I went into the bathroom and locked the door and I couldn't stop crying, you know. Just couldn't stop. I thought I was going to jump out the window there for a second."

"Angie."

"What?"

"I'm married now. I got married tonight."

She raised up on her elbow. "Go on," she said.

"No, I did." I touched her face. I wished I had a sister. I wished there was blood between us. "I married Son."

"You're not joking, are you?"

"No."

"Why, Rose?" she whispered.

"I'm going to keep the baby and I just didn't see how I could do it alone. If I married Son then I can stay here. This wouldn't be such a bad place to raise a baby."

She stared at me, her eyes open wide. She was completely awake. "I'm jealous," she said. "I'm happy for you, but I wish it was me." She looked down at her stomach, pushed at it with one finger. "You're doing the wrong thing. Nobody gets married like that, it's crazy. You did it because of Beatrice, not because you love him, but I would have done it, too." She looked at me. She wanted me to tell her how it could all be the same again. "If I had been the one to walk outside. If I was the one he found. I would have married him, too."

"I know." I was quiet for a second, waiting to tell her the rest. "I'm going over there tonight," I said finally. "I have to get things started now before I think about it too much."

"You married him," she said. "I figured you'd go over there." We looked at each other for a long time. I was moving to a little house not a quarter of a mile away. I would still be at Saint Elizabeth's every day. We would have been split apart soon anyway, when the babies were born, and knowing all of that I still could not stand to leave her. She scooted over in her bed and lay down flat on her back. "Come here," she said.

I lay down beside her. We were too big to face each other, but we lay there together and looked up at the dark ceiling and held hands. "It's going to be fine," she said. "It's going to be good, even."

"You too," I said.

"But I wish you weren't leaving. I wish we were going to be together."

After a while she pretended to be asleep, but I could tell she wasn't. I got up and took a few things, a clean dress, my toothbrush, some underwear. I would get the rest later. When I finally did leave, neither one of us said anything about it.

Son was in the kitchen with Sister Evangeline, having something to eat. When I came through the door she nearly threw herself at me. "This is just the way it should be," she said. "I was going to tell you, a million times, but I didn't." She clapped her hands. "I kept it all a secret all this time. I am so happy, Rosie. I've never been so happy. What a big day. I deliver two babies in the morning and my best girl gets married at night. There's never been a day like this in all the world."

"You knew?"

"Sure I knew." She waved her hand, dismissing me. "Of course I knew. I know all sorts of things."

"More than just the babies?"

"It's in my diary. The week you started working in the kitchen, I said, Rose will marry Son, sure as I'm born. Why, I don't know that you two had even properly met then. I had to drop my rosary down next to the stove. My rosary! That's how sure I was."

"I don't want to hear this."

"That's your problem, Rosie, you never want to know. All sorts of things going on out there and you don't want to know about them until they land on your plate."

Son sat at the table, smiling. He didn't care how it happened, only that it had. I was tired.

"Well, you two get going," she said, and gave me a little push toward Son. "I'll see you in the morning, if you're feeling up to work. You've had a big day today. You might want to take tomorrow off."

"I might," I said. I kissed her good night, even though I felt strangely angry at her for knowing my business. Then Son and I went home.

The house looked different than it had five hours before. It was my house now, at least to a small part. I looked around the living room.

"Are you Catholic?" I asked him.

"No," he said. "I'm not much of anything. Does that matter?"

"No," I said. "I was just wondering."

We took off our coats and stood in front of the fireplace, which was cold. "I could start a fire," he said.

"I think we ought to go to bed, probably."

"Sure," he said. "You must be tired. You can have the bedroom, I'll sleep in here. I fall asleep in here half the time, anyway."

"I know I'm no great find," I said. "But you might as well get used to sleeping with me. We're married. We've only got one bedroom."

Son looked surprised, as he had a hundred times that night. "You, Rose? Dear God, there was never such a find." He came to me and put his hand on my face. With the base of his palm against my jaw, his fingers curved all the way up the side of my head. And then he kissed me, very lightly on the side of my nose and then my lips, then on my lips again.

We went into the bedroom and I took off my clothes. I would not be embarrassed, I told myself. This was the body he had married, this is the one he would have to see. We kept the lights off, but the moon against the snow made the room seem nearly bright. "Look at you," he said. "Look how pretty you are."

"I'm not pretty," I said.

"You have no idea."

I slid in between the covers, not lightly, not sexy, and pushed my back against the wall. At least it was a double bed. Son took off his overalls and sat down beside me in his shirt and underwear. "You might as well get used to it," I said.

"It's been a long time."

"Well, nothing's going to happen, at least not for a while. Just sleep with me." I touched his back. A tree, a wall, a city.

He took off the rest of his clothes and lay down beside me. I saw something on his arm, a birthmark or a scar, and leaned over to look at it. It was a tattoo. It said Cecilia in green letters near his shoulder, a cluster of leaves beneath the name. "Who's Cecilia?" I said.

"Someone I knew a long time ago."

"You must have loved her, to put her name on your arm."

"I thought I did."

"Don't say that," I said quietly. "Don't change your past because of me. There's her name on your arm." I ran my fingers across the letters, up the C, over the e and the l, down to the a.

I could feel his skin tense beneath my hand. "That means you loved her."

"Okay," he said.

We didn't say anything for a while but didn't sleep either.

"It's going to be all right," he said to me finally. "We've done the right thing."

"Yes," I said.

"And it will be good for the baby."

"Yes."

"What are you going to name her? If you know it's going to be a girl, you must have picked out a name."

"No. I never did. I was always so sure I was going to give her up. I thought it would be better to not give her a name. I thought that would only make things worse."

"But you must have thought about it, even if you didn't want to."

"No, I didn't."

"So now you should think about it."

And I did. I thought about it for a long while. "Cecilia," I said finally. "I'm going to name her Cecilia."

"No," he said.

"It would be perfect. We'll tell her you had her name put on your arm the day she was born, that you loved her so much you went out and had her name written right here." I touched the tattoo again and he flinched.

"Don't do that, Rose. I'm asking you."

"Cecilia," I said. "That's her name."

SON

1

THERE ARE SO MANY pretty names for girls, Caroline and Emily
and Bess. Those are the three I thought of right off. Then there
are all the names you could choose 'cause you wanted to make
somebody else feel good. Angie, Evangeline, June. Or Beatrice,
since she was the one who brought us together in a way. She
could call her Elizabeth for the saint or Louisa for the hotel. In
the hospital gift shop, I bought a book called *Naming Your Baby*.
You wouldn't believe all the pretty names in there, ones you'd
never think of, like Madeline and Isabel. In the end, there was
only one name that wouldn't be right, which is the name Rose
had settled on.

Cecilia.

In the weeks before the baby was born, I begged Rose a hundred different ways to change her mind. Once I even tried putting my foot down. "You will not," I said over breakfast, and
looked at her straight enough to scare her, but I must have forgot
who I was dealing with. Rose don't scare. She don't even ruffle.
She just whisked my plate up off the table, her belly so big in
front of her you hardly know how she could move about at all,
and she looks at me as if to say, who are you to tell me what to
name my baby?

"Rose," I said, "listen."

"Come on now," she said. "I've got to get to work."

Before I know it she's got the dishes clean and her coat on
and she's out the door to make breakfast for twenty-five other
girls, none of them as far along as her. She didn't stop working
in the kitchen. She stayed there till the last possible minute, was
stirring up a birthday cake for someone when her own water
broke out on the tile floor.

Rose was a strong girl. She's the only woman I ever knew

who felt as big as me. Not that she's anywhere as tall as me, but her hands and feet are big and the bones across her shoulders are sturdy. When you find a beautiful woman who's small, small like Cecilia, there's something about her that makes you want to cradle her in your hands. You want to keep her in your pocket, and show her to people like a little secret that you own. But Rose's beauty was something that no one person could keep. It filled up every room she went into. I remember the first time I saw her, standing up on the porch with Angie. She put a shadow over every girl there. Her white neck, the length of her thighs against the worn blue cotton of her dress, the line of her jaw under her dark hair. I thought, what's she doing here? What kind of man would let her get away?

But I never asked her about that man and she never asked me anything about Cecilia, except whether or not I'd loved her. She was always staring at her name across my shoulder when we were in bed at night. She made like it was the tattoo she was really interested in. "Did it hurt?" she asked.

"I don't remember. It was a long time ago."

"But it must have hurt. Needles." She shivered.

"I guess it must have," I said. Pain is one of those things where the big ones just wipe the small ones away, so I really couldn't imagine a needle working in and out of my arm when I was seventeen could have hurt so much.

I loved lying in bed with Rose, smelling her warm skin, running my hand down against her sides once she fell asleep. Everything about her was big; her belly was a mountain, her breasts and legs were smooth and swollen and round. In bed with her I didn't feel lonely the way I did with other women who had fallen asleep beside me. Not that I'm saying there'd been so many, but there were enough to know. Sleep brings out the smallness in a woman, their little hands holding the edge of the pillow while they dream. I felt so huge beside them. I was afraid they would wake up and be scared to see me there. I never touched them while they slept. But Rose could hold her own against anybody. Even after the baby was born, when her body whittled down into its old self, she was still a match for me. There was something about Rose, not just her size but who she was. I could tell she'd seen some things. When we were married she wasn't yet twenty-four and I was forty-five. I'd seen plenty, more than God will forgive me for, but not more than Rose. Even knowing her as little as I did, I knew that much.

That first month was the only time in our marriage we were

ever alone, if you can call living so close to Saint Elizabeth's being alone. Me and Rose both stayed over there pretty much all the time, same as always. We were used to it that way. Some days it seemed like nothing had changed. I was still eating dinner in the big kitchen while she cleaned up, and as she washed dishes I would find myself looking at her breasts under her wet apron and then looking away so she wouldn't see. Then I'd think, that's my wife, and hell, I've seen her coming out of the bathtub in the morning, big as life. So I tried to tell myself it was okay if I looked, that I don't have nothing to be ashamed of, but it's hard for me to believe.

When a man gets to be my age, he don't much expect things will change. Winter and you press caulk into the windows, summer and you're putting up the screens. The pipes give way one by one. By the time you've repainted the whole place inside and out it's time to start over again. You're alone and you'll always be alone. It's so true it doesn't bear mention. You just stop thinking about it, the way you stopped thinking about everything after a while.

But then here comes Rose, after eighteen years of pregnant girls come and gone. After the first day I saw her I found myself looking for her. I hoped she would be there when I came in in the morning. I went to the kitchen at night to find her. It had been so long since I'd done anything like that that for a while I didn't even know I was doing it. Then all of the sudden I'm lonely at night. I couldn't remember the last time I was lonely. I would think of her, the way she pushed her hair behind her ear with one wet hand, the way she blew on a spoon of soup she was tasting for salt. I longed for her. Not like I longed for a woman at seventeen, not like I longed for Cecilia, where I wanted to feel her hands on my back and press my face against her neck. I only wanted to be near to Rose. I guess maybe I wanted the rest of it too, but that kind of longing had pretty much been worn out of me. I'd come to believe that part of my life was over.

So when I found her that morning in the snow and she came to my house and slept and woke up and said yes, she would marry me, everything changed. It was like the sun had set in the east, and suddenly nothing was like it was, even though everything was like it was. I can't explain it. It felt like I should be coming home to another house, living in a different state, that nothing of my old life should have stayed the same because I was suddenly a married man. But instead we went on just like before, except now the longing wasn't there. Rose was there, beside me in my bed.

We stayed pretty formal for a long time, always being polite to each other. You marry a person you don't really know and you're afraid of saying something that might run them off. But we got along fine. The only sore point between us was over the naming of the baby, which wasn't even a sore point with Rose 'cause she simply refused to see it as a problem. I couldn't seem to make her understand how badly I didn't want her to go through with it.

Five days before our baby came, Angie went into the hospital. She went right away, the very first pain that she felt, which I think is as it should be. I had taken a real liking to Angie, she was always one to stop and tell you a joke or throw out a big wave when she saw you coming across the field. Rose was a wreck right from the minute Angie told her it was time, rubbing her hands the way she does when she gets nervous. She insisted on taking her to the hospital. We put Angie's suitcase in the back, but the box she had with her she wanted to hold up front.

"I can't believe the way they listen to you now," Angie said, pressed between us in the front of the truck, the three of us all as big as houses. "It's like you're one of the sisters."

"That's an awful thought," Rose said.

"No, no, I mean, you've got that kind of power. The way you stared them down and said, 'No, Son and I will take her to the hospital.' " Angie laughed. "Like, la-di-da, I'm running this show now. Well, I think it's something, is all. You stay on, they're gonna be calling that place Saint Rose the Divine."

"I like the sound of that," I said.

Then Angie bunched up her face and grabbed on to my arm so hard I liked to drive right off the road. "God! What?" I said.

Rose reached over and smoothed back her hair, and Angie took a few short, quick breaths. "She wasn't lying," Angie said. "This is gonna hurt."

"Are you okay to make the drive?" I asked.

Angie laughed. "What if I'm not?" she said. "What're we gonna do then?"

When the two of them came into the emergency room the nurses like to took a fit, two girls so pregnant coming in together. Angie gave the nurse her box and said something to her about the letter that's taped on top of it. The nurse said that nothing could be left at the front desk, but Angie held her ground. Tired as she was she wouldn't get in the wheelchair until they promised to do exactly what she told them. The nurse took the box, and they started to wheel Angie through the doors, when all of a sudden she raised both arms over her head and called out for Rose.

"What is it?" Rose said, going to her.

Angie just smiled and shook her head. "Never mind," she said.

"What?"

"I was gonna say I changed my mind."

Rose was squatted down on the floor beside her chair and the two of them just stared at each other, their noses not six inches apart. I wasn't even sure what she meant, changed her mind about having it or changed her mind about giving it up. Then my wife leaned over and kissed her friend on the forehead, so sweetly and right that it made me look away.

Once Angie was gone the doctor tried to talk Rose into staying on, said her time was so close it was hardly worth the trip home. I didn't think it would be a bad idea. I wanted to see her have some rest. But she wouldn't hear of it. All she wanted to talk about was Angie. Every five minutes she was out of her chair, going to ask about Angie and the baby. They kept saying fine, fine, everything looks great, but Rose wouldn't settle.

"Come on and sit," I said to her. "You're going to wear out the floor."

"I hate this."

"Well, she's fine. You heard the doctor."

"She's too thin, too small." Rose started to tear up, but when I reached for her she moved away just slightly so that my hand fell down across her back and barely touched it.

We waited there all night and Rose never fell asleep, even though I'm sure I did. When the doctor came out, all solemn, you could see in Rose's face that she had already resigned herself to what he was about to say and was ready to take it. The cord had worked its way around the neck and by the time they knew, it was all too late.

Rose looked up at him. "You mean it could have been prevented?"

"No," the doctor said. "There was no way to tell."

"But if you'd known something was going to go wrong?" Her

voice was high, almost like she was about to start shouting at him.

The doctor looked puzzled. "If we'd known," he said slowly, "then yes, I guess we could have taken the baby cesarean, but you can't think about things like that."

Rose sat still for the first time, her hands folded between her knees, her head down. Finally she nodded. "All right," she said.

"You can see her for a minute if you'd like," the doctor told her.

Rose got up and started to follow him down the hall. She'd forgotten I was there, and so I just went along behind them. "Maybe she doesn't know," I said.

"She knows," Rose said, not turning around.

I almost went inside the room with her, but when I saw Angie's face, looking so small and pale against the starched white pillow slip, I stepped back. The doctor went on, reading a chart as he walked away from us. I sat down on a chair in the hallway, not wanting to listen but hearing it just the same.

"Hey," Rose said.

"It didn't go so good," Angie said. Her voice sounded dreamy, more tired than sad. They would have given her something. They would give her one good long sleep before she had to wake up and remember everything for the rest of her life.

"You're fine," Rose said. "That's what matters. You're just perfect."

"I don't feel it."

There was a long silence and I felt for Rose, wondering what it was she was supposed to say to her friend. I looked up and down the hallway. No one was there but one lone nurse, and she turned into a room before I could get a good look at her. I could hear her shoes squeak away from me and the door click shut behind her. It was late, but the fluorescent lights made it seem like high noon. I thought about how everything in that hall would always be just so. The brown and black tiles on the floor would always be scrubbed clean, the walls would always be the same dull green color. There would always be that smell of sweet soap, which was trying to cover something up, sickness and worse.

"Rose?" Angie's voice was sleepy, fading, a million miles away.

"What?"

"You knew, didn't you?"

"Knew what?"

"About my baby. Sister Evangeline would have known, she would have told you." She stopped for a while, and I held my breath. "It makes sense now, the way she was that day. I never saw her get upset with other girls the way she did with me."

"Of course I didn't know."

"I'm so stupid, why I never thought about it before. Never thought about it before because I'm so stupid, right?"

"Go to sleep, Angie."

"And there you were, watching me make all those stupid things and you said it was stupid, didn't you?"

"Angie."

"I'm not saying I blame you. I mean, what could you have done? You couldn't have told me. You wouldn't want to hurt me. But you could have told me. Maybe if I'd known I might have been able to do something about it, tell the doctors to watch out. Did you think about that, all that time you were watching me?"

I was on my feet, standing by the door. Rose's voice came quiet and steady, everything about it said, trust me, believe me. "I never knew this would happen. Nobody knows life and death, not even Sister. It's just a bad thing, an awful thing. There isn't any reason for it."

And then Angie started to cry and she said something I couldn't understand. I looked down at my shoes and felt something like a cold wind go through me because I knew Rose was lying. I didn't know from the way she said it, that's what worried me. The way she said it I never would have figured it out. But I knew Sister Evangeline, and she would know whether or not a baby was going to live, I was sure of it. Rose would be sure of it, too.

"That's right," Rose said. "You just cry."

I wanted to look around the corner, see them there. I wondered how her face would look when she lied. But I was intruding just being in the hallway, in the hospital. I should have been in Habit.

"I want to go home," Angie said.

"You will soon enough."

"I want to go home with you."

"You're going home to your mother."

"No."

"Go to sleep."

"Rose?"

"What?"

"Take the box of baby clothes. From the front desk, don't forget it. It was a lucky thing we both had girls, huh?"

"Go to sleep, now."

"Don't forget it, promise?"

"Promise," Rose said.

Rose stayed in a while longer, I imagine until Angie fell asleep. When she finally came out of the room she looked worn down. She took hold of my arm, not out of love but because she was afraid she wouldn't be able to stand up a whole lot longer.

Driving back from the hospital I couldn't help but think about our wedding, since that was the last time we were in Owensboro, but I didn't think it would be such a good idea to bring it up. It probably would have been best not to bring up anything at all, but Rose looked so tired and sad, staring down at her hands and not saying anything.

"It was best, your not telling her," I said.

"Not telling her what?" she said. Her voice was flat, like she was responding to some worn-out joke that everyone already knew.

"Not telling her what Sister Evangeline told you, about her baby dying. If Sister said that was the way it was going to be there wasn't a single thing that could have been done. That's fate. Divine fate. That's God's business."

"I didn't know," she said. "That's what I told Angie."

I looked right at her. I didn't care about the road.

"I didn't know anything," she said, and then she closed her eyes, which was her way of saying the conversation was over, even if she wasn't going to sleep.

When we went back to the hospital a week later Angie had already checked out and gone home to her people, but she wasn't the reason we were going up anyway. It was Rose's time, the two trips so close that in my memory they blur together. It's hard for me to sort out who had her baby before who sometimes. There was a day, when first I was at Saint Elizabeth's, I could tell you the delivery time of every baby to come through that place. I knew the length and weight and whether it was a boy or a girl. I would make a point to remember the weather on that day and the color of the mother's hair and what town she was from. That was when I felt a certain responsibility to all those babies, thought that they might come back looking for their true selves some day and appreciate a gardener who had a mind for facts. But it got to be too much is all, and it seemed cruel to remember one and not the other, so I just stopped trying.

This girl was to be one of them, this daughter of mine. The one her cousins would whisper about, the one who finds out years later, just by accident, that she is not herself at all. Was it not for so many bits of fate fallen into our laps, my daughter would have been someone else's daughter.

I was like Rose had been in the waiting room the week before, pestering every person in a white coat that went by. "I want to know about my wife," I said, the words so right in my mouth. My wife. My family.

"She's doing fine," they all said, and it bothered me, because it was the same way they told us Angie was fine.

The night my daughter was born I thought about her father, just that one time and not later. I thought about him because he didn't know. With just about every girl to come through Saint Elizabeth's, you can be sure the fellow knew, that she cried and he turned on his heel and left her there. For a long time I wanted to think that was true of Rose, but anyone who knew her at all could see she was a leaver, that she wouldn't know a thing about what it's like to be left. Somewhere out in California was a man thinking that right about now his baby was being born, but he didn't know where to start looking, so for just one minute I felt for him, and then I let it go. A child needs one mother, one father. Even if the job wasn't meant to be mine, it was now. I would be the only father she would have.

I went to the gift shop and bought myself a pack of Luckys. I didn't smoke much, but I figured with the baby around I'd need to quit altogether, so I was just going to sit in the waiting room and smoke a couple. No sooner did I get one lit than a nurse came out and said, "Congratulations, Mr. Abbott."

I stubbed out the cigarette and tossed the pack down on the table for the next poor guy who'd come to wait. "Everything okay?"

"Better than that," she said, real chipper, and I thought this must be a pretty sweet job, getting to come out and tell people their babies are born. If anything bad happens they always send out the doctor. "You have a beautiful girl, and your wife came through it all like a dream. She didn't even cry out, Mr. Abbott, not one time. I can't remember that happening as long as I've been here.''

I followed her down a long corridor and through a set of double doors that said, NO ADMITTANCE. "You can see her for a second," she said quietly, "but then you'll have to go. She needs her rest." She pointed over to a gurney where Rose was lying.

I looked down on Rose for a minute before her eyes half opened and she saw me there. She looked like she'd been to war.

"Hiya," she said.

"Tough time?"

She moved her head around, but I couldn't tell if she was nodding or shaking her head no. She reached out for my hand and I gave it to her. "Know what I did?" she whispered.

"No, what?"

"I told them I wanted to fill out the birth certificate." Her voice was so soft I had to bend down to hear her, until my ear was only a few inches from her lips. "The nurse says to me, she says, the father always does that, but I tell her, no, no, not this time." She smiled. She looked so proud of herself. "I saw her," she said.

"Saw who?"

"Cecilia."

"Please, Rose." I ran my fingers along the side of her face and down onto her neck. Her skin was still damp with sweat. "I'm telling you, there's no reason to do that."

"It's done," she said. "In ink. Don't worry about it, Son. It's a good idea. It's a pretty name."

I straightened up, and Rose closed her eyes and let her hand fall away from mine.

I walked down the corridor, following the pictures of storks painted on the wall. I went the way their beaks pointed me until I came to the large glass window. So many babies born on the same day in Kentucky. I tried not to look at the names right off. I tried to find the baby that looked like Rose all on my own, but every time I thought I had it right, it turned out I was wrong.

"Who are you looking for?" a nurse asked me.

"Abbott."

"Boy or girl?"

"Girl."

"And you're the father?"

I nodded and she smiled at me. That's what having a baby gets you, smiles from pretty women. She said I should follow her around the back and she tried to find a smock for me, but none came close to fitting. Finally, she decided just to drape a couple of them over my shoulders and she went away and came back with a baby wrapped up in a blanket. "Cecilia Abbott," she said, and put the baby in my arms. "Brand new, new as they come."

But Cecilia Abbott didn't look like her mother at all. She was pale in every way, with hair fair enough to be called white. It was impossible to believe she had been inside of Rose not an hour before, and now lived in the world without her.

"Take her," I said to the nurse, my voice shaking so that I surprised myself.

"No sir," the nurse said, and she laughed at me. "That's your girl now, you best get used to holding her." She led me over to a chair and sat us down. "Not so often we get a baby named quick as that," she said. "Why, we got ones stay here for days, their tags just reading, Baby Girl Smith or Baby Boy Jones. That always makes me sad for some reason. Seems like a body should get named right off."

"Seems so," I said, looking at my daughter.

"Cecilia is a pretty name. Kind of fancy, but I like that. Looks like she's pretty enough to be a Cecilia."

I looked up at her. "You think?"

The nurse ran one careful finger over the soft spot in the top of her head. "You bet," she said.

The nursery closed sharp at four o'clock, and all the babies were removed from the fathers. As soon as she was gone I missed her small weight, her tired face. I went to look in on Rose, but she was sleeping. Everyone was whipped, too big a day. So I went back to the window to say good-bye to my girl. I stood there with the grandparents, most of them younger than me, and waved because her eyes were open. She looked right at me, just for a second, but I swear to God she saw me there, and I loved her. It happened just that fast. It was so complete, so much love, that I realized that before that moment I hadn't loved her. I drew in my breath and felt myself getting taller. For the first time in my life I was glad to be so tall, because it gave me a better chance of protecting her. Something that small would need protection. I knew I could do that.

All around me young women in pink terry cloth robes held

the arms of young men, one of them wearing an army uniform, another a marine. They made faces through the glass and mouthed the words *Mama* and *Daddy* while they pointed to their chests. I saw myself in them. They were in love, too. All of us in love.

"Which one's yours?" a boy said to me. He was probably nineteen or twenty, but looked younger on account of his being so thin. His skin was broken out all along his hairline.

"That one," I said, and pointed to the plastic box where she lay as still as a chicken egg.

"Cecilia Abbott," the boy read from the card. He had to squint, even though the letters were big. "Well, she's a cutey, all right, and she keeps good company, too. That's my boy, right there in the crib next to her."

"Baby Boy Seidel," I said.

"I'm thinking of calling him Elvis," the boy said, and tapped at the glass lightly with his finger, until a nurse made a face at him from the other side and he stopped.

I figured it up in the car on the way over. It had been twenty-eight years since I last set foot in a tattoo parlor. And it was love that was making me go again this time, even though this time I wasn't drunk and wasn't seventeen and I was alone. But it was still Cecilia making me go, I am not a superstitious man. I did not believe Cecilia had come back to me in any way. This was for my daughter, a new girl, who happened to have her name.

The best places were always around military bases, but I sure wasn't going to drive all the way to Fort Campbell for a small job like this. There was a place in Owensboro, a colored woman who did them in her house. It had been years since I had heard about her; some guy drunk in a bar pulled up his pants leg to show me where he'd had the skyline of Memphis tattooed above a scar he'd picked up in World War II. I remember the buildings looked neat and orderly and that she'd left the ragged red trail of the bullet to be the Mississippi. "Got a sign in her front yard," the man said to me, running his finger over the rooftops like it was the first time he'd noticed them there. Says TATTOO. Just like a NO HUNTING or a FOR SALE, 'cept it says TATTOO. I always wondered where she found that damn sign."

There was nothing to say that she would still be there. I had met the man years ago, and there was no telling how long he'd had Memphis with him, but people around these parts don't tend to change much, unless of course they die. Sure enough, after driving around the other side of town for a while, I asked a colored boy out on his bicycle did he know about a woman did tattoos?

"Ma Mamie," he said, and motioned for me to follow. It's not easy, driving a truck slow enough to tail a boy on a bike. This boy, especially, as he didn't seem to be in any hurry to take me anywhere. We went up and down a few streets and then into an alley, where I saw the sign just as the man in the bar had described it. The boy was good to bring me to the door because it was getting dark and the place would have been hard to find otherwise.

"Kid," I called out my window. I wanted to give him a quarter, but he was sailing off over the crest of a dirt hill, not looking my way at all.

I parked the truck and got out. The way it was in Kentucky, in the South back then, was that going into a colored neighborhood was more or less like going into a whole other country. Your neighborhood could be on the edge, you could live three blocks or not even that, maybe just the distance of a field, be as close as from here to there, but the chances of you ever getting there, assuming your business was good, were about as much as you getting to California. Folks didn't mix, plain as that. There was no town meeting, no drawn-out line that said this is where you don't cross, but there was an understanding, and all good folks, colored and white, abided by that.

So when I had the opportunity to find myself on the other side, I looked around. That particular road was dirt and dark, but the snow on the ground spread around whatever light was left. I looked at the same porch on every house, each with a couple of chairs, a stack of empty bushel baskets, some firewood, maybe a flat of empty Coca-Cola bottles. I watched the curtains draw back, a face peer out and disappear. They wanted to know what a white man big as me was doing out in their road come nighttime, though it was clear enough whose house I was standing in front of. They wanted to let me know they'd seen me, that if anything was to happen, they would have seen my face.

It gets late so early in February, and I wanted to make it back to the hospital before visiting hours were over. I knocked on the door, and a girl, maybe fourteen, answered. She had to tilt her head back to see my face.

"Yeah?"

"I've come to see Ma Mamie," I said.

"You want a tattoo?"

I nodded my head.

"You got money?"

I told her I did.

With that she suddenly stepped back and pulled the door open all the way for me to come inside. She was wearing jeans and a thin yellow shirt with the sleeves cut off. There were twisted yellow threads hanging down on her shoulders. Her hair was brushed back hard into a high ponytail that was braided tight. "What're you gonna want?" she said, and pointed to where I should sit down at the kitchen table.

"The date," I said. "Just today's date."

"That's four numbers and two dashes. That's six bucks. You're gonna have to put the cash on the table where I can see it. Lots of folks seem real interested in paying for what they want until they've got it, if you know what I mean."

I nodded and put the money out on the table. I looked into the living room. There was a big console TV, a crucifix, an old divan. "I hope you don't make a lot of noise," she said. "My pop's asleep in the back. He's a security guard, works the night shift." She went to wash her hands in the kitchen sink. "One thing he don't like is being woken up before his time. Where you gonna have this tattoo?"

"On my shoulder."

"Then take your shirt off," she said.

I started to unbutton my shirt and then thought better of it. I didn't like the idea of taking off my clothes, any of my clothes, in front of a child. "Where's Ma Mamie?" I asked.

"I'm Ma Mamie," the girl said, not looking around.

I covered up the six dollars on the table with my hand. "That couldn't be true, unless you were making tattoos when you were four."

She dried off her hands and brought out a big fishing tackle box from the pantry. "You may have been to my mother before me. She was Ma Mamie, too. Both of us named Mamie, me for her and her for her mama and on back like that. All of us Mamies. When my mama died, I got the needles. That makes me Ma Mamie. Take your shirt off."

I thought about it for a while. It just didn't seem right. "No," I said.

"I'm good," she said, screwing in the needle on the little electric drill. "All the Mamies are good. That's because we learn from the time we're born, right away. I did my first tattoo when I was eight years old, on my brother. I had to kneel on his chest to give it to him, but it's there today, a little blue star, right there." She tapped the space between her breasts. "It's not half bad, either. If he was here I'd have him show you."

"How old are you?"

"Twenty-one," she said, and started to set up her pots of ink in a row.

"Like hell."

"Don't you talk ugly to me, mister." She didn't look up, but her voice was steady and low. "My pop is sleeping in the other room. I think you best bear that in mind." Then all of the sudden she jerked her head up, like it's all forgotten. "Time is money," she said. "Yes or no?"

It was good and dark outside now, and I needed to get going. If there was another place that did tattoos in Owensboro, I'd never find it before the end of visiting hours. I wanted today's date put on today, not tomorrow. That seemed like cheating somehow. This was the day my daughter was born. I unbuttoned my shirt. "Okay," I said.

I pulled down the top of my overalls and took off my shirt and sat at the kitchen table of a fourteen-year-old colored girl whose father may or may not have been in the next room.

"Cecilia," she said. "Not very good work, if you don't mind me saying."

"It was a long time ago."

"So where you want the date?"

I pointed just beneath her name. "Right there," I said, and tapped the skin.

"I can touch this one up," she said, touching the name the way Rose did. "I can make it darker, prettier. It'll look like new, only better."

"No," I said. "Just leave that one alone."

"I can still do this good," she said, her voice gone all dreamy. She started to wash my arm. "I'll just make it look like it happened all on the same day, both tattoos. I'll mix up a special ink so the new one'll look faded to begin with. You won't be able to tell, not till all the scabs come off, but then you'll see."

I looked at her and smiled. For the first time since I'd come in the door I felt like this would be okay. "That would be nice," I said. "Really nice."

"All us Mamies are pros," she said. "Genetic."

I heard the hum of the needle and looked away. I don't mind what happens, long as I don't have to watch.

It only took her a few minutes and she switched the needle off. "That looks good," she said. She blotted up the extra ink with a little towel and let me see. Cecilia, 2-6-69. It was good. "You want something else?"

"No," I said. "You were right. You do a fine job."

"Come on and let me do something else." She sounded girlish all of the sudden. She stood on one foot and twisted from side to side.

"I would, but I've got to get going. My wife's in the hospital. She's had a baby."

"How about just a little flower. I'm real good at flowers."

"Roses? Can you do a rose?"

"Like nobody," Mamie said.

"Then put a little rose there, under the date. That'll be for my wife."

She changed her needles and flicked the switch on again. "You won't be sorry about this," she said. "This is so pretty." I felt the needle cut into my arm and thought about Rose and Cecilia, everyone there on my arm now, everyone included. "Almost done," she said. "You're being good, just keep holding still."

But just then a woman walked in the front door and let out such a yell that the needle bit deep into my arm and then fell to the floor. Mamie screamed and the woman screamed again and it was all I could do to keep quiet myself.

"Goddamn you, girl, giving tattoos!" the woman said. She was a big woman, and her big wool coat and tall black fur hat and the two sacks of groceries in her arms made her seem all the bigger. Mamie stood behind me.

"He was in a hurry," Mamie said straight into my back. "He needed to get going. He couldn't wait."

"What kind of a fool are you?" she said, turning on me all of the sudden. "Letting a child give you tattoos? Get out of my house! Get out of my house!"

I pulled on my shirt and felt the blood on my arm soak through right away.

"Don't you want to see it at least?" Mamie said to her mother.

"I don't want to see nothing."

"I'm good," she said. "Good as you. Good as you ever were."

I rushed past the Mamie at the door and wondered for a

second if she had been the one who drew Memphis on the man's leg, or if that story was from a long time ago, and it had been her mother. But I didn't ask. I hurried outside and into my truck and turned on the heater because it always made such a racket and I didn't want to hear what they were saying anymore.

═══ 2 ═══

BEFORE ROSE there was Cecilia. She came before Saint Elizabeth's and Habit and my daughter. I was not a young man when I married for the first time: forty-five is better than half your life and the folks who know me would say I seemed older than that. But the first time I was in love I was young, young like I can't believe now, seventeen.

Truth is, I was in love with Cecilia a long time before that. I used to say I was born loving her, on account of the fact I couldn't ever remember meeting her. She is in the very first days of my memory. I can see her sitting beside me in Sunday school at the Lighthouse Baptist Church, cutting out stars. Or I see her in the store with her mother, Mrs. Stewart, touching all the bolts of fabric she walks by. I see her at the Fourth of July picnic, not more than four years old, wearing a yellow dress that tied behind her neck and saying the Pledge of Allegiance. Not that I always remember her being a child. Lots of times I think about her when she was seventeen.

I don't think of her hardly at all anymore. It just got less and less over the years and now it's been an awfully long time. There was a time if a man'd told me I would be able to go an hour, much less a day or week, without thinking of her, I would have said he was crazy. But truth is, months go by and she won't even cross my mind. Even in the shower, or while I'm getting dressed, and I know I must still see her name on my arm, I don't see it, or if I do, it's just letters. It doesn't tell me anything anymore. That's one reason, although, God, there are so many I could barely list them, why I didn't want Rose to name our daughter Cecilia. I thought it would stir things up, that every day for the rest of my life I would hear that name, I would speak it myself whenever I called her in to dinner or sent her off to school, and it would remind me of what I had worked so hard to forget. But it didn't, really. It became my daughter's name. When she was old enough to talk we would sit on the living room floor to try to get her to say Cecilia.

"Ce-ci-li-a," Rose would say, putting her face up near the baby's and pointing at her.

"Sissy," Cecilia said, and tapped her chest.

"Sissy come to Daddy," I said, and opened my arms. She ran right into them, climbed me like a tree, to bury her face in my neck.

"Don't call her that," Rose said, standing up. "It isn't her name."

"Well, it's the one she likes, and I'm siding with her." I rolled onto my back and put Sissy up in the air. "Airplane," I said.

"Airplane," she said.

"Oh great, that one she gets." Rose walked out of the room and left us there, making engine noises.

Rose was a good mother. She fed the baby just the way the Spock book said she ought to. She never complained when she had to get up in the night. She dressed her warm. But there was something that nobody talked about that I think ate away at her. Sissy looked as adopted as any child to come out of Saint Elizabeth's. She was blond curls and blue eyes and the doctor said she was in the lower range for size for her age. Her giant, dark-haired parents looked awkward and out of place in the little examining room. It didn't much bother me. For Sissy to be mine I had to make her mine, and I'd done that. But for Rose it was all supposed to come natural. Sissy looked too much like whoever it was Rose'd left behind, so in a funny way, it was more her that got reminded of the past than me.

There was no one thing that made me think of Cecilia. I just did from time to time, for no reason in the world. She would come to me in a dream, sit beside me on the bed and hold my hand and talk to me. She was still seventeen and I would always feel ashamed to have gotten so old. Other times I'd think I'd seen her, just a flash of some woman turning the corner or driving a car that was so much her it made my heart stop. Then just as quick the woman would look up and I would see her with light on her face and she wouldn't be anywhere close. Those things didn't happen much at all, but when they did, they shook me deep, and for a couple of days I'd be nervous and want to

keep to myself. I'd remember the whole thing, beginning to end.
It was like watching a movie you can't get out of.

When we were seventeen, Cecilia loved me. At eight she
loved me, ten she didn't, thirteen loved me, fourteen didn't. But
when we were seventeen she said she'd settled down. She was
my girl, that's the way we used to say it. I was only grateful. In
the years Cecilia didn't love me, I felt paralyzed. It was like
she'd taken part of me, most of me, with her when she left.
There was nothing for me to do but wait.

"It's over," she'd say, pulling her hair from the collar of her
coat with one hand. All I could think of was touching it, leaning
over to touch my face to her hair. "Don't," she'd say.

Cecilia would tell people she was five three, but really she
wasn't a hair over five feet tall. She had a way of seeming bigger
than she was, the way she walked with her head up and her
shoulders back. Folks thought it was funny, me being so much
taller than her. Course, then I wasn't nearly as tall as I turned
out to be. I was only six two. I had another growth spurt later,
not too long after I left Ashland City, Tennessee, when I was
eighteen. Cecilia didn't mind about me being so tall, though. If
anything, it was what kept bringing her back to me. She loved
to be carried. Once, when we were fifteen, we were watching a
fireworks show down by the river and she couldn't see, so I knelt
down and she sat on my shoulder, just balanced there like a little
bird. She was in heaven. She said it was a whole other world,
being up so far. If she could have had her way I know she would
have had me carry her everywhere, but she was worried about
how it was going to look, so we saved it for special times, like
when it was raining and she didn't want to get her shoes wet or
when we were coming home late from a dance and she was
wearing high heels and her feet got tired. And always when we
were alone, always when we kissed. She liked me to hold her
up in my arms like a baby. She liked for me to reach down and
pick her up and carry her someplace else, anyplace, so that when
she opened her eyes everything was different. Cecilia said it
made her feel like she was important, special. She said it was
the reason she always came back to me.

And I liked all of this just fine. Except that when I picked her
up, when I held her, I could always feel how small she was. Just
looking at her it was easy to forget. Cecilia was such a power-
house, and don't kid yourself about who was calling the shots
on things. I was always half afraid of her 'cause in a funny way
she was just so big, but when I picked her up she was of the

earth, if you know what I mean. She wasn't anything more than ninety pounds and I was the one who made every choice. It scared me, maybe because I could feel her as just a living thing, which meant it would be possible to lose her for good, or maybe I was afraid of hurting her somehow, like if I was to pick her up wrong I could break her accidentally. It's the same way I felt with Sissy when she first came home from the hospital. I would just barely touch my palm to her chest and I could feel her little heart beating inside her and it felt so small it would make me want to put her down and run away from her as fast as I could. But I didn't, not with Sissy or Cecilia either.

Folks that didn't know Cecilia very well all liked her, and the folks that did know her, like me and my family, liked her in spite of ourselves. She was sort of a silly girl, I guess. I can say that, looking back on things now. She'd change her mind a million times and always say she was right, and she was way too proud, considering we were all more or less from the same stock. But somehow you just couldn't hold it against her, like we all knew if we were her we'd be feeling pretty good about it, too. My folks tried their best to hate her. Truth is, they got pretty tired of the whole thing, me being happy or sad depending on whether or not Cecilia was coming around. They wanted her to make up her mind. They wanted me to have a little peace. Every time she broke things off, my mother would bake me a chicken with green peas and mashed potatoes. She'd call it comfort food.

"You're better off rid of her, Son," she said. "That girl's never going to settle. She wants to keep you hanging on, that's what she wants. You just can't give her the satisfaction."

I would just shake my head, trying to do what was supposed to come naturally: sit up, cut your food. I am forty-five. I have made it twenty-eight years in the world without Cecilia. But at seventeen it was impossible to think of a day without her.

Whenever she came back, smiling and forgetful, my family loved her with me. They tried not to, but Cecilia held them almost the way she held me. They all fussed over her smallness, her bright hair, her pretty hands. She was friends with my sisters. She drank iced tea with my mother after school and looked through pattern books. We all felt Cecilia gave something to us, and the price we had to pay was her constant leaving.

Our last year of high school, I was made fullback of the football team. It's funny to think how much that mattered then, to me and Cecilia both. You never think about getting old when you're seventeen. You never think about how it's all going to turn out, that you'll have a wife and a daughter and a job that takes up every waking hour. When you're seventeen, there isn't anything past a good spot on the football team. In a small town, it was as close as you were going to get to being God. I was just so much bigger than any of the other kids. I doubled up and played basketball, too, but it was the football that everybody cared about. Folks said straight out I was the reason we won. Not just big, but fast too. Cecilia would say some days it felt like there wasn't a place in town she could go where somebody wasn't talking about me.

"Not the team, not the game, just about you," she said.

That was the kind of thing that made her happy, made her hold to my arm in a crowd, which made me happy. She would sit on my lap in the front seat of my father's car late at night and let me kiss her, and I felt like nothing else ever needed to happen in the world. It would have been fine to stop everything right then. There was no other girl like Cecilia. There were girls who were prettier or less pretty, girls who were funny or bright, but at the heart of it, they were all the same, just like I was the same. In any crowd of people, Cecilia's face would always be the first one you'd see. It's almost like everyone else was there to be around her, arranged in such a way to set off her eyes, her mouth. I'm not even sure now that she was so beautiful, although then I thought she was. It was more that all of her ways were big. She'd built a momentum from being wanted by so many people, and the attention had made her kinder and meaner both.

For a long time folks talked about the war in Europe, and what Ashland City said was that we should just tend to our own. There would be no point in Roosevelt going into that, though Lord knows we would have done whatever he told us to. But in December of 1941, just as the football season was winding down, the Japanese bombed Pearl Harbor and we all changed our minds. I left the house that Sunday without my coat, even though it was past freezing outside, and ran all the way to Cecilia's. Her family was sitting around the radio. Her mother was crying. When Cecilia saw my face she jumped up and came over to me. Everything about her looked wound up, not so much scared, but like she wanted to go and fight herself. We went out into the kitchen and held hands and I told her I was going to enlist.

She smiled at me. I never will forget the look on her face at that moment. I remember everything, the dim light in the room, the long table, the yellow wallpaper with the green vines on it and the set of brass canisters along the counter and Cecilia wearing a pleated skirt and a pale pink sweater with a stitching of flowers around her neck and her hair was pulled back in a ponytail and her face was pure light. It's just like a movie, a movie that doesn't leave out one single thing. It was as if the Japanese had bombed downtown, and I told her I was going off to get them, right then, before they got to her street.

"Then I'll marry you," Cecilia said. "As soon as you get back from training. We'll get married and that way you'll know I'm waiting here."

It was settled just like that, without my asking. I didn't need to ask Cecilia to marry me, because my whole life was that question to her. Everything I did was by way of asking her to stay with me. "Then marry me tonight," I said. "Or marry me first thing in the morning."

She smiled and touched the soft hairs on the back of her neck. "I can't get married tomorrow, silly," she said. "I've got to get bridesmaids. I've got to get a wedding dress. I'm not going to get married every day of my life, you know."

I leaned down and picked her up and she wrapped her arms around my neck and I put my arms around her back and I held her there, breathed in her smell and the smell of that pink sweater. Rose asked me if I loved the girl whose name is on my arm. She said I must have, that the name itself was proof, so yes, I loved her. At that minute, at night in her kitchen, holding her up off the ground, I loved her like I have never loved anything again in my life.

I didn't want to wait for Christmas. I didn't want to finish out the end of the football season. The thought of graduating from high school seemed almost embarrassing, the sign of a man who did not love his country, or did not love Cecilia and want to finish basic training fast enough to get back and marry her. I enlisted the next morning, Monday, December 8, in the United States Marine Corps.

"You the boy's parents?" the sergeant said to my mother and father, who stood with me in the small office, which was crowded with boys I knew and their mothers and fathers. We had been in line for nearly an hour.

My father said they were.

"You'll have to sign him over, then. Seventeen we need consent."

The sergeant handed my father a form, and my mother looked at me. "You're sure about this," she said, just like she'd asked me the night before and again that morning in the car driving over. Her voice wasn't nervous. It wasn't that she thought my signing up was a bad thing, she just didn't want me to do it if I didn't want to.

"Sure," I said. I felt everyone waiting for us to get on with it.

"Boy's doing right," my father said, and handed the form to my mother. "If I was a younger man. Hell, bombing Pearl Harbor."

"You'll have to wait till the first of the year," the sergeant said, pushing some papers toward us across his desk. "We've got a crowd."

The three of us went out of the office, saying excuse me a dozen times just to get to the door. Outside in the bright December light we saw a line of boys snaking up the street and around the corner of the block. It looked like every boy in Tennessee was there.

It made me crazy to wait because it put off coming back, but then three days later they called and said there was room in Parris Island and that I should report in less than a week. I took the money I had saved and borrowed a little extra from my folks to buy Cecilia an engagement ring for Christmas. It was a nice diamond with a small blue stone set on either side, and when she opened the box, two weeks early, she jumped to her feet and kissed me.

Everything was a promise that had yet to be made good on: I would go to war and we would win the war and Cecilia would marry me and we would be happy. I never separated them, either. One thing was the other, they ran together in my mind. But those few days between the attack on Pearl Harbor and the morning my father drove me to Nashville to catch the bus to Parris Island were the happiest I ever had. The news of the war filled every free second, and at seventeen it all seemed like a movie that I was about to have a part in. The war did something to Cecilia. She loved the whole idea of it, the soldiers and the broadcasts and the articles in the newspapers. I believe that during those few days Cecilia loved me in a way she hadn't all the time we had been together before. I was going away and leaving her a war bride. It was the best thing she could have hoped for.

Every time she showed her ring the girls would fall around her in a circle, ask her how she would be able to manage once I was gone. But even when I loved her the most, I always knew Cecilia would manage fine.

"While you're gone you'll write me every day," Cecilia said.

"Every day."

"And you'll think about me. You'll miss me." Cecilia pressed against me and shivered. It was nearly midnight and we were standing by the edge of the Cumberland River and it was snowing. It was my last night home and we were pretending it was New Year's Eve. Everything had changed since I enlisted. Our parents never asked us what time we'd be home or where we were going. Everything we did was given a quiet blessing. "Pick me up," she said.

I picked Cecilia up in my arms and she put her head on my chest. Her hair looked so pretty, spread out against my dark coat. Her hair looked so pretty in the snow.

"You know what my resolution is?" she said.

"What?" I was only half listening. I was so full of looking at her, of feeling her chest go in and out against my chest while she breathed.

"In 1942 I'm going to be the best wife Son Abbott ever wanted," she said, and then she looked up and smiled at me.

I was trying to remember if I resolved to do anything, if there was anything I wanted, or wanted to be different. I couldn't think of a thing.

The next morning when I left, Cecilia stood on the front steps of my house, holding my mother's hand. She had kissed me good-bye before, but when my father started to pull away, she came toward the car and he stopped. I rolled down the window and she leaned inside and kissed me again.

"You're not going to go off and forget me, are you?" she said. But the question was so crazy that I didn't even answer her, I just ran two finger down along the side of her face. She was practicing for when I would go away to war. She was trying to get her good-bye just right.

"You know your mother and I have always liked Cecilia," my father said when we were a few miles from the house. "Not that we've always wanted to. That girl's given you a bad time over the years. But now that it's all settled, I'm glad about it. It's clear enough how you feel about her. We're just glad that everything's worked out. If this is any sign of what kind of a wife she'll be, you're going to do just fine for yourself.''

"Don't I know it,'' I said. I leaned my face against my hand, hoping there would be a little of her perfume left on my glove. All the way up I thought about her, not about the war, just that I had left her and now could set about coming back.

There isn't much I remember about the first three weeks of boot camp, other than how much we were all the same. They shaved our heads first thing, stripped us down and gave us clothes. They looked in our ears and down our throats, weighed us in and measured us up against a wall. When they gave us our shots it was like they were making us even on the inside too, making sure we would all be sick at the same time, well together.

I was good at doing what I was told. I had practice. When the coach said fake to the left, I did it, never once went right just to see what it would be like. My folks told me what to do and always said I was a good son, did my chores without being reminded. After school I had a job at the seed feed store, loading bags into the backs of trucks. One hundred pounds of sweet feed for horses, one hundred pounds of corn, twenty-five pounds of rabbit chow for the Henleys, whose daughters kept rabbits as pets. They told me where to go and that bag was over my shoulder. I did my job. No one told me what to do more than Cecilia, to wait for her by the lockers after school, to drive her cross town to see Jeannie Allbrittan, to wave to her from the basketball court. To leave her alone. To come back to her. The marines had nothing on Cecilia. So I got up at four-thirty in the morning and showered and dressed like I was told. I folded my leggings right and tied them right and ran for an hour before breakfast. I memorized my rifle, knew it in the dark, took it apart and put it together again and loved it the way they told me to. It was a Springfield 0.3., not what we'd have later on, when the battles came, but what we had for now. I knew about guns from my father. I'd shot deer with his Winchester since I was twelve. I was hoping for a beautiful gun, a good-looking pistol to wear on my hip. Where I came from, everybody had a rifle or a shotgun of some kind or another, but handguns, automatics or even old six-shooters, were pretty much just for the movies. I would say I was a good shot, but I had nothing on the boys in Parris Island. We were Southerners mostly, and lots of those boys had been hunting since they were seven or eight. They may have had a hard time making their beds just right, but they could shoot a fly on the other side of the mess hall with a .22. In Parris Island, the way I shot was nothing special.

All the guys in our company thought we would know each other forever, but the truth is I don't know what became of a single one of them, and none of them would know that I became the groundskeeper at a Catholic home and married a pregnant girl and said her baby was my own. In quarantine we only had each other. We thought we would go to war together, fight together, come home together. We thought we would build our houses in the same towns and talk at night the way we talked now. Maybe it was because we looked so much alike, and everywhere I turned, there I was, sometimes fairer or heavier and always shorter, but it was me. Maybe it was because we had never been away before and we didn't know that you could live with someone and not treat them as family. I wondered sometimes if it was that we were scared, and that was the thing that kept us tight, but I can't remember anybody who was smart enough to be scared. Now I'm older, and I know enough to be scared of all sorts of things, things that aren't even there, things that could never happen. But back then it was all Hirohito and Hitler, like their armies were nothing more than football teams from other towns, and you don't get scared of football teams, you just wait for your chance to go out there and lay them out in front of everybody.

In the bunk under me was a guy from Chapel Hill named Dee. He had two older brothers in the navy who'd already been shipped over to the Pacific. It was a big deal, Dee going with the marines.

"Nobody expected me to," Dee said, putting black polish on his boots and then brushing it off and then doing it over again. "But I just figured it was better, you know, spreading out a little."

I told him I just had sisters.

"Well, one of them sure likes you." He winked at me and stuck his hand deep inside his boot. "You get more good-looking envelopes than anybody here."

"That's my fiancée." I tried the word out. "Cecilia."

"You getting married? No kidding?"

"Before I get shipped out, one way or another."

"Sweet deal," Dee said. "Guy ought to have a wife waiting for him when he's off at war. I'll tell you if there was anybody I liked, even a little, I'd marry her in a minute."

"I like her just fine," I said. It was a wonderful thing, to talk about Cecilia to someone who didn't know her, someone who hadn't watched us grow up and seen her leave and come back like a seasonal bird. Dee thought I was doing her some kind of favor by marrying her. He didn't know how it was at all.

"Pretty?"

"You better believe it."

"Blond or brunette? Or God, she's not a redhead is she?"

"Blond."

"Good thing she's not a redhead. I have this thing for redheads. I might have to get on a bus to go and meet her myself if she was a redhead."

"Then she's safe," I said.

"You got a picture?"

I put down my boot brush and wiped my hands carefully on the edge of a towel. I had a picture of Cecilia in my footlocker, in the little space for personal things we could keep. It was the same picture I'd had of her for years, the one of her in her blue sundress. I looked at that picture so much I thought I'd pull her off the paper. But then I just lost it somewhere. I never knew what became of that picture. "Here," I said, and handed it to Dee.

He took it by the corner, careful, like me. He whistled. "She's a little thing. God, what a doll. Hey, Jim," he said, calling over to the guy in the next bunk. "Get a load of this."

Jim came over and took the picture. "Yours?" he said to Dee.

"Son's. What do you make of that?"

Jim took the picture and showed it to his bunkmate, a guy from someplace in the Midwest, Illinois maybe, and from there it started to go around, up one row of bunks and down the other. Even when I couldn't see it anymore, I could hear them saying our names, Son, Cecilia, whistling. Every guy wanting to be me, wanting to have Cecilia wait for him.

Dear Cecilia,

You don't know it, but you are very popular in Parris Island. I'm not the only one who dreams about you now. Your picture has been making the rounds and everyone agrees you are the prettiest girl we are fighting for. One fellow named Sam Dixon who is from Alabama came over to my bunk early this morning before inspection and asked couldn't he please see your picture again. I guess I'll have to be very careful now, so many guys who want to know where you are.

There isn't much I can tell you about what's going on here. Everything is a secret, most of the time even from us. Whatever we're doing I am mostly thinking of marrying you. Running in the hills in the morning or marching or peeling potatoes, I am thinking about you in a wedding dress and how you will be such a beautiful bride. I can't remember a week that ever went by that I didn't see you, but now it has been almost two weeks. I think of you so much it is hard to know what else I am doing. Marry me the first day I see you again.

I love you. I keep thinking there must be a better way to say it. I wish there was a way to tell you so that you would know that no one has ever loved a girl the way I love you.

                                              Son

Just after New Year's we got our first Cinderella liberty. I didn't know what that meant until the D.I. came in and told us that if we weren't back on the stroke of midnight, we sure as hell better plan on turning into pumpkins. In our lives there had been so much free time, but after three weeks in boot camp, twelve whole hours without instruction seemed impossible. We didn't know where to start because there was just so much. You'd have thought we would have wanted to be alone more than anything, because we hadn't been by ourselves, not even for a minute, since we arrived. But instead we went out the gate together and stayed in our groups all night. A uniform was your ticket back then, not like it is now, and when we went down the streets of Parris Island, it was, "Hello, Marine," "How's it going there, Marine," everywhere.

Dee was in our group, and Jim from the next bunk, and his bunkmate Perry from Illinois, and that guy Sam Dixon who liked Cecilia's picture so much. We wandered through town, feeling a little anxious about the daylight. It was night we were interested in, though nobody came right out and said it. I wanted to buy a present for Cecilia, and the guys were good about coming along with me. The five of us went in and out of dress shops, talking about sizes and the color of hair. All the salesgirls were sweet, and there was one who said she'd meet Dee for a drink after work. The other guys thought of girls they'd known at home, maybe somebody they just went out with a time or two, but now they wanted to buy her something. It felt good to have a girl to send a present to, any girl. I picked out a scarf with red flowers around the edge.

"If you want to write a note for that and give me the address I could just mail it for you," the salesgirl said. "If you want, that is."

"That would be good," I said. I thought about it for a minute and then wrote something down and handed it to her. She was a pretty girl, slim and dark-haired. I thought if she was all fixed up she would have looked a little like Ava Gardner.

"Would you like to go for dinner tonight?" she said, keeping her eyes down on the counter as she wrote out the receipt.

I felt my face flush and I hoped that none of the guys had heard her. "I can't," I said quietly, "I've got a girl." I tapped the scarf on the counter.

She looked up at me. Her eyes were brown. "Here?" she asked.

"No, Tennessee."

"So do you want to have dinner with me tonight?" She started to smile, but then looked away, like all of the sudden she'd lost her nerve about the whole thing. I felt bad for her. She was a pretty girl. I wondered then if that's what it meant to be in love, turning down invitations from pretty girls when you were away from home.

I thanked her for everything and we left. It was cold and snowing a little bit and we pushed our hands into our pockets and headed down the street toward no place in particular.

"I say we have dinner," Jim said.

Dee looked at his watch. "It's barely four o'clock."

"Well, it's too early to start drinking now. If we wait and have dinner later, it'll just cut into our drinking time." Jim was a sensible guy. He could always figure out how to do something, fix an engine or tighten his blankets to make a quarter bounce. If he said dinner was a good idea, then chances are it was. We were seventeen. We were always hungry.

By the time we'd eaten it was getting dark, and we figured we could raise any sort of hell we wanted. The first bar we went into a couple of guys bought us a round of beers and we took this as good luck. Sam and Perry shot pool while Dee and Jim and I split a pack of cigarettes. It's not that I'd never had a drink. I'd done some drinking in my day, but that was the first time it didn't matter. I wasn't breaking any rules, there was no worry in the back of my head about coming in late and drunk and seeing my mother waiting up for me in the living room. Now I was a marine out with my marine friends and I could drink what I wanted.

"You should see this guy's girlfriend," Sam said to the bartender, and put his arm around my shoulder. "Great big guy like this and he has this little bitty girlfriend." He held up his thumb and forefinger about an inch apart. "This big. And pretty." He shook his head.

"Who?" Jim said.

"Cecilia. Son's Cecilia."

"To Cecilia, then," Jim said, and raised his glass, and the whole bar raised their glasses and looked up and said, "To Cecilia," and we all whooped and hollered. The bartender filled us up again and we started talking about getting over to the Pacific to show those guys what for. Then just when we were all starting to feel a little lonely, the salesgirl who liked Dee came in and gave us all a wave. She came to our table and sat right down next to Dee and kissed him on the cheek. Suddenly I missed my salesgirl and remembered her as looking more and more like Ava Gardner.

"Betty," she said to Perry and shook his hand. She shook hands with all of us and asked us where we were from. Then someone put a song on the jukebox and she got up to dance with Dee, even though there wasn't really a dance floor. Jim and Sam and Perry and I watched them like they were a movie. We were all drunk, but Dee was drunk and dancing.

Then a guy around sixty came over and sat down with us and bought everyone a round of drinks. "I was a marine myself," he said when we raised our glasses to him. "The Great War. Hell of a war." We nodded.

"What's that on your hand?" Perry said. He probably wouldn't have asked that way, except that we were all so drunk whatever came to our minds came out of our mouths.

The man, who said his name was Louder, rolled up his shirt sleeve and showed us a snake that went all the way around his forearm. I could tell by the yellow and brown on its back and the diamond shape of its head that it was supposed to be a cottonmouth. Its red tongue was out, lying on the top of his hand. I wondered why anyone would want a cottonmouth on his arm. "This one's basic training," he said, tapping the snake on the head. "I got plenty others, but I'm not going to take my shirt off. It's too damn cold in here. You know what they say, can't be a marine without a tattoo."

And that was all we needed to hear, because nobody was

going to tell us we weren't marines. We were all out of our chairs and on our feet. I went to get Dee. "We're going for tattoos," I said. "Come on."

But Dee only pulled Betty closer and pushed his face into her hair. "You crazy?"

"Marines have tattoos," I said. "Are you a marine or what?"

"I'm a dancing marine." They did a sloppy half turn so that all of the sudden I was facing Betty. She gave me a wink. I wasn't sure what it was supposed to mean.

"We'll go without him," I said to the others.

"Without Dee?" Sam said.

"It's either that or no tattoos." I downed the last of my drink and then the last of Dee's drink, which he had left sitting on the table. It served him right.

"You boys know where to go?" Louder said to us when we were almost to the door.

We stopped, looked back, shook our heads.

He pulled himself into his coat and got to the front of the line. "Come on, I'll take you down there, but I'm not going to stay and watch. I never watch a tattoo. Not even my own."

It was nearly midnight, but Louder said the place stayed open late. "I oughta get a commission," he said. It wasn't too far from the bar, and I was glad since the cold was starting to creep up under my coat. There was a sign in the window that said, TATTOOS WHILE YOU WAIT. It was lit up like a soda shop, full of guys I knew and guys from other companies, all as drunk as me. They all said hello and tried to make room for us on the edges of chairs. The place smelled like rubbing alcohol, like gin.

"None of you planning on throwing up, are you?" a small, burly man said to us when we came in. We shook our heads. "Well if you are, go outside." He took a silent count of heads. "It's gonna be awhile."

"We've got until midnight," Jim said.

The man handed us books so we could pick out what we wanted. When his sleeves rode up above his wrist we caught sight of the edge of a world, the tails of things hanging down beneath his cuffs. He called for the next fellow in line to come behind the curtain. Louder looked around.

"Just like the old days," he said.

I was more sure than ever that this was the thing to do, what with so many of the guys there doing it. A fellow named Pinsky whose bunk was near the front of the Quonset hut stepped out from the back, buttoning his shirt. "They've got three guys working back there," he said. "You won't have to wait too long."

"Hurt much?" I asked him, and then was sorry because the question didn't sound very marine.

He looked at me, his eyes glazed over from bourbon or something else. "You bet," he said, and stepped through the door without a coat.

Jim and Perry went back first, Jim for an eagle with a flag twisted in his talons and Perry for a snake like Louder's, which seemed to make Louder happy. He stayed with us after all and talked about something that I couldn't quite hear. I was thinking about my tattoo, which would say Cecilia. I picked out the kind of letters I wanted. I thought of how happy she would be to see her name there, on my arm like it was on most every tree and park bench in Ashland City. I had carved it in so many places that it was almost a joke in town, every tree named Cecilia. When a very short man with smooth black hair and a careful little mustache called me back I told him what I wanted.

"Big or small?" he said. There was no interest in his voice. There was talk that they'd done more than a hundred and fifty tattoos since liberty began that afternoon. He was tired and didn't care about my love life.

"Pretty big," I said, "from about there to there." I marked out the place on my arm and he started to wash it off.

"Write it down," he said, and gave me a pencil and paper. "I don't want to make a mistake. My spelling's not so good."

So I wrote down her name on a piece of paper and held it up with my other hand while he worked. After every letter he finished, he checked it again.

His hand shook a little while he worked the electric needle, probably just from being so tired. When it was done I looked at it and for the first time I felt married, like the whole ceremony was done and Cecilia was mine. "That's good," I said to the tattoo man.

My voice seemed to startle him, almost like I woke him up. "Yeah?" he said. "You think?" He looked at my arm like he'd never seen it before. "It's not bad, really."

I tipped him a dollar over the price and went back out into the waiting room.

Jim and Perry were finished, but Sam was still getting worked on, so I sat down and waited with the rest of them. I was starting to sober up a little and was sorry for it. I could feel a sting in my arm that I hadn't before. Then Sam came into the waiting room with his shirt off. He was still as drunk as he'd been in the bar. He was smaller than the rest of us, but he'd kept up. It must have hit him harder. "Look at this," he said, and turned his shoulder toward us. That tattoo was a little red, but it was clear enough from where we sat. Jim and Perry started to howl. It said Cecilia.

"You son of a bitch," I said, and I went for him across the waiting room. All the chairs, the black and white tile floor, the pictures of tattoos taped to the wall, turned into a blur. There was just no stopping me, though I guess a few people tried. I was a fullback and I moved through the room of would-be marines like water and got to Sam. It was like somebody just handed him to me, and I had him by the shoulders and up in the air. I can still see his face above my face. It was pale and red and a little broken out. His blue eyes were rimmed with water and there was a pain and fear I hadn't seen before. "My arm," he said, crying. "My arm. Put me down."

But I didn't put him down as much as throw him down, through the curtain and onto the table where someone I didn't know was having the word *America* carved into his chest. The tattoo man I'd tipped five minutes before looked at me like someone he'd never seen before in his life.

"I'll call the Shore Patrol," the burly man said. "Stupid, drunk bastards."

So then I went for him, hating him exactly the way I had hated Sam a minute before. All I wanted to do was fight, that quick I'd gone crazy, seeing her name like she was the one who put it there. Jim took hold of my arm and so I turned to go for him, but when I saw his face he said, "Son, hey. Son," and I heard him. "We need to get out of here now," Jim said.

Perry went and picked up Sam and helped him into his shirt. We were all so good at getting dressed quick in those days, and the four of us were out the door, and it was all forgotten. We were running together, stumbling half blind and laughing at what, I can't imagine. I never saw Sam's tattoo again.

The next morning was a hell that nobody accounted for, 'cause the day went on same as ever, four-thirty wake-up, four-forty-five run. Each beer and whiskey was with us as we went through our course. And nobody's arm felt like lifting a field pack either.

It's the day *after* liberty that folks should talk about, but I guess it doesn't make as good a story.

It was that day I got my assignment to stand guard duty, midnight to four A.M. I wasn't any too pleased, seeing as how all I was thinking about was the night's sleep I'd be having, but there was no arguing with the marines. At eleven-thirty I got up and got dressed in the dark, careful not to wake up Dee in his bunk, took my rifle, and headed out into the night. I was lucky, since it wasn't as cold as it had been the night before and it wasn't raining. Actually, it was a pretty night, and standing guard wasn't too bad as long as you could stay awake. It was the first time I'd been alone and so I walked back and forth in front of my post and thought about Cecilia. With all that time I could think of her as long as I wanted to. It felt like a luxury, like a bath, to remember whole conversations we'd had without anyone interrupting. I'd tried to do it at night, but I was always so tired I just fell asleep after a minute or two. I imagined our wedding, the Lighthouse Baptist Church done up in flowers. Magnolias were her favorite, but there'd be no way of getting them that time of year. In the summer I'd go around cutting off magnolia branches. I took so many I had to start doing it at night. I tried to get them mostly out of the woods, but a lot of the good trees are the ones growing in people's yards. Then I would go and leave them on Cecilia's doorstep, their stems bound together with twine, so many flowers they made their own tree.

That's what I was thinking about when I heard the jeep drive up. I snapped up straight, worried at first that I'd been thinking so much and that my thoughts had taken me too far away. I felt like my thoughts of Cecilia were spread out on the ground, that I had been caught touching her clothes.

"Halt," I said, trying to make my voice sound like something a person would halt for. "Who goes there?" I pointed my rifle out toward the bright headlights of the jeep.

"Corporal of the guard."

"Advance and be recognized," I said. I still couldn't see him with the lights in my eyes.

He turned off the jeep and got out and I blinked, trying to adjust to the darkness. "What's your name, marine?" he said.

"Sir, my name is Wilson Abbott, 276559, sir."

"Abbott, what is the first general order?"

I was relieved, 'cause that was the one I could always remember. I told him I'd walk my post in a military manner. I told him the whole thing.

"At ease," he said.

These were the sweetest words in the language back then. It meant that things were going to be all right. I took a step to the side and looked at him.

"Corporal of the guard come to smoke," he said, and tapped a Camel out of his pack and lit it. "Not too bad out here to-night."

"Sir, no, sir."

"Anything to report?"

"Sir, no, sir."

He probably wasn't more than nineteen or twenty, but on that night he was so far my superior that I couldn't imagine we could have gone to high school together. He pulled on his cigarette, leaned back his head, and blew the smoke straight up. Bill Lovell was his name, I remember that. I waited and tried not to watch him, thinking he would finish his cigarette and go on, but he seemed to make it last and when he was finished, he lit another one off its end. He took the one that was done and field-stripped it, flicking off the burning end, scattering the tobacco, and rolling what paper was left into the smallest ball you could imagine.

"You smoke, Abbott?"

"Sir, yes, sir."

"Well then, have a smoke with me." He took a cigarette from his pack, lit it, and handed it to me. I can't describe this so that it would make any sense to someone who hadn't been there, but this was just short of a miracle; the corporal of the guard giving me a cigarette at my post. I took it and thanked him. "Where you from, Abbott?"

"Sir, Ashland City, Tennessee, sir."

"Never heard of it."

"Sir, no, sir," I said. I wanted to ask him where he was from, how long he'd been there, but I didn't want him to think that if he gave me a cigarette I'd take it as a sign that I could do anything I wanted, so I just kept quiet and enjoyed the smoke.

He looked around the camp. It must have been three in the morning. Nothing was moving, nothing awake. Then he looked at me. "It sure would be a shame if you had to shoot anybody with that weapon," he said. "Springfield was fine in the Great

War, but you'll need better than that to fight Tojo. I hear his boys have weapons we haven't even thought about yet."

"Sir, yes, sir."

The corporal of the guard stripped his second cigarette. I did the same.

"Seems to me they should be giving everybody side arms, like this," he said, and pulled a gun out of his holster. ".45. Now there's a weapon to fight with."

It was a hell of a gun. If you didn't want to shoot somebody with it you could use it to hit him over the head and kill him just the same. I'd seen pictures of them, but I'd never been up close to one. Right there, in his hand, you could tell it would have nearly the kick of my Springfield. All the power without the size.

"You interested in weapons, Abbott?"

"Sir, yes, sir."

"I figured, you being from Tennessee. Tennessee and Texas, there're two states that know from firearms." He pulled the slide back and forth, ejecting four rounds. They popped out of the chamber and made a dull sound when they hit the dirt. "When you do this," he said, "you're taking off the safety and putting back the hammer. See? Now it's ready to go. Course, there's another safety here, in the grip. This weapon does all your thinking for you." He put the .45 flat in his outstretched hand. "I can't let you hold it," he said, "but it's heavier than you'd think it would be." He moved his hand up and down slowly, like he was a scale. "Nearly five pounds with the clip in. Just right, just enough to give you something to hold onto."

I would have loved to have that gun.

He put one finger through the trigger bar and spun it around his hand, then caught the gun by the butt and held it still again. "Pretty good, huh? Comes from watching all those Westerns."

"Sir, yes, sir."

"I've been working on my draw," he said, and put the gun back into the holster. He reached down, flipped the top of the holster up, and pulled it out fast in one clean movement. He pointed it down, then put it back in the holster, looked away for a minute, and pulled it out again. "I'm fast," he said, "but not really fast enough. I've seen guys who do this"—he pulled the gun out again, a little better that time—"you can't believe the weapon was ever in the holster, they get it out so fast. The secret"—he pulled it out again, this time tensing up a little—"is just to do it over and over again and then—" He pulled

the gun out and it discharged. He had hit the grip safety and
the trigger at the same time. I heard the loud crack and
smelled the sharpness of the gunpowder before I felt it. The
round went into my left knee with such force it knocked my
leg clean out from under me. I fell to the ground like a stone
and there was a sound of all my breath coming out of my
lungs and Billy Lovell looked at me for that second and I
looked at him and we knew, that in different ways, it was all
over for both of us.

=== 3 ===

MOTHER CORINNE never liked it, Rose staying on and working in the kitchen the way she did, but Rose just wouldn't go. It wasn't three days after Sissy was born that she just bundled her up and took her into breakfast. I went over with her. "You don't need to do this," I said. "You should have some rest, stay home with the baby. You don't need to be working." But she didn't even look up at me. She was putting diapers in her overnight bag and trying to find her scarf.

We went in together through the back door. Once we got there I knew why she was doing it. Sister Evangeline lit up like a Christmas tree. The second she saw Rose and the baby she started to cry, her hands pulling at her rosary. "Lookee," she said. "Oh, Mother Mary, lookee at this one here." She wrapped her arms around Rose and put her head down next to the baby, kissing her. "I never get the babies," she said, not stopping to wipe her face. "All the girls come here and I can see so much promise, but then everybody goes away. I've tried not to mind, but now I can tell you, I do. Every one of them I miss."

"I'm here," Rose said.

"I wasn't sure. I mean, I was sure, everything in me said this baby was going to stay, but then I thought maybe I just wanted it so bad, maybe I was trying to will it so. I got confused." She smiled at me, standing over near the door. "Old women. You know me, Son."

"She wouldn't leave you," I said, because then I knew it was the truth. "I tried to get her to stay at home, but she wouldn't have it."

"Well, you should stay at home." She reached up and slapped Rose a couple of times on the cheek, too hard, I thought. "You should be in bed." But the joy in her voice said very clearly,

155

You're fine, you should be right here. "They sent me a new girl when you left. Penny. Sweet girl, but she's no Rose. I'd forgotten how to cook with you around. All those years of doing everything and now I can't boil an egg. And Penny, sweet girl, she can't do a thing, either. I was starting to think I'd be out on the streets, an old nun looking for work. But you're hungry, all of you. You," she said, and touched Sissy's nose. "Sit down, I'll make you breakfast."

"You sit down," Rose said, and dropped the baby in her arms like she was tossing a handbag on the sofa. Sister Evangeline and I both took on the same panicked look. "I'm going to make breakfast."

"Well, what am I going to do?" Sister Evangeline said.

"Take care of Cecilia, I guess," Rose said, and went to tie an apron on.

"I don't know about babies anymore."

"You know more about them than I do," Rose said. Then she set about her job, just like nothing had happened. She took out the bowls and the eggs and the flour, the cups and spoons. She forgot about us, or at least tried very hard to look like she had. I ate the plate of pancakes she set before me.

"I need you to take the baby over to June," Rose said to me. "June?"

"She's going to keep her for me, for a while, during the day."

"I thought you'd keep her here."

Rose shook her head. She kept on cooking. With Rose it was always a meal for twenty-five. "I don't want her around here. In fact, I want her out before the girls start waking up. It's too hard for them to see a baby. Believe me, I know what I'm talking about."

"But how's June gonna feel about this?" I said. Sister Evangeline had the baby and was bouncing her up and down.

"I called her and worked it all out. She's thrilled. You know June. She'd love to have the baby around."

"I talked to her, too," Sister Evangeline said. "She can hardly wait."

I stewed for a minute. I didn't like it, the baby not being with Rose. I didn't like not knowing either. I was the father. That ought to count for something.

"You need to get going," Rose said to me. "Girls will be up any minute."

I leaned over and took my daughter out of Sister Evangeline's arm. Such a tiny bundle. Such a little round weight. I wanted to keep her with me but there were so many things to do. I was the one with the paying job in the family. "All right," I said. "But we'll talk about this later."

When I got to the door Rose stopped me. I thought that maybe she couldn't stand it now that she was watching her go. "Son," she said. I turned to her. Sissy was asleep like an angel. "Take the diaper bag."

I carried the baby over the pasture to June's house. It was cold and I kept trying to keep her head covered up without smothering her. Who would have thought I'd be walking across this pasture with a baby? My baby. The bag of bottles and soft clothes swung from my shoulder. My daughter slept and woke, twisting up her mouth as she watched the sky pass over her head. It was early, barely daylight, but when I came up the steps June threw open the door, fully dressed.

"Well, let me see this," she said, and stretched out her arms.

I gave Sissy over to her and she just couldn't get enough of it. I thought she'd push the baby clean into her chest. "Son Abbott," she said. "If I had known the day I met you what good things you'd bring to my life, I would have taken a mind to marry you myself."

"You're smarter than that," I said.

"Not smarter," she said. "Just too old. God, will you look at this one? All my life I thought a baby would come to me. Just didn't count on it taking so long." She stepped inside the house, and I saw a bassinet set up in the living room, right in the center of things where June could keep an eye on her all day. She didn't waste any time getting herself set up.

"This seems like an awful lot of bother for you," I said.

"Don't be a fool."

I sat down on her sofa, made myself to home for a minute. "If you ask me, it's Rose who should be doing this. There's no point in her going back to work."

"The point is that she wants to. If she wasn't meant to stay at home it would only wind up worse in the long run. She told me on the phone, it's only while this one's real little. It's hard for those girls, seeing new babies when they're so close to having one of their own. It's confusing. Once some time goes by and things settle down, she can stay over with Rose during the day."

"I don't like it," I said.

"Well," June said, running her finger along my daughter's cheek. "I do."

I stopped in a couple of times during the day to check on

things, but everybody seemed happy as larks. Once I went by and found Sister Evangeline there, changing Sissy's diapers on the kitchen table. "Everything else in the world gets modern," she said to me. "Babies stay just the same."

I thought a lot about the two of them, both past sixty and finally getting to have a baby of their own. I was glad for them. I could see it was no burden. But still, I wished it wasn't my baby they had.

At the end of the day Rose and I went over to June's and took Sissy back. June acted like we were tearing her heart out of her chest.

"She'll be back in the morning," June said.

"First thing," Rose said.

June watched us walk back toward our house beside the hotel. "This isn't right," I said to Rose, Sissy fussing a little in my arms. "Leaving her with someone else, not paying her any attention."

"I feel sure Cecilia got more attention today than most children get in a lifetime."

"I just don't like it," I said.

She stopped in the snow, halfway between Saint Elizabeth's and our house. We looked at each other in the darkness. The stars behind her head looked like a decoration for Rose. "I'm tired," she said quietly.

And I didn't say, see there, I told you; and I didn't say, that's what you get; I said, come on then, let's get you home.

The next morning when I was on the second floor finishing up work on a sink, flat on my back and staring up at the curved underside of a washbowl, Mother Corinne came in.

"Son," she said. "I won't have this."

I sighed, sat up, and wiped my hands. I'd gotten good at being careful not to hit my head on things. "Rose?" I said.

"She's not a resident anymore. She shouldn't be here."

"She's my wife now, Mother."

"Then she should stay at home as your wife. I'm none too pleased about the way all of this went. It wasn't the time to talk to you before, but I'll have you know this is a great disappointment to me. I trusted you, Son. If I'd known you were going to be picking out girls for yourself I would have dismissed you years ago."

I stood up, because Mother Corinne used her size to bully

people. "Since we both know that's not so, I think it best we just don't get into it."

She flushed a little bit. "The point of this conversation is your wife's continuing to work in our kitchen, which is unsatisfactory."

The thing you had to do if you were going to deal with Mother Corinne was forget about her being a nun. I used to let her get by with a lot of stuff, took all her guff for years because she was supposed to be a woman of God. You had to deal with her as straight as she dealt with you, or you were dead in the water. "The way I hear it told, the food went downhill fast with Rose gone. Sister Evangeline can't do it anymore. She hasn't been able to for years, and she can't have a different girl coming and going for each meal. She needs someone to look after her, and she wants that someone to be Rose. As for my feelings, I'd tend to agree with you. She's not getting paid and she's working like a horse, which don't make much sense to me. I'd say we should all be thankful for what's set before us."

Mother Corinne mulled on this for a minute. She was not one to set her teeth so far into something that she couldn't let go when presented with the truth. "There will be no salary for her, not if she's not asked to be here, but if she wants to help, for a while," she said, "then I suppose that could be arranged, but her daughter will have to stay at home. This is no place for children. Surely even you would be able to understand that."

"I understand that fine," I said. "Sissy is staying with June Clatterbuck."

"Then this conversation is concluded," she said.

"Except for this: when you want to get rid of Rose, you go tell Rose. Not me." I turned the cold water faucet. Water came out. "Fixed it," I said.

Mother Corinne nodded toward the sink and left me there. I didn't scare her and I didn't try to. We'd been around each other for so long and we both admitted, at least to ourselves, that we were dependent, me on the work and her on the worker. But Rose was another story. She didn't need anything from anybody, and if you tried to tell her what to do, chances were she was going to tell you to go to hell.

Sissy was pure joy, as smart and loving a child as God's made. Being around so many people while she was growing up made her friendly.

"Children are like pups," Sister Evangeline told me. "The

more people picking them up and playing with them, the more people they'll grow up liking in their life.''

By the time she was three she'd started coming over to Saint Elizabeth's for lunch, and when she was four she was pretty much around all the time. It happened gradually, so that even Mother Corinne was used to her. She still went over to June's every day, but it was almost like she was too busy to spend the whole day with one person. All the girls wanted their time with her. They wanted to brush her hair and read her stories. They wanted a little chance to mother if they weren't going to get to be mothers in their own right. At the hotel she was the center of the world, and it made her sweet, where another child might have turned spoiled.

With all the excitement that came from spending her days at Saint Elizabeth's, Sissy must have found the evenings dull, two quiet parents and a little house. Her mother read cookbooks at the kitchen table, or did a little straightening up. I used to wonder if Sissy would forget who her mother was, with so many mothers. Once or twice I caught the girls trying to get her to say Mama to them. But Sissy knew. If she fell and scraped her knee, it was Rose she ran to crying, and if she painted a picture she was proud of, it was Rose she wanted to see it first. And Rose would always turn down the flame under the pot she was working on and listen to her for a minute or pick her up under one arm to wash out her cut in the sink.

"You know you shouldn't be running in the halls," she would say matter-of-factly, not scolding, but just passing something along. "That's how these things happen."

Sissy would sniff a little and touch her cut lightly.

"Don't touch it," Rose said. "That's why I washed it in the first place." She got out the small first-aid box she kept near the stove and put a Band-Aid on. "Repaired," she said and lifted her off the counter and put her down on the floor, but Sissy held on to her neck like clinging ivy. "Come on now, your mother has to work."

"Kiss."

"Okay, kiss." Rose kissed her. "Now scoot, go scare the nuns."

"Kiss."

"Kisses don't grow on trees, you know. I've got to get to work." She kissed her again, quickly this time. "Out of here." She pried Sissy off her neck and sent her off to a whole stream of girls who waited to see her Band-Aid and kiss her for it.

* * *

Rose just never seemed to have much time for Sissy. Every last thing, from a chicken in the oven to the sad story of one of the girls, came first. One night we were lying in bed, not sleeping, and since it was what I was thinking about, I finally asked her. "Why did you keep Sissy?"

"What do you mean?" she said, tired, her thoughts someplace a long way from that bed and that night.

"Why did you go through everything to keep her? Why didn't you just let her go like all the other girls do?"

She sat up on one elbow and stared at me. "What an awful thing to say. Cecilia's my daughter. I kept her because she was mine."

"But you weren't going to keep her. I'm not trying to make you mad. You came here because you wanted to give her up and then you didn't, you married me, you stayed here, and now it all doesn't seem to matter very much, and sometimes I wonder why you did it, is all. I just keep thinking, it couldn't be because you wanted to spend the rest of your life cooking at Saint Elizabeth's, or even because you wanted to take care of Sister Evangeline. Those are good things, but they just aren't enough, not to change so many lives around. Don't look at me like that, Rose. All I'm saying is, I wonder, that's all."

Rose got out of the bed. "I can't believe you," she said. She pushed her hands through her hair. She'd gotten thin in the last couple of years and it made her face sharper and so beautiful I could hardly believe it sometimes. "Are you not happy?"

"No, I never said—"

"Do you want us to leave?"

A tightness came up in my throat. "Oh, Rose, Jesus, you know I love you. And Sissy. Dear God. That's not what I meant."

"This is what I'm supposed to do: be married, raise my daughter, do my job. This is my life." She was slapping her hand against the bedpost, punctuating every word with a slap. "I don't know how to do this another way."

"I'm sorry," I said. "I'm sorry. Come back to bed."

"No," she said. She stood in her nightgown by the window, shivering.

"Please. I was wrong to say it. I never should have brought it up."

"You think I don't love her. Well, to hell with you." She took her pillow off the bed. "I'm going to sleep with Cecilia." She went into the living room and left me alone in a bed I had been alone in half my life. I could still feel her warmth in the blankets.

The next morning Sissy was in heaven. All the way to Saint Elizabeth's she held Rose's hand. "Mommie slept with me last night," she told me for the fifth time. Rose had braided her hair. She almost always waited and let Sister Evangeline braid her hair. "And Mommie's going to sleep with me tonight," she said.

"We'll see," Rose said.

I did love Rose. I loved her strength and her pride. I loved the way she just got things done and never cared what anybody else might think about it. I loved the look that came over her face when she helped Sister Evangeline up from her chair or when she talked to one of the girls or when she closed her eyes and prayed. I loved the feel of her body beside me in bed at night and the way she brushed her hair without looking in the mirror and the shape of her fingernails. I thanked God for her and hoped that she would stay with me in Habit for the rest of our lives, but I could do without her. What I mean is, I could conceive of that loss, life with no Rose. It would be a terrible thing, but I had lived through losing a woman before and if it happened I could live through it again. It was Sissy I flatly could not do without.

The love for a woman and the love for a child are not the same thing. With a woman, there's always the sense that they're loaning themselves to you. You have to remember that they could go at any time, and if a man's smart he never forgets that. He's just grateful for every minute she's there. But a child you come to expect. Their love is so much like breathing that it's a part of you, a leg, a lung. The look on Sissy's face whenever I came into the room was something I now depended on, the feel of her arms wrapped around my neck, the way she called for me when she was scared in the night. After she was born I never thought about her father again because in the center of my bones I was her father and no one will ever tell me that me being the one to make love to Rose nine months before Sissy's birth would make me any more so. When new girls came to Saint Elizabeth's and said, Who are you? What is your name? she always said, Cecilia Abbott. That's who she was. Abbott. Mine. I couldn't see how Rose could be more of a parent than me. Didn't I rock her to sleep? Didn't I tell her stories and show her the woods and buy her penny candy in town? Didn't I love her with my whole life? That one night Rose slept with Sissy was the only time she

threatened to take her away from me. As mad as she was, I think
she saw it would be the one thing I'd never come back from.
Even if Rose didn't love me, she didn't hate me either.

There were always so many girls coming and going, I never
knew how they kept a balance. Every time a girl went off to
Owensboro, a new one appeared at the door, flat-stomached,
suitcase in hand. When one would disappear, sometimes Sissy
would think to look for her. "Where's Stella?" she would ask
her mother.

"She's gone off to have her baby."

I don't know. I'm old-fashioned. I didn't like a four-year-old
having to spend every day thinking about who was having babies
and where they came from. I'd get flustered when Sissy would
ask me why everybody had a baby but us. Rose, on the other
hand, wasn't bothered by anything.

"Why do they have to go away when they have the baby?
Where's the baby then?"

"In the hospital," Rose said, pinching in the edges of a pie
crust, or maybe it was a tart. Nothing was a plain old pie with
her anymore.

"The baby lives in the hospital?"

"No," Rose said, "the baby goes home to its parents."

"Then why don't they come back?"

"This isn't their home. This is just a place girls go to get
ready to have a baby. Like a chicken sits in a nest. This is the
big nest for pregnant girls."

Sissy thought about it for a while. "But we live here all the
time."

"That's because I'm the keeper of the nest," Rose said. "If
I went away, nobody would get dinner."

Sometimes, if it was somebody Sissy especially liked, she
would sulk for an hour or two once she realized that girl was
gone, but she always got over it. There were so many girls in
the world.

Just before Sissy's fifth birthday, a girl named Alice came to
Saint Elizabeth's. Sissy took to her like a duck to water, the very
first day Alice arrived. There were many girls over the years
that Sissy fixed herself to, and because Alice was the first, we
used the name to mean anyone Sissy loved. "I think this one's
an Alice," we would always say when Sissy came in, talking a
mile a minute about some girl who had just arrived. It would be
hard to say exactly why Sissy settled on Alice, the first Alice.
Maybe it was because she was getting older and she didn't want

to spend her days with so many different people anymore. Sissy was at a point that she needed one mother, and since her own mother wasn't available, and she was getting too big for Sister Evangeline and June to pick up anymore, Sissy chose Alice.

There was nothing so out of the ordinary about Alice. She was more of what they called a hippie girl than most that came through. She wore her blond hair long and straight with bangs that fell into her eyes. She wore a lot of beads around her neck which Mother Corinne was quick to talk her out of. But it was 1973 by then, and we were used to seeing all kinds, not like the old days when the girls were all nervous and well mannered. Once the sisters had given her some clothes and talked her into combing back her hair, she looked a lot younger than you would have thought at first. Whenever I saw her, I would think to myself that she was somebody's daughter. That was the kind of look she had.

It was Sissy who introduced us to her. I was in the kitchen, having lunch with Rose and Sister Evangeline after everybody else had eaten. Sissy came in holding Alice's hand.

"There's my big girl," Sister Evangeline said. "Where's my kiss?"

Sissy came over and kissed her. "This is my friend Alice," she said, grabbing hold of Alice's hand again.

"Nice to meet you," I said. I shook her hand and brought her a chair that was over next to the walk-in. I noticed that she had on the same old blue cotton dress Rose was wearing the first day I saw her standing on the porch drinking tea. It was big on Alice, and she had an old cardigan sweater wrapped around herself. Seeing that dress again made me feel so in love with Rose that my face turned red. I wondered if she would remember it, but it wasn't like Rose to remember something like a dress.

Sister Evangeline said hello, and Rose got up to get Alice a cup of coffee from the stove. "Alice is my best friend," Sissy said. "Right?" she asked.

"You bet," Alice said.

Sissy got out of her chair and sat in Alice's lap.

"Cecilia," her mother said. "Don't climb all over people like they were furniture."

"She's all right," Alice said, and looped an arm around her waist.

Sissy stroked the blond braid lying over one shoulder. "I look just like Alice."

We all looked at the two of them, sitting there together. "You do," Sister Evangeline said. "Now that you mention it, you do."

"Alice is from Katie's," Sissy said.

"Cadiz," Alice said.

"But she lives here now," Sissy said.

Alice bounced her knees up and down a couple of times. "You bet."

"When did you get in?" Rose said.

"Just last night. It took me longer to get here than I thought it would. I shouldn't have come so late."

She smiled at Sissy and tickled her side a little to make her squirm. I liked Alice. She seemed more like she'd just come into the Hotel Louisa than Saint Elizabeth's. It was almost like nobody had told her that this was a home for unwed mothers and she was there because she was one of them. If she felt uncomfortable about the whole thing, she didn't let on.

"I'm going to show you the lookout now," Sissy said, and jumped onto the floor. The lookout was a balcony off one of the third-floor suites. It gave you the best view of Habit for your money.

"Maybe Alice isn't finished having coffee," Rose said.

Alice took another sip and put down her cup. "Now I'm finished," she said to Sissy. "It was nice meeting everyone. I'm sure we'll see plenty of each other."

"The kitchen is the place to be. If you ever need anything," Sister Evangeline said, "why, you just come to the kitchen." She leaned out and patted Alice on the hip.

"I will," Alice said, and got up to leave.

"Did you have your interview with Mother Corinne yet?" Rose said.

Alice smiled. "That's why I'm dressed like this."

"I never get to girls in time," Rose said. "I should convince Sister Bernadette to bring everyone in here first. Did she give you a hard time?"

"Nothing much."

"I hope you didn't tell her your husband died."

"What?"

"When she asks what happened to the father, everybody says they were married but their husband died in a car crash."

"Really?" Alice said. She tilted her head to one side and gave a small shrug. "I just told her it was none of her business."

* * *

Alice was good for Sissy, she settled her down. Other girls passed her around, mothered her for a spell and then let somebody else have a chance, but when Sissy spent time with another girl now, it was clear that she was just on loan from Alice and should come back as soon as possible.

"Alice and me are going to Egypt," Sissy said one night when I was tucking her into bed.

"Egypt," I said. "That's pretty far away."

"You bet," Sissy said. "That's how we like it."

"Won't you miss your old dad?"

She thought about it for a minute. Sleep was dragging down her eyes. "Yep," she said dreamily.

It was Alice who started teaching Sissy how to read, even though she already knew the alphabet. She taught her how to tell time and cut snowflakes out of sheets of paper. I wondered at what point it would all start to bother Rose, since all Sissy had to say anymore was Alice this or Alice that, but she didn't seem to notice. It was all the same to her, one girl or two dozen girls paying attention to her daughter. But it worried me. Rose would say, everything worries you.

"Is it dead?" Alice asked me. She was standing down under a sycamore tree I was sawing on.

"Naw, just a little bit. Lightning hit it, here. See? Mother Corinne's always worried that somebody's going to hurt themselves, tree'll fall on their head or something, so I just go ahead and saw the branches off right away. Don't really need to, though, nobody comes all the way out here."

"I do," Alice said.

"I guess you do." It was a nice day, too nice for March. Spring had come on early and strong and stirred everything up. It wasn't even the end of the month and there were daffodils. You could count on it, sometime in April it would snow and kill everything off. That's the way it worked in Kentucky. "Where's your shadow?" I asked her.

"Cecilia's asleep. Out like a light. I've never seen a kid who sleeps that hard."

"She sure is crazy about you," I said, reaching over for a smaller branch. It's not often I have to use a ladder, but these were pretty far up.

"She's a sweetheart, no doubt about that."

"Well, we appreciate it, me and Rose, all the stuff you've done for her."

"It's good for me," she said. Alice pulled on her braid for a while and then twisted it around her fingers. "There's something that's on my mind, Son," she said.

I looked down at her, but she was staring off toward the back pasture. Alice had gotten big overnight, the way girls around here will do. One day they just look like they've got a little belly and the next morning they're full-blown pregnant. I came down off the ladder. "What's that?"

"Cecilia's been asking me to teach her to swim this summer. I'd told her awhile ago about the lakes down where I'm from in Cadiz. You know Cadiz? Lake Barkley and Kentucky Lake right there together. I told her about how everybody there knows how to swim as soon as they know how to walk and she tells me she doesn't know how to swim and would I promise to teach her." She stopped for a minute and pulled on her hair again. "The thing is, I won't be around this summer, and I'm not sure she understands that. It makes me think that maybe I've done her a disservice, getting so close to her and all."

Alice looked so young standing in that field where everything else was growing alongside of her. I felt like she was just a baby, closer to Sissy in age than a few years younger than Rose. She was a good girl. "What about you?" I said. "Maybe there's been a disservice done to you, too. It won't be so easy giving her up."

Alice smiled. "But that's what we do here," she said. "We give things up. For me it's just a matter of fact, but I'm twenty, Cecilia's five."

I wanted to ask her how she got so smart by twenty, but I guess it was clear enough that she'd had a tough go of things. "It'll be hard for her, no doubt about that, but I think she's better off knowing you than not. I think it would be worse if you pulled away from her now than waiting a couple of months until you had to."

She nodded her head and dug her hands into the small of her back. "Good," she said. "That's what I wanted you to say."

"It'll walk you back," I said.

"Stay with your work. That's all I needed to talk about."

"This tree would be happier if I left it alone."

She nodded her head and we walked back to Saint Elizabeth's without talking. Alice seemed to be concentrating on everything very hard, the field and the sky and the edge of the woods that

led to my house. It was almost like she was trying to memorize
it all, get it fixed in her mind so that when she was gone she'd
have something to remember all this by. I just stayed quiet and
left her alone.

"I'm going to see if Cecilia is up from her nap," Alice said
once we got inside.

"Sure," I said. We went our own ways, and I was feeling
better for having talked to her, not that I thought things were
going to be any easier now, but it seemed better, having them
out in the open. I went into the kitchen to get myself a glass of
water and found Rose sitting at the kitchen table talking to some
woman holding a baby in her arms.

"Son!" Rose said. "Look at this. Angie's here." I had never
heard Rose sound so happy about anything.

"Hey, Son," Angie said, and got up and kissed me. Her hair
was shorter and combed neatly and she didn't have on any dan-
gling jewelry, but it was Angie all right, still as skinny and wiry.
Still looking seventeen.

"How have you been?" I said. I was so happy to see her.
Rose and me both had done so much worrying about Angie over
the years that we just gave up talking about it.

"Bad for a while, then real good," she said. "It was like I
was telling Rose. I was down for so long after I went home. I
kept wanting to call but my mother said that I should put the
whole thing behind me, you know, past in the past and all of
that. Then once I cheered up and I realized that my mother was,
as usual, full of shit, I felt embarrassed that so much time had
gone by without me calling, so I didn't call because of that. But
this is Duane, this is my son." She held the baby up and jiggled
him around a little until he looked at me. "I figure a baby is a
new start, clean slate. So here I am."

"Angie married Duane," Rose said.

"Who's Duane?"

"This guy I used to go with a long time ago, before I was
here. Everything was such a long time ago." She laughed.
"God, it's weird being back. You still in the kitchen, Mother
Corinne still in her office, pregnant girls still running up and
down the halls. Girls are always going to get knocked up,"
Angie said. "That's just a fact."

"Did Duane ever know"—Rose tilted her head to one side—
"about all this?"

"Nope," Angie said. "And he never will. That's why it was
hard for me to come and visit. I told him I was visiting a cousin

in Lexington. It would be pretty hard to explain that my best friend is someone I met in Saint Elizabeth's if I say I've never been here. I should have called, but I wanted to surprise you. If you're gone, I figure you might as well make a big deal out of coming back."

That was when Alice and Sissy came in. "Mommie, Alice and me are going to have tea on the porch."

"Alice and I," Alice said.

"Not just yet. Come here and say hello to my friend Angie, Mrs. . . . What is your name now?"

"Tyler," Angie said absently.

"Mrs. Tyler. Mrs. Tyler and I were friends before you were born."

Sissy came up and looked at the baby carefully. He was a good baby, quiet and settled like she had been.

"She's so big," Angie whispered. "I never thought she'd be so big already."

"You'll see," Rose said. "That's the way it goes."

"Maybe we should go on outside," Alice said. "What do you say, give the grown-ups some time to talk."

"Wait a minute," Angie said. She gave Duane to Rose and got down on the kitchen floor on her knees. She took the barrette out of Sissy's hair and smoothed it down with her fingers, then clipped the barrette back into place. "There," she said. Her voice was shaking a little. "Now you look better."

Sissy touched her hair.

"What do you say?" Rose said.

"Thank you," Sissy said. She looked at Duane again. "Bye, baby." She started to go and then stopped, suddenly remembering why she had come in in the first place. "Can I sleep with Alice tonight?"

"Here?" I said. "All night?"

"It's okay," Alice said.

"No," I said. "I don't want you over here all night."

"Sister Bernadette said yes. She said yes if it was just once," Sissy said.

"Fine," Rose said. "As long as Alice doesn't mind."

Alice and Sissy went out through the back door and Angie stayed on the floor for a few more minutes. I turned to say something to Rose, but Angie beat me to it. "I never thought about her getting big like that," she said, but not really to anyone. Then she shook her head and smiled at Rose. "She must look just like Thomas, 'cause she sure doesn't look a thing like you."

The words hung in the air for a minute, and none of us knew for sure what to say. Rose turned her face toward the baby, but I don't think she saw him. Then finally Duane started to fuss a little and Angie took him back and everything went back to the way it was before.

"I'll let you two alone," I said. "I know you have a lot of catching up to do."

"It was good to see you," Angie said. "I think about you, Son. You were so nice to me, that night you drove me to the hospital. I never thanked you for that."

"Don't think about that," I said, but I didn't just mean that. I meant everything. Don't think about any of it. I kissed her again and touched the baby's cheek and headed outside, back out to the field to pick up the branches of the sycamore tree.

All the way there I heard his name. It was better before, when I didn't know his name.

Angie and Rose stayed late in the kitchen that night and Sissy was with Alice and I went home and felt sorry for myself. Being alone is something you have to be good at to enjoy and over the last five years I had forgotten how. I started to pull out the couch to make up Cecilia's bed, and then saw what I was doing and felt foolish. I decided I would build her a bedroom as soon as I was sure the spring rains were over. Her own room on the side of the house. She was getting too big for sleeping on the couch and as little as any of us were home we never saw the sense in moving. I didn't like being home without her, and I was mad at Rose for letting her go so easy.

I heated up some soup for dinner and ate it standing up next to the sink. Then I washed my bowl and went on to bed.

When Rose came in I woke up, even though she was trying to be quiet. "Is it late?" I asked her. I was glad I was up, I wanted to tell her about Sissy, that she should care a little bit about where she was spending the night.

"Not too bad," she said. "Midnight."

"Angie's driving back this late?"

"She called Duane, she told him she was having fun so he told her to stay awhile." Rose's voice sounded light and girlish. I watched her take her dress off in the dark. She sat down beside me on the edge of the bed, wearing her panties and a bra. "We had such a good time," she said, and put her hand over my hand. "I had forgotten how nice it was to have—" but she didn't finish her sentence. She ran her hand absently up and down my arm. "Did you miss me?" she said.

"I did."

"That's good to know." She looked at me lying in the bed. She ran her finger up my arm and down the center of my chest. "I said good night to Cecilia. I tucked her in. Alice's roommate had her baby, so Cecilia had her own bed. She said, tell Daddy good night." She put both hands flat out on my chest and leaned toward me. I watched her breasts curve down into her bra. I watched the way they moved with her breath. I thought of how I had been alone a few hours before and now here Rose was, with her hair falling forward on her face, close enough that I could smell the warmth of her. I put my hand back behind her neck and brought her face to mine.

So many girls came and went over the years, after a while it seemed like everybody only stayed for a few days. You get one of their names, and the next time you think to ask someone says she's been gone two weeks already. I wished I was better at this. I used to be.

Alice managed to slow time down. We all got used to her, came to like having her around. But by June it was clear she wasn't going to be there much longer. I tried to tell Sissy, Alice tried. We explained to her about the baby and that when it came Alice would have to go just like everybody else, but Sissy wouldn't hear it. It was summer and she was running all over the place. It was hot that first week in June and Alice had to stay inside near a fan. The weather made her sick, her ankles were swollen. She was sad in her last weeks, as if she suddenly understood after all that time what she was there for. Sometimes when she watched Sissy from the window she looked like she was going to cry, even though Alice wasn't the kind of girl you'd think of as crying.

"I want you to have my parents' address," she said to me one afternoon. "Write me a letter every once in a while and let me know how she's doing. This place is hell," she said, printing out the street name on the back of an envelope. "Who would of thought I'd want to stay on?"

Alice left in the middle of that same night with Sister Bernadette and Sister Serena.

Rose and I talked it over at breakfast. "We have to tell her now," Rose said, "before she starts asking where she is."

I twisted a napkin up in my hands. "She's going to be so hurt."

"It's not you hurting her. It's not anybody hurting her. This is the way things go around here."

Sissy came in and looked around. "I can't find Alice," she said.

"Come here," Rose said. Sissy came over to the table, and Rose pulled her up into her lap. "Alice had her baby last night."

Sissy's face lit up. "When are we going to see it?"

"We can't," Rose said. "Alice is gone. You knew that she would have to leave once the baby was born."

"She's coming back," Sissy said.

"She can't, sweetie. That's the way the nest works. You knew that."

Sissy looked horrified, like you do the first time you lose something in your life, the first time you understand that things can be lost. "She's upstairs," Sissy said, and was up in a flash, but I caught her with one wide sweep of my arm. She buried her face in my chest and cried, worse than she had as a baby, worse than she ever did with a fever. Her back heaved up again and again against my shirt and I rocked her and made clucking sounds. "Alice isn't gone," she sobbed.

"Alice is fine," I said. "She's A-number-one-okay. She just had to go with the baby." I wanted to eat her pain, take it into me and make it my own.

"I want her to come back," she cried.

"I'm sorry," I said.

"I want my mother," she cried.

"Here I am, baby," Rose said. "I'm right here."

But when Sissy looked at her she turned her face away. "No," she said, crying like it was the end of all the earth. "I want my mother."

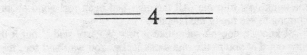

4

I TRIED TO STAY in the marines after I was shot. It was almost like somewhere in the back of my mind I knew that things would be worse, even worse than the hospital and doctors, once I got home. The bullet and the knee were nothing compared to what was coming. Remember, this was 1942, when everyone was going off to war, and the ones who came back to their hometowns wounded or crippled came back that way because they'd been fighting, not because they were screwing around on a marine base in the middle of the night.

So the first thing I said when I woke up in the hospital was, how long before I'm healed up and you can ship me over? It was stupid, because I knew the second that gun went off there wasn't going to be any war as far as I was concerned. The military takes their time in these sorts of things. Even when they knew how it was all going to go as clear as I did, they waited a couple of extra weeks to make sure. Or maybe they forgot for a while and then remembered. But finally I got the word and it was medical discharge. The hospital was pretty much empty. I had a whole ward to myself. It was so early in the war, guys hadn't been shipped back yet. I lied. I told them I had a feeling that when this thing healed up I was going to be good as new, so why didn't they just keep me around awhile and let me do what I could.

The marines may be slow to make up their minds, but once they do they never changed them. Even if I healed up all the way, they said, the chance of reinjury was too great. The hole in my knee was something that I'd have with me, to one degree or another, for the rest of my life.

And that was true, 'cause my foot turned in some and gave me a limp, but it doesn't bother me now unless the cold turns bitter. Even then, I don't think about it. I know there's some pain in my knee, but I never stop and think about where it came from.

I was entitled to a disability check. Seventeen dollars a month.

My parents drove all the way to South Carolina to pick me up. It took four marines to get me into the back of the station wagon, my leg stuck out straight. One of them was Perry, from the bunk next to mine. All the guys had been real good about coming to see me in the hospital.

"I know it doesn't seem like it now," Perry said, "but it'll turn out that you're the one that's lucky. You wait and see, the rest of us will go over there and get shot in places a whole lot worse than the knee."

"Don't say that," I told him. "This is good luck for all of you. Now one of us has been shot, the rest of you stiffs get off scot-free."

Perry asked me if I'd write to him every now and then. He didn't say it, but I knew it was because he didn't get a lot of mail, and I did write to him, pretty regular, until he was killed in forty-five. He survived several landings in the Pacific, but his luck ran out on Okinawa. He stood at the gates of the base and waved good-bye as I drove away with my parents.

"Everybody at home's been worried sick about you," my mother said. "It was in all the papers, even in Nashville. That boy, Bill Lovell—"

"Don't," I said.

"That's the last person he wants to talk about," my father said.

"It isn't that," I said. "It's just it was an accident, is all." I looked out the window and remembered everything we passed from the bus ride coming up. I hadn't even been gone long enough to forget the landscape. "There's no sense looking to place blame."

"Cecilia'll be awful glad to see you," my mother said.

"I got her letters."

"She said she was going to wait at our house until you got home, that she'd stay there all night if she had to."

I wanted to see Cecilia. I wanted to press my face into her hair and close my eyes. That was the part that made it all so crazy. Here I'd been waiting all this time to go away so I could get back and marry her and now I was coming back and I didn't want to be. It wasn't that I didn't want to marry her, I did more than ever. But I felt like I'd let her down, her personally, by getting shot in Parris Island instead of some island in the Pacific. I was never such a fool that I didn't know it was my enlisting that made her want me. We had a deal in a way, even if neither of us came out and said it. You make me proud and I'll be yours. Now that I wouldn't be living up to my half, I wondered if she was planning on living up to hers.

"You suppose she'll still want to go through with the whole thing?" I said.

"The wedding?" my father said.

"The wedding, sure, what with all of this."

My mother craned around in her seat so she could see me. "Oh, Son, you don't know what she's been through. You don't know how she's cried. We've all had our doubts about Cecilia, but I can tell you, things are different now."

"It's all made her grow up a lot," my father said.

"You wait and see," my mother said. "That's one thing you won't have to worry about."

I leaned my head against the backseat window and closed my eyes. Me and Cecilia getting married. I believed them, you know, I really did.

When we got home it was nearly three in the morning. It was a little harder getting out of the car than it was getting into it, on account of the fact there were no marines around to give us a hand, but we did it and I was up on my crutches and standing in front of my house. That's what I remember, trying to get up those steps the first time. I came into the living room and Cecilia was asleep on the sofa and I felt like it had been years since I'd seen her and for a minute I was glad about the way everything had gone because it meant I was getting to look at her asleep.

My mother went over and shook her shoulder gently and said, look who's here. Cecilia sat up and smiled faintly and looked around like she didn't know what she was supposed to be looking for. "Son," she said, almost surprised. "You're home."

I nodded, too glad and tired and miserable to say anything. She got up and put her arms around my waist and held me, and my parents stood and smiled. She felt warm, like a blanket wrapped around you in one place. Then my mother drove her home to her own house, her own bed, and my father helped me up the stairs to mine.

I hadn't been gone ten weeks, but when I woke up the next morning from a dream of Billy Lovell crying over me in the dirt, I felt too old to be in that room again. Nothing had changed, my high school pennant and one from Vanderbilt, the maple bed, the red bedspread, the rug and the curtains and Cecilia's junior class picture framed on the nightstand. I'm not saying I'd grown up so much since I'd been gone, though I had some to be sure. It was more that I didn't think I'd be back this way. I was going off to war and now the room was someplace I was supposed to visit and not live. I would come home from the war and marry Cecilia and we would live in a house of our own, a double bed, pots and pans, a radio. It was past ten o'clock, I had slept so late. I thought of all the guys, having run already, through with breakfast, and drilling on the grinder by now.

My mother knocked once on the door and then came in and sat on the edge of my bed. "You sleep all right?" she said.

I nodded. "Yourself?"

"Fine, having you back." She patted my hand. "I have some good news. I called Mr. Franklin, the principal, last week, once we knew for sure when you were coming back, and he said you can come back to school. The teachers will help you make up the work you've missed so that you can graduate on time. Truth is, they probably won't make you do all of it. He didn't come right out and say that, but it was the feeling I got."

"I can't go back to school," I said, not even thinking about it.

"Why not? You're home now."

"I'm too old to go back to high school."

"That's ridiculous," my mother said, standing up. "You aren't any older than you were when you left. You won't be any older than any of your friends. You'll graduate with your class, Son, right on time. You're going to have to make the best of what's happened."

But my friends, Joe Logan and Gary Allbrittan and Randy Todd, would all be gone. They left when I did, or a few days after. By the end of the year pretty much everyone had signed up. "I'll think about it," I said.

"There isn't anything to think about," she said. "Now come on and get up and get dressed. Cecilia called and she'll be here before too long. Do you need help?"

"No. Why isn't she in school?"

"It's Saturday," she said, and shut the door.

I struggled around with my clothes for a while, but it was all a little harder than I thought it would be. I was used to the nurses being there. Once you get over feeling embarrassed all the time you can see they're a whole lot of help. My leg liked being left alone, me on my back, it up on pillows, and no more movement than whatever breezes came through the room. The business of getting up and getting my clothes and twisting myself around trying to get into them set off a pain I hadn't felt in weeks. I sat back down on the bed and lifted the heavy cast up with both hands. I looked at it, lying there on the unmade bed. It wasn't my leg at all.

Then my father came in and he looked at it too. "Come on," he said, and he looped one of my arms over his neck and pulled me up slow. "Girlfriend's coming over," he said. "We might ought to get you in a tub first." My father was a big man, though not as big as I turned out to be. That year he would have been thirty-nine, since he was only twenty-two when I was born. It's something, to remember my father young like that, knowing I'm so much older now than he was on that day. We crowded into the bathroom, him and me and my cast, and he shut the door.

"Don't think I don't have any idea what I'm doing," he said, pulling my pajama top over my head. "I gave you plenty of baths in your day. Course, that was all a long time ago." He leaned over and turned on the water, slipping the little rubber stopper into place. He kept checking the temperature with his wrist. "Sit down here," he said, and eased me down onto the edge of the tub. "We don't want a lot of water."

The room must have felt good, it must have been warm, with the heat on and the steam from the bath and two grown men, but the only thing I remember feeling was ashamed. I don't know why now, because it was only my father, but at that moment I had let him down, too. Sitting half naked on the edge of the bathtub I wanted to cover myself. "I think I can take it from here," I said.

My father stepped back to get a good look at the whole picture. He was a contractor, he knew how things worked. "I can see you getting in okay, but I can't see you being able to get out."

"I'll manage."

"Well, chances are you would, but here's the thing, your mother was going to do this first and I stopped her, said I didn't think it was such a good idea. So if I mess it up, you know who'll be raising hell."

I nodded my head. He was right. I got good at doing things for myself, once the leg could stand to be jostled around a bit, but in my first week home I was dependent. I needed help. "Get out of these," my father said.

I lifted up my hips and he pulled down the bottoms of my pajamas and then carefully took them off my foot and then the cast. Then he put his arms around my chest and helped me to lower myself into the water, being careful not to get the cast wet. It wasn't hard, it didn't go much past my knee. "What in the hell is that?" my father said.

I looked over and saw him staring at my shoulder, at Cecilia's name. All the scabs had come off it while I was in the hospital. The nurses, who liked to tease me about it, took real good care to keep it clean. I thought that even as they said they didn't approve, they wouldn't have minded seeing their names on the arms of fellows they knew. "I got a tattoo," I said.

"I can see that."

"It was first liberty," I said. "We'd all been drinking."

My father sat back on his heels. "I thought about getting one of those, long time ago. Never got around to it." He looked again. "I wouldn't show your mother anytime soon, least not till she's through worrying about your knee." He smiled and shook his head. "You go off to boot camp and get yourself tattooed and get yourself shot. Most people don't do that much in a whole war."

By the time Cecilia came I was dry and dressed and sitting on the couch downstairs with my leg up. I wanted to run to her, pick her up and hold her, take her places we could be alone, tell her every thought I'd had those last ten weeks, every time I'd said her name aloud. But my mother came in with a tray of coffee and my sister Martha ran into the room to say hello. Cecilia was wearing the sweater I had given her for Christmas last year.

"I'm sorry I was so asleep when you came in last night," she said, sitting down on the edge of the couch, near my waist.

"It was late," I said.

"I barely even remember you coming in. I'd been waiting all that time and then when you finally came home I didn't even wake up all the way."

"I was pretty tired myself." I wanted to kiss her.

She looked at my cast for a minute, tapped the plaster lightly with one fingernail. "Does it hurt much?"

And I knew right then, though don't ask me how. She was planning on calling it off. I don't think she even knew it yet. My eyes kind of lost their focus, like she was still sitting in front of me but I couldn't quite see her anymore. "No," I said. "It's fine."

"Everybody at school's been worried. Your mom says you're coming back."

"I don't know yet. The leg's better off staying still."

"I could bring you the work," she said, and then for a second she caught my stare. It was right there. When a person has left you as many times as Cecilia left me, you could see it coming from miles away. The first thought of going makes a sound as clear as somebody saying your name. She laughed and turned her eyes up to the ceiling. "Stop that," she said, "you're embarrassing me."

"You're still wearing your ring," I said.

She held up her hand so that the stone caught the sun and let it go in little white circles around the room. "Why shouldn't I be?"

"You should be. That means we're going to get married. I want to get married now," I said. I wanted to keep saying it, like reminding her would make a difference.

Cecilia ran her finger up and down my cast. "We'll get married," she said. "Don't worry about that. Just worry about getting better. Once this is off we can talk about getting married."

"This isn't going to be off for a while," I said.

Cecilia just smiled. "What difference does it make?" she said. "We're not going anywhere."

Sometimes I try to imagine what life would have been like had I married Cecilia. I believe, in my better moments, that there is a plan and things go not the way we want them to but the way they should. If my life hadn't gone the way it did, with me finally leaving Ashland City, I never would have come to Habit. Then maybe Rose wouldn't have found someone to marry and maybe she would have given Sissy up and that was the thing that made all the events in my life up to the day she was born make sense. Before that, it hadn't come together, I hadn't been able to see things as part of something larger, the way my father would have. I could only see my own grief. But Sissy made everything worthwhile, suffering in the past, hard times ahead of us. It all made sense because it meant she stayed with us. Before, the only thing I'd wanted was a life that God did not intend for me to have. I suffered the loss of things that were never mine, a house with Cecilia, children and neighbors and anniversaries. Until I met Rose, I could never see how the whole thing fit together.

* * *

How much trouble my leg gave me exactly is hard to say, be-cause I told everyone it gave me so much I might have come to believe it. Too much to go into town, too much to try and drive, and too much to go to school. We were in the war now, and one by one there were names in the papers that we knew or the name of someone we didn't know but who lived in the next town, or dated your cousin once, or had your same last name. These were the ones who died, whose bodies came back or didn't. Every day I read the paper I would feel ashamed all over again, not so much for being alive, but for not having taken my chances right-fully. No one ever said this to me, even gave me the smallest cause to think it was true, but I was sure that people were think-ing by now that I had shot myself as a way of getting out. Some days I half wondered if I had.

I kept thinking the knee would take a turn and I would get back in. It was going to be a long war, everybody saw that now, and I thought there may still be time for me, but the knee wouldn't go along. Even when I finally got to moving around pretty well on my own, I could tell I was a long way from running off a landing craft onto a beach. Years off.

My school agreed to let me work at home, and every day Cecilia would bring me my lessons and the notes she'd taken in class. In truth, I was glad to have the work to do. It kept me busy. I was really a much better student those last months than I ever had been before. I sat at the kitchen table all day now, my leg stretched over several chairs, and I read books and worked long math problems in a notebook. My mother never bothered me. Until three o'clock every afternoon she treated me like I was in school.

Then at three Cecilia came. All day long I would watch the clock and think about where she was, in science class, in his-tory, at lunch, walking over the school lawn, stopping to talk to a friend, winding her way slowly toward my house. At first she would get to the house quickly, half out of breath. She would tell me what everyone had said and done that day, acting out both sides of every conversation. She would hold my hand as she talked and sometimes her engagement ring would slip to one side and bite into my fingers.

But there was a war going on, and it didn't take long to see men who had been hurt while fighting. I imagine she met men, too, ones who were just getting ready to go off. Me and my leg, stretched out in my parents' kitchen, didn't look quite as interesting, and Cecilia started to come late. Some days she didn't come, but sent somebody else instead.

Time went by slowly and winter seemed longer than I had ever remembered it being, but by the spring I was just wearing a light brace and could get around pretty well with a cane. I'd go for short walks through the neighborhood at night, waiting until it was late enough that I wouldn't have to stop and explain myself to everyone I passed. Sometimes I would stand stock-still in the driveway and shoot free throws into the hoop my father had put up on the garage when I was ten. Every time the ball went through, one of my sisters would run and catch it and bring it back to me.

Sometimes I would ask Cecilia about the wedding, but she would always say, when your cast is off or after graduation or not until you find a good job. We were breaking up, but the thing was, it wasn't like all the other times before. We were breaking up but she wasn't leaving. Cecilia sat the closest to me when my parents were in the room, and when I went for walks she wanted to come with me. And since I wanted her, needed her more than I ever had before, I took every act of kindness as a chance that things would work out after all.

But when we were alone she'd nearly pull her hair out in frustration. By the last month of school it was all she could do to drop my books on the table and go.

"I don't know why you can't pick up your things yourself," she said one day when she was giving me a math assignment. "Everyone knows your leg is fine."

"It is?"

"You're going to sit right there for the rest of your life, let everybody else take care of you. Well, not me. I'm not going to do it."

"You think this is all a joke? You think I should go down and reenlist?"

Cecilia looked so angry. She was hugging her notebook to her chest. I watched the ring on her hand. It was always there. I hadn't seen her take it off once, not since I put it on her. "Yes," she said slowly. "That's exactly what I think."

I tensed the muscles in my leg. Tense, release, tense, release, just like the doctor told me. "I want to," I said. "There's nothing in the world I want more. It's the only thing that could make half a difference to you, so you've got to know by now that I'd do it if I could."

She wouldn't say a word. Her face was as cold as anything I'd ever seen in my life.

"What I want to know," I said quietly, because in truth a big part of me didn't want to know, "is why you keep coming around. If this whole thing is making you so crazy then why do you bother?"

"What am I going to do? Have everyone in town say I broke off my engagement because you got shot?" She pulled out a chair and sat down at the table across from me. "It's all I ever think about. People at school, my parents, they keep saying how they all know this must be so hard for you and how great I am, helping you along. I hate it, you know? I really hate it. I feel sometimes like I'm already stuck in a marriage and I'm not even married yet." Then all of a sudden she looked up and stopped talking. It was like she realized that she was saying these things to the enemy, the person she was trying to get away from. She picked up her books and left without so much as a good-bye.

This is how crazy I was: I thought, if that's the reason she's staying, at least she's staying.

The principal of our school, Mr. Franklin, came to the house to give me my exams. He seemed to understand my not wanting to come back, and so he never suggested it, even though by that point everyone knew I could have returned to classes. "I've been going over your work, Son," he said, bringing out a file of papers I'd written. My mother put a cup of coffee down on the table for him and then left the room, even though it was clear she wanted to stay. Mr. Franklin spooned two sugars into his coffee. "I think you should consider college. You've done very well, now that you've stopped concentrating on athletics."

It's nothing but sheer vanity that makes me say this. Rose, I bet, would laugh if I told her that someone once said that I should go to college. But Mr. Franklin did.

The weekend before graduation it turned fiercely hot out of nowhere. Late May, nobody could figure it out. My mother was up in the attic getting down the last of the summer clothes, packing the sweaters away in mothballs. My father was working a lot, because that's the busy time of year for contracting. Cecilia came by when she knew my family was going to be around, because she'd come to a point where the idea of being alone with me was more than she could stand. As much as I tried to figure out what to do about it all, I couldn't. The truth is, I had started to hate her a little. I looked forward to her visits less and less. I was feeling half as trapped by the whole thing as she was. But it never occurred to me that I could have come not to want her. That wasn't the way it worked between us. I wanted her and she decided. That was the way things went.

So on that hot Saturday when she showed up at the house and found me on the couch reading, I'd just as soon she hadn't come at all. I wanted to find out what was going to happen in the next chapter, and she was working so hard to make it clear to me that she was sorry she was with me that I was half ready to throw the book at her. Then my father came in and said to her, "Cecilia, will you please get this boy out of the house? Take him down to the quarry, get some sun on him. He looks like the underside of a rock."

"I can't swim yet," I said. "It doesn't sound like much fun."

"You don't have to swim," my father said. "Just get some air, get out. Take the station wagon. Cecilia can drive you."

Cecilia looked at me, told me in her way, get me out of this. "That sounds like a good idea," she said.

"Cecilia doesn't have her suit," I said.

"So she'll borrow one from Martha. You're sounding like an old man, Son. You can't spend your whole life indoors."

So Cecilia went up to my sister's room and put her swimsuit on and then put her clothes back on top. I had to ride in the backseat with my leg up because my knee still didn't take to being bent. I waited for her in the car and when she got in she didn't say anything and I didn't say anything, she just drove to the quarry.

What I remember best was the heat. It felt good, the way the first few hot days will after a long, wet spring. The sun seemed to go right into your bones and work the winter out of you. I spread a blanket out on the ground and tossed my book down. Everything took me twice as long then, and Cecilia only stood there and watched. "I can't believe nobody's here," she said. "A day like this."

"It's early," I said. I pulled my shirt off over my head and stretched out on the ground. Cecilia took off her dress and stood there for a minute in my sister's bathing suit, which was too big for her. "What's that on your arm?" she said, leaning closer.

It was her name. I had never told her about the tattoo. I figured I would show it to her on our wedding night.

"Jesus," she said, reading it over and over again. "How could you have done that?"

"It was when I was in boot camp. I was drunk."

"Jesus." She walked away, toward the water. "Does anybody know about it?"

"My father's seen it, the guys in boot camp, a couple of nurses. That's about it."

"Your father's seen this? I can't believe you. Who would do a stupid thing like that?"

"It wasn't a stupid thing. We were getting married, I was in love. I got a tattoo." I started to stand up, but I don't know why.

"Stay there," she said, her voice full of anger. "Don't talk to me. Don't look at me." She walked into the water and then turned around again. "That's my name," she said. "You can't just go putting it wherever you want." And then she was gone, underwater, swimming out toward the center of the quarry.

I looked at her name for a while, tried to remember what I had been thinking that night. I loved her. I loved her even as she was swimming away from me, even as I was hating her. That's the way it is, when you've loved somebody your whole life. It's like a direction you go in, even when you don't want to go anymore. I lay back on the blanket and closed my eyes and felt the sun on my face. I listened to the sound of Cecilia's even strokes through the water and occasionally the sound of her diving from one of the rocks and thought, she'll stay out there her whole life rather than come onto dry land with me.

I read for a while and then lay on my stomach to watch Cecilia swim. She had been out there a long time. I don't know if an hour had passed, or two, but my skin was tight and red and I shaded my eyes with my hand to watch her dive. I thought that she must have gone down deep because she didn't come up. Then she did, came up and flipped her wet yellow hair aside and waved her hand and I started to wave to her. I couldn't remember if I was angry at her at that moment or not, and then she was gone again, back under the water. I found my cane and stood up. My leg was stiffer for lying still. Again she came up and her head was thrown back and her neck was long and wet in the midday light and smeared with a bright streak of red coming down from her forehead. Her mouth made one terrible round O. She was pulling air in, as much as she could get before going down again, which she did. The water set itself right almost immediately, smoothing over the place she had been so quick it was like nothing was going on at all. Nothing was wrong. It was like watching something very far away, something that had happened years before, even while it was happening right in front of me. She broke the surface again. She didn't make a sound, other than the splashing, because she wanted to save her lungs for taking air in, not forcing it out. Her wild eyes passed over me and suddenly I understood. That was still Cecilia and I was still here. It wasn't yet something that had happened, but something that was happening, and even as I understood this I stood there. I took a full minute to watch her suffer and watch her want me as I had wanted her all my life. Then I went into the water with my shoes and pants and brace.

The leg pulled down, but I was swimming. I did not see Cecilia. She had said as much with her eyes, that that had been her last time up. I dove down, let the weight of the leg carry me, and felt along the bottom in darkness. Huge rocks jutted up and I traced around them with my hands. The water made its own world, and I remember thinking this is where I'm going to die. I pushed myself up again and breathed like Cecilia. I made sure it was the right spot and then went down to feel the silt and rocks, some branches blown in by storms. I felt the pressure of the water, the way my leg pinned me there to the bottom. I came up again and gulped the air and thought how much bigger I was than Cecilia, how much more these lungs could take in. The third time down her hand brushed my face, not at the bottom but resting on the top of some branches, and I took it and pulled it up with me, forced her head above the water as if it would make a difference and I screamed, "Somebody help me." I was pulling two weights back, Cecilia and the leg and they both wanted me under. I put one arm beneath her arms and pulled myself backward, calling again and again until someone called back. A family I could barely see crested the hill when we were still twenty feet out and by the time the man had made it to the edge of the water, we were pretty much there. He only had to get wet up to his knees pulling us in.

I knew those people, they went to church with us. There was a basket of food on the ground that they had dropped and the mother was pressing her two children into her skirt so they couldn't see Cecilia's face, which was cut along her left temple. Her mouth was still in that same O. I lay back on the bank with her on top of me. Martha's swimsuit was half falling off of her it was so big, as if the water had made Cecilia even smaller. The man, Mr. Thompson, I can't remember now what he did for a living, he was trying to pull my arm off of her but I couldn't seem to help him. He was pushing on her chest, pushing her back into my chest, trying to work the water out of her lungs.

Her hair spread out against my chest, so much longer and darker than it was when it was dry. The wife asked should she go and call for somebody but the husband said no, we should take her in ourselves.

"Come on, Son," he said. "Get up now." He helped me up and Cecilia just came with me and I knew the day was hot but I couldn't feel it anymore. I took her legs in my other arm and we walked back toward their car. The mother stayed behind. She wouldn't let the children in the car with us and they were crying. My knee was starting to swell and I was ashamed that I even knew how much it hurt.

Mr. Thompson opened the door of his car for me. "Come on," he said. He was a young man but he looked so old to me. He was sweating and his hair was slicked down against his head. "Get in the car," he said.

But I couldn't. I just stood there.

"Son," he said. "We need to get going."

"I'm soaking wet," I said. "I'll get your car all wet." It was the first thing I had said and my voice felt strange coming out of my mouth, like it had been months since I'd tried to speak.

"Don't worry about that." He helped me inside. He put us in the back, where we'd have more room. There were a couple of toys on the floor, a yellow dump truck, some other things. When I sat down Cecilia's head fell back against my shoulder and I remembered one night we were coming home from a football game and she was starting to get a cold and got so tired waiting for me to shower and change that I said I'd carry her home. When I picked her up in my arms she went to sleep right away, like a baby. I carried her home and took her in the house and her mother didn't say a word, but led me upstairs to her room. I laid Cecilia in her bed and watched her mother take off her shoes and cover her up with a blanket and we both backed out of the room together so we wouldn't wake her up.

The cut on her forehead didn't look so bad. It wasn't bleeding at all. It looked as clean as a tear made in paper. She was just so white, all her skin was cold and puckered from the water. All her skin was showing with just that bathing suit on, her legs and arms, her neck. I had never seen so much of her before, and it made me look away. I rocked her a little and said "Shhhhh," but I can't imagine why.

Mr. Thompson didn't say anything driving over, or maybe he did. He was driving fast and people were blowing their horns at us. We got to Dr. Smith's office and there was a lot of commotion once we got inside. People who'd been waiting to see the doctor were trying to take her out of my arms but I just couldn't let go of her. Mr. Thompson was crying then, I saw him.

"She drown," he said. "Son here tried to save her but she hit her head and drown the quarry."

It was the middle of the day and still so pretty outside. Even inside the light was coming in everywhere.

Then finally Dr. Smith came up to me and said, "If we're going to help her, you're going to have to let her go." And I heard help her, and my arm fell away and he took her off so fast. Martha's swimsuit going through the door. It was pink and nubby and soft and too big for Cecilia. I don't know what made her think it would fit.

They put me in, too. They wouldn't let me go home. Mr. Thompson went back to the quarry for his family. The nurse took me to a little room in the back where I took off my clothes and lay down. She said she was going to have to give me something for my knee. And then she did.

For the second time that year I was in the local papers as the victim of the worst kind of luck. Except this time I was a hero. One paper even said, "Marine Risks All in Attempt to Save Wife's Life." So many people got it wrong that I started to realize they were doing it on purpose. It sounded better to say we were just married. The people in Ashland City felt real bad for me when I got shot, but as time went on and their sons went to war and I was home in my parents' house, maybe they thought my deal wasn't so tragic after all. At least I was safe. But when Cecilia died, a wave of grief went up from every corner of the town, and the grief was as much for me as it was for her. I had loved her for as long as anyone could remember, for as long as I could remember. And when she had finally agreed to marry me everyone was happy and they said no one had ever waited for a girl the way I had and no one deserved her more. Our wedding would have been so crowded that people would have had to stand on the steps outside the church, they would have spilled out onto the street, all of them waiting to catch sight of us because they felt in some small way like they had a personal stake in the whole thing.

Folks made two casseroles, two hams, two pies, one for Cecilia's family and one for mine. They told the story to one another in our living rooms: Son had fallen asleep. His leg had been giving him a lot of pain that day and he could hardly walk. He fell asleep while Cecilia was swimming. It was such a hot

day, not like May at all. Anyone crippled, anyone outside on
such a day would have fallen asleep. But when she called out he
woke up and ran right into the water, forgetting about the leg
and the brace, forgetting that he could barely walk and couldn't
swim at all he went right into the water and pulled her out but
by the time he got there it was too late.

I stood in the kitchen. As much as I tried not to hear them,
as softly as they spoke, I must have heard it fifty times.

When they came up onto the shore he couldn't let go of her,
of her *body*. Yes, that's what Jim Thompson told me. He just
lay there and held her and he kept saying, somebody help me,
even after they were on shore and she was dead I know, it breaks
my heart, too.

The weather stayed nice all week, not as hot, but warm and
clear. The day that they buried her was so nice that it just made
no sense at all. There were enough flowers blooming already to
do the whole thing up real pretty. Those are the only two things
that I remember about that day at all. The flowers were nice and
the weather was nice.

People were getting used to the whole idea of funerals in
1942. My suit was hanging on the back of my closet door all the
time, one memorial service or another. But that was soldiers
dying, and while I don't mean to say that isn't as bad, it was
something you were ready for in a way. Cecilia drowning caught
everybody off guard. It just wasn't the time for that kind of loss.
No one took it well, my father least of all. He couldn't get past
the fact that he had sent us out there, talked us into going when
clearly neither of us wanted to. He blamed himself so bitterly
that I came close to telling him the truth. He wasn't the one who
killed Cecilia.

Over the years I came to live with this, came to believe even
that maybe there was a difference between killing someone and
watching them die. But at the time it was as good as if I'd held
her under the water myself, took her into the quarry and pinned
her there and watched her look up at me with disbelief then fear
then not at all. For days after her death I waited for the sheriff
to come for me. I would hear him telling my father at the door,
I would hear my father say no. When he came for me I never
knew what I wanted, if it would be better to go along and have
it be over or would there still be time enough for me to run out
the back door and get away. Tall and lame both, I couldn't have
gone too far. I didn't want to go to prison, that was the truth.

Even if it meant having some peace from my own nightmares, I was too afraid.

The other thing I dreamed about was this: saving Cecilia the first time she went under. In the dream I went into the water and pulled her out, pushed the water from her chest like Mr. Thompson did, but this time her eyes flicked open and she saw me and was thankful. At that moment Cecilia would have loved me the way she had on Pearl Harbor Day, except this time she owed me her life and so the love never changed. For a long time I believed this would have been true, and then I came to realize that, true or not, she was dead and I'd never have the chance to know for sure.

I never did tell either of these things to anyone. I just got quieter. It didn't take long for me to forget I had ever been anything but happy with Cecilia. I could see it on every tree I went by, her name carved in like a reminder of something to do. I could see it on my own shoulder, and I got to where I couldn't stand it anymore.

By the fall my knee seemed about as good as it was going to get and I told my parents I was leaving.

"Leaving for where?" my mother said.

"Doesn't matter." I couldn't bring myself to sit down at the table with them. I stood by the stove and pushed my hand through my hair over and over again. I talked to my folks so little back then that I'd already put off going for a long time because I didn't know how to tell them exactly.

"You can't just go," my mother said, sort of half smiling 'cause she was trying to keep it all from getting away from her. "We need to know where you are, how you're doing."

"I'd tell you if I knew," I said, slowly. "I just don't."

"These are hard times, Son," my mother said. "Hard times for all of us. There's been more pain for you than anyone thought possible, but it won't be different anywhere else. You're better off here, with people who love you."

My father was looking inside his cup of coffee, moving the handle back and forth as he listened. "You go if you need to go," he said. My mother looked up at him and lost the end of her smile. I looked up, too. "I want you to stay," he said. "But she's everywhere. I know that."

I felt such relief at that moment that I almost changed my mind about going. The fact that someone had seen it too, my father had seen it, gave me the closest thing to joy I'd had since her death.

If he understood, then maybe he knew this too: when she died they lost me. I would have to go away. A better man would have seen things through, stayed in town and sorted it all out. People die, terrible things happen. I know this now. You can't pick up and leave everything behind because there is too much sadness in the world and not enough places to go. But at seventeen, I didn't understand, and so I left.

For a long time I stayed in Tennessee, sometimes dipping down into Alabama or up into Kentucky. Once I got as far as Indiana. I can't much remember what I did where, it all pretty much runs together in my mind. Work was easy to find because I said I was a marine and had been shot. I had a limp to prove that. There was a shortage of men my age, so there was always something for me. For this same reason, women were easy to find, too. Some I stayed with for a night, others a week or two. I stayed until they wanted me to leave or, worse even, until they wanted me not to. I know I should have cared for them more than I did, but it just wasn't in me. All I wanted was to keep going. I didn't mind not having one place to live, I thought it was right. I didn't make friends or enemies either in that time. I did my jobs well, and people said so. I was good at carrying out orders.

Then one day I was hitching to Owensboro for no reason in particular and the truck I was riding in broke down near Habit. I walked into town and asked around about work and some people said if I had the stomach for it I should go down to Saint Elizabeth's. The folks in Habit didn't cotton much to Catholics back then, or to pregnant girls without husbands, though in those days they were mostly girls who got in trouble right as their fellow was going off to war and then he didn't come home.

I walked a couple of miles in the direction they pointed me and came on a neat little white house off of the road. It was smaller than I thought it would be and in good shape, which meant there wouldn't be a lot of work. I knocked on the door and a woman in her forties who was still good-looking answered.

"Evening," I said. "Is this Saint Elizabeth's?"

She laughed a little. "No, no," she said. "Over there." She pointed to a break in the woods. "In the back pasture, that way. You looking for somebody?"

"Just work."

She nodded. "I thought so. You don't look like the regular customer they get over there."

My face flushed and I turned away from her.

"You should give them a holler," she said. "They're good people. Always looking for somebody to do things."

"Much obliged," I said, and started to turn off the porch.

"You from around here?" she said.

"No, ma'am."

She looked at me hard. "I didn't think I recognized you. This is a small town. I guess I know about everybody."

"Yes, ma'am."

"We could use some new blood around here."

I nodded. "I'll be heading over there, then," I said, but when I got into her yard she called me back again. I turned around.

"What's your name?" she said.

"Son."

"Well, Son, I'm June. When you go over there, you tell them June Clatterbuck says to give you a job."

"Obliged."

"Then you come back here later and tell me how it went, you hear?"

I said I would, and I did. June Clatterbuck was the first friend I made in Habit.

I'll never forget the sight of the place, the very first time I laid eyes on it from the entrance of the drive. I forget how pretty it is. It's all just work to me now. But that night it was around six o'clock and just getting dark. The light caught in every one of the front windows and made it seem half on fire. Saint Elizabeth's was far and away the biggest place I'd ever seen in my life, and when I walked up toward it I was really hoping there'd be something for me to do so I'd have the chance to look around some in the morning. That and the fact it was getting late and I needed a place to sleep.

It was a smaller operation then, seven girls and Sister Evangeline and another Sister named Mary Joseph, who has long since passed away. Sister Evangeline was mother superior back then, but since there were just the two of them, she never brought it up to anybody.

I rang the bell, and Sister Mary Joseph answered the door. She smiled up at me. She was a real sweet woman, Sister Mary Joseph, and she said, "What can I do to help you?" That's just what she said, first thing, and that's the way she meant it, too. So I told her I was looking for work, and she said I'd have to talk to Sister Evangeline. She asked me my name and told me hers. "She's having supper now," she said. "We're all having supper. Have you eaten?" I told her I hadn't, and with that she opened the door wider and let me in. You've got to remember this was a long time ago, when folks treated each other decently without knowing them.

I followed her into the dining room where everyone was sitting together at one table. The seven girls looked down at the napkins in their laps when Sister Mary Joseph introduced me and I remember I felt so awful, like I'd caught them all half dressed or something. Back then we used to say a girl was in a family way, and the thought of that seemed so sad because here were all these girls with no families to speak of. I wanted to tell them that I should go, or at least wait in the other room until they were finished eating, but I was so embarrassed that I couldn't even speak, and when Sister Mary Joseph led me to a chair there was nothing I could do but sit in it and accept my plate.

Sister Evangeline must have been around fifty then, but she was still pretty much the same. The little tuft of hair that stuck out from the front of her wimple was brown instead of white and maybe she wasn't as heavy, but she chattered a lot and filled up people's plates with food they weren't hungry for. She tried to ask me some questions over dinner, but it was all I could do to choke out the smallest yes or no. After a while she just gave up.

"Maybe Mr. Abbott will help with the dishes tonight and give you girls a rest," she said after we had eaten our tapioca pudding.

Sister Mary Joseph gathered the girls together and led them out into the lobby. Not one of them said a word. I helped Sister Evangeline pick up the plates and took them into the kitchen. It's almost impossible for me to think about that kitchen now without Rose being in it, but this was 1944 and Rose hadn't even been born yet.

"You don't need to do the dishes," Sister Evangeline said once the door swung shut behind us. "I just thought it might be better for us to talk alone."

"I'd like to do them," I said. It always made me feel better, doing something to earn my keep. I turned on the hot water and stacked them in the sink.

"What kind of work are you looking for?" she asked. She was wiping down the counters but not paying a lot of attention to what she was doing and she kept missing spots.

"I'll do whatever you've got, wiring, plumbing, painting. My father's a contractor. He taught me how to do a little bit of everything."

She nodded. "That's what we need around here, a little bit of everything. I could pay you out of petty cash for a while, then write the bishop and see if there's money for bigger jobs. We've needed help around here. It's been hard getting somebody from town."

"I don't need to stay on," I said. "I'm really just passing through." I ran a couple of plates under the water and stacked them in the dish rack.

"Headed where?"

"No place special," I said, and then I was worried 'cause I didn't want to sound like a vagrant. "I like traveling, is all."

"And you don't like the war?" she said, but in a nice way.

"I got shot in the knee," I said. "I'm not much good to them anymore."

She nodded. "I see," she said. "But you didn't get shot in the war."

I never said exactly. I always liked to tell it so people would think that's what I meant without my having to lie. "No," I said. "I was shot in basic training. It was an accident."

She smiled and patted my hand. "Don't mind me," she said. "I'm just interested. You, for example. You don't seem like someone who's been to war, which is why I asked you that. That's the kind of thing that's easy to tell about a person."

"You can tell things about everybody?"

"No, no." She waved me off, trying to pretend for a second like she was shy, but she couldn't make it work. "I know a lot about babies, they're my specialty. But sometimes I can tell things about grown people. There are things anyone can tell, if they pay attention. Like you're not a traveler. That's not your nature at all. Everything about you says that you're the kind of man to stay in one place. Now what about that?"

"Maybe," I said, not feeling too comfortable. "I used to be, but people change."

"Exactly," she said, very happy, like we were playing some sort of game where the point was for her to guess things about me. She picked up a plate and dried it a little and then set it back in the rack like maybe she'd decided she wasn't so interested in drying after all. "So what we know about you is that you used to be a person who stayed in one place, and that place was Tennessee because I can tell from your accent. I'd even go so far as to say middle Tennessee. Then you enlisted for the war because you wanted to defend your country. You seem like a good man, and that's what a good man would do, but there was an unfortunate accident and you were sent home for your knee to get better. And after that, something happened, that wasn't about the war or the knee and that was the thing that made you a traveler. The bad thing was something else entirely.''

I stared at her. My hands were in the water but they weren't washing dishes, they were just in the water and all of the sudden the feeling was so familiar that I felt those same words come up in my mouth, Help me, somebody, but instead I said yes, it was something else.

Sister Evangeline looked at me straight in the eye and said, ''And that something wasn't your fault.'' And then she put her hands down in the water and held my hands.

5

EVER SINCE I got married and Sissy was born, I never saw Miss June as much as I would have liked. Work kept me busy, same as ever, but now instead of spending my evenings wandering around, hoping to find somebody who was up and maybe willing to sit and talk for a while, I stayed at home. It was the only time I got to really see Sissy and Rose, when they weren't surrounded by a dozen different people pulling on them and wanting their attention. Course, I was going over there a lot, picking Sissy up or dropping her off. We went to June's for dinner every once in a while, and Rose got over to see her some. Sissy was ten then, and she and June got along real well, but I hardly got over there just to visit the way I used to and I felt bad about that. I looked after her though. I always cleaned her gutters in the spring and put her storms up for her in the fall. I kept up with her lawn just like the rest of the property. But still, I should have sat with her more. All the time she put in with me when I didn't know anyone in town. Until she died, I'd forgotten how much I'd relied on her.

It came quick, a stroke. "I don't mind a stroke," Miss June told me once, "so long as it takes me out clean. What I'm afraid of is one that will leave me crippled up, dependent on somebody." It came to her over lunch and she died in her kitchen. Sister Evangeline found her at two o'clock when she went over to watch their show together like they did every afternoon. She came into my workroom, not going fast or even out of breath.

"June's dead," she told me.

I looked up. The sun was square behind her and I couldn't see a thing. "Dead?"

"In her kitchen. You better come on."

I put down my screwdriver and balanced myself against the workbench. "You call an ambulance?"

"She's dead," Sister Evangeline said, "not sick."

I walked back through the pasture with Sister and she held onto my arm. No one could be sure how old Sister was, though by my calculations she must have been well past eighty by then. She didn't seem more than seventy most days. It was only when she was up and around for too long that I even thought about her age. "Why don't you wait back up at the hotel?" I asked Sister.

"No sense you going alone," she said. She puffed a little bit, so I slowed down. She took small, careful steps and what with her being five feet tall and me just at six seven, it was hard for us to get matched up.

We went in June's front door, which was open on account of the weather being so nice. Everything in her house was neat, put right in its place. The sun fell over the living room carpet and showed up how the cabbage roses had faded. "In here," Sister Evangeline said, and walked into the kitchen.

June was lying on the floor and her chair was turned over. The way her mouth was tensed made me think she'd felt some pain at the last. Sister Evangeline squatted down and closed June's eyes with two fingers. Then she picked up her hand and held it for a minute. "I wish it was me," she said kind of matter-of-factly.

"Don't say that."

She stayed down there awhile, just watching her. "Help me up, Son. I never should have gotten down like this." I leaned over and put my hands under her arms to straighten her up. She was a solid little thing, no doubt about that. "You take her in and put her on the couch so she looks comfortable and I'll call the funeral home." She sighed, looked at the table, and then smiled. "She was eating liverwurst," she said, pointing to the sandwich still sitting on the plate. "That's good."

I picked June up and carried her into the living room like Sister told me. She didn't weigh any more than Sissy. It was an awful thing to never really have the chance to hold somebody until she was dead. I put her on the couch. She did look better there.

"Hank's coming over," Sister Evangeline said, hanging up the phone. "He said we should wait here with her. It won't take him five minutes." I helped Sister down into the chair that had been June's and then sat down myself.

"This is awful," I said.

"People die," she said. But I knew it was even harder for her. June was old. Not quite as old as Sister, but old enough for her to talk about the way things had been in these parts when they were growing up. They were friends. Going to June's every day was what Sister looked forward to, and now that was gone. June was gone.

"She wanted to be a Catholic," Sister Evangeline said to me. I was surprised, I guess, seeing as how much trouble the Catholics had given the Clatterbucks over the years. "A hundred times she said that and I used to always say I'd give her instruction, but she just couldn't seem to get around to it. It was almost like she was scared. I should have pressed her, maybe."

"Naw," I said quietly, "can't press a person on something like that."

She nodded. "I guess that's right." Then she bent her head down toward her chest and she said, "Eternal rest, grant unto her, O Lord, and may perpetual light shine upon her. May her soul and all the souls of the faithfully departed rest in peace. Amen." She kept on saying it, over and over again, until Hank came up from the funeral home.

By the time we got back to Saint Elizabeth's, Sister Evangeline was pretty worn out. "What's wrong?" Rose said, soon as she saw us. She was fixing dinner and pots were boiling all over the place. Her apron was covered in flour.

"June's dead," Sister said. "I'm going to lie down."

Rose moved toward her, but Sister put up her hand. "No, honey, I'm fine. I'm just tired is all. Let me go on. Son'll tell you what happened." She moved off down the hall with her little shuffling steps.

"June?" Rose said.

I nodded my head. "Just this afternoon."

Rose sat down and I took her hand. "Poor Sister," she said, and then added, "poor June."

They buried her with her family, just the way she wanted. All the girls came, even though most of them had never met her. They had all read the plaque in front of the hotel. Everybody felt they owed June the respect. It was always strange to see the girls outside of Saint Elizabeth's. When they were in the hotel or just walking around the grounds, I never noticed them being pregnant. After a while, you know, you just stop seeing some things. But whenever we went out it was like every girl was standing in a spotlight, and all together they made a wall of round bellies that was nearly impossible not to stare at. The dresses only really fit on one or two of them. The others were wearing things too big or too tight, like they had grown some on the bus coming over. They bowed their heads and said their prayers and tried to ignore the people who were staring at them. Habit and Saint Elizabeth's didn't have occasion to mix much, but June Clatterbuck's funeral was something that brought out everyone from both sides of town. Things had gotten better. People didn't mind the sight of pregnant girls the way they used to. The nuns still made them uncomfortable, their long white dresses and their habits flapping behind them like bed sheets on a line, but since there were television shows about nuns now, and a movie from time to time, people were a little more accustomed to the idea of women who were married to God.

I stood there with my hands folded. The town stood on one side of the open grave and we stood on the other: pregnant girls, nuns, and one man too tall to blend in anyplace. Miss June would have gotten a kick out of it, her funeral making such strange bedfellows.

"Right beside her mother and father," Sister Evangeline said to me. "She never got over missing them, not till the day she died."

"Jesus owes us nothing," the preacher said, "and still He gives us all. He gave June Clatterbuck her life for more than seventy years. He gave us all June to know and love. We have witnessed His goodness through her." He looked at our side for a minute and then back to the ground. "Hell awaits the sinners," he said. "June walks with the Lord."

Sissy leaned over and scratched a mosquito bite on her ankle. She'd been crying off and on. I wanted to pick her up, but she only would've fussed at me. "I'm not a baby, Dad," she'd say every time I tried to pick her up now. It was true, she was getting so big you would have thought she was twelve, all legs and arms. She went to school in town and most of her friends and their parents were there. I could tell she was a little embarrassed standing with us. She would have liked to have been on the other side with the Baptists, even though she was taking being a Catholic very seriously because the nuns were always giving her rosary beads and holy cards and she liked those things a lot. She'd been good through the whole funeral, stood up straight and was quiet. She didn't complain about having to wear a dress or her stiff shoes like she did when she went to mass in the ballroom or up in Owensboro. June was the first one to see Sissy turn over and she heard her first words. Sister Evangeline fussed with Sissy's hair, picking at it like it was full of straw, and Sissy didn't even seem to mind that.

"Sad stuff," Sister said.

Sissy looked over at the place where the ground was dug up. "Why isn't he saying any of the prayers right?" she whispered to me, but I put my finger to my lips and she was quiet.

As soon as the service was over Mother Corinne clapped her hands twice to gather everyone together. "All right, girls," she said. "We need to start back." You could tell Mother Corinne didn't take to things not Catholic. It made her nervous, standing in the Baptist cemetery with a preacher.

We all climbed on board the Baptist Sunday school bus to go home. They'd sent it for us, which I thought was real decent of them. The last of the Clatterbucks was gone. The last real proof that there had ever been a spring that healed the sick. It would all be the church's now, just like the church had been saying it was all those years.

Sissy wanted to sit next to Rose on the bus. It was funny how I could always tell what she was thinking. I don't know if it was just because she was mine or if all kids were easy to figure out. She was trying to get in line right behind her, but then at the last minute Rose stepped back to wait for Sister Evangeline and help her on. Sissy sat down next to me and then kneeled on her seat, peering back to watch Rose.

"Can we go swimming later?" she asked her mother.

"You don't go swimming after a funeral," Rose said. "Turn around and sit down."

"Then I can't see you."

"So you can't see me," Rose said. "I'm not going anywhere. Sit."

Sissy sat down and swung her legs back and forth. I figured she was wishing she was behind Rose now so she could kick the back of her seat. That was the kind of thing Sissy loved to do to drive Rose crazy. Sissy didn't seem to care if the attention she got from her mother was good or bad, as long as Rose knew she was there.

"I hate this," Sissy said, but I didn't know what she meant: hated the funeral or death or her mother or having to ride home on a bus. She picked up my arm and arranged it over her shoulder until she was comfortable. "I wouldn't ever want to be buried," she said.

"I know what you mean."

"What if she wakes up later? What if they're wrong about her being dead."

"They weren't wrong," I said. "I saw her. I made sure they didn't make a mistake."

"Everybody makes mistakes," Sissy said.

The lawyer who called was from Owensboro. There wasn't a lawyer in Habit, which was fine by me. He said I should come up and talk to him about June Clatterbuck's will.

"What about it?" I said.

"You've been left an inheritance," the man said.

Wills depressed me, more than funerals even. The idea of dividing things up once a person was dead gave me a weird sort of chill.

"Come tomorrow," the lawyer said. "You and your wife should both come."

"I can't go to Owensboro," Rose said when I told her. "Who'll make lunch?"

"I'm sure somebody could do it."

"No," she said. "Whatever it is, you can take care of it. It was good of June to think of us, but I don't see any sense in both of us taking the day off to go sign papers."

"It might be good for us, taking an afternoon off. We never do get up to Owensboro anymore."

The truth is, Rose and I never went anywhere anymore. Rose never went anywhere. She cooked seven days a week, three meals a day. She didn't get sick or take vacations, she didn't even miss breakfast every now and then. She always had a couple of girls to help her, chopping things or washing dishes, but it was her kitchen now. Sister Evangeline stayed with her all day, but mostly in an old armchair I'd moved in from the card room. She'd sit and shell peas and talk to Rose. Sometimes she'd tell her what she'd like to have for supper, or she'd make a banana pudding just to keep her hand in things. Mother Corinne avoided the kitchen whenever possible, coming only rarely to complain about something. She still gave the grocery money to Sister Evangeline, who gave it to Rose. I knew it worried Mother Corinne, how much they needed Rose to do things now. She was always hoping the bishop would send her another sister who would take things over in the kitchen, somebody she could scare into doing what she wanted, but nuns were hard to find. Girls didn't sign up the way they used to and the ones that were already around were getting old.

I used to tell Rose all the time that I thought she was crazy, she should take some time for herself.

"I must be doing what I want," she said. "God knows, they're not paying me for it."

"But you need to do other things. Why not go back to California? Visit your family. You've never gone back out there."

Rose turned away from me. I was breaking our agreement, saying things like that. We didn't talk about things that came before Habit. Sometimes I wanted to know. It's one thing for us to not have known much about one another when we got married, but it had been ten years. In a way, I thought nobody knew more about Rose than me. I knew every mood she had and how long it would last. I knew how she moved and where she went and when she wanted to be left alone. But as time went by, I started to wish I knew the rest of it, too. Sometimes I thought I'd even be willing to tell her what had happened to me, tell her everything, if it would have made her talk to me. It wouldn't have. I doubt Rose really cared about what I'd done before.

So I drove on up to Owensboro the next morning by myself and found the lawyer's office, three doors down from the justice's office where we'd been married. I wondered if it was still the same guy. I thought about stepping inside to see, but then didn't. I wore my suit, just like I had to June's funeral.

"Mr. Abbott," the lawyer said, and shook my hand. He was a young fellow with dark, combed-back hair and glasses. "Will your wife not be joining us?" he asked me.

"Not today."

"That's too bad. This is good news. It's nice to have everyone together when the news is good. Were you aware of the fact that June Clatterbuck owned a good deal of property in Habit?"

"All the land at Saint Elizabeth's," I said.

"That's correct. The Catholic Church owns the structure of Saint Elizabeth's, but the land itself, her personal home, a barn, that was all hers."

"That's right," I said.

"She's left that to you and your wife, Mr. Abbott. The land and the house."

I shook my head. "That couldn't be right. There must be other Clatterbucks."

"Two nieces in Indiana. Some money has gone to them, but the property is yours."

I sat there for a minute and pulled at the cuffs of my shirt. "Then it was supposed to go to the church. They always wanted that land, acted like it was theirs all along."

"Well," the lawyer said, "that wasn't what Miss Clatterbuck wanted. We spoke about this on several occasions. The fact is, the church is on very weak grounds, so to speak. Water rights, access rights, those all belonged to Miss Clatterbuck and now to you. With a certain amount of effort and money, I don't think it would be impossible to get rid of them."

I put up both of my hands. I didn't want to hear it. "That's not what anyone wants."

He seemed relieved. "Fine then, all the better. It will take some time to draw up the papers, but no one's contesting this decision. Miss Clatterbuck had discussed this with her nieces before her death."

"It looks like she told everybody except us."

"I don't think she wanted to say anything," he told me. "People can be like that about wills."

I signed a few papers and shook his hand again before I left. I was planning on having a sandwich before I drove back, but now it seemed best to just get on home.

"Rose," I said, "come outside. I need to talk to you."

"How did it all go?" Sister Evangeline said. She smiled at me with her lips pressed tight together, like she could barely keep from laughing out loud, and I knew all of the sudden that she knew. I smiled and shook my head at her.

"Come in here and tell me what happened," Rose said. "I want to watch the soup."

"The soup can watch itself," Sister Evangeline said. "You made him drive up to Owensboro alone, now at least take a minute to talk to him."

Rose sighed and took the spoon out of the pot and set it on a saucer. "It's like living with your mother," she said.

"That's right," Sister said.

Rose came outside and closed the door. It wasn't too hot that day and everything was green on the count of good rains all spring. "What is it?" she said.

"I want to take a little walk."

"Then go on," she said.

"A walk with you."

"In your suit? Go home and change first."

"Sissy isn't home from school yet?"

"She's in a play, she won't be home till four. What is this, anyway? Was there a problem at the lawyer's?"

"Don't you want to know what she left us?"

"I hate to ask," Rose said.

I thought how in a way we could be alike, both thinking it was bad luck to want anything from a will. "Come on," I said. I took her hand and she let me take it. Rose knew when to give in on things. I didn't ask her for very much at all, so maybe she just decided this once she'd go along on my walk. We went past our house, down through the back pasture, where the stories say the spring used to be. I remembered one night when me and Rose walked down there, the first time I took her to meet Miss June. I remembered another time when I found her in the snow, half out of her head, and took her home with me.

"It's pretty here," I said, stopping in the middle of the field. It was good land. I'd always thought it would be good for horses.

Rose shaded her eyes and looked around. Maybe she was thinking of things that had happened out there, too. "Same as ever."

I sat down in the grass in my suit. I felt a little guilty, because right at that moment I wasn't feeling bad about June's death. I was happy for what I'd been given. "This is ours," I said to Rose.

"What is?"

"All this." I waved my hand out in front of me. "June left us the property. Everything underneath Saint Elizabeth's. Everything you're looking at in all directions."

Rose looked at me. You just don't see Rose looking surprised. She never cared enough to look surprised about things. "She left it to us?"

"All of it. Her house, too."

Rose sat down next to me and picked at the grass for a minute. "My God," she said, and shook her head. We sat there for a while, with our arms crossed over our knees, and watched the land to see if it had changed somehow.

"I came here almost eleven years ago," Rose said, staring straight out in front of her. "I was going to be here six months."

"I was going to be here three days," I said. "And that's been more than thirty-five years."

We were quiet for a while, just taking it all in, and then Rose said, "They ought to put up a sign, warning people."

* * *

Rose went back to the kitchen to work, but I just couldn't settle down. I wanted to walk over every inch of the land and look at it again. Thirty-five years I had been tending to the trees and pulling the ivy out of the flower beds. I watched fields sit empty so many good summers and thought they should have let me put out corn or soy like I asked but Mother Corinne said I shouldn't take the time away from work. In the fall every maple on the south hill would turn red and in the winter the drive would still need shoveling, but it would all be different now.

I was fifty-five years old when June died, and in those fifty-five years I had owned nothing, not the house that I lived in or the truck that I used for hauling. I can't say that I ever thought about it too much, at least not the way other men do. When I was growing up, I always thought about the things I wanted in terms of what Cecilia and I would have together. Then she died and my whole notion of the world went with her. I just never thought about things like that anymore. If I gave my life over to working on my own land or somebody else's, it didn't really make a difference to me. By the time I got married and Sissy was born, I was set in my ways. I never thought about getting something for them.

But having it fall to me the way it did changed things. I just kept looking at the ground, the same dirt and the same tough grass, but no one could tell me to get off of it now. I wasn't beholden to anyone, not Mother Corinne or the church. It was no one's kindness that was letting me stay on. I could get old and not worry. I could die and Rose and Sissy wouldn't have to worry.

I went over to June's house and went inside. It felt strange, not knocking. The last time I'd been there was the day she died. I took a hard look around, made note of how much sun came in and how tight the window casements were sealed. I ran a finger over the rose-covered wallpaper in the hall. I studied the light fixtures. There was a bedroom downstairs that had been June's and two more large bedrooms upstairs. I'd never been upstairs before, and I had to bend my head down to keep from hitting it on the low sloping ceiling over the staircase. Both of the rooms were made up real pretty, like June was expecting someone to come and stay, but I didn't remember her having guests. I sat down on the edge of the bed and folded my hands. I thought about waking up here every morning from now on and I put my feet up on the bed and stretched out. It was just starting to get dark outside. The girls would be coming off the porch of Saint Elizabeth's pretty soon and in for Rose's dinner. None of them knew that all they had been looking at belonged to the cook. This would be a good room for me and Rose. Sissy could be right across the hall. When she got older and wanted more privacy she could move into the bedroom downstairs, and after she grew up and got married and I got too old to climb the stairs, I could move into that bedroom.

I walked back down and looked at the kitchen. It was plenty big enough. I could make new cabinets and tear up the linoleum on the floor, make it someplace Rose would want to be. Then every once in a while we'd eat dinner at home, the three of us. I stopped and read a note taped to the refrigerator. "Milk, tomatoes, Cheerios, corn meal," it said. I pulled it off, folded it, and slipped it inside my suit pocket.

I headed back to Saint Elizabeth's in the dark and went inside through the kitchen door. Rose was sitting by herself at the table with her feet propped up on a chair. She was staring out the window at the dark. It wasn't often that a person got to see Rose sitting still, and I watched her for a while.

"Where's Sissy?" I said finally.

She looked up at me, almost like she'd been waiting for me. "She's eating with them tonight," she said, and tilted her head toward the dining room.

"You getting used to all this?"

"It's a lot to think about," Rose said.

"You bet."

"Look at you," she said. "You're still in your suit."

"I went over to June's and looked around. I'm thinking we should move over there. It's a lot bigger. I figured I could pack up all her personal stuff and send it to her nieces. I don't know. The lawyer could tell us what to do."

"We could go there, I guess," Rose said. "I've been thinking, I don't want to tell Cecilia about this."

"About what?"

"The inheritance, the land. I don't think it's a good idea." I sat down next to her at the little table. She kept looking off out the window. "She's too young. She's better off thinking that we don't have anything," Rose said. "She'll work harder, then. I don't want her to spend her life planning on staying here. She shouldn't think there's any reason for her to stay. There isn't. But if she knew that this was all going to wind up being hers, she might not ever look any farther than the end of the drive-way.''

I wanted to tell Sissy. I wanted to pick her up in the air and swing her around and give her the land as a gift. ''I don't want to lie to her about it, though,'' I said. ''I don't think that would be right.''

''Why not?'' Rose said. ''We lie to her about everything else.''

''Jesus, what a thing to say.''

Rose put up her hand. ''No,'' she said. ''Forget that. I'm sorry. Tell her we're going to move to June's because it's bigger. Tell her Saint Elizabeth's owns it. I don't think she'll ask any questions anyway.''

Rose got up and peered through the swinging door to see if everyone was about finished eating. I just sat there, staring at my hands on the green-topped table. ''I am her father,'' I said quietly.

Rose stopped and looked back at me over her shoulder. ''I didn't mean it that way,'' she said.

''I know what you meant,'' I said. ''I'm always here. Every day for ten years. Don't tell me I'm not her father.''

''Yes,'' she said, like suddenly she understood what I was saying. ''Of course you are.''

When Sissy came home from school the next day I walked her over to June's and told her which bedroom would be hers. She was in fourth grade then and smart as a whip. She acted just like me, going through a house she'd been in all her life like she'd never seen it before.

''What if it's haunted?'' she called out from the bathroom, where she was turning the shower off and on.

''June wasn't the haunting type,'' I said. ''Even if she was, she'd haunt the creek bed, not the house.''

''I can't imagine living in somebody else's house is all.'' She opened the hall closet and looked inside. ''This is full of coats.''

''We'll have to box everything up.'' I looked inside. It looked like there were coats from her whole family, like everyone who had ever been there had left a coat behind.

''Mom wants to do this?'' Sissy said.

''I don't think your mother much cares where she sleeps, as long as she doesn't have to walk too far to work.'' I took a gray felt hat off of the top shelf and put it on Sissy's head. She folded back the brim in the front.

"How do I look?" she said.

"Good," I said, and nodded. "Very good." I couldn't help but think she'd never be pretty like Rose. Sometimes I would stare at her so hard while she was sleeping, trying to see the smallest bit of her mother, in the eyes or around the mouth, but Sissy just looked like Sissy, no one else.

Everything happened so slowly at Saint Elizabeth's that to see a change you had to wait and watch for years. But that's what I'd done and so I knew things. The girls were getting younger. Every year had one girl who set a new record. We'd had them seventeen and then sixteen. Over time a few more started to keep their babies. The state said we had to have a psychologist and a social worker come down with the doctor once a week. The sisters held regular classes for the girls so they could keep up with their studies. They came from farther away. Not as far as California, but you could tell, these places were shutting down. There were fewer and fewer places a girl could go.

Other things had changed, too. Sissy got so big that most of the girls stopped trying to baby her. Sister Evangeline passed out the futures of unborn children without a thought to getting in trouble, and Mother Corinne got used to Rose, but she never liked her. She always acted like Rose was some kind of hanger-on who'd give up one day and go home. She never thanked Rose for the work she did or how she took care of Sister Evangeline.

So when Mother Corinne found occasion to come into the kitchen every now and then to fuss at Rose about something, buying expensive olives or a new blender, Rose let it go. I'd been there before and seen it happen, Mother Corinne would be ranting and raving and half the time Rose wouldn't even look up from what she was doing.

But once we got June's house cleaned out and started to carry our things across the back pasture, Mother Corinne decided to take offense at everything Rose was doing. You couldn't blame her in a way. All those years she'd been acting like the land was hers and then all of the sudden it wasn't. She didn't hold it against me or Sissy, but the thought of Rose having it drove her half mad. Except that Mother Corinne didn't really get mad, she just got firm and found ways of talking to you that made you feel small and smaller. One day just before we moved in, right after lunch, she came into the kitchen looking like her eyes were on fire.

"All through that meal I had to sit there and watch the waste," she said to Rose, the soft veins on her temples coming up. "There was twice as much food on every plate as the girls could eat. That's food that will be thrown away." Her hands moved like quick knives in the air. Sister Evangeline and I sat at the table and watched. We hadn't seen her like this in a long time, but Rose hardly noticed.

"I didn't see plates coming back with food on them. No more or less than usual," Rose said.

"I don't know where you come from," Mother Corinne said. "Who taught you to lie the way you do."

Rose started to turn away from her, then all of the sudden she cocked her head a little to one side, like she was trying to hear a song playing on the radio in the other room. She had a heavy wooden spoon in her hand and she turned back to Mother Corinne. "No more," she said. Her voice was low and steady and she moved the spoon slowly back and forth like she was blessing her.

"I won't have this," Mother Corinne said, not hearing her, not knowing that anything had changed. But I knew it and Sister Evangeline knew it. Rose had changed her mind about what she was going to take.

"Leave," Rose said.

"You won't tell me where to go," Mother Corinne said. "You're here through my good graces, you and your daughter both."

Rose raised up her spoon and Sister Evangeline said, "Rose, you come here!" and Rose turned around. Mother Corinne looked at the three of us in horror, like she didn't know who was worse. She was too angry to speak. I had never seen her so mad. But when she got to the door Rose called out to her.

"My good graces," Rose said. "Not yours."

After that, I don't remember Mother Corinne coming into the kitchen again. It was a big hotel. You could avoid someone forever if you wanted to.

The first night in the new house I went to tuck Sissy in. "Here we go," she said.

"You brush your teeth?" She nodded. "Say your prayers?"

"Twice."

"That's the way you're supposed to do it." I sat down on the edge of her bed and pulled the sheet up under her chin. I looked at her there on her white pillow, her hair all spread out like a fan, and I thought about June's father. He had died before I ever came to Habit, but June loved to tell stories about him, how he had saved her life. He would have watched his daughter bent with fever in this house, maybe in this room, and thought about how he'd do anything for her.

"Show me where I am," Sissy said. She hadn't asked me that in more than a year. When she was little she used to say it all the time. It meant she wanted to see my tattoo and read her name on my arm.

I took off my shirt and pulled up the sleeve of my undershirt. "Right there," I said.

"So you'll never forget my birthday."

"Not unless I don't take a bath that day," I said.

"Cecilia and Rose," Sissy said.

"Both of you right there." I tapped my arm.

"But the rose isn't right because the tattoo girl's mother came home before it was finished and she got scared and dropped the needle," she said.

She used to make me tell the story over and over again. "When I was born you went to Mamie's house and had her put my name on your arm and the day I was born and a rose for Mom."

"You've got a good memory," I said.

"You've told me about a million times," she said, sounding sleepy.

"Good night."

"And if you and Mom had had a bunch of kids, you would have put all their names on your arm, all the dates. And if you'd had even more kids you would have gone to the other arm and then your legs, and then your back."

"Good night."

"Until they'd be putting the names on the soles of your feet and the back of your neck. Charlie, Thomas, Mary, Douglas, Lee Ann, Susan, Octavia."

"Octavia?"

"I go to school with a girl named Octavia."

"Good night," I said, and closed the door but not all the way.

"Good night," she said.

I went across the hall and got in bed with Rose. She reached up and turned off the lights. I kissed her good night on the forehead, but she didn't say anything.

That night I dreamed about Cecilia. It was a dream I hadn't had in a long time, the one where she comes and sits down on the edge of the bed.

"How you doing, Son?"

"Okay, I guess. Good, really. This is our house now. We moved. You look good." She was wearing a dark green dress, one I'd never seen before.

"I look just the same," she said, and ran her fingers through her hair. Her hair was just the way she used to wear it. It was a real forties style, neat and waved. I liked hair that way.

"Have you been doing all right?"

She nodded, she seemed a little more tired than usual, but like I said, it had been years since I'd had this dream. "Not a lot happens, you know? I think that's the point of the whole thing." She leaned over and touched Rose's cheek gently with the back of her hand. "She has such nice skin," Cecilia whispered. "She's just so pretty. I wish she wasn't so pretty."

I looked at my wife asleep beside me. Her steady breathing was a comfort. "She's no prettier than you," I said.

"We're different," Cecilia said. "I always thought you'd marry someone like me."

"Who's like you?" I asked, and took her hand.

Cecilia bent her head down a little and smiled. She always needed to know she was special. "I'm going to go and look at your daughter," she said. "Is that all right? I won't wake her up."

"Sure," I said. Dying had made Cecilia humble. She was easier to get along with, but I kind of missed the way she used to be.

She gave my hand a squeeze. "You take care of yourself, now," she said. "Get some sleep."

"You too," I said. She got up slowly, like she didn't really want to go, but she did. She waved to me from the door.

When I woke up it was pitch-dark and I felt scared to death. I never got used to those dreams and I thought it was bad luck to have one the first night in the new house. I sat up in bed and tried to adjust my eyes to the light. There was a woman standing at the foot of the bed wearing a dress. I could hardly breathe. "Cecilia?" I said.

"She's asleep," Rose said. "It's just me. Go back to sleep."

I reached up and turned on a lamp at the bedside table. It took me a minute to find the switch because I wasn't used to it. "Why are you dressed?"

"I'm going to go home," she said.

I honestly had no idea what she meant. "California?"

She smiled and shook her head. "I'm going back to the old house. I can't sleep."

"Don't be silly, Rose. Come back to bed."

"No," she said softly. "I need to get going."

I got up and pulled my bathrobe on. She had her little suitcase in her hands and she saw me staring at it.

"I just needed a few things," she said.

I followed her downstairs, through our new living room and out onto the front porch. "If you don't like it here, we'll go back," I said. "We don't have to stay here. The other house is fine."

"Go back to bed, Son," she said, walking down the stairs. "Don't worry about anything. Everything's fine."

I took hold of her hand and she gave me a funny little smile that I knew meant I was supposed to let go. She didn't say anything else or look back over her shoulder and there was nothing I could do but watch her walking away, getting smaller and smaller in the dark field. There were so many stars out and somehow it just made me crazy, the night being so pretty like that and her leaving. It was happening all over again. She was going and I was letting her go. I stood on the porch and waited until from far away I saw a little light go on in the front room of the house I had lived in thirty-five years. I sat down on the steps and kept my eyes on that light, thinking, that's where my wife is.

═══ CECILIA ═══

$$=== 1 ===$$

I SAW HER when I came home from school. She was standing in front of Saint Elizabeth's reading the sign, so I knew what that meant. When I was a kid I used to run out as soon as I saw somebody at the sign but my mother told me to leave them alone, let them come in on their own time. When I passed this girl she sort of looked up a little and I nodded at her and smiled and she went right back to reading. It wasn't like she was snubbing me or anything, that's just the way they are.

I went in and was talking to Sister Bernadette at the front desk. She had a letter for me from my pen pal in Spain, who, thank God, had been writing to me in English. My Spanish is rotten. We were matched up through our schools because we were both fifteen, girls, and studying each other's language, though clearly one of us was more successful at it than the other. Sister Bernadette was telling me that when she was in convent school she had a pen pal who was taking holy orders in Italy. "Her name was Maria Theresa," Sister Bernadette said. "We lost touch after the war."

I tapped the letter on the desk. I liked getting mail here better than at the house. Not that I got any mail except from Sylvia, who, according to her letters, had a life even more boring than mine. Sister Bernadette put everybody's name on a key box behind the front desk and sorted the mail out like she was the postmaster. She wrote the names on masking tape so they could be peeled off easily and replaced with new ones. There were some things about the old hotel that were cool, like the attic and all the boxes behind the desk. "Got a new customer outside," I said. I checked out the stamps, which were infinitely better than American stamps, plus it took like five of them to mail a letter.

Sister Bernadette went to the window and raised up on her toes to look over the top of the half sheers. "Poor thing," she said. "She's been there two hours now. I wish she'd come inside."

I shrugged. "At least the weather's good."

Sister nodded, and with that the door opened a little bit and the girl crept inside. It was like she'd heard us talking about her. I dropped down on the couch and slid my finger underneath the flap of the envelope. I was trying not to listen and trying to listen while the girl whispered to Sister Bernadette. She was really thin. It was hard to imagine being that thin and pregnant too. She had a ton of red curly hair that was caught up in a ponytail holder. It looked more like bundled kindling than hair. I started to read Sylvia's letter. It was all about her father acquiring more goats. She used the queerest words. Acquiring goats.

"Wait here, dear," Sister Bernadette said. "I'll see if I can't get Mother Corinne."

The girl came over and sat down on the couch next to me. I shouldn't say next to me. She sat on the same couch as me but as far away as possible. She looked like she was going to be sick, and let me tell you, it's happened before. I've seen girls throw up in their purses waiting to be interviewed. The first three months and then again in the last month. That's when everybody throws up. She looked up and saw me there for the first time.

"Hi," she said.

"Hi there." I smiled again. She looked like a rabbit caught in a trap. Her eyes darted from side to side, but so fast you could barely tell it was happening. We were the only two people in the lobby. It was the standard nap hour at the baby farm.

"I'm Lorraine," she said, and stuck out her hand like she was trying to get my vote.

"Cecilia." I leaned over the couch, not exactly getting up, and shook it. I always feel so stupid shaking people's hands.

"I just got here," she said. She was checking out the carpet and the horse paintings. This was not a girl who'd been in a big hotel before. Not even a shabby one.

"I know. I saw you outside."

"Oh," she said, and nodded, thinking it all over.

"Don't worry about it," I said. "It's fine. Everybody here is nice enough." I wasn't so good at the Welcome Wagon stuff. There was a time I got into it, but after a while you figure it out: everybody comes and everybody goes.

"Oh, it looks nice. That nun"—Lorraine pulled at a few of her curls and I was impressed by the way they sprang right back into place when she let them go—"she seemed nice."

"Very nice," I said. She smiled and I smiled, and then the whole thing got a little awkward. I didn't want to just stare at her, and I didn't want to get up and leave. "I'm going to read my letter," I said, and held up the light blue airmail paper like it was proof of something. Not that Sylvia's father's latest goat acquisition was really burning a hole in my curiosity. Sylvia didn't get out too much. She had never been to a bullfight. I don't mean to stereotype or anything, but what's the point of living in Spain if you never go to a bullfight?

"Don't let me keep you," Lorraine said, and made a sudden jerking motion with her hand, like she was trying to catch a glass of water she'd just knocked over in the air. It made both of us jump a little. "Nervous," she said, and then looked like she was going to cry. I've seen that too.

I put the letter back in its envelope. "Don't be nervous," I said. "Look, I'll tell you." I checked over my shoulder to see if Sister Bernadette had come back. Not that she wouldn't agree with what I was going to say, but she wouldn't like to hear me say it. "Mother Corinne is a little bit of a hard ass. Not awful, but it's best to get off on the right foot. Are you Catholic?"

"No," Lorraine said, her eyes getting absolutely round with terror. "They told me at state social services—"

"Ah," I said, cutting her off. "That's not the point. You don't have to be, but it makes things easier. Just tell her you are."

"But I'm not."

"There isn't a test. She won't ask you to say the stations of the cross or anything. It's just"—I turned my eyes to the large portrait of Saint Elizabeth over the front desk, the crucifix over every door—"polite or something. If you don't want to do it, don't do it. They won't kick you out."

"Anything else?"

My mother probably didn't even know I knew this, even though I'd seen her take a hundred girls aside and tell them. "The guy who got you pregnant. Don't say he's dead. Everybody does that. It makes Mother Corinne crazy."

Lorraine put her hands under her thighs and sat on them like they were cold. She was quiet for a minute. "I was going to say that," she said finally.

"See?"

"So what do I tell her?"

"I don't know. Tell her the truth. Or tell her you don't remember."

"What did you tell her?" Lorraine said.

All of a sudden I was the one who was wide-eyed. I started
to explain, I opened my mouth, but then Sister Bernadette was
there to take her back to the office. "Wish me luck," she said,
and picked up her bag.

I sat there, absolutely frozen. I felt like I had just been mistaken for some escaped mass murderer. I felt like I was going
to be sick, but that would only have proved her assumption. No
one had ever, ever, mistaken me for one of them, not even as a
joke. The lobby felt small and airless. I thought I was going to
pass out.

I got up and went outside. It was May, four days from summer
vacation. I wanted to go home, to my home, where I lived with
my father. I cut through a hole in the hedge and started out
across the back pasture. Halfway to the house I dropped my
books and Sylvia's letter and the sweater I hadn't needed all day
and fell down in the grass. There's maybe a week in every year
you can do this. It comes after the mud has dried up and before
all the bees are out.

I had never had sex, and not because I was so righteous and
good. No one had asked me.

If someone had asked me, though, I'd like to think I would
have said no. Let me tell you, I've seen it. From day one I've
heard the stories of girls who said yes. He was going to marry
me, he promised. People tell me things you wouldn't believe.
It's like there's a sign over my head: CONFIDE HERE. But who
else are they going to tell? Going to tell a nun how it makes you
feel to have him look at you and say your name? Going to tell
another pregnant girl? Big chance of sympathy there. Better to
tell some kid who's around and probably won't remember. But
I do remember. There's a recorder turned on somewhere inside
me. Everything stays. Mary Claire, who couldn't sleep alone
during thunderstorms and so checked me out from my mother
like I was a library book, told me she'd done it at thirteen.
Cheryl told me that she always believed it couldn't happen your
first time, but she'd only done it once and there she was. She
also said it hurt.

There had always been a huge gap between me and the girls
who came through Saint Elizabeth's. They were older and away
from their families and stuck in the middle of a big adventure
they hadn't planned on having. I was never one of them. That

was because of sex. It showed on me. I looked into the mirror and saw Virgin and they saw it, too.

So there I was, lying in the back pasture with my head on a geometry book, thinking this: things are changing. Now they're going to start thinking I'm one of them. It was like seeing an eclipse when it never occurred to you in your wildest dreams that the moon could block out the sun. Not that I'm saying I'm the sun or anything. I'm the caretaker's daughter. I'm the cook's daughter. I'm not one of them.

"Sissy!"

I about jumped out of my skin. I sat up like a shot and saw my father running across the field. My father has a bad knee, so it's not often you see him running anywhere. "What!" I called out.

"Jesus, girl, you scared me half to death." He stopped about ten feet away from me and put his hands on his bent legs and started to pant. He went red then white then red again.

"I scared you!" I stood up and went to him, put my hand on his back. "What is it? What's wrong?"

He shook his head and took a couple of deep breaths. "I just saw you lying there," he said. He stopped and wiped his forehead with his sleeve, then he sat down. "Don't ever do that."

"Do what? Think? Be alone? Lie down?" I sat down next to him. He didn't look good, really. "Dad. Hey, Dad. Look, I'm fine."

He nodded, closing his eyes. "You're fine," he said.

I waited for him to say something else, but he seemed too busy breathing. I scratched the knee of his overalls. "You're scaring me," I said quietly. "Here, lie down a second. It's nice out here. See? That's all I was doing. The bugs aren't out yet. Just lie down."

My father did what I told him and stretched out in the moss and bluegrass. He took one huge, long breath, held it and then let it go. "This is better," he said. "I'm okay now."

"Were you looking for me?"

"No, I was just going home. I wanted to find my ball peen hammer. I thought it might be at home."

"It's in the junk drawer," I told him. I put my hand just above his face to keep the sun out of his eyes. "Next to the fridge. I saw it there yesterday."

"Good girl," he said.

"You feeling okay?"

He opened his eyes and smiled at me. "I guess I shouldn't run. Or I should start running. One or the other."

There was something about the fact that my father was so big that made it scary to see him lying down. It was like, moving around in the world, you didn't notice how much space he took up. But when he was still like this he looked like a tree that had fallen over and wouldn't ever be able to set itself right again. He'd turned sixty last year. The sisters threw him a big party. Most of the kids I went to school with had grandparents who were sixty, not parents.

"What were you doing out here?" my father said. "Getting some sun?"

"Just thinking."

"Anything interesting?"

What was I going to tell him? That I was thinking about sex? That I had just realized I could be an unwed mother? "I was thinking maybe we could have dinner at home tonight. I'll cook for a change. How about that?"

My father looked up at me. It unnerved me, the looks he could give. "What's your mother going to say if we don't go to dinner?"

"Gee, I think she'd have to notice we were gone before she could say anything."

"Sissy," he said, his voice suddenly going stern.

"Okay, okay. I'm not trying to start anything. I'd just like a night away from the baby farm is all. A little time at home."

He nodded and I saw some relief in his eyes, but maybe just because I wanted to. He must get tired of it. He's over there all the time. "That's fair," he said. He took another deep breath and then stood up. "Come on and walk me home. Show me where the hammer is."

I got up and tied my sweater around my waist and got my books together. "I got another letter from Sylvia," I said.

"Another one? That girl must have an awful lot of time on her hands." He reached over and took my books. I didn't want him to carry them, but I knew it would only make him feel worse to treat him like he was feeble or something. "What's new in Spain?" he asked me.

"Nothing," I said. "I've about decided that Spain is the most boring place in the world."

When Dad and I got to the house to look for the hammer, I knew right away my mother had been there. There was a skirt folded up on the kitchen table and a new bar of clear yellow hand soap next to the sink. She still came by every now and then, almost always when she knew we'd be gone. She would leave some small offering: apples, a dishtowel, magazines. Dad noticed right away. He took everything as a sign of something good.

"Look at this," he said, and held up the skirt. It was short and violet with kick pleats. She had made it herself. "This is pretty."

I took the skirt from him and put it back down on the table. "I'd never wear that color."

"That color is fine for you," he said. He looked down at the skirt and ran his hand over the cloth like it was a sleeping cat. "She must have made it."

"So she made it," I said, and opened the refrigerator, not looking for anything.

"Be nice," my father said. He wasn't telling me, he was asking me. Please, be nice about your mother. It was important to Dad's complex system of denial that Mom and I got along. That way he could believe that we were just a normal, happy family who were temporarily living in separate houses.

"I am nice," I said, shutting the refrigerator door. "We don't have any food. Can you take me to the store?"

He wagged the ball peen hammer in the air. "Got to get back to work," he said. "You and I can have dinner any night. Maybe we just ought to eat at the hotel."

I could feel a bad mood coming on. I'd made up my mind. "No," I said. "I'll go over and borrow some stuff. I want to cook."

He sighed and slipped the hammer into the bib pocket of his overalls. "Suit yourself," he said. He smiled and patted my head. My father was so much bigger than me, than everyone, that it didn't seem condescending when he patted my head. It was like that was the part of everyone he mostly saw. It made sense that it was the part he'd feel the most affection for. "You're okay?"

"You bet."

"I'll be home by six, then." And with that he went out the kitchen door and across the field. His gray hair looked coarse and bristly in the sunlight. I'd cut it way too short again.

I went up to my room and tried on the skirt. The truth was, I liked it. She at least had good sense about how long things ought to be. I stood in front of the mirror and looked at myself, trying to see what Lorraine had seen. I turned to the side and pulled the skirt tight over my stomach. I stared inside my eyes so hard it scared me and I had to look away. Kicking off my shoes, I climbed on top of my bed to see my whole body in the mirror over my dresser. I was looking for my mother, looking for cheekbones and long legs and a wide mouth. I could have looked all day and not found a shred of evidence. Once when I was twelve I accused my parents of adopting me. I had it all worked out in my mind: they hadn't been able to have children of their own. They had grown close to one of the girls there. The girl died, but just before she did she begged my parents to take me and raise me as their own. The girl who was my real mother died in the arms of the mother who raised me. Or didn't raise me, as the case may be. I thought about my dead mother, how she was skinny like me and not quite tall enough. She had my dirty blond hair and pale skin, a very slight overbite. She was a good dancer, even though she was shy. I thought about how heartsick she would have been to know the many ways this woman she gave me to, entrusted me to, had let me down.

After months of fantasizing about this so hard that I was absolutely positive, I went to my parents with my story. My mother, without saying a word, pushed her chair back from the table and left the kitchen. My dad looked pale, so pale I was sure I was right. "I'm right," I said in her absence.

"Of course you're not right," he said helplessly.

A few minutes later my mother returned and slapped a piece of paper down on the table. "Birth certificate," she said matter-of-factly. "Proof."

I read it over carefully. My mother's name, Martha Rose Abbott. My father's name, Wilson Eugene Abbott. My name, Cecilia Helen Abbott.

"Helen's a stupid name," I said. I was furious about losing that good dead mother I had imagined. It was as if she had been murdered.

"Helen is my mother's name," she said, folding the paper back up and slipping it into her apron pocket.

I hung the skirt in my closet and pulled my jeans back on. Then I headed over to Saint Elizabeth's. We had worn a path between our house and the hotel. Like goats, my father and I followed the same trail back and forth a dozen times a day. Sometimes the sight of the field rubbed bare in a line would make me angry. I'd walk in the grass two feet beside it for no good reason.

I went in the kitchen door to avoid seeing any of the girls. I wasn't in the mood. Sister Evangeline was alone, sitting in her big armchair near the stove. Soft yellow tufts of stuffing came out of the arms where she'd worn the fabric through. It was getting to be the time of year when it would be too warm for her there. Then my father would move her chair closer to the open window and then finally next to the door of the big walk-in refrigerator when it got really hot in July and August. "I'm like a little houseplant," Sister Evangeline would say whenever my father picked up her chair with her still in it and moved it to the next logical spot. "I just need to be kept in the sun."

Not too far from her comfortable chair was a wheelchair folded up and resting against the wall. That was a recent addition. Sister could walk, but not for very long. She wouldn't sit in her wheelchair during the day, though. She thought it made her look like an invalid. My mother helped her back and forth between the two. If Sister Evangeline was asleep in her chair, my mother would just pick her up in her arms. My mother had started buying staples in large bags years ago; fifty pounds of flour, fifty pounds of rice. She bought entire flats of canned tomatoes from a wholesaler in Louisville. She saved the place money and worked up the shape of a bodybuilder to boot. My mother was two inches shy of six feet tall, and the sight of her walking down the hall with Sister Evangeline asleep in her arms always made me want to cry.

"Hey there, lambchop," Sister Evangeline said to me, wide awake and happy for company. I leaned over and gave her a kiss, and she slapped my cheek hard enough to make me think she'd live forever.

"How are you feeling?" I poked a long strand of white hair back up under her coif.

"Good," she said. "Old. Nothing new there. God made this body, and He's going to get His money's worth out of it." She laughed a little at her own joke. "What about you?"

I shrugged, unfolded the wheelchair, and sat down next to her. "Fine, I guess. I'm in a mood."

"Sweet Lorraine," Sister said.

I'd grown up with Sister Evangeline. My mother said she was the first person at Saint Elizabeth's to hold me. So let's just say I was used to this kind of thing. "Lorraine," I said.

"Listen, pet, you have some sympathy. This isn't any sign from God, this is just Lorraine coming in and having a lot of other things on her mind." She stopped and tapped the side of her head for effect. "Things besides you. Imagine that! She'd be thinking of things other than you." She took my hand and patted it hard, but none of this was improving my mood. "Don't be sour. This is your trial. I've known it from the day you were born. Folks forget that a place that's easy to live in can be hard to grow up in. They're not the same thing. There was always going to come a time when you'd be mistaken for one of them. It will happen again. You've got to remember, they're good girls, same as you. Only difference is the babies. You're just going to have to steady yourself."

What Sister Evangeline had to say didn't cheer me up so much as just being around her did. She told everyone their problems were silly. She sweetly dismissed everything that was laid out before her. I guess when you get to be that old you have a better sense of what a real problem is. "Give me a saint," I said.

"What is the date today?"

"May fifteenth."

Sister Evangeline closed her eyes for a minute and folded her hands in her lap. This was her favorite game. When I got upset when I was little or did something well, she would give me a saint as a reward. Now she waited for me to ask her so she could show the things she still remembered.

"May fifteenth is the feast day of Saint Isidore, the farmer. He lived in Spain and watches over your friend Sylvia."

I pulled my legs up into the wheelchair and put my head down on my arm.

"He was very poor. Poor all his life He always worked for the same man and was a faithful servant. He had a wife, too"— she looked at me to make her point—"also a saint. When Saint Isidore guided his plow he talked with God or his guardian angel or to other saints. But I shouldn't say other saints, since he didn't know he was a saint himself at that time. That's the tricky part about being a saint. If you ever think of yourself as one it throws you out of the running. I've known people who thought they were saints, plenty of them, and believe you me, they were anything but." She stopped.

"Saint Isidore," I said, guiding her back to her story.

"Every moment of his life he was with God. Once he carried a bushel of corn to the mill to be ground into flour and it was winter. On the way he saw the branches over his head were filled with tiny birds, all starving to death in the cold. So Saint Isidore opened his sack and poured half of it on the ground, even though his friends made fun of him for being so sentimental. When they arrived at the mill, his sack was full again, and when it was ground, his corn turned into twice the meal. That's the way God works. He rewards the ones who give things away."

"They made him a saint for feeding the birds? That doesn't sound especially sainted."

Sister Evangeline waved her hand in the air, dismissing my stupidity. "Of course not. There were plenty of other things, things his spirit did after he was dead. It's just that the part with the birds is the part I really like. That's the part that speaks well of God, that He would notice what was done for birds." I remained unconvinced and Sister Evangeline smiled at me. "It will be the last, great project of my life to make a Catholic out of you," she said. "That's why God's keeping me alive so long."

"I am a Catholic," I said.

"A better Catholic, like Saint Isidore."

"You want me to be a saint?" I asked. I was incredulous. I tried to imagine myself, Saint Cecilia, starving in a garret somewhere, giving my last crust of bread to some pathetic, needy squirrel. Wasn't there enough to worry about already?

She read my thoughts like they were running on a screen over my head. "Why not shoot high?" she said. "I remember the day you were confirmed. I stood beside you and you said your vows and I was so proud of you, I thought, this girl could be a saint."

"Please."

"It's not impossible," she said.

Just then my mother came into the kitchen, her hands full of radishes. "Take these for me," she said, and held out her hands to me.

I took the radishes, their roots clumped with dirt, and put them in the sink.

"Don't you think Cecilia could be a saint?" Sister Evangeline asked.

My mother dropped her chin to her chest and looked up, the way she did whenever she thought things were simply ridiculous. "Cecilia isn't a saint. She's a person, just like the rest of us."

I would never expect my mother to think I could be a saint.

"Saints are people first," Sister Evangeline said. "They're just very good people. You could be a saint, Rosie. Any of those girls in there, all of them. It's possible. A person just needs guidance, they need faith. And you should get that faith from your parents. You should be telling her these things, Rose, not me." Sister Evangeline turned to me, but spoke a little louder to be sure my mother would hear. "Rose is a good Catholic. She just keeps it all in here." She tapped her chest. "Like it was a private thing." She looked up at my mother. "God is not a private thing, Rosie."

"I'll remember that," my mother said.

But Sister Evangeline missed the sarcasm in her voice and settled happily back into her chair. "Good," she said. "Good."

Sometimes I thought about becoming a nun to irritate my mother and make Sister Evangeline proud of me. Either. Both.

"Rinse those off, will you?" my mother said.

"I'm only staying a minute," I said, turning the water on the radishes. The dirt washed away from their tangled roots, sending muddy streams toward the drain. "I just need to get some food."

My mother nodded, going off into the pantry for one thing or another.

"I'm going to make dinner at home tonight for me and Dad."

"You're not eating with us?" Sister Evangeline said. It was the sound I was hoping to hear in my mother's voice. It was disappointment. It made my mother look out of the pantry, first at Sister, then at me.

"Why aren't you eating here?"

I felt trapped. There was no way to say something that would both hurt one and please the other. "Dad seemed so tired," I said. "I thought it might be better for him to stay at home."

"I saw Son outside not ten minutes ago," my mother said. "He's fine." She looked at me, maybe just to figure out what I was up to, but she really stopped and looked at me. Sometimes days and weeks can go by without this happening. At that minute I wanted so much to touch her, just her hand or her sleeve.

"I just want to," I said quietly.

"She's growing up," Sister Evangeline said.

And I wanted to tell her no, I'm not. Everything is exactly the same.

2

THE FIRST MORNING after school let out for summer vacation I slept through breakfast and lunch both. There was never much food in our house because my dad and I never ate there. We had food for television watching and midnight snacks, preferably things that wouldn't go bad too quickly since we were slow making it all the way through a bag of something. When I woke up hungry at one o'clock that afternoon I found a jar of popping corn, no oil, two Pop-Tarts, and a bag of prunes. I started over to Saint Elizabeth's.

My mother was alone in the kitchen, eating a sandwich and staring out the window. My mother refused to read while she was eating. She thought it was bad manners, even if you were alone.

"Where's Sister Evangeline?" I asked.

"Asleep," she said. "She had a bad night last night. There was something wrong with her stomach."

"She's all right though?" I stopped, my hand on the door of the refrigerator.

"Fine," my mother said. "Don't worry so much."

I found some chicken salad in a Tupperware dish and sniffed at it just to annoy her. I knew full well she'd never leave anything to go bad.

"I'm going to teach you to drive," my mother said. She didn't say it to me, but she must have. There was no one else there.

"I'm too young to get a license. You have to be sixteen."

"It takes a long time to learn how to drive. You should work on it this summer, while you're out of school. By the time your birthday comes around you'll have it down."

"I'm sure Dad will teach me," I said carelessly, pressing the chicken salad against a slice of bread with a fork.

But my mother liked to teach me to do things. She showed me how to bone a fish with one pass of the knife, how to truss a turkey, change the oil in a car, do taxes. Instruction seemed to be her only method of communication as far as I was concerned. "No," my mother said. "I thought of that. He wouldn't be able to sit in the front seat if it was moved up close enough for you to drive. Besides, he'd be too nervous. Just because a person knows how to drive doesn't mean he knows how to teach someone else how to do it."

It was one thing that my mother was forever missing my attempts to be close to her, but the fact that she didn't get my digs at her either made me insane. "I'll have to get a learner's permit."

"Don't be silly," my mother said. "This is driving, not brain surgery. You don't need to take a test to learn how to drive."

"We'll have to do it in the Dodge," I said.

"The truck will be fine."

"Dad uses the truck," I said, "and the nuns use the station wagon. We can't have regular lessons in either one of those. Besides, if you want to teach me to drive it seems like it should be your car at risk." The truth was, I just wanted to ride in that car. Dad had built a shed for it next to the house when I was still a baby, and my mother had kept it pretty much locked up ever since. She was always turning it on and sitting in it to keep the engine in good shape, and once when the tires rotted through she bought new ones, but the car never went anywhere.

She sighed and ran her hand through her hair. "All right," she said, picking up her plate and washing it off in the sink. "Finish up your lunch."

"We're starting now?"

"Good a time as any."

Maybe we were both nervous. I knew I was, but with my mother it would have been hard to tell. She wasn't talking. She never talked to me unless she had something specific to say, some piece of wisdom to impart. She never said the weather was nice but warm for May. She didn't ask me how I slept or if I was excited about being out of school. My mother would have thought it was a waste of time, stating the obvious. The truth was, we didn't get along. Not the way my friends in school all stopped getting along with their mothers when they hit fourteen. We'd never gotten along. It wasn't that we fought, exactly. We hadn't even progressed that far. She had figured out long ago that Saint Elizabeth's was full of women who were hungry to mother, and I had figured out that nothing short of setting myself on fire in the front lobby would have gotten her attention. The unspoken pact was that we ignored each other. That much we had down to an art.

She was forty that summer, but she didn't look that old to me. My mother was the kind of person whose age would have been impossible to guess. Year after year she stayed the same, thin and tall and straight. On nice days she would sit in the sun on the kitchen porch of the hotel and shell peas, so she always managed to have a little bit of a tan. Her hair stayed the same too, she cut it herself in a straight line under her jaw. It was nearly brown enough to be black. When she pushed it back behind her ears like it was that afternoon, she looked like she could have been twenty, just coming home from college.

My mother had on a red long-sleeved tee shirt with the sleeves pushed up above her elbows and a blue cotton skirt she'd made herself. Everything about her seemed perfect, the way her collarbone raised up above the rounded neck of her shirt. The way her hands were narrow and her fingers were long and thin. The way she walked with her head up, never looking around from side to side. The way it seemed the fact of her beauty had never occurred to her and so made her more beautiful. None of it, not lip or tooth or ankle or eyelash had come to me. And I wanted it. And I knew she would think I was ridiculous for wanting it. And I knew that if I asked her, and if she could give it to me, she would pull her beauty over her head and hand it to me like an old dress. "Take this," she'd tell me. "It never did me any good."

We lived in Habit, where no one locked their doors when they went out or when they were home at night, asleep in their beds. My mother raised up the door on the garage. "Keys are in the car," she said. My father had had the car repainted a couple of years ago as a birthday present for her. It looked like something out of a time capsule sitting there. Like it was 1965 in that garage and the car had just rolled off the showroom floor.

We both walked to the passenger side and stood there. "Other side," she said to me.

"What?"

"You're driving."

"I don't know how to drive."

"I know, that's what this is about."

"But I can't drive the car," I said. I started to get nervous, remembering suddenly her rule for instruction in all things: you have to do it yourself.

"Go on," she said, making it clear she didn't have all day to stand there. "Get in."

"Please," I said. "Just let me watch you for a while. Talk to me and let me watch you, then I'll drive."

She shook her head. "You've been watching me drive your whole life. Enough's enough."

"But I wasn't paying attention before." I looked at her. "Mom," I said.

She smiled a little. I never called her that. I never called her anything at all. "Go," she said, and got in the car.

I walked around and got in on the other side. Why hadn't I been paying attention all those years? I was always so happy to be a passenger, looking out the window, counting phone poles. I remember when my mother taught me to swim. She'd take me down to the Panther River and wade me out until the water was over my head, then she'd push me away from her again and again until I found a way to stay afloat. She was so serious about me doing it on my own that I really thought she'd let me drown trying. "Won't you at least back it out for me?"

"What are you going to do, call me for the rest of your life every time you need the car backed out? R," she said, pointing to the letters above the wheel. "Reverse."

She told me how to start it up. How to give it a little gas and let the engine warm itself. She told me how to work the pedals and what all the letters stood for. She was animated as she talked to me over the sound of the car's low idle. "Check your mirrors every time," she said. I made a point to remember that, remember everything. I knew she wouldn't tell me twice.

I looked over my right shoulder the way she said and crept into the field as slow and straight as possible. My hands were sweating and I thought they would slip on the steering wheel.

I looked at the field for the first time as a driver and thought that this wouldn't be a bad place to start. The ground was pretty even and the grass was short. There was really nothing to hit, unless I went into the house or the garage.

"D," my mother said. "Drive."

I shifted the car into drive and we started slowly to go forward. I kept it so slow that the sensation was more like rolling than driving, which was fine with me.

"Steer," my mother said, and tapped the wheel with her finger. "Get the feel of it."

As I turned the wheel the world turned with us, and we started to make our first big circle around the field. "Is this right?" I said. I hit the brakes for no good reason, and we both lurched forward in our seats. I thought I couldn't listen and steer at the same time.

"This is fine," she told me, and I started forward again. My mother was smiling. She rolled down her window and pushed her elbow out. "I should start driving more," she said. "I love this car." I looked over at her. "Eyes on the grass," she said, and pointed ahead. She didn't say anything about my speed, she just let me creep along. "I used to drive a lot," she said. "Just for fun. Not going anyplace."

"Did you ever take me?" I asked. I loved the idea. My mother driving, me as a baby in the seat beside her. The two of us going no place together.

"No, no. This was a long time ago, before you were born."

"When you lived in California?"

She nodded, not seeming at all bothered by the mention of the past. I was in eighth grade before I ever knew my mother wasn't from Kentucky. I was writing a social studies paper on California, and my father told me to ask my mother about it because she was from there. "That's right," she said, tapping her fingers lightly on her door.

I was so amazed by this day. I was out of school. The sky was perfect blue and a breeze was coming out of the hills. I was driving, not just any car, but my mother's car. And my mother was with me, talking to me as if it was something that happened all the time. I felt lucky enough to gamble. With my mother, one wrong question could blow the day to hell. I turned the wheel to take us along a line of trees, not too close. "Did your mother teach you how to drive?" I said.

My mother laughed. "God, no. My mother was horrified when I learned how to drive. She not only didn't drive, she wouldn't even ride in cars. She was scared to death of them."

"Why was she afraid of cars?"

"My father died in a car accident," she said absently. "It happened when I was very young."

It took my breath away. Until that afternoon I knew this: my mother's father was dead and she was not in touch with her mother. That was the information issued and there were to be no questions, as it was personal. My mother didn't answer personal questions. As her daughter I was no more

entitled to information about her life than a checkout girl at
the supermarket. Now here we were and for no reason at all
she told me how her father died. "Do you remember him?"
I asked tentatively.

My mother was quiet for a while and I thought I had gone too
far and spoiled everything. But it turned out she was only thinking about my question. "For a long time I thought I did, but
now, in truth, I'd have to say no."

My mother talked in her car.

If there is an explanation for this in all of science, I can't
imagine what it would have been. She didn't talk in my father's
truck or the nuns' station wagon. She didn't talk on buses. But
in that blue Dodge Dart that was hers alone in all the world she
sat comfortably. She folded her legs beneath her. She even put
her foot up on the dashboard for a minute. She smiled and
stretched and said whatever came into her head. It was almost
like the car was her house, only she was never like this in her
house.

I kept on turning the wheel, making slow passes by my
mother's house. I liked driving. God, I loved driving. I would
have been happy spending the whole day going around in
circles.

"I think that should about do it for today," my mother said.

I inched toward the garage and held my breath as I put the car
inside. Once the car was safely back in its shed, the ignition key
turned to off, everything went back to the way it was.

"I need to get dinner started," my mother said, looking at
her watch. "I didn't realize it was so late."

"You bet." I got out and shut the door. I thought she would
say something, I don't know what. She looked at me from the
entrance of the garage.

"You coming?"

"Yeah," I said, and closed the door behind us. I didn't care
if that was all. That was enough, and it sure was a lot more than
I'd been expecting.

My mother moved away when I was ten years old. Or maybe
we moved away. It didn't seem to be a decision as much as
something that just happened. We all went to June's house
together. I went to bed that first night with both of my
parents across the hall and when I woke up it was just my
father.

For a long time we all pretended that nothing had really happened. My mother was there in the kitchen of Saint Elizabeth's every morning, making our breakfast along with everyone else's. She'd throw out a couple of excuses to keep us at bay: she still had some packing she wanted to do; she was having trouble sleeping at the new house; she was planning on coming on Friday or Monday; next week. At first she was in the new house a lot. I'd find her there when I came home from school, cleaning out the oven or hanging some drapes she'd made. "I was working on these so late last night," she'd tell me. "I just fell asleep at the old house." Her sewing machine was at the old house. It made more sense to her to sleep with her sewing machine than with us.

But as time went by, it became clear she wasn't coming back. She didn't even bother giving us excuses anymore. A couple of times after she first left I spent the night with her, like she was a girlfriend or some distant relative I was going to visit. I'd put a change of clothes and a toothbrush in a plastic shopping bag and walk over to the house we used to live in. But it didn't work. My mother was just the way she'd always been, and I'd thought, for some crazy reason, that on those nights she would be different. I thought she'd ask me to sleep with her. She'd fix my hair. Instead she came home late, read her books, and planned her menus. She'd look up every now and then and say something like, "Which sounds better to you, carrots or wax beans?" As soon as I'd said carrots she was gone again.

Those nights I'd sleep in my old room but never sleep. I'd think about my dad, alone in our house. I'd feel his sadness coming across the field like a hand in the dark. I was angry with him back then, even more than at my mother. I thought he should have said something, to her or to me, somebody. He should have said to her straight out, Rose, have you left us? Are you never coming back? I want to know why. He should have told me she was gone for good and saved me all that wondering. But he did nothing. He just stepped back and let it happen. He let her go.

After a while I forgave him for it, though, even if I never said anything. I came to see that that was the way it was with my mother. There was no way to make her do anything. It would have been sadder to ask and watch her look up for a second and then away, or maybe to not even look up at all. It was better for us to hope for as long as we could. Those were good days, in a strange way, the days we thought she was always just around the corner, like prosperity or Christmas.

That night after dinner when we were home I asked my dad. "Have you ever driven the Dodge?"

"Sure," my father said. "A couple of times when the truck was in the shop, and when I had it painted. I drove it then."

"But did you ever drive with Mom?"

He thought about it for a minute. "Maybe. Not that I can remember offhand. Why do you ask?"

"She's teaching me to drive," I said, sitting down on the arm of the sofa. "I don't know why I'm asking."

"God, learning to drive." He shook his head. "I can't believe this."

I looked through our front window and couldn't see a light on across the field. She was probably still at Saint Elizabeth's. Sometimes, if Sister Evangeline wasn't feeling well, my mother would sleep on a cot in the little room next to hers in case she needed something in the night. "Did you know her dad was killed?"

"Your mother's?"

"In a car accident," I told him. I slid down off the arm to sit beside him on the sofa. I felt like I was gossiping, repeating something I'd overheard about the love life of a movie star. "She told me today when we were driving. He was killed when she was really small. She doesn't even remember him."

"No," my father said slowly, "she never told me that."

Then suddenly something occurred to me, how pretty my mother was, how young she seemed. There was my father, past sixty now. I always thought he was waiting for her to come back to him, but maybe it wasn't like that. Maybe he could never really believe she had been with him at all. Maybe he thought it was inevitable, her moving away, like their time together had been some kind of fluke and he was just happy for what he got. I thought I probably shouldn't have said anything about her father. Pointing out the things he didn't know would only make it worse. "It isn't a big deal," I said. "I just thought it was interesting."

"It's sad," my father said, and turned to look out the window like I had done only a minute before. He was wondering if she was all right.

I had been so excited about her telling me something, anything, that I had forgotten that part of it. It was sad.

That night I couldn't sleep. I kept thinking about my mother's father. I tried to think of him as my grandfather, but that word seemed so impossible. He must have been a young man when he died. He must have barely been used to the idea of being a father. He was still getting up in the night to come and sit beside my mother and watch her sleep. At the most, he might have imagined her someday being old enough to go to school. He never would have thought then that she could grow up and have a daughter of her own. He couldn't have believed that his baby would have a baby old enough now to drive. I made his face like my mother's. He was handsome and tall with a straight nose and blue eyes. He sat on the edge of her little bed with his hand on her back so he could feel her breathe. He looked at the faces of the dolls lined up beside her and the striped yellow wallpaper he'd hung himself before she was born. He looked at his sleeping daughter and said her name. The part that I couldn't get over was the way he didn't know anything that was going to come. That she would grow up to be so beautiful. That she'd keep everything to herself, like the most basic facts of her life were all secrets. I wondered if maybe that was why it was all a secret, because she had been so disappointed by his not being here. I imagined that one night while he was sitting on the edge of her bed she woke up, just a little bit, and saw him there. She wasn't much more than a baby, maybe two or three at the most. She opened her eyes and saw her father watching over her and said nothing, just went back to sleep. It was that safe for her then. But later, maybe just a week later, she woke up and he was gone. Just like that, and night after night that followed he was gone. Days he was gone. He didn't know that was coming either. He had no idea that he would die in a car. I didn't know if it was his car, if he was alone, if it was his fault.

I got out of bed and went to the window. My mother's house was still dark, but I didn't know if that meant she'd gone to bed or never come home at all. I thought that if something had happened to her I wouldn't know about it until morning.

I missed my mother's father. Is that even possible? Maybe I had fallen asleep for a while. Maybe I was like her, just waking up and looking for him to be there. I wondered how it would have changed things for all of us if he had stayed home the day he was supposed to die in his car. How his decision to go out for something small, something like coffee or orange juice which everyone could have done without, had changed things for all of us.

I went down the hall, into my father's bedroom. He slept with his door open. He was always afraid that something was going to happen to me in the night. That I'd be sick and call for him and he wouldn't wake up. I stood by his bed and looked at his shoes underneath the straight-backed chair, his overalls folded over the chair, his shirt hanging over the back. There was a picture of my mother holding me as a baby framed on the night table. She was trying hard to smile, but you could see in her eyes how much she hated having her picture taken. There was a paperback mystery novel, a box of blue Kleenex, reading glasses. I can't tell you the comfort I took in these things. They were always there, just exactly like that. He was facing away from me. The covers were pulled up to his neck even though the night wasn't cold. I watched his breath go in and out, as regular as a clock, until I felt better. And I did feel better, because he was something I understood. He was something that didn't change.

I was just through the hedge and heading up the path to Saint Elizabeth's the next morning when I saw Lorraine sitting on the front porch, waving at me like a mad woman. "Hey there," she called.

"Hey," I said.

"I've been looking for you all over the place. You're never around." She looked so much happier than she had on that first day. I had forgotten about her, really, how upset I'd been by the whole thing. I sat down next to her on the steps.

"I'm around all the time," I said. "I just usually come and go out the back. I don't actually live here."

"I know," she said. "That nice nun, Sister Bernadette, told me. Your parents work here."

"That's about the size of it."

"I thought when I met you in the lobby that day you were . . ." She opened her hands over her lap and laughed. I just couldn't see being sixteen, pregnant, and so damn cheerful about things.

"Nope," I said.

"Well, I wanted to thank you, for being so nice and all. That was a bad day, you know. My sister said she'd drive me up here but I took the bus like a dummy. Sometimes I get it in my head that I have to do everything by myself. I didn't tell Mother Corinne that Homer was dead. I wanted to thank you for that, too.''

"Sure," I said. Homer?

Lorraine looked out over the lawn. "It's so pretty here. I wonder if the babies ever stay in town. I mean, I wonder if the local people adopt them or if they're shipped off to places like New York.''

"I don't know," I said. I'd never thought about where the babies went, or where the girls went. I used to, when I was little, but then I stopped. I imagined if all the babies to come out of Saint Elizabeth's stayed in Habit the town would be pretty well flooded by now.

"If they don't tell me where my baby's going, I may just take a mind to keep it. You can keep your baby here. There're places in Texas where I hear they make you give the baby up, even if you change your mind halfway through. I wouldn't go there. I wouldn't go someplace that said I couldn't change my mind.''

I was feeling a little uncomfortable about this whole thing. I didn't like talking about what happened to the babies, it just made me sad.

"Where're you from?" I asked Lorraine, not because I was so interested but because I wanted to change the topic of conversation.

"Alabama," she said. "Birmingham. It seems pretty far away now, I'll tell you.''

"Why didn't you go someplace in Alabama?''

Lorraine looked at me like I was crazy. "There aren't any homes in Alabama. This is the last one in the South. These places started closing down years ago, that's what social services told me. There's not such a call for them anymore. It's not a big deal to have a kid on your own these days. Everybody wants to have a baby now, you know?''

"I guess I never thought about it.''

Lorraine took my hand and put it on her flat stomach. "Can you believe there's something in there?" she said.

I left her there on the front porch. She said she wanted to see me again, maybe walk into town and have a Coke, and I said sure, but I don't know that I meant it. Something about Lorraine unnerved me. I could still feel the warmth of her skin beneath her dress. She talked to me like any girl would if she was in the desk next to mine. She was like someone asking for answers in the middle of a math test. Even with Sister Bernadette telling her different, she didn't seem to understand I wasn't one of them.

I went past the lobby and the dining room and through the big swinging doors into the kitchen. Sister Evangeline was back in her chair, which Dad had recently moved next to the window. My mother was at the stove, making Cream of Wheat, so Sister must have slept through breakfast. She was the only person that my mother was willing to cook for after a meal had been served.

"Hey," I said, and kissed Sister Evangeline's cheek. "Are you better?"

Sister nodded. "Still a little tired, but the worst is behind me. How about you, angel?"

"Don't change the subject, we're talking about you. What was wrong?"

"She's turned into such a worrier," Sister Evangeline said to my mother.

"She gets it from Son," my mother said.

"There's no telling what was wrong, just a little bedevilment. I'm at an age where it doesn't need to be a thing anymore. My body just goes on holiday, like the banks."

I looked at her hands and saw that one of them was wrapped in gauze. "You cut yourself?" I touched her fingers, which looked nearly as white as the bandage and the white skirt they were resting on.

"This, I don't know. Who cuts themselves in bed? It's nothing big, though. Doesn't hurt." She held up her hand so that it faced me, palm out. "Your mother wrapped it up. Didn't she do a nice job?"

"It looks pretty professional," I said. I ran my fingers along the top of her bandage. Sister Evangeline was my grandmother. She was my aunt and my cousin. I wouldn't think about her age. If anything happened to her, it would be like losing all the family I had outside my parents.

"Mom's teaching me how to drive," I said.

Sister Evangeline beamed. She was like Dad. She took every piece of news that my mother and I were doing something together as a sign of change. "Oh, that's good. Rose loves to drive. That's her hobby, you know, that car. This will be good for her, for both of you."

My mother spooned the cereal into a bowl and brought it over to Sister Evangeline on a tray. "I don't know how teaching Cecilia to drive is going to be good for me," she said.

"It gets you out. It puts the two of you together." Sister Evangeline was always saying things to me and my mother that I could see her saying to either one of us, but not when both of us were in the same room. I looked at my mother, who didn't look at me.

"Eat your breakfast before it gets cold," she said. "You're getting thin, that's half your problem right there. You need to eat more."

"Everything tastes the same these days," Sister Evangeline said, blowing on a spoon of cereal to cool it off. "It's taken all the fun out of it."

"Do you have time for a lesson now?" I asked my mother. It shouldn't have mattered to me, I wasn't doing anything all day, but I wanted to get going. There were things I wanted to know.

My mother looked at her watch. "This is as good a time as any, I guess. You're all right?" she said to Sister Evangeline.

"I'm popular," she said. "There'll be girls in and out of here all day. You two go."

So my mother and I headed off to the car. I didn't say anything on the walk over. I was superstitious. I believed that the secret was to do our talking in the car. Outside of the car we should remain as normal as possible, which is to say, not talk.

I got in on the driver's side, turned the key, and slipped into reverse.

"What are you doing?" my mother said. "The car isn't warm."

"Sorry." I could actually feel my heart beating faster. I checked both my mirrors and sat up straight. I waited until the idle dropped and then I slowly backed out of the garage. Then we were out in the bright field. I went all the way around without saying anything. I tried to look like someone who was concentrating hard on her driving.

"That's good," my mother said.

I went around another half field for good measure. "I've been thinking about your father," I said, keeping my eyes straight in front of me, my speed down.

"My father?"

"Well, yeah. I mean, he would have been my grandfather. I've been thinking about that. I was wondering what his name was."

"Calvin," my mother said.

"How old were you when he died?"

"Three, I guess." My mother straightened out her skirt with her hands. "I used to think about him a lot when I was growing up, when I was your age, but then I stopped. Sometimes, every now and then when I read about someone in the paper who died in a car accident, then I'll wonder about him." She stopped and shook her head. "This is a morbid topic of conversation to have during a driving lesson."

"Did your mother ever get married again?" Every word out of my mouth felt like a step farther out onto the ice. I kept thinking she would tell me to pull the car over and just get out. She would just take her history and her privacy back to the kitchen.

"My mother did get married, but not for a long time." She stopped and thought about it for a minute. "It was almost twenty years, I guess. I'd already left home. It was good for her, though. I think she was happier being married." She leaned her head on her hand.

What I wanted to know about the most was her mother, but I couldn't imagine her ever telling me anything about that. My mother stared out her window, watching the same things go by again and again. I wondered if she was thinking about her father.

"I used to drive a lot," my mother said.

"Where did you go?"

"Anyplace. That was never the point. I just liked going. I used to go anyplace that I could get to in a day."

She trailed off and was quiet for a while. I didn't so much care about my mother's driving, but I wanted her to keep talking. "Where was the best place you ever went?"

"I drove all the way to Carmel from San Diego once. That was pretty great. I rented a hotel room by myself and sat on the bed for about five minutes, and then I checked out and drove all night to get home again. It was a stupid thing to do. I was so tired by the time I came in. But I think about that hotel room all the time. It was so nice. There was a bed near the window and you could open the shutters and look at the ocean. Carmel-by-the-Sea, that's the full name of the town. Do you ever wonder why you remember some things so well and not others?"

"Sure," I said, but I never had.

"You asking about my father makes me think of that. I don't remember him, but I could tell you everything about this hotel room I stayed in for five minutes eighteen years ago. There was a wood floor with a blue braided rug. Brass bed, white chenille spread. It was room number twelve. Why in the world would I know that?''

I felt like she was really asking me, and I didn't know what to tell her. ''Maybe it was a lot of fun,'' I said.

''It was,'' she said, looking out her window. ''It was fun.'' We were quiet for a while, and I knew that pretty soon it was going to be over for the day, and maybe tomorrow she wouldn't be talking. I wanted her to tell me everything. ''I've about had it with this field,'' my mother said. ''I think it's time we branched out a little.''

I stopped the car and turned to face her. ''Where do you want to go?''

''I don't know,'' she said. ''It doesn't really matter. Let's just get on the road.''

''Road driving?''

''Sure.'' She reached over to me and for some reason I jumped back. It caught me off guard. ''God, you're nervous,'' she said, and looped a piece of my hair behind my ear.

I looped the car onto the dirt road that ran from my mother's house down to Saint Elizabeth's and out onto the Green River Parkway. We passed my father and I waved to him from my open window.

''I'm driving, Dad!'' I called out, and he waved back.

I pulled up behind Saint Elizabeth's and stopped again. ''Let's get Sister Evangeline,'' I said. ''She never goes anyplace. Let's take her with us.''

''Wait here,'' my mother said, and got out of the car. She ran up the front steps and I waited for her, the car idling. I was as happy at that moment as I could ever remember being in my life. I slapped the steering wheel with my palm and turned on the radio, but I couldn't get anything to come in.

Then my mother was there, holding Sister Evangeline in her arms like a bundle of laundry. Her arms were around my mother's neck. ''Open the door,'' my mother said.

I got out and ran around to the other side of the car. Sister got in herself, and my mother leaned over and got her settled. Then my mother and I got back in. We were laughing, the way girls laugh when they're doing something bad. It wasn't bad, but it felt that way.

''Look at this,'' Sister Evangeline said as I pulled out onto the road. ''Cecilia driving.''

''You bet,'' I said.

"Where are we going?" she asked, leaning forward for an answer.

"Nowhere," my mother called back loudly so that the sound of her voice wouldn't all fly out the window and onto the road.

$$=== 3 ===$$

MY FATHER walked in the front door just as I was getting ready to go out. His face was covered in blood. His hands stayed at his eyes. He kept wiping them over and over again just to see for a second. His white shirt was dyed red, starting at the neck. It was soaking down, making the bib of his overalls a dark blue-brown. There was blood in his hair and on his shoes. He took one step inside the house, realized that he was getting blood on the floor, and stepped back out onto the porch. I didn't know whose blood it was at first. It didn't occur to me for a full minute that it could have been his.

"Dad?" I said, and held out my arms to him. He wiped his eyes again and again, trying to see me there. He cocked his head to one side. He looked like he almost remembered me. Like he couldn't quite place my face.

"Cecilia?" he said.

Then he fainted there on the porch. He didn't go over straight, he just sort of folded, sank to his knees and then to his hands and then fell over to one side. He turned over a chair on his way down, one that he'd been working on refinishing in the evenings. He'd been holding onto the back of it to help him stand up. It wasn't until my father said my name that I could really register what was going on, how bad it was. My father had never called me Cecilia in his life.

I started doing a million things at once. I squatted down beside him and then stood up again. I pulled his legs out from under him so he was lying flat on his back. I touched the top of his head. I ran inside and took three pillows off the sofa and put them under his head. I ran into the kitchen and then just stood there for a minute, looking around, trying to find something that would help. I looked at the teakettle and the potholders hanging

over the stove. I looked at the tablecloth. I saw the blood on my
fingers and wiped it off on my shorts. I got a glass of water. I
took the dishtowel off the refrigerator door and wet it, then I
started to go outside again. I came back and pulled the tablecloth
off the table, sending the blue china sugar bowl flying halfway
across the room. When it broke the sugar swept over the floor
like a layer of frost.

I ran back to my father and put the glass of water beside him.
The red was working its way across the pillows now, turning all
the flowers and leaves a darker color. I wiped his face with the
dishtowel. The blood had caked at the corners of his mouth and
around his eyes. His forehead was cut clean across in a straight
line and the blood was still pulsing from the edges of the cut. I
couldn't imagine where he had cut himself like this, if he had
fallen and hit his head on the front steps, if there had been an
accident. I lifted up his head in my hand. It was so much heavier
than I thought it would have been and that's when I first realized
I couldn't move him inside. My father was the one who picked
people up. Always when a girl's time came and she felt she
couldn't walk, my father carried her to the car. He carried me
everywhere when I was little. I saw him picking up Sister
Evangeline in her chair and moving her across the room like it
was nothing. But who in the world could carry him? I slid the
tablecloth under his head and wrapped it around like a towel,
making it as tight as I could. Maybe it hurt him, because he
raised up his head and opened his eyes a little.

"Lie still," I said, even though he wasn't trying to go anywhere.

"You all right?" he said.

I nodded. He was asking me because I was crying.

He took hold of my hand. "Get your mother," he said. But
I just sat there, stupid. "Go," he said.

At the word go I was up like a shot, running down the front
steps. I slipped on something wet and came down hard on the
path, on my knees and one hand. The gravel dug into my skin
and I tried to get up again. I was clawing at the steps to get up
and then a second later was running on the goat trail that con-
nects our house to Saint Elizabeth's. I was running as fast as I
had ever run anywhere in my life. I wasn't wearing my shoes.

I came up the steps of the back porch and through the door
like a shot. I came into the kitchen wild, out of breath, yelling
for my mother.

"Cecilia!" Sister Evangeline said.

"Where's Mom!" My voice was so loud. It had to be loud enough to be heard over my breath.

"What's happened to you?"

"Dad fell," I said, though I didn't know if he had fallen. "Dad's hurt."

"Your mother isn't here." She stood up, shaky, and came to me. "She's gone with Mother Corinne and Sister Bernadette to take some girls to the doctor." She took my hand and turned it over, palm up. When she touched it I sucked my breath in. A pain went all the way up my arm. "Call an ambulance," she said.

I went to the phone by the door and dialed the hospital in Owensboro. We all knew the number. Girls had babies around here every day. We all knew the number by heart.

"I'm in Habit," I said when someone answered, but then I was crying and I couldn't make myself stop. Sister Evangeline took the phone from my hand.

"We're at Saint Elizabeth's," she said. "We need an ambulance." There was a pause and I looked at her. "Yes," she said and waited. "Yes." She put her hand over the receiver. "Can you drive there? He says it will be a lot faster if someone can drive him up."

"Mom's not here," I said.

"Can you drive there?" she said to me again.

I looked at her. Her face was clear. She was looking at me so hard that it made me calm down for a minute. "Yes, I can drive."

"She'll drive him there," Sister said into the phone. "Yes."

Sister Evangeline hung up the phone and put a hand on each of my arms. "Listen to me, Cecilia. You pull yourself together right now. You're the grown-up now. Do you understand me? No tears." She wiped beneath my eyes with her thumbs. "I'll wait for your mother. I'll send her up just as soon as she comes, but for right now it's on you."

I nodded at her.

"Go on now," she said. "Give your father my love."

I went out the kitchen door, fast but more careful, and who was standing there but Lorraine.

"Sweet Jesus," she said, looking pale herself.

"Come on," I said. "Help me."

We went up to the shed and I backed out the car. I did what my mother said. I looked behind me. I kept it straight. It was strange to feel the rubber pedals under my bare feet, and I curled my toes around the top of them. Lorraine sat beside me, looking at me like I was a maniac. "What's going on here?" she said.

"My father's been hurt," I said. "We have to take him to Owensboro."

"Hurt," she said. "Hurt like how?" She reached over to wipe off one of my knees with the hem of her skirt.

"He cut his head," I said.

"Oh," she said, sighing. "It's not like a heart attack or anything."

"No," I said, and felt better then for some reason, thinking of something worse that it wasn't. "Do you know how to drive?" I asked her, suddenly hopeful.

"No," she said. "Christ, don't you?"

"Yeah," I said.

I cut across the back pasture, driving through the dried creek bed where the spring used to be. I was too scared about other things to be scared about driving. I pulled the Dodge right up to the front steps and got out of the car. I left it running, the door wide open. Lorraine crawled over the bench seat and out my side. My father was still there. I don't know why this surprised me. I had been afraid for some reason that he'd be gone.

"Dad?" I said. I tried to kneel beside him but my knees hurt when they hit the wooden planks. I came up again then squatted down on my toes. The tablecloth was red in the front, but not all the way around. I took this to be a good sign. "Dad," I said again, "Lorraine's here."

"Hi, Son," she said. All of the girls called my father by his first name.

Dad's eyes blinked open and he smiled at me. "I'm feeling better," he said. "Hi, Lorraine," he said. He didn't look at her.

"You're going to have to help us get you in the car," I said. "Can you get up okay?" Not that I knew what I was going to do if he said no.

"Sure," he said, keeping still. "I just passed out. The sight of blood always gets to me, even when it's mine. I don't think it was anything so big." He sounded so conversational, chatty, like we were talking about baseball scores or something. "Is your mother here?"

"She'll be right behind us," I said. I looked up at Lorraine, who was holding onto the porch railing, looking sick.

"I'm not so good with blood myself," Lorraine said.

"Get over it," I hissed at her. "Come here, get on the other

side of him." Lorraine came and stood on the other side of my
father. She stared at me like an idiot. "Take his arm," I said.

I counted to three and then Lorraine and I pulled and Dad sat
up. He touched his hand to his head. "I'll be fine," he said.
We got him on his feet and over to the porch railing. We were
only steadying him. We stood beside him, one on each side,
and helped him down the steps. He put his arm on my shoulder
and leaned into it with his hand. "Lie down in the backseat.
Put your head up against the door." My father seemed so relieved once he was actually in the car. I got one of the couch
pillows, one that wasn't as stained as the others, and leaned over
the front seat and put it under his head.

"This is good," he said to me. "Everything will be fine
now."

Lorraine got in on the passenger side and I closed my door.
I remembered again that I didn't have any shoes on and thought
for a minute about running upstairs for some, but I just wanted
to go. I turned the car onto the dirt road and headed out past
Saint Elizabeth's to the Green River Parkway.

Once you get on the parkway, it's pretty much a straight shot
up to Owensboro, but I was used to driving with my mother.
She told me when to speed up and slow down, when it was safe
to go.

"You really shouldn't be driving, honey," my father said from
the backseat.

"I thought you knew how to drive," Lorraine said. "Look,
I'm going to have a baby—"

"Don't be stupid," I said to her. "I'm driving, aren't I?" I
should have been nicer to Lorraine. The truth was, I needed
her.

"She's a good driver," Dad said. He was coming around, I
could tell by his voice. Dad had never driven with me before.

"What happened to you?" I said, glancing back at him in my
rearview mirror. There were too many cars on the road. My
hands were sweating. I thought there was a chance I would kill
all of us, me and Dad, Lorraine and her baby.

"It was just dumb," he said. "I went into the basement without turning the lights on and I walked straight into a low beam.
Forty years I've been going into that basement. You'd think I'd
know where everything was by now."

"You cut your head at Saint Elizabeth's?" I couldn't believe
this.

"In the basement," he repeated.

"And you walked all the way home? Why didn't you go up-stairs and get help?"

"I didn't think it was that bad. I knew it was bleeding and I didn't want to walk in and scare one of the girls."

"That's so nice," Lorraine said.

"It is not nice!" I said. I was panicked. I saw my father walking across the back pasture, half blind. I saw him falling down in the grass, nowhere close to the house. I wanted to pull the car over to the side of the road and scream at both of them. "What if I hadn't been home?" I said. "You could have bled to death! You could have just lay there on the front porch all day." I tightened my hands around the steering wheel.

"Don't get so upset," my father said. "Nothing bad's hap-pened."

But something terrible had happened. I was driving a car I wasn't so sure how to drive to a place I'd never driven to. I had seen my father covered in blood. I saw him fall down right in front of me. I saw that he was old and that I couldn't pick him up. I saw a way that he could die.

"I've never been to Owensboro before," Lorraine said. "I was sick the last time everybody went up for mass."

There were signs for the hospital. I didn't have any trouble finding it. I pulled into the emergency entrance, barely missing a parked car on my left side. There were men there waiting with a wheelchair. They didn't look like they were waiting for anyone in particular. One of the guys was sitting in it, smoking a ciga-rette. They helped my father in while Lorraine and I stood and watched. I gave one of them the car keys. I was happy to be rid of them.

"I love this hospital," my dad said. "This is where you were born."

I rolled my eyes behind him. A nurse came up and started asking us questions. She handed me a clipboard with a pile of forms pinned on top. She stared at me for a minute and then came back with another wheelchair. "Sit down," she said to me.

"Sissy," Dad said. "Is something wrong?"

"Nothing's wrong," I said. "It's your blood. You go on." I kissed my father on the cheek, just below his red turban, and then they wheeled him away.

"Sit," the nurse said.

"Sit down," Lorraine said, and put her hand on my shoulder, guiding me into the chair. The nurse bent over and looked at my knees and my hands. "You might need a stitch or two yourself." I straightened out my legs and looked at my knees. There were long stripes of blood going down my shins and onto my feet. My feet were incredibly dirty.

She took me back to an empty room and washed out the cuts with soapy water while Lorraine stood behind me and patted my hair in a way I found unbelievably annoying. The nurse swabbed the cuts with iodine, which hurt like hell, and then wrapped everything up neatly. "You'll be okay like that," she said. "It wasn't too bad, once I got them all cleaned out. Just sit for a while, okay? No running around."

Lorraine wheeled me back out into the lobby, taking the red vinyl chair beside me for herself. One of the orderlies came up and gave me back the car keys. We sat there quietly, just soaking it all in. Things with my father weren't so bad. He was fine, like he said he was. People cut themselves all the time and sometimes they pass out. No big deal. But what I kept hearing was Lorraine saying heart attack. I thought of my father's heart, attacking him from the inside, the two of us in the house alone, and what could I do but stand there and watch him? Something had shifted imperceptibly between us in those few minutes on the porch. All these years my father had been wondering how he was going to take care of me, how he was going to protect me from things. I remember how nervous he was when I was old enough to walk to school alone. He walked behind me, staying a block or two away the whole time, trying to hide behind trees and not realizing they just don't make trees that big. I knew he was there, Christ, everybody knew he was there, but I kept my eyes straight ahead. I was old enough to walk to school alone. If he wouldn't let me, then I'd just pretend.

But now I'd seen him look old. I'd seen him grab for something and fall down just the same, and I didn't begin to know how I was going to be able to protect him from things. It was just the two of us in that house. Even though my mother lived just across the field, it would not be close enough. I wouldn't be able to count on someone else and my father would be counting on me.

"Guess this is where I'll be soon enough," Lorraine said, patting her stomach.

Just the sound of her voice was jarring. I was too far away in my own thoughts to remember that she had problems of her own to worry about. I was always forgetting Lorraine was pregnant. She wore loose tops and as far as I could tell she wasn't showing at all. She just seemed too dumb to be pregnant, too much of a kid. She wasn't like the girls who came to Saint Elizabeth's. Those girls seemed glamorous, even when they weren't much older than me. "You nervous?" I said, picking at the edge of the gauze around my hand.

Lorraine twisted up her mouth and looked down the long green corridor to the double doors where they took people away. "Sure," she said. "I don't know. I mean, it's still a long way off, a lot of things could happen."

"What? Like your boyfriend coming back?"

She laughed. "He wasn't exactly my boyfriend. Naw, I mean something else. I don't know what, but something. I've been kinda getting into this whole Catholic thing here, praying to saints, confession, miracles. I've been taking communion and praying to Saint Theresa." She reached down inside her shirt and brought up a medal on a silver chain. "See, that's Saint Theresa, the little flower. Sister Bernadette gave it to me. She told me to just keep praying and everything would work out all right."

"You're not supposed to take communion," I said. "You're not even Catholic."

She dropped the medal back into her shirt but kept one finger on top of it. "Nobody knows that except you. I don't see how it could make any difference anyway. What kind of saint would Theresa be if she only paid attention to Catholics?"

I wanted to tell her she shouldn't bother. I'd seen it. All of it. Girls who thought they were going to be saved and girls who thought they would keep their babies in the end. Nothing works out. But then I figured it wasn't my place. If wearing a medal made her happy, then what the hell difference did it make to me?

Then all of the sudden my mother came in with Mother Corinne. The two of them were walking up the hall about ninety miles an hour. "Over here," I said, waving.

"You're in a wheelchair!" my mother said. "Sister Evangeline said it was Son. My God, what's happened?"

I stood up to show them I could. My mother was wearing a dress because she'd been at the doctor's. It just that minute occurred to me they must have been in Owensboro that morning. They must have driven back. "I'm fine," I said. "I just fell and scraped my knees."

"She's really fine," Lorraine said, like she was some kind of Greek chorus or something.

"Dad hit his head in the basement and cut it up pretty bad, so I brought him up here."

"You drove here?" my mother said.

"Well, what was I supposed to do, wait for you to get home?"

"You shouldn't have brought Lorraine," Mother Corinne said, her hands locked together in one angry knot. "She's a minor. She's the responsibility of Saint Elizabeth's."

"She needed my help," Lorraine said, looking down at the floor.

"You never should have driven here," my mother said. "You don't even have a license."

"What is this? I was the one who was home. I was the one who did what they were supposed to do."

"I'm driving Lorraine home," Mother Corinne said, and put a heavy hand on Lorraine's shoulder like she was some kind of juvenile delinquent. "The two of you can work this out yourselves."

"I did need Lorraine," I said furiously. "She helped me get him in the car. I needed some help, and Lorraine was the only person who was home. Don't make her feel like she's done something."

Lorraine looked up at me and a wave of pure gratitude came over her face. "I'll see you at home," she said quietly, and the two of them went down the hall. Mother Corinne's skirts swung out to the side when she walked and nearly swallowed Lorraine up whole.

"I know this was hard for you," my mother said once they were gone. "But you should have thought things through. You should have just called an ambulance and waited. You could have done a lot more damage to everyone by driving here."

I'd been good through all of this. Ever since my father said go, I'd done this whole thing and held it together and been okay, but now all of that was gone. I didn't want to be the one to have seen him hurt. It should have been her. She should have been the one who was there. I wanted to know exactly where she got off telling me that I'd done anything wrong. "Don't you tell me what I can and can't do," I said, trying to keep my voice down. "You can't be gone all the time and then waltz in here like you're somebody's mother and tell me what I'm allowed to do."

"Watch your tone," my mother said, holding her voice as even as Mother Corinne's.

"No," I said. I took a step toward her. "Think about it. What if I hadn't been there? How many days do you think he would have been lying on the porch before you noticed he was missing? How long would Dad have been dead before you swung by the house to say you needed a light bulb changed and so you wanted him to come by?"

My mother stared at me, her cheeks flushing, and right then I wished she'd hit me. I wished she cared enough for once to just do something.

"I'm going back to see your father," Rose said, turning away.

"I'm sure he'd love that," I said.

I watched her walk away from me and wished my eyes could burn holes in her back. You'd have thought that enough had happened for one day without having my mother decide to play responsible family member. It was one thing to put up with her endless indifference, but to have her act like she actually gave a rip since it was convenient to do so was more than I could stand. I sat in my wheelchair and kept my eyes trained on the swinging doors at the end of the hall. Any minute now she'd walk through them and I'd go right up to her and tell her she could go to hell for all I cared. She'd done a rotten job. She had never for a minute put me first. Jesus, look around you, I'd say to her. Saint Elizabeth's is full of girls who can't raise their children. At least they're kind enough to give them away.

My mother came through the doors at a fast clip, put her hand on my shoulder, and whispered in my ear, "Your father isn't feeling well so you just pull it together until we get home. No fighting in front of him."

"You're worried about me upsetting Dad?" I said, but she put up her hand to stop me. They were wheeling my father into the hall. He had a thick pad across his forehead and a layer of gauze wrapped around his head. He looked like a war hero, a general, coming home from battle.

"There's my smart girl," Dad said to me. I went to him. I picked up his hand from the armrest and felt better that quick. I had my father. If not my mother, my father.

"You should have seen this one," he said to my mother, and kissed my hand. "She's going to be a nurse. No, she's going to be a doctor. She knew exactly what to do. She was a professional straight through. She even drove up here, can you believe that?"

"She told me," my mother said.

"Cool as a cucumber. I wouldn't have believed it. She didn't get it from her dad, that's for sure. You put me in a crisis like that and I just fall all to pieces. This one's got a real head on her shoulders.''

The nurse wheeled us to the front door. ''Where's the car?'' my mother said.

''Some orderly parked it when we came in.'' I dropped the keys in her hand and pointed to the far side of the parking lot. ''Over there. Somewhere.''

My mother wrapped her hand tight around the keys. ''Wait here,'' she said. ''I'll just be a minute.'' Then she headed off into the dark.

''I'm so proud of you, Sissy,'' my father said.

''You scared me to death.'' I looked out over the parking lot. It was so quiet out there. No one was coming into the hospital. No one was sick.

''I told the doctor what you did. He said you did everything right. I guess some people are just born knowing things. June was that way.'' He put his hand on my hip and pressed me against his chair. ''You know, this is crazy, but when I hit my head I thought it was June's house I was going to, not just her house, but to June, like she was still there. That's 'cause if a fellow was to hit his head, June would be the most logical person to go to. She was solid, like you are. That's what I was thinking about when the doctor was stitching me up, how much you've turned out to be like June.''

I looked down at him. I'd never thought about that. It was a nice thing to say. Nobody was a better person than June. But for some reason it gave me a shiver, too. June was stuck there, like all her niceness wouldn't let her get away.

''Maybe it's because she had you when you were a baby,'' my father said. ''I was against it. I can tell you now that you're older. I thought it should have been your mother taking care of you when you were little. But Rose knew, she knew there was something June had to give you, and she was right. There isn't a person in the world I'd be prouder to see you grow up to be like.''

Then my mother drove up in front of us and I held my father's hand while he got up out of the chair. ''Let me sit in the back,'' he said. ''I'll get some rest back there.''

I waited until he was in the car and then closed the door and went to get up front. My mother kept her eyes straight ahead as she pulled out onto the road.

On the way home we told the story of my father's accident again and again. He told my mother what had happened. I said

what I'd thought, about it not being his blood when I first saw
him there. My mother looked pale as we went over the details,
like maybe the whole thing upset her. But it could have just been
that it was dark and she looked whiter against the night sky.

"How many stitches did you get?" my mother asked.

"Fifty-seven," he said. "Can you believe that? They'll be in
for two weeks, the doctor said."

I watched her drive. She was so casual about it, the way she
only looped one wrist through the bottom of the steering wheel.
She watched my father in the rearview mirror while they talked.

"That girl, Lorraine," my father said. "She sure was nice."

"She was a big help. Now she'll probably get in all sorts of
trouble for not telling anybody where she was going."

"That's ridiculous," my father said. "I'll talk to Mother Corinne about it. I'll just explain it to her. She'll understand."

"I hope so," I said, looking at my mother's profile against a
row of passing streetlights. She had missed dinner. I thought it
might have been the first time she'd ever missed fixing a meal
at Saint Elizabeth's.

My mother drove us right to our house and parked the car
there in front of the stairs. She looked around slowly, taking it
all in. She stared down at her feet. The door was wide open.
"Good God," she said, walking up the porch steps on her toes.

Dad and I got out of the car and followed her up. I could see
now it was blood I had slipped on. It went across everything
like a thin coat of paint. It was all exactly as we had left it. Three
stained pillows, the dishtowel soaked and red, a glass of water,
the chair overturned. "What a mess," my father said.

"Don't worry about it," I told him. "I'll clean it up. It looks
a lot worse than it is."

We went inside and my father lay down on the couch. I brought
a pillow out of the spare bedroom for his head.

"I'm going to get us something for dinner," my mother said.
"Will you be all right while I'm gone?"

My father looked up at her and smiled. "Of course," he said.
"I'm here," I said.

My mother nodded and went back out the door. "Two minutes," she said over her shoulder.

"What are you two fighting about now?" my father said after
she'd left.

"We're not fighting."

"Okay," he said, and sighed. "I'm tired enough to just believe you tonight.'' His eyes flicked down for a second and then back up again. ''I may go to sleep for a minute.''

''You do that,'' I said. I pulled an old green afghan that had been June's over him. ''I'm going to straighten up some.'' I leaned over and kissed the top of his head, but he didn't say anything.

I got a bucket of soapy water and a brush from the kitchen, switched on the front porch light, and went outside. It was turning into a nice night, clear and a little cool. I threw the pillows and the towel onto the lawn and got to work on the wood. The blood came up easy, but there was a lot of it. I kept finding new spots every time I thought I'd finished. It made me think about my father, how I would take care of him. This was nothing, but it felt like the start, and I was going to have to figure out how to get ready for it. I wouldn't be getting any help from my mother. You could bet on that.

I was still mad at her, but a little less so. Maybe I was just tired. I wanted to be able to stop hoping that she would turn into something else. I wanted not to want her so much anymore. It was getting old. Every time something happened to make me feel close to her again, even something as stupid as driving lessons, she was always waiting right around the bend with a new way to prove to me how little the whole thing mattered to her. You'd think a person would learn after a while. That's what amazed me about myself. I was so damn slow to learn.

I sat down on the steps for a minute and wiped off my hands on my shorts, which were already about as covered with dirt and blood as a piece of clothing can get and still qualify as fabric. I saw the chair lying on its side and reached over and grabbed a leg to set it right again, when I saw something written underneath it, on the bottom of the seat. *"Merry Christmas to Rose, from your friend, Son. 1968."*

It was a nice chair. It had been in my mother's house for as long as I could remember. Dad had been stripping the varnish off of it so he could do it over again. I never knew he'd made it. I didn't know it was a present for my mother. I reached under the chair and touched the carved letters. I ran a finger over Christmas, Rose, Son, 1968. I was born in February of 1969. He would have given her this chair just before I was born. But it was signed, your friend, not, your husband, or, with all my love. It was sweet. It was like something my dad would say. He wanted to be her friend more than anything. That's what he was trying to tell her even then.

My mother came up the stairs, her arms full of bags. "Careful," I said. "They're wet."

"Oh," she said, and put the bags down on them anyway. "Where's your father?"

"He's asleep," I nodded back toward the house, "on the couch."

My mother sat down beside me on the stairs. "I didn't realize at first how bad this whole thing was. I thought it was just a little cut." She wrapped her arms around her knees like she was cold. "I talked to Sister Evangeline. I shouldn't have said that about you driving. You had to, I understand that now."

I shrugged and wiped up a spot of blood I'd missed. We were both quiet for a long time. There had always been things I'd wanted to say to my mother, things I'd wanted to know, but I'd been raised by my father who taught me through everything he did that my mother was someone I'd be better off not bothering too much. Sitting there on the porch I just didn't care anymore.

"Why did you move?" I said, looking straight at her.

"Move where?"

I pointed across the field to the little house with no lights on. In the dark it was barely a smudge at the edge of the woods. If you didn't know what you were looking for you'd never be able to see it at all. "Over there. Why don't you live with us?"

"I don't see what this has to do with your father's accident," my mother said flatly.

"It doesn't have anything to do with it, really. I just wanted to know. I've always wanted to know." I thought about it for a minute. "Maybe it does have something to do with it," I said.

My mother looked at me. I could see her thinking it all out, which way to go with this. "That's between your father and me," she said.

I shook my head. "If it was between you and Dad, that would mean that he understood, and if he did he would have told me. No," I said. "I want the real reason."

"It's personal," she said, her voice cooling off like the night.

I wasn't afraid. The day had been too much. I had been so afraid since the moment I saw my father's blood that this seemed like nothing suddenly. It was like finding out that dog you had walked three blocks out of your way to avoid every day of your life had no teeth, and in one second you go from being scared of something to maybe even feeling kind of sorry for it. Maybe. "It is personal," I said. "It's personal to me, my life. You're my mother, the man on the couch is your husband, and yet all we seem to be to you are two more mouths to feed. I just want to understand. It's not even like you hate us. I mean, I think I could deal with that. I could get over it. But you don't hate us, you don't even know we're there. Most of the time I feel like I'm either irritating you or boring you to death and I really want to know why."

My mother held her back so straight all the time, even when there was nothing to lean against. "I said I was sorry about the car. I made a mistake. If I'd known your father was so badly hurt I never would have said what I did."

I slapped my hands down hard on the porch and the sound made both of us jump. "You just won't do this, will you? You won't tell me. I'd really gotten to the point that I thought the problem was that I was afraid to ask, but that isn't it at all. I'm so far beneath you, you don't even think I deserve an answer."

She was quiet for a while. "No," she said. "It's not like that."

"Then what is it like? What? Tell me why I'm wrong. Tell me what it is you want." I felt like I was being pulled off the steps, like every force in nature was trying to get me to say, to hell with you, and stalk off into the night. But I fought it. I didn't want to make it that easy on her.

"I guess I always thought that just being here was enough. It's been so hard for me to stay sometimes." She kept her eyes fixed across the field, on her house, the place she wanted to be. "I kept my promises and did what I said I was going to do. Sometimes I fight," she said, and put her fingers on her chest, "just with myself. The part that wants to go and the part that promised to stay. When I moved back to the old house it was because I thought I was going to leave altogether." She waited. Every word seemed to be a burden for her, like she was lifting them up one by one and handing them to me. "Nothing had happened, really, nothing had changed. It was just that I wanted to go again. All these years I thought I'd done a good job because I'd found a way to stay, but I guess if you didn't know those things to begin with, it wouldn't have looked like I was doing anything especially heroic. It probably doesn't look that way even if you do know those things."

"It's that awful for you? We're so bad you have to fight just to stay on the property?"

My mother smiled a little, like I had made a joke. "It isn't you at all. It's just me." She reached out a finger and ran it down along my arm. It felt so strange. "I don't know why things didn't work out better with you," she said. "There were always so many people around who wanted you. So many mothers. I just guess I didn't have it in me. I'd done such a bad job being a daughter. I never could get over that. Maybe I'd been wanting my own mother back for so long it never really occurred to me that I was supposed to be one, a mother. But I shouldn't have given you away, Cecilia. I'm sorry about that."

"You didn't give me away," I said. But she had. That was exactly what she'd done.

"I'm not like you," she said quietly. "I don't think about things the way you do. You give me a lot of credit I don't deserve." She wrapped her arms around her waist, as tight as I had ever wanted to be held. "You think I'm holding things in, fighting them back. The truth is, I don't ever think about the past. It took a long time to learn not to, and now I just don't. I don't ever think about it. I'd do just about anything in the world to avoid thinking about it. The past should stay behind you, where it belongs."

I looked at her, her beautiful face. I felt tired and sad and it was as strong as the anger I had felt before. I had never thought my mother needed my help, and now that I could finally see that maybe she did, I had no idea what to do for her.

"Come on," she said. "Come inside and help me make dinner."

I wanted to say something nice, but I didn't know what. "I'm not mad anymore," I told her.

She smiled at me. She looked relieved, even though I knew she had forgotten I had ever been mad. "Good," she said. "I'm glad."

My mother and I got up and carried the sacks of groceries into the house, quietly past my father. I picked up the pieces of the sugar bowl and swept the floor, and my mother found a new tablecloth in the linen closet. We didn't talk much while we were making dinner. I should have asked her other things, about her mother and what had happened, but it was enough for one night.

When dinner was ready I went into the living room and woke my father up and he said he felt better. The three of us sat at the table together and talked about little things, girls who were about to have their babies and my pen pal, Sylvia, in Spain. We talked about the garden my mother wanted to put out this year, and my father said he knew a place that would be perfect and would till up the soil for her. It was the first time in my life the three of us had had dinner together. Just the three of us, in a house that was ours, and I kept thinking it was the first time things had felt normal. There was my father with his head sewn up and my mother just having told me her life was a joke and I finally felt like things were a little bit normal.

LORRAINE made herself right at home. She showed up in the afternoons, flopped herself down on the couch, and put up her feet. "I think Robert De Niro is cute," she said. "I like older men."

"We're talking about De Niro now?" I brought a bag of potato chips in from the kitchen. Lorraine needed salt. She practically took it straight from the shaker. Lorraine was salt by this point. The doctor was always checking her to see if she was all right, but she was fine, just hungry. "What happened to the other one? What's his name? The one yesterday."

"Too light, I decided. Men should be dark. Italians. Al Pacino." She took the bag and tore it all the way down the middle. It was clear she wasn't planning on rolling it back up later on.

I owed Lorraine, no doubt about it. But in all fairness to her I don't think that's what she was thinking of when she decided to make herself a permanent fixture in my house. The truth was, Lorraine just seemed to like it better here than at Saint Elizabeth's.

"They're all so serious over there," she said. "I mean, give it a rest. How many hours in the day can you discuss the size of your ankles?"

It wasn't what she'd done for me, helping me with my dad and taking the heat from Mother Corinne. It was just that we'd spent this time together, and now she wanted to be friends. She'd wanted to be friends all along. After the accident she started showing up and asking me to go for walks. Then she just started coming in and getting comfortable. Sometimes she'd come by right after breakfast, or come home with me after dinner, running half the way back to make bed check in time. Lorraine's roommate was a girl named Loelle, who divided her time equally between reading romance novels and sobbing. "Loelle," Lorraine said. "Do you think she made that name up or what?" She ate a potato chip and ran her finger down the inside edges of the bag, fishing out the salt. "Not that I haven't tried talking to her, but she's one of those people that likes to cry alone."

I guess my feelings for Lorraine had softened a little bit. She still got on my nerves, but it was summer and I was pretty bored. Summer at Saint Elizabeth's could be deadly. After years of having people tell me everything about their life, it was nice to have someone I could talk to for a change.

It wasn't just me that Lorraine was interested in, she wanted my whole family. My father, who liked just about everybody anyway, took a special interest in her after our trip to the hospital. The fact that she had taken up residence on our couch and in our refrigerator seemed like the most natural thing in the world to him. He even made a point of buying the foods she liked: chips, pretzels, olives, canned anchovies.

"Jesus, Son," she said when he came home from having his stitches out. "It looks like someone hit you in the head with an axe."

We were watching "Jeopardy," keeping score on the back of an envelope. I looked up and saw him standing in the doorway, a red crease in his forehead which went straight across above both eyebrows.

"You think?" he said, touching it lightly.

"I don't think," I said, and threw a couch pillow at Lorraine. We'd had to buy new ones. I couldn't get the others clean.

"It gives you character," she said. "It makes you mysterious."

I could never get used to the way she talked to my father. It was almost like she was flirting with him. Not that she was, I don't think, but it embarrassed me to death just the same. Dad never seemed to notice.

"They did a good job, I thought," he said. "The doctor said it will fade some. It won't wind up being this bad."

"It isn't so bad," I said, even though it was. "We'll put some vitamin E on it. I read where that's supposed to make the difference."

But Dad just shrugged and headed out to the kitchen to find his tape measure. "Just one of those things," he said.

"You didn't need to make him self-conscious about it," I whispered to Lorraine.

"He's not self-conscious," she said. "You're just crazy."

Lorraine was famous for saying whatever came into her head.
There was no processing a thought with her. Something would
occur to her and a split second later it was out of her mouth.

My father wasn't the only member of the family she was
trying to endear herself to. She had signed up to be the helper
in the kitchen and liked it so well she wound up putting in twice
the hours of any of the other girls. Sister Evangeline had already
told her she was going to have a boy. Lorraine joked about
calling him Cecil for me. "Cecil Stone," she said, because
Stone was her last name.

My mother liked Lorraine as well as she liked anybody else
in the world, which is to say fine but not with any particular
warmth. Lorraine, on the other hand, was fascinated by my
mother.

"I can't imagine having Rose as a mother," she said. "She's
very mysterious." Mysterious was one of Lorraine's favorite
words. Robert De Niro was mysterious. The hotel was mysterious. My mother was mysterious. "I bet she had a lot of lovers
when she was young."

"She's my mother, for Christ's sake. Can't you give it a rest?"

"She wasn't always your mother," she said, trying her best
to sound worldly. "She did have a life before you, you know."

Lorraine liked to make it sound like she and my mother were
together in that other life, being beautiful and young, sitting in
cafés in Paris, drinking espresso and making daring eyes at the
waiters. She probably saw the two of them under a red umbrella,
exchanging sex tips or something. Lorraine wanted to be close
to my mother, but I could have told her she was out of luck.

Nothing had really changed with my mother after we talked the
night of my father's accident. I thought it would somehow. I
even thought that she might stay over, move home. But after the
last dish was in the dish rack, she said good night and headed
out across the pasture. My father stood out on the front porch,
waving, then just watching her go. He was so happy that night.
Having his head split open was well worth it to him if it meant
we all sat down together as a family and had dinner. But for me
it felt even worse. I was wanting her again. I was wishing she
would stay.

We still had driving lessons, and in the car she was more
inclined to talk. "I don't know why you want to keep having
lessons," she said when I asked for one a few days later. "You

drove all the way to Owensboro by yourself. What more can I teach you?''

"It was a fluke," I said. "It doesn't mean I know anything."

So every two or three days she'd agree to go out with me. We drove around in circles: east to Reynolds Station, south to Pleasant Ridge, north to Philpot. She told me about dates she went on in high school, working in a candy factory, the ocean. But mostly what my mother wanted to talk about when she was in the car was the car itself, driving.

"I picked up a hitchhiker once," she said.

"You're kidding me."

"No, I did. And if I ever catch you picking one up so help me God I'll kill you, if he doesn't do it first."

"Where was this?"

"In Texas, I think, maybe west Oklahoma. He was going to some little town in Arkansas. His name was Billy. I always wondered what happened to him. He was such a sweet kid."

"What happened?" I asked, thinking of what Lorraine had said about her. Suddenly I was wondering if it were true, if my mother had had lovers, maybe even hitchhikers.

"What do you mean, what happened? Nothing happened. I drove him to his parents' house, I had dinner, spent the night, and then went on."

"You spent the night?"

"Get your mind out of the gutter," she said mildly, looking out her window. "You've been spending too much time with Lorraine."

At least she noticed who I was spending time with.

My mother reached into the glove compartment and shuffled through a stack of maps the size of a phone book until she found a pair of sunglasses. She wiped them off on her skirt and slid them on. You could tell they were from the sixties, with the big white frames. They'd been in that glove compartment for so long they'd come back into style. In sunglasses, my mother looked like a movie star. She leaned back in the seat and tilted her chin up toward the light. "Driving is the most important thing you can learn," she said. "It's the secret of the universe."

I was a natural behind the wheel, my mother said so. I'd been driving less than a month and already I was passing people, easing into other lanes, getting onto the off ramps at just the right speed. I dreamed of making a cross-country trip, just the two of us. Always staying inside that blue car, where we were completely at ease with one another. Completely alone.

Of course, the driving lessons put Lorraine beside herself. "This is great," she said right off when I told her I was going to keep practicing. "I don't know how to drive."

"And you never will," I said, trying to find my sneakers under my bed.

"But I want to come."

"You can't come," I said. I sat down on the floor and pulled on my shoes without unlacing them. "Listen, this is nothing personal." I didn't try to explain it further than that. I didn't entirely understand it myself.

But if there was one thing Lorraine couldn't bear, it was being left out. She asked again in the kitchen one day, with my mother and Sister Evangeline standing right there so I wouldn't be able to make a scene, but this time it was my mother who said no. "I'm not a driving instructor," she said. "I'm just teaching my daughter how to drive. There's a difference. As soon as Cecilia gets her license I'm sure she'll teach you."

So Lorraine waited for us, looking as sad sack as was humanly possible. She was always doing something ridiculously thoughtful when we came in, like cleaning out the big walk-in refrigerator at Saint Elizabeth's.

"Have fun?" she said, a damp rag in her left hand.

I looked to my mother for a little support, but she had already clicked back into place. Without her sunglasses she was the cook again, oblivious, busy.

"Lorraine's been here all afternoon, working away," Sister Evangeline said. "You girls should be outside, have some fun. It's too nice a day to be stuck in the kitchen."

"You want to do something?" I asked Lorraine, but she kept her head deep in the refrigerator. Her feelings were hurt. She'd been lonely all afternoon. She wanted me to tempt her outside. "Come on," I said. "We'll go lie out. We'll get some iced tea and take it out in the pasture."

"What?" Lorraine said. She poked her head out for a minute. "Did you say something?"

"I said you needed some sun." Why did she have to go through this every time? "It's the middle of summer, you look like a sheet."

"Go to the Panther," my mother said out of the blue. I could never believe she actually heard what was going on around her.

"How are we going to get there?"

"Drive," my mother said. "You drove to Owensboro. I guess it wouldn't kill you to drive to the river."

At this, Lorraine was in full swing. "I haven't been swimming all summer."

"Just be back before dinner," my mother said. "No sense getting everyone in trouble." Somewhere along the way my mother had decided I knew how to drive and the fact that I didn't have a license didn't seem to figure into her equation at all. She'd never been pulled over by the police, so police didn't figure in either.

Lorraine and I went back to my house and I lent her a swimsuit. She changed in the bathroom and came back with the suit on under her clothes. We found a couple of old towels and a bedspread nobody ever used. We packed some food, mostly things with salt, and a couple bottles of Coke and headed off to the car. By one o'clock I was back out on the road.

Habit sat pretty much in the fork of the Panther River. You could hit it going about ten miles north or ten miles south, though everybody knew that south was better. The river pooled in a couple of places and was deep enough to swim in without touching bottom. The current was slow and there were flat banks. It was the place that you wanted to be from the first day of summer. The place you had to drive to get to.

We unloaded our stuff and spread our towels out on the grass. It was good and hot and I decided I wanted to build up a sweat before I got in the water. I pulled my shorts off and my shirt over my head and stretched out. Lorraine sat down beside me and watched the boys who were swimming in the river.

"Take your clothes off," I said. "You're going to get weird lines that way."

"I'm fine," she said.

One of the boys came out of the water, shining like a new car. He waved to me. Andy LeBlanc from my school, a year ahead of me. I waved back, thinking there was no way he would have known who I was. Then I thought that maybe he was waving just because I was a girl in a swimsuit, sitting on the bank of the river. He probably didn't even know we went to school together. For some reason that made it even better.

"You know him?" Lorraine said.

"Sort of."

Andy dove back under the water, leaving a bright wake behind him.

Lorraine hugged her knees up to her chest and shivered like she was cold, which would have been impossible. "I hate my hair," she said softly, and not especially to me.

"What are you talking about?" I reached out and took a big handful of Lorraine's hair. I pulled on it lightly and then let it go, watching it spring back into place. It was the most remarkable thing at the river. On a bright day like this, it looked like she was sitting in a spotlight.

"I want hair like yours. I hate my hair. I can never get it to lay down." Her voice was so unbelievably sad that it made me sit up and look at her. "It ruins everything," she said.

"What's wrong with you?" I said. I held my own hair out to her. It had stopped being blond. It had turned to a color the magazines called dishwater. It was straight as a poker and hung past my shoulders in a curtain of mediocrity. "Look at this. Nobody wants this hair. People spend their whole life dyeing and perming so they can have your hair and they still don't have your hair."

And then Lorraine was crying. Not hard, but it was strange to see her cry at all because for all her moods, she wasn't the kind of person you thought of as a crier. She was trying to hide it, but her face turned so red. It made her freckles stand out across the bridge of her nose. "What is wrong with you?" I said.

She wiped her nose on a corner of her towel. "I just want to go swimming," she said helplessly.

"So we'll go swimming." I wasn't getting it at all.

Lorraine watched the boys shooting up out of the water like beach balls that had been held under against their wills. They hollered out with every splash, cut upstream in straight lines. They turned and flipped, threw the water above their heads in a fountain with both hands. It was like a show just for us. Maybe it was. "I don't want to be pregnant anymore," Lorraine said. "I'd rather be you."

I looked at Lorraine, who kept her eyes ahead. I looked at her wild, brushfire hair, her pale skin, her straight nose, her narrow back. She must have been four and a half months by then. Sometimes I could see the start of a little belly when the wind blew back her dress. I thought about how she had had sex. That somebody had wanted her in that way. She had wanted, been wanted, been desired. She knew things I didn't even have words for. She kept her clothes on and her knees up. She wouldn't let them see what I knew and forgot over and over again.

"Before," she said, still watching the boys, "you should have seen me. Man, I'd have them right here, every one of them. All I ever had to do was walk around, give a couple of looks, say

hey. You wouldn't believe it, the way I could make them jump."
Her voice was soft, like somebody telling secrets about someone
else. It was the voice you used to talk about other girls, not
yourself. "They said I was good, too," she said. "I was good."

I felt like I was out in the water, not knowing how to swim.
I didn't know what to say to her. I told her I was sorry. It came
out sounding like I thought somebody had died.

"I made my mother sick, she worried about me so much. We
fought like cats. She said this was going to happen. You're going
to get in trouble one of these days, was how she'd say it." Lorraine smiled at me. "I guess this is trouble," she said.

"I guess," I said. Idiot.

"So I've decided," she said, smiling bigger now, laughing a
little, "that I want to be you. That's nothing new. Everybody at
Saint Elizabeth's wants to be you."

"Right."

"Of course they do. You've got good parents and a nice house
and a whole flock of doting nuns. You're the queen of the show
around that place. You don't make anyone feel like a freak."
She leaned toward me and added in her best, dramatic whisper,
"You're a virgin."

"Says you."

"Please."

I laughed. It was a sore point with me, but at that moment it
sounded like a benefit. "All right," I said. "But I still can't see
that being me would solve your problems."

"Other people's problems always look better than mine." She
pulled the medal out from inside her shirt and dangled it in front
of her chest. "Saint Theresa's problems look better than mine.
Dying of something beautiful and dramatic as a young nun, that
wouldn't be so bad."

"Except for the part about being dead," I said. "Don't be a
fool, Lorraine. Take off your shirt and go swimming."

"That's what you'd do if you were me," she said.

"That's what you'd do," I said. "If anybody gives you trouble
I'll just hold them under."

"Go on," she said. "I'll watch you."

"I don't want to go on. Come in the water with me, just—"
I stopped, I wanted this to be easy. "Forget it for a little while."

"Swim," Lorraine said, her voice getting serious again. "I'm
going to have a Coke."

And for some reason I got up and left her there. It seemed
mean, but I was more afraid that she would think I felt sorry for

her. I didn't. Sorry maybe for what had happened but not for
her. Lorraine was born to land on her feet. It was written all
over her.

I waded into the water. It felt all the colder because I was so
hot by then. The boys parted like the Red Sea, like a school of
fish I had frightened away with my hand. They swam to the
other bank and watched me. Let them watch. When it was deep
enough I held my breath and went under, my eyes closed tight.
I swam down until I touched the bottom. I stayed down as long
as my lungs would let me and imagined them all wondering
where I had gone. I came back up and waved to Lorraine on the
shore. I half thought she'd change her mind, come into the water
with her round stomach pushing at my blue swimsuit, but she
stayed where she was.

"Swim!" she shouted at me. "I want to see you doing some
work out there."

When we got home it was still early. The tops of our shoulders
were burned, my wet hair was matted into one giant ball from
riding with the windows down, and Lorraine had gone back to
normal, which is to say, whatever had surfaced for a minute at
the river had slipped back under again.

"I'll come over after dinner," she said.

"Sure." I thought I should have said something else. Something like my father would say, easy and comforting. But nothing came to me. Lorraine was pregnant. What was I going to
do, tell her she wasn't? I waved and walked back to my house
to take a shower. There was mud up both my shins.

"You look like you've been out clearing a field," my father
said to me as I came up the front stairs. He was finishing that
chair he'd been working on before his accident. My mother's
chair. He was putting on the last coat of varnish. The wood was
redder now than it used to be. It looked good.

"Lorraine and I went swimming down at the Panther," I said.

My father put his brush down. "The two of you?" he said.

"Sure, Mom let me drive."

"You didn't go with somebody?"

"I went with Lorraine."

"With an adult. I've told you this. I don't want you swimming
unless you go with an adult." I couldn't believe the way his
voice went up. It was something I'd only heard him do a couple
of times in my life. My father was really angry, and in a way it

was more interesting than anything else, seeing as how my father never got angry.

"We're old enough to go swimming," I said. "There were lots of people there. It wasn't like I was going by myself in the middle of the night."

Then everything changed. My father could be like a movie sometimes, with everything playing out across his face. He wasn't mad at me anymore and he felt a little stupid that he'd gotten so mad in the first place. "I just hate the water," he said. "I'm acting crazy."

It was true about my father and water. He wouldn't go near it. He had to hold his breath when he drove over bridges. It was because he didn't know how to swim. "So you're crazy," I said. "The next time we go swimming you can come if you want."

He went back to his chair, and I went upstairs and stood in a hot shower until all the hot water was gone. Sometimes I felt like my father and I were locked in a battle of worrying. Maybe my mother was right. Maybe that was the way I was most like him.

It was three days before I could get my mother to agree to another driving lesson, and once she did agree, she wound up not going. We were all set, headed out the door, when Sister Bernadette came in and said there was mail for both of us. My mother and I went to the front desk and each got a thin envelope from our key boxes. Mine was from my only correspondent. Featherweight blue paper from Sylvia in Spain. My mother looked at hers for a minute, turning it over in her hands, and then slipped it in the pocket of her skirt.

"You're going to have to go without me," she said.

"I can wait until you read that," I said, opening mine with a finger underneath the flap.

"No," she said. "Not today." And just that quick she turned around and was gone, not to the kitchen, but out the front door. I went after her. Driving was not something I gave up on easily.

"Hey," I shouted from the front porch.

She was headed toward her house, the little house we used to live in together. She stopped and put her hand over her eyes, blocking out the sun to look at me. "What?"

"I want to go," I said. "Come on."

"I can't," she said, but she kept standing there, looking at me. I didn't know if she was trying to make up her mind about whether or not to come back inside or what.

"Mom?" I started to come down the stairs toward her, but she waved me off and went on.

Now I was in a bad mood. I sat down on the steps to read my letter.

Dear Cecilia,
   I haven't heard from you in a long while now and stand expectant at my mailbox. I am hoping that you are robust and that your silence is not caused by illness.

I folded the paper back up and returned it to its envelope. I wasn't up to Sylvia just then.

I killed the day as best I could, reading one of my father's mystery novels and being mad at my mother for blowing me off. I wanted to skip dinner, stay at home, but by four o'clock I found myself heading back to Saint Elizabeth's to see if they needed any help. The days in summer were endless, every one of them felt like a week.

If I had money I'd turn Saint Elizabeth's back into the Hotel Louisa. All the pregnant girls in the world could still come, but I'd make it just like a hotel, with room service and elevators. I'd put a pool in the back with a big covered cabana where they could dance. They could just dance with each other if they wanted. It would be all right because who was ever around to see? My father did a good job of holding things together, but it was too much for him. It would have been too much for anybody. There should be someone there who did nothing but put in gardens. It should have been a wonderful place.

When I got to the kitchen Lorraine was there, slicing away at a stack of bell peppers. The food had changed a lot over the years. Now it was all about health, what you could eat when you were pregnant, special diets. Even the standard iced tea had been replaced by some mint decaffeinated stuff that tasted like watered-down mouthwash. Sister Evangeline was all the way over by the refrigerator now. The two of them were talking about Saint Theresa when I came in. Lorraine wanted to get it exactly right, the way saints went about solving the problems of your life.

"I've been praying a lot," Lorraine said. "I'm just wondering if it's better to stick to one saint or move around."

"Move around," I said, taking a slice of pepper. "Cover all your bases."

"Couldn't hurt," Sister Evangeline said.

"Where's Mom?"

"She's been in and out of here all day," Sister Evangeline said. "She hasn't spoken a full sentence since lunch."

"What do you want me to say?" my mother said, and we all turned and looked over at the broom closet near the pantry. There she was.

"When did you get back here?" Sister Evangeline said.

My mother stepped out into the kitchen and scared me half to death. She looked absolutely wild-eyed. "Awhile ago," she said, and locked her fingers behind her neck in a way that made her seem especially girlish.

"You've had some news," Sister Evangeline said, not asking her but telling her.

"No," she said.

"Don't lie, Rosie." Sister Evangeline sat up in her chair. She was the mother now.

"Just leave it alone," my mother said.

"Tell me," Sister Evangeline said.

"We can't talk about this." My mother raised her voice ever so slightly. It would have been enough to send me running home, but Sister Evangeline didn't even blink.

"Girls," Sister said. "Why don't you go outside for a while?"

I looked at Lorraine, who gave an almost imperceptible shrug of her shoulders and put down her knife. "What is this?" I said.

"Just go," my mother said to us.

"I want to know what's going on," I said.

And just that quick my mother turned on me. "You can't know everything! Goddamnit, Cecilia. You don't get to know everything about everyone."

I stared at her. I could feel a wave of tears coming up and I bit down hard on my back teeth to keep them in. "I was just asking you a question," I said. "I just wanted—"

"Go on, honey," Sister Evangeline said. "Let your mother and I talk for a minute. This isn't anything. You and Lorraine give us a few minutes. We'll finish dinner. By the time it's on the table everything will be fine, okay?"

I nodded. I didn't know what to say anymore. Lorraine and I walked out like ghosts, into a day that was still too bright.

"What was that all about?"

"Did it look like I had any idea what that was about?"

"I've said it before," she said, walking through the pasture toward my house, staying on the goat trail I seemed to go on a hundred times a day. "Your mother has a past. She has secrets."

I was about ready to kill Lorraine.

We watched "Jeopardy" and the early news and waited for six o'clock to come. I tried to see it in my mind. The girls would be drinking that lousy tea now. My mother would be setting the tables alone because Lorraine and I were here. She would be putting the dressing on the salad, slicing the chicken, putting out pitchers of water and milk. The same silver pitchers they'd used when it was a hotel. Everything would be ready and it would all be exactly the same. We would serve dinner. We would eat together in the kitchen, Sister Evangeline, my mother and father, me. Lorraine ate with the girls. Mother Corinne didn't like her to eat with us. Normally I wouldn't care, but tonight I was glad. I wanted to hold my family in place. I wanted to watch them.

And when sports was over and we went back, it was all exactly like that, except it wasn't. Something had happened while we were gone, something that my mother knew and Sister Evangeline knew, but the rest of us were kept from. My father didn't notice. He ate his chicken happily. He pushed his potatoes against his fork with his knife and chewed.

"I'm thinking I'm going to take all the shutters off and strip them. All of them. I may take them up to Owensboro and have them sandblasted. Some of the girls have been saying the shutters are flapping around at night, keeping them up. It seems like it would be better to get them all painted and rehung before I think about nailing them down."

My mother didn't eat her dinner. She moved it around on her plate, from left to right and then back again. It was like she couldn't eat it until she had turned it into a configuration she could stand. "You got a letter today," she said, out of the blue.

"From Sylvia," I said.

"Really," Dad said. "How's she doing?"

"I didn't finish it. I forgot. There was so much going on this afternoon."

"What was going on?" my father said.

"I don't know. What was going on, Mom?"

She wouldn't look at me. "Nothing," she said.

Whatever it was, it had Sister Evangeline upset. She was the one who did most of the talking at dinner and tonight she was quiet. She kept her eyes down. I thought that her color looked bad. The bandage was back on her hand again and it seemed like she was falling apart. It was one of the days she looked as old as she was.

After dinner my father and I started the dishes, but my mother told us both to go. "I'm in the mood to do dishes," she said.

Dad wiped his hands on a towel hanging over the stove. "I guess that's it for us then," he said.

"I'm going to stay awhile," I told him.

He nodded. "Suit yourself." Then he smiled at my mother. "The chicken was good," he said. He headed out the door and she did nothing to stop him. She didn't go and put her arms around his waist. She didn't kiss him. Not that she ever did those things but for some reason I kept expecting her to.

"You never do go," my mother said to me. She didn't sound mad, only tired. "I remember when you were little, you were always afraid you were going to fall asleep and miss something. I used to say, Cecilia, nobody can stay awake all the time and you'd say, I do. I think it was years before you ever believed that you really fell asleep. You thought you were awake all the time."

"I don't remember that," I said.

"Do some dishes," my mother said. There were girls coming into the kitchen, carrying stacks of plates. The ones who were really pregnant, the class of July, stayed in the dining room. Once you were that big you didn't have to do things like bring your plate to the kitchen anymore. Lorraine talked about that a lot. It was something she was looking forward to.

Lorraine brought her plate in and stayed to help dry. She was wondering too. She didn't want to be too far from the action. But after a while my mother sent her off. "Go on, Lorraine," my mother said. "You've done enough."

"I don't mind staying," she said.

"There's no point." She raised up her hands like she was presenting the kitchen, introducing it to us. "It's all been done."

Lorraine left grudgingly, and then my mother turned to me. "Bedtime," she said.

"It isn't even dark outside."

"My bedtime," she said. "I'm tired." My mother usually went to bed pretty soon after dinner because she got up so early in the morning, but seven-thirty was pushing it even for her. Sister Evangeline sat quietly, running her rosary around in her hands. She didn't say anything, not even good night.

I should have told her I wanted to stay. I did want to stay, but I went on home like she told me to. I said good night and went home. I told my father that I wanted to read, but all night I sat up and waited for the light to go on in my mother's window. It didn't.

Hindsight is a remarkable thing. When I look back on that night I tell myself I knew she was going, but I don't know that I knew anything, really. I didn't see the lights of the blue Dodge as she pulled it out of the little shed my father had built for it when I was still a baby. I didn't see them turn onto the road or which way they went. The only thing I knew for sure was that when I got up the next morning, my mother was gone.

5

I WANTED TO LOOK for her, but where do you look for someone in the world? It's such a huge place, and I thought of all of it. Interstates and highways, four lanes down to two. Rural routes and back roads and streets and alleys. There were so many places to drive. So many places to get out of the car and go inside. Every city and town, every field. Every house in each of those cities and all the rooms in those houses. My mother could be in any one of them. She was lost, like a ring you swore you'd never take off but did, put it in your pocket, and the next thing you knew it was gone. The places to begin looking are as many as the breaths you took in a day. More than that. She could be anywhere, and by the time I got there, she could be someplace else again.

I called the police. They asked me, were there any signs of a struggle?

No.

Any indications of foul play?

No.

Had she been depressed lately, moody? Was there any reason to think she might be leaving?

She was my mother. There were always signs she might leave.

Was there a note?

Yes. Two actually. The first was more of a list.

July 3d. Breakfast: Oatmeal, toast, strawberries (use the ones we have, they're getting soft). Lunch: Chicken salad with al-monds and white grapes (in blue Tupperware, bottom shelf), carrot and celery sticks, black olives, sponge cake. Dinner: Catfish (broil it), red new potatoes with parsley, steamed spin-ach, cornbread, tapioca pudding.

*July 4th. Breakfast: Banana walnut waffles. Be sure to put
out cold cereal too.*

It goes on, a full two weeks, complete with assignments of
who should do the cooking. It's pretty long. You don't need to
read all of it. There was a lot on the Fourth of July. She wanted
there to be fried chicken, potato salad, baked beans, apple pie.
The stuff she always made on the Fourth.

The other note was to us, everyone together, her husband and
daughter, Sister Evangeline, all of Saint Elizabeth's. All on one
note.

Everyone,
  *I am sorry that I am leaving so suddenly, without saying
good-bye. I'm doing a bad job with this and at the same time
don't know another way to do it. I won't hope that you'll
forgive me, or even that you'll understand. I only hope that
you will find it in your hearts to wish me well and love me as
I love all of you.*

                                                   Rose

Not to sound bitter or anything, but part of it isn't true. The
part about her loving everyone. She just didn't.

The police took this down, but they told me there was nothing
they could do. I could hire a private investigator to find out
where she was, but they couldn't make her come back. Unless
the car wasn't in her name. We could track her down for that,
they said.

But of course, the car was hers.

My father sat on the front porch of our house, his hands folded
between his knees, and watched. Maybe it was for her to come
back but maybe he was just watching in general.

"Hey," I said.

"Hey," he said.

It had only been a day, not even twenty-four hours, but it
seemed pretty goddamn clear that hope was not in order. "What
do you think?" I said, and he must have thought I said, what
are you thinking? What I meant was something else entirely.

"I was thinking about this girl I used to know when I was
growing up and how she was in an accident and died. It was
terrible, you know? The worst thing that could have happened?"
He kept on watching the field, at least the piece of the field that

was right in front of him. "The whole town had their hearts broken. Everybody loved this girl. We all thought we'd never get over it. But we did, because she was dead." He stopped, as if he was trying very hard to figure out the point of all this. "Your mother's not dead," he said to me finally.

With all my heart I wished I could have comforted him. I wished I could have put my arm around his shoulder or sat on his knee and told him that we'd get through this. I wished I even could have lied to him and said I thought she'd come back. But I didn't do anything. I just stood there until I couldn't stand there anymore. Then I went down the steps and across the field without saying a word.

It was getting to be dinnertime. Someone would be putting together the meal she'd mapped out. I hadn't eaten all day. When my father came back from breakfast and woke me up to tell me about the notes, I lost my appetite. I wasn't looking forward to going to the old hotel, for all the obvious reasons: I didn't want to be reminded. I didn't want sympathy. I didn't want to hope that she would suddenly be there the way people are in movies. But I'd put enough together to know that Sister Evangeline was the person I needed to talk to. Dad said he hadn't seen her, that she was spending the day in her room. So I went down the hall and knocked on her door.

"Sister?" I said. "It's Cecilia."

It was quiet and I thought she might be sleeping, but then a voice came from the other side of the door, telling me to come in. She was sitting up in bed, fully dressed, her legs straight out in front of her. It was the room I used to take naps in when I was little. My mother would put me there while she cooked because it was so close to the kitchen. "You already know everything," she said.

"I know she's gone."

She looked like a doll, propped up in bed. She looked like someone had left her that way and she had no choice but to stay there. "I begged her not to go. I told her it was the wrong thing to do, but you know your mother. She has a mind of her own about things. You can't tell her anything."

"How could you not have told me?" I said, knowing perfectly well how. It was my mother she loved first. It was my mother whose confidence she would never break.

She looked at me, as sad as my father. "How could I have told? You make a promise to someone, you have to keep it.

Nobody could have made her stay, pet. Not once she made up her mind.''

But I believed I could have. Me, who never talked to my mother outside of a car, who she never came to for anything. I really thought that I could have made the difference. ''Why did she go?''

Sister Evangeline sighed. ''Your mother's a good woman. No one ever brought me the joy that she did. But everything with your mother was a secret. I used to tell her, if you tell another living being, you won't have that weight to walk around with all the time. It'll be easier. But she thought her life was a house of cards, you know, you take one card out and the whole thing comes down. She didn't tell me. There were things I knew, just from knowing. I knew she didn't like to think of everything she'd put behind her. If you get everything wrapped up just right and you leave it alone for a long time, then one day a little piece of it breaks off and comes back to you, it's seeing the dead. I think your mother thought she'd seen the dead, and it scared her bad.''

''What dead?'' I said. ''What are we talking about here?''

''I don't know the details,'' she said. ''I just have feelings.''

I was so angry just then. Angry at Sister and my father, but so blindingly angry at my mother that I couldn't stand it. I wanted to scream. I wanted to scream at her for leaving me but she was gone.

''Come sit here with me,'' Sister Evangeline said, patting a place on the bed beside her.

''No,'' I said.

''Cecilia,'' she said. She had a way of saying my name when she was trying to coax me into something. She said every syllable as a separate word. She almost hummed it. Sa-ceel-lee-a.

''I'm going to go now,'' I said.

''No,'' she said. ''Come here.''

I went and sat down on the edge of the bed, the very edge. She reached over and took my hand and squeezed it, but I wouldn't squeeze back.

''I'm not being a very good nun today,'' she said. ''Other days, I'd tell you how God works, how we don't always understand His ways, but that they are always for the best. I know it's true, but today, it isn't in my heart and it shames me.'' She held my hand tighter. It hurt a little. ''Today I'm a selfish old woman and I'm as sad as I've ever been because I want things that I can't have. This isn't what I want, and so I hate it. There's not a thing in the world I can do to get Rose to help me because she's already gone, but you're here, pet, and I'll tell you, you're going to have to help me. I know you're torn apart, but I can't have you go away from me too, especially not now, because I just couldn't stand that.'' She took my chin in her other hand and turned my face to hers. ''This is what you're going to have to do: you're going to have to be the one to remind me how God works, how He gives us what we need. You're going to have to be that thing for me and I'm going to be it for you. I can't miss Rose and miss you too. It's too much. It's too much for anybody.''

I felt like crying, but I was so tired and so hurt that I knew if I started I wouldn't be able to stop. So I put my legs up on the bed and put my head in her lap and Sister Evangeline ran her fingers through my hair while she looked out the window. ''What is today?'' she said.

''July third.''

''Then God has told us something after all,'' she said. ''This is the feast day of Saint Thomas, doubting Thomas. He didn't go with the other apostles to see the empty tomb of the Lord, and when they told him, he didn't believe. He said, 'Except I shall see in His hands the print of the nails, and put my finger in the place of the nails, and put my hand into His side, I will not believe.' So when Christ came back, and they were all alone, He said to Thomas, 'Put in thy finger hither, and see my hands; and bring hither thy hand and put it into my side. And be not faithless, but believing.' And Thomas fell to his feet and cried, 'My Lord and my God.' But you know what Jesus said to him, pet? Jesus said, 'Because thou hast seen me, Thomas, thou hast believed. Blessed are they who have not seen, and have believed.' ''

Later that night, after someone had made dinner and someone had cleaned it up and put the plates away, I went to my mother's house. I don't know what I expected, exactly. I thought something would be different, but it was all the same. I hadn't been to my mother's house very often, and I was never there alone, unless she sent me over from the kitchen to pick up a recipe book she had left on her nightstand. Of course, I knew it all from living there when I was young, and she hadn't made any changes since my father and I had moved across the pasture five years ago. I remembered it as being a wonderful place when I was growing up. I loved the smallness, the way the kitchen and living room were just one big room together. The way you could sit on the couch and see everything. It was exactly the opposite

of Saint Elizabeth's, which had a hundred places to be lost in.
The little house made us close, if only because we were always
right next to each other.

But now I saw it as my mother would have, coming home
alone night after night. It was just a place she slept. A place she
brushed her teeth and read her books and waited for time to
pass. My mother didn't have a television or a radio. She kept a
phone in, in case Sister Evangeline needed something in the
night, but I doubt she ever called anyone. I don't remember her
ever calling us, or that I called her. All those years, but she
hadn't done anything to make it her own place, no framed pictures or little, stupid things that people kept on tables beside
couches. It could have been a cabin that people rented over the
summer, it could have been anyplace. It didn't bear her marks,
and now that she was gone it was like she'd never been there at
all.

I went into the kitchen and opened the cupboards. There was
a jar of instant coffee, a jar of sugar, a box of saltines, peanut
butter. There wasn't a full set of anything: two glasses, one cup,
four spoons. In the drawer next to the stove I found an open box
of Marlboros. I never knew my mother smoked. How could I
not know that? I took one out of the pack, turned the front burner
of the gas range on high, and lit it. I had smoked once or twice
before, after school, at a slumber party. I never liked it. But this
one I drew in and held until it made me cough, and even then I
kept on smoking it.

I took the cigarette into her bedroom and turned on a light.
The bed was made, everything was put away. I lifted up the
bedspread and looked underneath the bed. There wasn't a slip-
per, an earring, a Kleenex. There wasn't even dust. It made me
wonder if she'd ever been there at all. I sat down on the bed and
smoked, flicking the ashes onto the cupped rim around the base
of the lamp. I should have gone and gotten a saucer, but it didn't
feel that important. I set the cigarette down and went to look in
her closet, her drawers, and was so relieved to see her clothes
there that I nearly said something aloud. I was the private investigator and this was my proof. She had left behind everything
she didn't think she'd need. I took dresses off the hangers and
held them to my face. I could smell her in the clothes, even
though I'd never really thought about my mother smelling like
anything before. She didn't wear perfume or lipstick, but she
was there just the same, sweet and floury, a little bit of laundry
detergent. I pulled out a dress I knew, one that was cotton with

a pattern of green leaves so small that from a distance it didn't even look like a pattern. She'd made it herself. She'd made almost everything here as a way of passing the time when she came home. The dress would have been too big for me. My mother was so much taller than I was. But I set it aside anyway. I took sweaters and a beige slip. I took a pair of stockings. There wasn't much there, and after ten minutes of trying to make choices I put it all out on the bed. I would take all of it. Even then it would fit into one shopping bag.

In the bedside table I found a blue ballpoint pen, a stack of unused postcards with generic sunset pictures, a roll of stamps. I added these to my pile. I thought for a minute about putting it all back, leaving this house exactly as she had left it so I could come back for the rest of my life and touch her things and smell them where they were. I decided that was sick. I wanted them with me. I wanted to shorten the dresses and wear the sweaters too big. I wanted to wear everything until they turned into things that were mine. I found a bag in the kitchen, folded all of it up, and put it inside.

I didn't find anything with writing on it. Not even in the trash cans, which I went through carefully. My mother checked her books out of the little library in Habit and returned them all promptly, so there wasn't a book to see if she'd underlined anything or written, How true! in the margin beside her favorite passages the way the sentimental girls in my high school did.

I went into the bathroom and opened up the medicine cabinet. There was even less there. A bottle of aspirin, an unopened tube of toothpaste, a jar of hand cream. I took these, too.

I'll say this much, she took the things I gave her, or she was careful to throw them all away awhile ago or take them out in the woods somewhere to bury them. The tin charm bracelet I bought her for Christmas when I was nine, the giant blue mixing bowl, the cashmere scarf I'd saved for, all of those things were gone. I was grateful. I think it would have killed me to find them.

I couldn't help but think there would be something for me, even if there wasn't something from me. There would be a note hidden carefully in a place where only I would find it. She wanted it that way, so she wouldn't hurt anyone else's feelings. Or maybe it wouldn't even be a note. Maybe there would just be some sort of cryptic message that I would have to put together. It would tell me where she was or why she'd gone, but even though I went over the place, slid my hands between sofa cushions, looked beneath the ice cube tray in the freezer, I found nothing.

I was in the hall closet, trying to see in a shelf above my head, when I heard the door open. I spun around so quick I nearly lost my balance and saw my father there, both of us surprised to be caught, both of us disappointed because we thought it was someone else who was surprising us.

"I saw the light on," he said. "I thought I should come over and check—"

"I'm just going through some stuff," I said.

He came in and sat down on the couch. I didn't know what was happening between us, why grief had made us so awkward all of the sudden, but I couldn't bring myself to ask. "Did you find anything?" he said.

"Nothing, really. Some clothes, some bathroom stuff. I'm going to keep the clothes, if you think that would be all right."

He turned to me. "Of course," he said. "All of this is yours. You don't need to ask for anything."

"It feels strange," I said. "Like I'm stealing things."

"You're not," he said. "Don't be silly."

And then we were just quiet for a while, looking around. "I lived in this house for more than thirty years," my father said finally. "And now I feel like I've never been here before. It's the damnedest thing."

"Come on," I said, picking up the bag. "Let's go home."

We were careful to turn out all the lights so if we were to see them on, later, we would know something had happened.

But nothing happened. Lorraine took over in the kitchen. Sister Bernadette gave it a shot, Sister Loyola, even Mother Corinne went in a time or two to try and make a sauce, but the girls seemed to do a better job. My mother had left files of menus, recipe books tagged with white slips of paper. Sister Evangeline kept her place in the kitchen and as it turned out, she'd been watching all those years. She could direct the girls fairly well, telling them what to do next. At ninety she had reclaimed her kitchen.

I went there to see her and to see Lorraine, but I wouldn't have anything to do with the food. It would've been too easy, me stepping into the spot my mother had left. Too easy for Mother Corinne, who had never given her the time of day to begin with. The kitchen was not going to be my fate in life, and I knew this was a place that could swallow you whole and never let you out. So when I could stand to be there at all, I only watched, kept people company, and sat on my hands.

Three days after my mother left, Lorraine came to my house early in the morning. She just came right in and woke me up, took hold of my foot and shook it until my eyes slit open.

"Get up," she said.

I sat up slowly and tried to swallow the taste in my mouth. "What?"

"Hair dye," Lorraine said, and held up a brown paper bag. "I'm going to dye your hair."

"The hell you are," I said, half awake.

"No," she said, "I am." She pulled the sheet back and dragged me out of bed, down the hall to the bathroom.

"Stop this," I said. "I'm not up yet."

"I know." Lorraine put the toilet seat down and had me sit on top of the lid. She wrapped a towel around my neck. "If I waited until you were up you wouldn't do it. Think of this as a surprise party for your hair." She ripped open the package and started to mix the contents of two small bottles together. "I already read the directions," she said. "It's highlights. Paint-on. If you like it we'll go to a full color job. I've been thinking about this, ever since that day we were at the river. You said your hair was dishwater, that was your word." She grabbed a section of my hair and began to dab on some god-awful-smelling stuff with a brush that looked like it had come from a bottle of Liquid Paper. "Before you said that, it didn't look so bad to me, but since then—" She made bold streaks down in front of my face, and I just sat there, dazed. I don't know why I let her do it. "Well, I can see it now. It's a little flat. You can get a lot of depth through color."

Lorraine painted away. She was careful. She was trying to do a good job. "You need to do something different every now and then," she said, sounding like a busy hairdresser handing out pat advice. "This is really going to be you."

"You're just trying to make me feel better." I appreciated the fact that she wasn't talking about my mother. The truth was, Lorraine loved my mother, and in a funny way I imagine she missed her almost as much as I did.

"Of course I'm trying to make you feel better, idiot," Lorraine said. "Believe me, you'll have plenty of time to make me feel better later on."

"Scheduling in a depression?" I asked.

Lorraine, in her favorite gesture, stepped back and opened her arms to reveal her round stomach to the world. "I imagine I'll be getting less and less cheerful about this as time goes on," she said.

I stopped and looked at her. She looked like a painting, some eighteenth-century Italian Madonna. The light fixture over the sink put a pale glow around her head. "Are you worried?" I said.

"You bet," Lorraine said, and turned her attention back to my highlights. "You bet."

The color was me. After she timed the dye and held my head under the faucet for a rinse, she blew it dry. I could see what she'd been talking about. The color had been flat before. It was better now. Lorraine was so proud of herself. "I like it," I said, looking at the two of us in the mirror. I was sort of a blond again. A streaky blond.

"I knew you would. You never let anybody do anything for you," she said. "I have to trick you if I want to do something nice."

Lorraine insisted that I go back to Saint Elizabeth's with her so people could admire her handiwork. Besides, it was getting to be time to start lunch. Lorraine seemed to bloom under the weight of her new responsibility in the kitchen. She made up a careful list of all the special diets girls were on. No sugar for Mary Carol, who had developed gestational diabetes. No salt for Paula, whose blood pressure ran high. "I'm not a good cook," she said. "Not like Rose, but I'm not bad. Anyone who can read can cook all right if they pay attention, but I think if I stick with it I might really be okay at this."

"Why would you want to be? Who cares?" I saw cooking as a trap, something that no one should aspire to. As long as you knew how, you'd be condemned to a life of waiting on other people.

"Everybody wants to be good at something," Lorraine said. "They need me here now." Lorraine kept her hair tied back tightly when she was in the kitchen. She braided it into a rope down her back and used barrettes to catch the pieces that sprung out from her head.

"Sure they need you. They need you to do a job they should be paying somebody for. If they don't need you, they'll need somebody else."

"Ah," Lorraine said smiling. "But just think, if it's not me, that somebody else could be you."

Even if I refused to take over what my mother had left behind in the kitchen, I did fill her place in other ways. I hadn't realized all she had done for Sister Evangeline. She took care of her clothes, she helped her dress. She steadied her when she went from chair to wheelchair to bed. I did that now. It scared me at first. I didn't like seeing her look fragile. I didn't like the way she felt so shaky at times and had to lean heavily on my arm. What bothered me most, of all the stupid things, was seeing her without her habit in the morning. Her hair was thin and long and it fell around her shoulders until she could get it into a bun. Her hair seemed wrong to me somehow, not like I'd imagined it at all. It made her seem delicate, vulnerable.

The other thing was the way she talked about my mother when we were alone together. Out in the kitchen, with all the people milling around, her name hardly ever came up, unless it was somebody saying, How did Rose make her white sauce? or, Where did Rose keep the cardamom? But alone with me, Sister Evangeline could go on and on about little things that made me want to jump out of my skin.

"Your mother was practical. Not like me. I'd do the same things over and over again and never think how to make them better, but your mother had a sharp mind." I was looking under the bed for her left shoe, not finding it anywhere. "By the time I was eighty, I had a hard time with shoelaces. Arthritis, see, in the finger joints. Some things I can do just fine, but those shoelaces, well, there were mornings I'd just want to cry I'd get so frustrated. So you know what Rose did? She went right out and bought me loafers. Her own money, too. Didn't go to Mother Corinne or anything. Loafers! Why didn't I ever think of that?"

"I don't know," I said. The shoe was under the dresser, no telling how it got there, but sitting there with that shoe in my hand, thinking about how my mother had gone out and bought it just out of logic or thoughtfulness, got me all choked up. That's how it would come back to me, her leaving. In little ways you never would've imagined.

It was my father who seemed to be coming to terms with things slower than the rest of us. Unlike Sister Evangeline, who was anxious to talk, he wouldn't say her name after the first few days. That absence of a name was so much clearer, and sadder, than the talking. He was quiet in general. He'd always been quiet, but this was different. He stayed so busy now. He decided not to take the shutters to Owensboro and pay to have them sandblasted. Instead, he took them all off and stripped them by hand on the lawn near his toolshed. I brought him his lunch outside because he wouldn't come in to eat it. He wouldn't stop even that long. I left him thermoses of iced tea, bottles of water, hoping that he would at least have sense enough to stop and take a drink.

"Can't you do that in the shade?" I said, my hand over my eyes.

"I can see the little bits of paint better in the bright light," he said.

"Yeah, but you're going to have a heat stroke. It's hotter than hell out here."

He stopped for a minute and wiped his neck and forehead with a handkerchief. He was soaked. His scar had gotten darker from being out in the sun so much. It was so angry and red that it looked like it had happened just the minute before. "Can you stay?" he said.

"I brought my lunch." I sat down in the grass and brought two sandwiches out of the bag. My father was the one person I'd still cook for, especially now because he liked to eat at home.

The grass wasn't good to sit in anymore. It was too late in the summer. It was coarse and dry and so alive with bugs that you felt like you'd landed in the center of their universe no matter where you sat. But I didn't mention it.

"Egg salad," he said. "Great."

And we sat there, the two of us, on a day hot enough to melt metal, and ate our lunch. We must have had a million things to say to each other, but we were quiet. In truth, it was still better being together, even when we couldn't talk.

This is the dream I had at night: I am in a restaurant. It's no place I've been before in my life. I'm with some friends. In the dream I know them well, but they are not people I really know. They say that some friends of theirs I haven't met before are coming to eat with us. After a while three women come in and sit with us at the table. One of them is my mother. I start to say something, to shout, to jump across to her, but she holds me in my chair with her eyes. She gives me this smile that says, just pretend, just play along with this. It's a wonderful feeling, being on the inside of a secret with her. I give her back the slightest nod. When we are introduced we shake hands, we say our names, Rose, Cecilia. We say how happy we are to meet each other. All through the meal we are careful. We speak to each other, but never too much. We don't exchange knowing glances or fix our eyes. We are in complete conspiracy, and I am happy.

"Cecilia? It's Sister Bernadette."

"Hello, Sister," I said, and felt a little wave of panic because it was rare that anyone from Saint Elizabeth's called me on the phone. "How are you?"

"I'm fine, dear." She hesitated for a moment. "There's a man here at the front desk. He's come to see your mother."

"My mother?"

"I was wondering if you could come over and speak to him. I can't find Son anywhere."

"Sure," I said. "I'll be right there."

To the best of my memory, my mother had never had a visitor, other than her friend Angie, an old Saint Elizabeth's graduate she had been especially close to. I'd called Angie first thing when my mother left. She said she hadn't heard from her. She sounded sad enough about the news that I believed her, too.

I had been lying on the sofa, reading my second detective novel of the week, when I got the call. I was wearing shorts and a Murray State tee shirt. My recently highlighted hair was pulled up in a ponytail that had gotten more than a little ratty over the course of the day, but I didn't want to take the time to change. Someone who was looking for my mother might know something about her. Or maybe he was an investigator. Maybe she'd done something or something had happened. The more I thought about it, the faster I started walking.

The man who sat in the lobby of Saint Elizabeth's was no detective. Not unless he had the most ingenious cover in the world. He was small-boned and blond and tired-looking. He wore little metal-rim glasses and a pale blue suit. He had his jacket on, even though it was a hot day.

"Cecilia," Sister Bernadette said. "This is the man I was telling you about. The man who's looking for Rose. This is Cecilia Abbott," she said to him. "This is Rose's daughter." I could hear the relief in her voice, relief that I was there now and could handle this thing she didn't know what to make of.

The man stood up and shook my hand. He was staring at me so hard. I knew he was looking for a piece of her in me, a piece I didn't possess. "I'm Thomas Clinton," he said. He kept looking at me. "I'm sorry," he said. "I never knew Rose had a daughter."

I nodded. "That's me," I said. I thought about it for a second.

"Clinton? Are you a relative of my mother's?" Did she have a brother? A cousin? I wished to God I knew. "Clinton is my mother's maiden name."

"I tried to find Son," Sister said, looking a little nervous. "I don't know where he is."

"No telling," I said to her, and then to this man. "Do you know my mother?"

"I did," he said. "A long time ago." He waited a minute and then added, "Is she here?"

I looked at Sister Bernadette, who looked helpless. She hadn't told him anything. "Let's go in the kitchen," I said. "I'll get you something to drink. We can talk."

Thomas Clinton followed me back to the kitchen, which thankfully was empty except for Lorraine. She was peeling potatoes.

"Hi there," Lorraine said, and wiped the strips of peeling from her hands. The man shook her hand and I introduced them.

"Mr. Clinton is trying to find my mother," I told Lorraine.

"So she is gone," he said. "I thought it was something like that, when the sister wouldn't say where she was." He sat down at the kitchen table. He looked sick with sadness. Lorraine brought him a cup of coffee he didn't ask for and he thanked her. "Has she been gone a long time?"

"A week," I said.

He looked a little hopeful at this news. "So she'll be coming back?"

"No," I said. "I don't expect she will." The man must have known my mother because he took this news as disappointing, not surprising.

"Where do you know Rose from?" Lorraine asked, pulling her chair up to the table to make herself one of the family.

"I was married to her," he said.

I looked at him again. I don't know what I thought exactly at that minute. What do you think? I sat down at the table, and Lorraine brought me a Coke from her secret stash in the pantry. "When?" I said dully. I was thinking maybe a year ago, three or five. I was thinking that maybe he lived nearby and she went to him at night after she left the kitchen. Two husbands. It was possible for her.

"It was a long time ago, before she ever came here. It was in California." And then he added, as if it would explain everything, "We were young at the time."

I was trying very hard to take it all in, but it was strange enough just having a man in the kitchen, much less my mother's ex-husband. You just didn't see men at Saint Elizabeth's. Every now and then someone who was lost or had a flat tire and needed to use the phone, but even that caused a little ripple in the daily routine.

"So you and my mother are divorced?" I said. "I'm sorry to be so dense about all this. She didn't ever talk much about her past."

"Technically, no, we're not, but it isn't an issue," he said quietly. "I never remarried, so I never followed through with a divorce. After a certain number of years I imagine these things dissolve."

"I think that all you have to do is put an ad in the paper," Lorraine said. "Publicly announcing it or something. Or maybe you say you aren't responsible for their debts. If the person doesn't get in touch with you, you're divorced."

I gave her a look that suggested she should keep the editorials to a minimum.

"I never minded it," he said. He was quite possibly the most painfully shy person I had ever seen in my life, which is saying something because we get a lot of shyness coming through here. He talked all right, but he kept his eyes down. He held onto his coffee cup like the last flotation device on a sinking ship. He was still wearing a wedding ring.

I had so many questions I could barely think of where to start. "Why did you come now?" I said.

"Rose's mother died," he said, and then he looked at me and suddenly his face flushed. "I'm so sorry," he said. "That's so thoughtless of me, just telling you like that. She's your grandmother. I'm sorry. I'm still not used to this, Rose having a daughter. She was a wonderful woman, Helen."

"Helen," I said. My middle name. She told me it was for her mother. Helen was dead.

"I looked for Rose for years after she left, and then, after time—" His voice sounded almost confused, as if he was trying to remember how he could have let such a thing happen. "I stopped trying. I came to understand this was what she wanted. Helen and I were always close. She was a wonderful woman. When she died, her husband gave me a box of postcards from Rose. The postmarks were different for a long time, but in the last five years they've all come from here. The town was so small. It wasn't difficult finding her, once I had something to work with. I was sorry Helen hadn't given me the cards earlier

I respect your mother's privacy, but it would have been good if she could have seen Helen before she died. It would have meant a great deal to Helen.''

"You mean none of you knew where she was all this time?'' My mother was too smart to forget about the postmarks. She wanted her mother to find her, but her mother didn't get the clue.

Thomas Clinton shook his head.

"But when she left—'' I stopped, not knowing exactly how to say this. "A long time ago, what did she tell you then?''

"She didn't tell me anything,'' Thomas Clinton said. "She was just gone.''

There was an awful silence after that. The three of us sitting there, all looking away. "I guess I should go try to find Son,'' Lorraine said. She wanted to go now, to be out of the kitchen and all of this for a minute, and I couldn't say I blamed her. She excused herself and was out the door.

"I can't believe you just missed her,'' I said. "It seems too crazy. You looking all these years and then getting here the week after she goes.''

He crossed his hands over his knees. His shoulders seemed to round into themselves. "I'm afraid that's my fault,'' he said.

"How could it be your fault?''

"I wrote to Rose when Helen died. I wanted to tell her in person. I didn't want her to get the news in a letter after all this time. Rose and Helen were very close, very, very close. I don't know your mother anymore, but I couldn't imagine how she would take the news. So I wrote and told her I was coming out to see her, just to talk to her and then I'd go.'' He stopped and took a deep breath. "I would have liked to see her.''

"So she left after she got the letter from you.''

Thomas Clinton looked so sorry. It was the only word I could think of. "You must think I've done something awful to your mother,'' he said. "I've done something to make her hate me this way, but I don't know what it was. I never thought I would have scared her off. It's been such a long time.''

Now that he said it, I could see that it did make perfect sense for me to think he was a monster. That he'd been cruel to her, made her the way she was. It occurred to me that here was a person you could blame anything on and he'd accept it, just because you told him to. But I knew my mother. I knew how she stood and how she walked. She wasn't the person who was afraid. This man sitting at the kitchen table, saying he was her husband, seemed as frightened as anyone I'd met. "My mother wasn't a big one for explaining things," I said. I didn't want to pass it off right away. I'd need to think about this, about everything, before I figured it all out.

"Maybe I shouldn't have written," he said. "But that seemed wrong, after all this time. It took me a long time to drive. I have a problem," he said. "With my inner ear. I can't fly anymore. It was a long drive."

I just kept staring at him. I really couldn't help myself. He had been married to my mother. He had seen her as a young girl. He had held her. He knew my grandmother. He had been to the house where they lived. Time was going so slowly. Lorraine had been gone forever. Every sound in the kitchen became louder, the refrigerator kicking in and out, the slight, tapping noise of the wind blowing at the screen door. I kept wanting to ask him if he heard these things, or if it was just me. "Do you want some more coffee?" I said.

He looked carefully at the contents of his cup and then shook his head. "I'm sorry," he said. "I know this must be very hard for you."

But the person who it would be hard on was coming through the door with Lorraine. I could tell by my father's face that she had told him everything on the way over. He was sunburned and tan all at the same time. His overalls were soaked in sweat and there was green paint on his hands and shirt from the shutters. The scar on his forehead was frightening somehow, dangerous. He was twenty years older than Thomas Clinton and twice his size. My father looked afraid. He looked scared to death. It didn't strike me until that minute that it wasn't just that my mother used to be married to both of them, she was still married to both of them, and God knew where she was now.

"Wilson Abbott," my father said, and reached out his hand to the stranger who was standing now, coming toward him like a shadow.

"Thomas Clinton," he said, and took his hand.

=== 6 ===

WE ALL STOOD THERE, sizing each other up. This wasn't one of those moments in life you're ever really prepared for. My father was stone silent. Usually I knew what he was thinking, but on this one I didn't have a clue.

"I apologize for this—" Thomas Clinton stopped to search for his words—"intrusion," he said. "If I had known—" But he didn't finish his sentence.

"I understand," my father said, though I could not possibly imagine that he did.

"It was Helen's death," Thomas Clinton said.

"No, of course," my father said. "Anyone would have done the same thing."

After that we just lapsed into silence. Not even Lorraine could come up with something to say. It had taken Thomas Clinton more than a week to drive from California to Kentucky. When he got there he found out his wife had married someone else, had a grown daughter, and had left them, too. He was tired. As tired as a person could possibly be.

"Why don't you stay the night?" I said to him, as much just to talk as anything. There were things that needed to be got at, stories to compare and piece together. But it clearly wasn't in him to do it now. "You can stay in my mother's house. You'll have a lot of privacy."

My father looked just slightly uncomfortable, but I knew him. He'd take anybody in. Thomas Clinton put up his hands politely, as if it were a tea party and I was trying to press the last slice of cake on him. "No, no," he said. "I've taken up enough of your time as it is. I'll stay in a hotel, if you could recommend one to me. I would like to get some rest before I start heading back."

292

"This is a hotel," I said. I realized that I wasn't just being polite. I wanted him to stay. I didn't have any relatives, no cousins or uncles dropping in for holidays. Even though I knew that being my mother's first husband didn't exactly make him part of the family, it was the closest thing I'd seen. "Just stay the night," I said. "Get some rest now and then come back and have dinner with us."

My father nodded at Thomas Clinton. He wasn't smiling exactly, but everything about him was reassuring. He was telling this man it was all right. He should stay.

Thomas Clinton ran his hand over the back of his neck. "All right," he said.

"Good. I'll take you over there," I said. "Do you have bags in the car?"

"Let Lorraine go," my father said. "I need your help with the shutters for a minute."

"The shutters?"

"I need you to help me pick the paint out," he said.

Thomas Clinton shook my hand again, and then my father's. "We'll talk more later," he said to my father.

"Sure," my father said.

Then Thomas Clinton left with Lorraine so she could settle him into my mother's house. I was thinking how glad I was I'd taken her clothes out of the closet.

"What about paint?" I said to my father once we were alone.

"Come on outside," my father said.

We walked around back to the toolshed, where the shutters for the whole hotel were lined up on the grass like doors into the center of the earth. My father was always careful about not leaving them down too long in the same place and stacking them all upright in the evenings when he was finished. He was afraid of killing the grass.

"You okay?" he said. "With Mr. Clinton and all." He raised up the corner of a shutter with his foot and checked beneath it.

"It's a shock, I'll say that much." But not a bad shock for some reason. I was perversely excited about the whole thing. I thought that maybe, finally, I'd found someone who would tell me about my mother. "Did you know about him?" I said.

He shook his head. "We should have talked more, your mother and I. But this . . . no, this surprised me. Maybe I didn't know her." My father paced down to the end of the row of shutters and then back up again. The shadow he threw down in the late afternoon sun was bigger than some of the trees. I guess it was a lot harder for him than it was for me. Maybe he and my mother were never legally married. Maybe you couldn't be, if you were married to someone else.

"He seems nice enough," I said tentatively. "Pretty depressed, but okay."

"Sure," my father said. He stopped then and looked at me. "Your mother and I," he said slowly. "We were married pretty much right away, right after she came here. Right after we met. And then we had you. It was all pretty quick."

"I didn't know that," I said, not getting his point exactly.

"All I'm saying is, maybe we shouldn't tell Mr. Clinton that. It might make it harder for him, to think she got married again right away."

"How could I have told him if I didn't even know?"

My father looked over his shutters. "Tell him you're fourteen, just if he asks."

"What?"

He turned to me. Everything about him was nervous. He put his hands on my shoulders and rubbed little circles on my collarbone with his thumbs, like I was a prizefighter going in for another round. "Don't you see?" he said. "If he knows how old you are, he'll know that your mother and I were married right away. I think that would be wrong."

There was only one reason he wouldn't want Thomas Clinton to know how old I was. She must have gotten pregnant before she and Dad got married. She must have had to get married. My head was spinning. It was possible, I guess, that she had left Thomas Clinton for my father. I tried to figure out how the distance between California and Kentucky came into all of this. Someone wasn't telling me the truth, not by a long shot. "You and Mom had to get married," I said. "Because of me. That's what you're saying."

My father looked at me with panic in his eyes. "No," he said. "Sissy, that's not what I mean. Don't make so much out of this. All I'm saying is it looks like Mr. Clinton has enough to feel bad about right now."

But it was my father who had enough to feel bad about right now. He wasn't going to tell me anything, that was for sure. "Okay, Dad," I said, because it was important to him. "If he asks, I'll tell him I'm fourteen."

"I'm sure he won't ask," my father said.

I went back to the kitchen and told Lorraine my theory. "Why else would he want me to pretend I was younger?"

"Maybe it's the reason he gave you," she said. "Maybe it was just close is all. You know Son, he lives in fear of hurting anybody's feelings. He's just trying to spare the guy a little grief."

"But think about it, my mother blowing her whole life for one passionate moment. She marries someone she doesn't love because she has to."

"Really," Lorraine said, twisting her hair up to the back of her head and tying it in a knot. "I don't think your mother did a whole lot in her life that she didn't want to do. She was mysterious, I'll grant you that, but I don't think you should be making a major case out of this. There's too much going on right in front of you."

"Like the fact she has two husbands," I said.

"Married to two men," Lorraine said, and sighed. "My God, not even I could have come up with that one."

"It's pretty unbelievable."

"Poor Mr. Clinton," Lorraine said. "The way he looked around when we went inside her house. It would have broken your heart. If somebody just told me this story, and I didn't know any of the people, I'd say he'd done something to her, hit her or run around or something. But not him. I think he's still in love with her." Lorraine put her head down on the kitchen table. "It makes you wonder if there are any others."

Other husbands? Leave it to Lorraine to give me something new to worry about.

All afternoon I thought about Thomas Clinton, lying in the bed that a week before his wife had slept in. Was he going from room to room, touching the things he knew she must have touched? Where had he met her and where had they gone together? I didn't need to ask him if he still loved her, because that was implicit in everything about him. Just the fact that he was here. Even though she walked out on him without a word, he still couldn't bear the thought of her getting the news of her mother's death alone. He would rather drive cross-country in the middle of the summer to tell her himself, put his arm around her shoulder, give her his handkerchief. Then he would have gotten in his car and gone home, if that was what she wanted, and stayed on if she wanted that instead. He was in love with her. No one was questioning that. You had to wonder what it would be like to be able to inspire that kind of love.

"Thomas Clinton," I said to Sister Evangeline as I helped her out of bed and into the wheelchair so I could take her out into the kitchen. "Mother was married to him before Dad. Actually, she's married to both of them, but Mr. Clinton doesn't seem to think that's such a big deal."

Sister Evangeline nodded and sighed. "A husband," she said. "I thought that's all it probably was. Poor Rose ran off just because she has two husbands. I wish she'd told me."

"Well, you're not supposed to have two, you know." Sister Evangeline never ceased to amaze me. This was big news, the biggest we'd ever seen at Saint Elizabeth's, which was a little hotbed of scandal in and of itself. "What would the church say about something like that?"

"The question is, what would God say, and that's between your mother and God. It's none of our business." I sighed and knelt down to slip her loafers onto her feet. "How's your father taking all this?" she said.

"It's hard for him, I can see that, the whole thing makes him nervous. But he's taking it okay. Mr. Clinton is a nice man. There's something about him, like he's just so harmless or something. I couldn't imagine getting mad at him."

"Do you like him?" Sister Evangeline asked me. I looked up and found her leaning over in her chair. Her face was so close to mine that I could see my reflection in her glasses.

"I like him fine," I said.

"I'd like to meet him," she said. "It would be like meeting part of Rose, before I even knew her."

I asked my father and he said it would be all right for us to have dinner in the kitchen of Saint Elizabeth's so that Sister Evangeline could eat with us. It would be a relief because in our house, with no one else, the three of us could drown trying to make conversation. At Saint Elizabeth's there would be Sister Evangeline and Lorraine. Even if we had nothing to say to each other, we'd at least have things to talk about. If we ate dinner late, at seven-thirty, the girls would be through eating and things would have quieted down some. I wrote a note telling Thomas Clinton what time I would pick him up, but I felt stupid when I got to the house. I remembered when I was little and I used to pick flowers and take them to my mother's door. I would leave them on the front steps and knock and run. My hands would sweat like crazy, like for some reason they were sweating now. I leaned over and slipped the note under the door. I started to run away, I did, but then I thought that was just ridiculous.

What would my mother say if she saw us there, having dinner together and evoking her memory like it was all some sort of séance? And yet she must have known this was how it would go. She knew both her husbands as men who would never be less than gracious in the face of social collapse. She knew, she must have, that we would all be peaceful and overly polite. That was the thing that made her run. If she could have counted on anyone to balk, to refuse, to blame, she might have found a way to get through it. But the thought of those painfully good manners must have filled her to the top with guilt. Because there would be no one there to punish her, she was left with the worse fate of having to punish herself.

I washed my hair and put on a dress for dinner. My father was at the kitchen sink, still working on getting the paint out from under his nails with a wire brush and Lava soap. He was wearing dark, pressed pants and a white shirt.

"You look nice," I said.

"Should I wear a tie, do you think?" He held up a dripping hand in front of his chest.

"No, you look fine." I took a hand towel from the refrigerator door and gave it to him.

"My hands look terrible," he said.

"They're fine." I looked at them hard. I went under his fingernails with mine, dislodging little flecks of paint. I brought a bottle of lotion from the sink and worked some into his hands. "See?" I said. "There, good as new."

"Thanks," he said. He touched the top of my head.

"I'm going to go over and get Mr. Clinton," I said.

"I can go," my father said.

"It's no big deal. I said I'd do it. You go on over and check on Lorraine, make sure dinner's okay."

My father and I went to the front door. "Sure I don't need a tie with this?" he asked again.

"Positive." We went down the steps together and then parted halfway across the field.

It was so insane, my father worried about his clothes, the nervousness in his voice. He was afraid he would lose her to this man. He was so busy worrying that, for a little while at least, he had forgotten she was already gone.

I knocked on the door of my mother's house and Thomas Clinton answered it. He was still wearing his suit. He even had the jacket on. It looked better somehow. I wondered if he had found my mother's iron or if he had one of his own in the trunk of his car. "Did you get some rest?" I said.

"I did."

I didn't come in the house. I waited at the door for him. "Should I lock it?" he said.

"Not here. Nobody locks anything in Habit." The light was just beginning to turn as we crossed the pasture and headed up toward Saint Elizabeth's. We were both trying to get a better look at the other one while keeping our eyes as straight ahead as possible. I kept wanting to say, stop, let's just look. We'll both look. But we kept going.

"It's awfully nice here," he said. "It must have been a good place to grow up."

"It's hard to say. I guess it was. Kind of dull, not like California."

"But it's quiet here." He stopped for a second to look around. It was like he was trying to figure out exactly where the quiet was coming from. "I like that. California is pretty noisy now."

"Where do you live?"

"Oh, I'm still in Marina del Rey," he said, like I was asking him if he'd moved.

"Is that where you and my mother lived when you were married?"

He nodded. "It's changed so much. Rose would never recognize it now. We'd made a down payment on a house just before she left. If we hadn't bought it then I never would have been able to afford to stay there." He looked at me, and then looked down at the ground. "Did she ever go back?"

"To California?" I asked.

He nodded.

"Not that I know of. No," I said. "I'm sure she didn't."

"It doesn't matter," he said, but he sounded relieved. "I was just wondering." If someone is gone, it's better to think of them as far away. I knew that.

It was such a pretty time of night. The sky was a bright dark blue and there was still a little bit of color at the west edge of the field from where the sun was going down. All the lights in

Saint Elizabeth's were on and as we approached it, I thought it was the Hotel Louisa. It looked like there was a wonderful party inside. We went up the back steps into the kitchen.

"Hi there," Lorraine said, smiling at Thomas Clinton.

"Hello," he said, and then to my father, who was standing behind her, "hello."

"This is Sister Evangeline," I said. "She was my mother's best friend."

Thomas Clinton reached down and shook her hand as she sat in her chair. Don't ask me how I knew this, it was something about the look on his face when he saw her: he was a Catholic down to his bones. There's a way a Catholic looks at a nun, even more than at a priest, like she's a holy relic or something. The Shroud of Turin sitting in a chair. "Sister," he said.

When he tried to straighten up, she didn't let him go. She held his hand, in fact, she covered it with her other hand, as if she was trying to make it safe. "I'm sorry for your troubles," she said.

He smiled a little and nodded. He understood. They both did.

"I asked Mother Corinne, and she said we could have dinner in the dining room tonight since everybody's out already," Lorraine said.

I looked up at her and felt a sort of panic. I didn't want Mother Corinne to know about Thomas Clinton, who he was really. Not when she thought so badly of my mother. But Lorraine caught all of this and smiled at me. "I told her you had a relative visiting from out of town," she said.

When Saint Elizabeth's was the Hotel Louisa, the owners, Mr. and Mrs. Nelson, sat at the same table every night. It is the round one that sits in the alcove of the window and looks out over the pasture, the front section of which was a formal garden back then, and the edge of the woods. The way the dining room is designed, this table is set off from the others. You really can't help looking at it. It's where the nine-month girls sit now. The head table, the best. It's their reward for being pregnant. Their reward for being so big and uncomfortable. When this was the Hotel Louisa, there was a special set of everything used for that table alone. The silverware was plated with real gold, the linens came from Ireland, the crystal was so heavy that Louisa would only drink out of white wine glasses. There were pink orchids on that table every night. Those were her absolute favorites. You can see them in the background of every portrait that was painted of her.

The Nelsons would invite anyone who was very important to sit at their table with them, mayors who were visiting, bankers, every now and then a movie star, the one who was never the star of the picture but whose face you saw everywhere and seemed so familiar. On the night that the hotel opened the Clatterbucks came and they sat at this table. June told me about it, how she made herself a yellow organdy dress and her father bought her a pair of shoes that were dyed to match. "There was music all night long," she told me. "Two bands, so that when one of them got tired the other would just step right in and start playing the same song. It never ended." It was the only time the Clatterbucks ever ate at the hotel.

"All these years I've been here and I've only eaten in this room twice," my father said. "The first night I came here and on my sixtieth birthday." Then he turned to Thomas Clinton. "Course, I'm in here all the time, painting, steadying tables, keeping up with things."

"I remember the night you came," Sister Evangeline said. "You couldn't look at the girls, you were so embarrassed."

"I thought I'd be here a couple of days, a week at the most."

"Things don't always work out like you think they're going to," Thomas Clinton said, and even though I knew he didn't mean anything by it, it put a kind of shadow over everything.

"Dinner's good," I told Lorraine. "You're getting the hang of this."

"I'm not Rose," Lorraine said, not caring a whit about saying her name to this nervous crowd. "But I'm getting there."

"Rose was a good cook?" Thomas said.

"The best," my father said. "She cooked three meals a day, every day she was here."

"That's funny," Thomas Clinton said absently. "I don't really remember her cooking at all."

"It's hard to imagine Mom not cooking," I said. "What was she doing if she wasn't cooking?"

"Driving," Thomas Clinton said. He got a look on his face like the old men in town get when they're telling war stories, like it should be an awful memory but it's been so long ago it's turned into something else. "I couldn't get her out of the car to save my life. Rose was a born driver. There were times I would think I never should have taught her how."

"You taught her to drive?" I said.

Thomas Clinton nodded. "I remember the day she got her license."

"She taught me to drive," I said. It made me so happy. For just that minute things fell into a line. Things made sense.

"She didn't drive so much," my father said. "When she was here."

It was like candy, talking about her this way when we were all together. We all knew we shouldn't, that at any second it would flip over and be too much. We could get angry or brokenhearted at one wrong turn, so we stopped. If people do have more than one life in a lifetime, they should be careful to make sure the different versions of the past never overlap. My mother had tried to do that, and when she knew she couldn't hold the two worlds apart anymore, she left.

"What will you do when you leave us?" Sister Evangeline asked.

Thomas Clinton ran his finger idly along the side of his dinner fork. "Go back," he said. "I have some time. School doesn't start for almost two months."

"You're a teacher?" I said. I had never thought to ask before what he did.

"Math," he said. "I guess I should try to have a vacation, go and see something. I don't know. It doesn't seem very appropriate."

"But you won't keep looking for her?" I said.

Thomas Clinton looked at me, and I knew from the expression on his face that that was exactly what he had been planning on. "No," he said. "I wouldn't know where to start."

"Go away for a while," my father said quietly. "Take some time off. Go fishing on your way back, through Arkansas. Great fishing in Arkansas. Do you fish?"

"I have," said Thomas Clinton.

My father nodded. "Then that's the ticket," he said.

After dinner my father went into the pantry and got a bottle of Jack Daniel's off the top shelf. It had been a Christmas present to him from all of the girls a few years back. He made a big deal out of hiding it because Habit was dry, even though nobody cared about those things anymore. He and Thomas Clinton stood out on the porch and had a quiet drink. I couldn't hear what they were saying from the kitchen, only the soft thud of the moths flying into the screen door, attracted by the light. Lorraine cleared the table, and I took Sister Evangeline into her room. "I'm tired," she said.

"It's late."

"That man," she said. "Have you ever seen anyone so sad?"

"No," I said.

She pulled the bobby pins out from the sides of her coife and slipped it off of her head. She scratched her scalp. I saw that the bandage was back on her hand. She'd put it on herself and not done a very good job.

"Is this bothering you again?"

She nodded. "I don't know what it is."

I went into her bathroom and got some Bactine, the box of gauze, scissors and tape. "Let me," I said, and sat down beside her on the bed. I was scared as I took the dressing off, scared that it might be bad. But it wasn't bad. There was just a neat little hole in her hand, like she'd stuck herself with something. "How did you do this?"

"I can't remember," she said. "It just showed up. It only bleeds a little sometimes. I just don't want to get a mess on the sheets."

I squirted it with the Bactine and wrapped it up again. I tried to make it neat, the way my mother had. "That's better," I said.

"It would be nice if he had something," she said.

"Who had something?"

"Thomas," she said.

"Like what?"

"I don't know," she said. "Something of his own. Something to hold on to. Like me and Son have you and you have us. You have to feel for the ones that are alone."

"Maybe we should ask Mr. Clinton to stay," I said, because all of a sudden it made perfect sense to me. He could live in my mother's house and take her place at the dinner table.

"Things don't work that way, pet," she said. I knew that, but it didn't mean I didn't want it.

I helped Sister Evangeline into her nightgown and hung up her dress. "Say your prayers," I said to her when I got to the door. It was a joke. I said it every night.

"Stay a minute," she said.

I came back to her bed and stood next to her. "What is it?" I said.

Sister Evangeline looked out her window and saw the half-moon on the other side of her curtains. I saw it too. "I miss her," she said, her injured hand folding around mine. "I miss her something awful."

* * *

Once Sister was asleep, I went back down the hall to the kitchen. "About time," Lorraine said. "Half the dishes are done already."

"Sorry," I said, tying a dishtowel around my waist. I looked out the kitchen window onto the back porch. "What do you think they're talking about?" I said.

"I know what they're not talking about. I can tell you that much."

"I'll kind of miss him," I said. "I don't know why. It sure as hell is awkward. He just seems so lost."

"I know what you mean," Lorraine said, and handed me a plate to dry. "It's like he's familiar or something."

"That's the problem with this place," I said. "Everybody leaves." As soon as it was out of my mouth I realized what a stupid thing it was to say. Lorraine was leaving, too. Not for a while, but she'd go. I never knew how I always managed to forget that about the ones I liked.

"You know what," Lorraine said, resting her soapy hands on the edge of the sink for a minute and staring out the window. "Sometimes I really think I'd just as soon stay."

By the time we'd finished up my father and Thomas Clinton were gone and Lorraine went upstairs to her room with Loelle and I went out into the night alone. I was halfway across the pasture when I stopped and sat down. Then I stretched out in the grass and looked up at the stars. The whole thing seemed a little funny. Funny because it wasn't so bad, when by every right it should have been. It was just a dinner. That was the thing my mother should have seen. How nothing was a big deal, we just ate. Then afterward the two men had drinks on the porch and we stayed inside, talking and cleaning up. I felt nearly hysterical, because really, it was dull. If anyone had come by they never would have known there was anything unusual about the picture. That was the way things worked. When you were looking for the big fight, the moment that you thought would knock everything over, nothing much happened at all.

My father had left the porch light on, and I turned it off when I came inside. I went upstairs and stood by his bedroom door for a minute. I didn't think he would be asleep already. His back was turned to me and I watched his steady breathing. Maybe he felt better now, knowing that it wasn't just him, knowing that it wasn't anything he had done.

"Dad?"

He rolled over and squinted at me. "You okay?" he said.

"I'm fine," I said. I stayed in the doorway, my hands against the frame. "I just wanted to tell you I was home and say good night."

"Good night, Sissy," he said.

"Dad?"

"What?"

"What were you two talking about out there? I know it's not any of my business, but I was wondering. You were out there a long time."

"Fishing," he said. "We were talking about trout fishing."

"Not Mom?"

"God, no."

"But he's okay, isn't he? He's a nice enough guy."

"Yes," my father said sadly. "He's a good man." Then he sat up on one elbow. "Give your old man a kiss good night."

I walked into the dark room, keeping my hands out in front of me even though I could see pretty well. I sat down on the edge of his bed and my father held me to him. "You're my girl," he said.

"You bet," I said.

I went into my room and saw the light in my mother's house was still on. Thomas Clinton was up, and I thought about calling him or maybe going back over, even though I didn't know what I would say.

When I woke up the next morning, the first thing I thought was, I've missed him. I didn't get a chance to say good-bye. I threw on some clothes and ran over to my mother's house. I was almost at the door before I realized how crazy it all looked. It wasn't even much past dawn. I didn't know why I was up. My sneakers were soaked through from dew and they made a light squishing sound when I walked. I wanted something, an address, a phone number. If we were both keeping an eye out for her, well, then our chances were doubled, weren't they?

Then Thomas Clinton opened the door. Just opened it, like he was expecting me. He was wearing a different suit now, a darker one. He was wearing a blue tie with a red stripe running through it. He said good morning.

"I'm sorry," I said. "I shouldn't be here so early. I don't even know what time it is. Is it early?"

"Not really," Thomas Clinton said.

"I just woke up and I thought you'd be gone and I wanted to tell you, you know, good-bye and everything."

"I was sitting at the table," he said. "That's why I saw you."

We stood like that for a while. Him inside, me in the wet grass. "Why don't you come in," he said.

"Sure," I said.

He had a little bag, not much bigger than a good-sized briefcase, sitting next to the door. I wanted to tell him that he shouldn't be driving cross-country in a suit, but then I guessed it was his business. "I found some coffee," he said. "In the cupboard. Would you like some coffee?"

"Okay," I said. He had been looking for things, too.

"I wanted to tell you again, how much I appreciate everything you've done. You've been very generous, all of you."

"It's not like you were any trouble or anything," I said. "We don't get many visitors in Habit. We're always glad when people come by." I sounded like the board of tourism.

Thomas Clinton set a cup of coffee in front of me on the table and I knew he must have just washed it out after having his coffee because my mother only had one cup. "Would it be all right if I asked you a couple of things?" I said. "Things about my mother?" I looked down into the cup of coffee and caught half of my own reflection there. "She didn't tell me a lot. I mean, you probably figured that out and everything."

"Sure," he said. "Shoot."

"Did my mother have any brothers or sisters?" I said.

"No."

"Any other family?"

"Some cousins, I think. Joe would know. I'll write his address down for you. He'd be glad to hear from you."

"Did she—" I stopped for a minute because I didn't know exactly how to say this. "Did she want to be anything, do anything special?"

He shook his head. "Your mother loved to drive, aside from that, no, I can't remember anything." Thomas Clinton tapped his fingers on the table, thinking for a minute. "I have something you might be interested in," he said. He went over and brought his suitcase to the table, then he opened it up and took out an envelope with pictures in it. "This was our wedding," he said.

There, in case I had doubted it, was proof that my mother had been married before. She looked so beautiful I couldn't take my eyes off of her. She looked happy in a way I had never seen her look, not even once. She was wearing a slim white suit with two big buttons at the collar and a wide-brimmed hat. Her gloved hands held the arm of a man who was clearly the young Thomas Clinton. He looked even happier. It was a picture of two people who had meant to be married forever.

"I have a couple of them," he said. "This is her graduation picture from high school. This is her, in front of the apartment building we lived in when we first got married. That's San Diego. This one, here, that's in Marina del Rey."

There were half a dozen of them. A picture of my mother in front of the Pacific Ocean, waving. Her hair was wet, she must have just been swimming. She was wearing a suit that was covered in flowers. No one was ever so beautiful.

"I like to travel with these," he said. "So I can show them to people. Ask if anyone had seen her." He tapped the one of her standing in front of an apartment building he told me was in San Diego. "That one," he said. "That's my favorite."

There were two pictures of Helen, my mother's mother. In one of them she was young and looked very much like my mother, only a little bit smaller, more delicate somehow. In the other she was older. She was sitting in front of a Christmas tree with a man. His arm was around her waist. "That's Joe," Thomas Clinton said. "Helen's husband."

I wanted to look at the pictures forever. They seemed to make up for everything, secrets and lost time. Here I could hold her in my hand and look and look, like I was drinking her. I could stare at her the way I always wanted to but didn't because she would catch me and put her hands on her hips and say, "What?" like I wanted something. But I didn't want anything. I really wanted only to watch her.

"You can have one," he said. "I'll have copies made for you when I get home, but if you want to have one now, you can."

I couldn't pretend. I couldn't say, oh no, really, that's okay. I wanted one. I wanted the wedding picture, but I thought that would be wrong. I wanted one I could show to my father. "This one," I said, taking her high school picture. It was the best one for me. It was the picture before either husband, when she was just herself.

Thomas Clinton nodded. "That one's nice," he said. He drew the others neatly toward him and put them back in their envelope. "I left my number by the phone," he said. "You'll call me if you hear anything? I won't come back. I don't want you to worry about that. I'd just like to know."

"Sure," I said. "You do the same." I was pretty sure I understood better than he did that she wouldn't be coming back, even if I'd only been without her a week and he'd been without her for years.

I walked him out to the car, the picture of my mother in my shirt pocket. "I should say good-bye to everyone," he said. "It's just so early."

"I'll tell them," I said. I could see that he wanted to get going. He didn't want to face us all together again.

"Well," he said, and held out his hand to me. I shook it. "It was nice to meet you, Cecilia."

"You too," I said.

Thomas Clinton got in his car and drove down the road toward the Green River Parkway. He put his hand out the open window and waved to me, and for some reason I had such a tightness in my chest when I watched him go. Maybe I was just tired of all the leaving, or maybe it was his sadness I felt as he went back toward California alone. At least it was daylight and he had said good-bye. Then all of a sudden I remembered I didn't know what my mother's maiden name was. All this time I'd thought it was Clinton. The car was already gone. I would have to write to him.

I wanted to sit down in the middle of the road and stay there for the rest of my life. Whenever someone came by and said, Hey, Cecilia, what're you doing there in the road, I'd tell them, missing people was a full-time job, being sorry about what was gone was going to take every waking minute now, so much time and energy that I had no choice but to stay right on that spot until they all decided to come back. I meant it as a joke at first, but then I looked down at the gravel and I really thought about it. I couldn't wait for them. They weren't coming back. I'd been trying all my life to figure out what was going on, with my mother, with all those girls that come and then go away. But now I wanted to forget. Right then I decided, as much as I'd wanted to know before, from here on out I didn't want to know at all.

Over near the shed I could see my father working on his shutters, down on his knees, scraping away. I waved to him but he didn't see me. As I was walking up toward Saint Elizabeth's, I started thinking about Lorraine. Don't ask me why, but I had this sudden picture of Lorraine and her baby staying on and me taking care of them. Lorraine was in the guest room and I was walking through the kitchen of our house, holding the baby on

my hip. It all looked so real in my mind, not like it was going
to happen, but like it had already happened and I was only
remembering it. And I knew then that that was the thing Lorraine had been talking about, her sign from Saint Theresa, the
thing that would work itself out if she just had faith. It was me.
I was her sign from God.